P9-DIY-192

ADVIKA
and the
HOLLYWOOD WIVES

ALSO BY KIRTHANA RAMISETTI

Dava Shastri's Last Day

ADVIKA
and the
HOLLYWOOD WIVES

KIRTHANA RAMISETTI

GRAND CENTRAL

NEW YORK   BOSTON

This book is a work of fiction. Names, characters, places, and incidents are the product of the author's imagination or are used fictitiously. Any resemblance to actual events, locales, or persons, living or dead, is coincidental.

Copyright © 2023 by Kirthana Ramisetti

Cover design and illustration by Sarah Congdon.
Cover copyright © 2023 by Hachette Book Group, Inc.

Hachette Book Group supports the right to free expression and the value of copyright. The purpose of copyright is to encourage writers and artists to produce the creative works that enrich our culture.

The scanning, uploading, and distribution of this book without permission is a theft of the author's intellectual property. If you would like permission to use material from the book (other than for review purposes), please contact permissions@hbgusa.com. Thank you for your support of the author's rights.

Grand Central Publishing
Hachette Book Group
1290 Avenue of the Americas, New York, NY 10104

Grand Central Publishing is a division of Hachette Book Group, Inc. The Grand Central Publishing name and logo is a trademark of Hachette Book Group, Inc.

The publisher is not responsible for websites (or their content) that are not owned by the publisher.

ISBN 9781538709276

Printed in the United States of America

For siblings, including mine

And friends, including yours

ADVIKA
and the
HOLLYWOOD
WIVES

CHAPTER ONE

It Happened One Night

ADVIKA SRINIVASAN COULDN'T TAKE HER eyes off the Oscar. It was tottering on the edge of the bar, its golden bald head catching the light in the midst of a swirl of conversations and shouted drink orders. As she nodded at requests of "martini" directed to her face and "Scotch, neat" to her chest, Advika still found her gaze drawn to the gold statuette, disbelieving that something could seem so magnificent and mundane at the same time. Only when she was making a martini for a pink-haired woman wearing a feathery blue dress did she stop to wonder why an Academy Award was perched there for so long. By the time she poured four glasses of champagne and a tray of tequila shots, it was gone.

The awards show had ended an hour ago. Yet new waves of people kept streaming into the Governors Ball from the nearby Dolby Theatre, and as this was the first official after-party following the Oscars, the undulating, sparkling mass all seemed intent on getting drunk. Luckily for Advika, her station was out of the way of the main scrum, situated next to the unofficial smokers' patio at the far north edge of the ballroom. She liked that this gave her an outside view of the revelry, which was spotlit in violet by an impressive array of lotus-shaped lights twirling above.

Interspersed amid the tuxedos and haute couture gowns were flashes of gold. That was where most people were clustered, around the people clutching trophies, their faces overtaken by enormous smiles. Advika envied their joy—the kind so pure and overwhelming that it's impossible to hide, so why bother trying. She shook her gaze off the throng, willing herself to focus on her job, so that there would be another job, and another one after that.

The steady stream of patrons to her bar continued for another half hour before finally dissipating. As she contemplated taking her break, someone arrived at the party whose presence electrified the crowd, and they all seemed to surge en masse toward the movie star—because of course it was a movie star.

"What's going on?" said Dean, her co-bartender. He towered a foot above her, which meant his body odor drifted down on her like a treetop shedding leaves.

"Ramsey Howell," Advika said. She briefly spied the actor's blond hair and the Oscar in his hand before he was swarmed by well-wishers. An awed, excited chant of "Ramsey's here" went up and circulated in the air, a low, persistent buzz that kept heads swiveling in his direction.

"Oh!" Dean scratched behind his ear. "Um, be right back, then," he said, bending down to shout in her face. But instead of walking to their break area, he joined the party guests flocking toward the actor.

"Wait! No." But it was too late. Dean's scarecrow height and narrow shoulders quickly disappeared among the people crowded into the ballroom.

Dean was a newbie, but she hadn't pegged him as a total amateur. How did he even get this gig? Advika wondered, hopping from one foot to another, her toes numb from having squeezed them into black one-size-too-small loafers she had hurriedly purchased hours earlier from Payless. She gripped the edge of the bar with slippery fingers and debated whether she should take off her shoes, worrying that once she did, her feet would rebel against going back in.

With Dean's desertion, there went Advika's hopes for taking her break. To distract herself from her foot pain, she imagined that she was one of the party guests rather than a mere bartender. If Advika were invited to the Oscars, of course she would be there as a nominee. And as long as she was daydreaming, she might as well make herself a winner too. She didn't know much about designers beyond the big names: Versace and Oscar de la Renta and Ralph Lauren. But for her moment in the spotlight, Advika would choose an up-and-coming Indian designer, and the form-fitting gown would be a brilliant shade of crimson with tasteful gold accents, which she'd wear along with stylish but comfortable shoes—maybe a custom pair from Converse? Her makeup would be simple—just soft, red lips and winged eyeliner. It would be the kind of look—dramatic, elegant, a touch whimsical—that would get her on all the best-dressed lists, despite being a mere screenwriter.

Usually, when Advika let herself daydream about winning an award, it would be about the speech she would give: touching yet funny, eliciting laughter from the front row of A-listers, and by the end of it, they'd be wiping away tears as they applauded. The camera would then cut to Advika's handsome partner, who would jump out of his seat and give her a standing ovation, as everyone around him marveled at how supportive he was of her. It was a fantasy she had envisioned for herself since her junior year of high school, and the shape of it had barely changed over the past ten years. (The one swap she made was having Emma Thompson present her the award instead of Brad Pitt.) But to be at the Governors Ball, in the midst of actual winners high on their own achievements, watching several famous women exchange embraces in between gabfests, gave Advika a new, aching dream. She didn't want to just win; she wanted to be a part of all this. Not just a tourist, given a day pass into the Hollywood dream, but an esteemed member of this community, ensconced in an inner circle.

More revelers arrived at Advika's station. She forced a smile as she looked past the twentysomethings who seemed to be around her age, standing on her outraged toes and trying and failing to spot Dean. As she busied herself pouring drinks for the impatient partygoers, who obviously didn't know or care that she had to handle their orders by herself, Advika thought of her most recent screenplay. She wanted it to be good enough to get her into this room as a guest, or at least the guest of someone successful. But even though Advika loved her screenplay and replayed the scenes in her head constantly (while driving to work, at work, in the shower, and making ramen for dinner), it didn't mean that anyone else would too. The screenplay was by far the best thing she had ever written, and as far as Advika knew, she'd be the only one ever to read it.

"Can you, like, do a heavier pour?" A brunette with heavy bronzer and a miniature nose told Advika after she handed her a Negroni. "We're not at some cheapo bar."

"Of course. Sorry." When confronted by rude customers, Advika avoided eye contact at all costs. Because if she didn't, she would see the smug expressions on their (almost always white) faces and lose it on them.

"These people, man," her date laughed, scratching his chin with his middle finger.

The group walked away without giving her a tip. Advika stifled a groan, her body tense from the new surge of pain biting her feet. She wiped away a thread of sweat above her upper lip, feeling as if everyone in the ballroom had seen how those guests had made her feel lesser than. An encounter like that only magnified how small her life had turned out. Especially on a night like this, when there was no way not to be attuned to the disparity between the haves and have-nots, the famous and the nobodies, the beautiful people and those who served them.

An Oscar, wearing a cape fashioned out of a black cocktail napkin, popped up inches from Advika's nose.

"Scotch and soda. Por favor."

She jumped back, startled. A silver-haired man with an elegantly undone bow tie grinned at her, and he was still holding his statue up, as if the award were asking for a drink. At the same time, a large group of bearded men, their faces flushed as they hollered and clapped each other on the back, made an unsteady beeline toward her. Judging by their science teacher looks and puffed-up bravado, she surmised they had been favored to win the Academy Award for something technical—special effects, or perhaps sound mixing—but lost in an upset. Advika made a *pfft* sound, annoyed and nervous about the approaching drunken horde. The silver-haired man saw where she was staring, and turned around to speak to them.

"Gentlemen, why don't you…" was all she heard him say. The beards looked at her quizzically but then collectively turned away, leaving her alone with the strange, handsome man. In the ballroom's dim lighting, he sort of looked like a tall, lanky George Clooney from the *Ocean's Eleven* poster, as if he too starred as a charming rogue in heist films. Even though the man was at minimum twenty years older than her, Advika found herself magnetized by him. He had the cocky yet endearing confidence of a movie star headlining his own hit franchise, training all of his attentions on her as if she were his co-star instead of an extra. *He's very keen on you*, her sister, Anu, would have told her if she were there, in a dramatic fake British accent punctuated by a giggle.

"I was here earlier, but you didn't notice me," the man said, flashing a dazzling, gap-toothed smile. "So I thought it might help if I dressed him up a bit. It's a little vulgar, isn't it, for him to parade around without a stitch of clothing?"

"I...guess?" Advika poured his Scotch and soda, and as she handed it to him, their fingers briefly touched, giving her a pleasant jolt. "Congratulations, by the way," she said, nodding at his award.

"Oh, this?" He chuckled. "It's always nice to win one. Shows that the folks here still tolerate me well enough." He turned around and briefly surveyed the crowd. Three women in black gowns and sensible pumps stood in a semicircle a few feet away. Advika noted how they took the man in, as if he were a gallon of ice cream on a sweltering day. She briefly made eye contact with the one in the middle, an older blond woman who had been actually biting her lip while staring at him. The woman (a talent manager, likely, or some kind of studio flack) looked away, embarrassed, and Advika returned her attention to this man who apparently made the over-forty ladies salivate.

The man swung back around, and the women huddled together to whisper.

"I like it over here. It's not too crowded, and I don't have to shout to be heard. Maybe I'll hang out here for a while, help fend off other drunken losers. Wait, that's not kind. Nonwinners." He gave her a crooked grin.

"Sure," Advika said, carefully rocking back onto the balls of her feet to give her toes some relief. Where was Dean? Everything below her ankles was about to mutiny.

"You're on the job; maybe we shouldn't bother you." The silver-haired man cocked his head to indicate he was speaking on behalf of himself and his statue. Advika caught a glimpse of the name emblazoned on the bottom, but with the lighting so dim, all she spotted was the letter *J*.

"No, it's fine." As if Advika would tell an Oscar winner to leave so she could take her break already. Not that she exactly wanted him to leave either—even though she had no idea who he was. Advika's pain was clouding her thinking, which was surely why she didn't recognize him. But by the way the industry women, who were inching forward with birdlike steps, were wowed by J, he must have had some power in Hollywood. He didn't carry himself like a sound mixer or composer or film editor, all of whom Advika had served that night, creating a game for herself by trying to determine their jobs based on their behavior and snippets of conversation. J was a Somebody with a capital *S*, but he didn't strike Advika as a director. Perhaps he was a producer?

"Excuse me." The blond woman had practically leaped over to J's right, her elbow knocking into his Oscar. "I just wanted to say congratulations. I adored your film."

J turned to face her while smoothly pushing his trophy away from her arm. "Is that so?" He took a sip of his drink and then flashed Advika a bemused look, raising his eyebrows and making a "yikes" expression with his lips. Advika responded by giving him a small smile and a shrug. Their fleeting, wordless exchange was oddly invigorating. Advika was used to being invisible in situations like these, mini-dramas that lasted for the entirety of people waiting for their drinks. But J acted as if this woman had intruded on the two of them.

"Your movie was so deserving," she gushed. "I'm so glad all this Oscars So White nonsense didn't ruin your chances."

"Seriously?" Advika muttered under her breath.

"It's just a travesty, how that tweet hashtag thing was trying to take attention away from the nominated films. I'm sorry, but you can't nominate an actor because he's Black, brown, green, or whatever." The woman shot Advika a withering look before retraining her gaze on J. "It should just come down to the performance, don't you think?"

Advika kept her face neutral with all her might, stopping herself from reacting more than she already had. She was supposed to be the equivalent of wallpaper at events like this. But it was disappointing that despite the amount of conversation about diversity and representation that #OscarsSoWhite had received in the weeks leading up the awards show, this awful comment was the only mention Advika had heard about it all night. She snuck a glance at J. Would he agree with this idiot woman? Advika steeled herself for his response, waiting to be let down but hoping not to be. And based on the way the woman was staring at him with furiously blinking eyes, they were both equally curious about what J would say.

But J offered no reply. Instead, he merely gave Advika another knowing look, the corners of his mouth briefly pricking up. Advika sagged with relief. J thought she was a nitwit.

"My name's Lynn, by the way," the blond woman persisted. She held out her hand, which J shook as if touching raw meat. "We met at the SAG after-party last week?" Then Lynn turned to Advika. "Champagne, with a splash of vodka. But it has to be top-shelf." The dismissive tenor of her voice went silken as she returned to J. "So listen. I'm not usually this bold, but my friends"—and here she gestured at the two women watching them with rapt attention, their feet slipped out of their heels—"put me up to this. They know I've had the biggest crush on you since—"

"My dear, I'm not interested. But thank you." J took his Oscar and stepped to the side, where Advika had just poured a dollop of her bar's cheapest vodka into Lynn's champagne flute. Lynn grabbed the glass like a microphone, large drops spilling out as she stomped away. J chuckled under his breath.

"That really doesn't happen to me anymore," he said out loud, more to himself than Advika. "At least not that overt." J shook his head and ran his fingers over the lapel of his tuxedo jacket. "What were we talking about?"

"You said you'd look out for me, help me fend off the sad sacks who didn't win Oscars like you." *Are you flirting?* Anu's voice popped up in Advika's brain.

"Ha," J responded. He raised his finger and mouthed, *One sec*, as he pulled out his phone from his breast pocket. As J turned his back to her again, Advika admired his silhouette: lean, yet also broad shouldered. He almost looked like an Oscar himself, except the trophy had a rectangular head and J's was more squarish. He had what Advika liked to think of as "Goldilocks height": not too tall, not too short, but just right. If they danced together, she wouldn't have to wear flats or stand on her tiptoes. Instead, Advika's chin would graze J's shoulder, which meant he could press his cheek against hers as they danced. Advika slammed her palm hard against her forehead, as if she could push the absurd concept of dancing with J out of her mind.

He swung toward her once more, then pretended to tip his hat at her, as if he were a cowboy wearing a Stetson. She blushed. Advika waited for him to say something, her gaze going to his bow tie, too nervous to meet his eyes. But J said nothing, only taking another sip from his drink. Surely he couldn't be waiting for her to speak. What could she possibly even say? Advika pulled her foot out of her right shoe and pointed it behind her, as if she were a flamingo. The agony of one foot diminished while that of the other increased. So she was already in a highly agitated state when she realized that J was now peering at her chest with the intensity of someone taking an eye exam trying to read the letters on the last row. Living, and especially working, in LA meant receiving these kinds of glances on a near-daily basis. But to be outright stared at in this audacious manner was so bizarre she wanted to laugh.

"No name tag. So I guess I'll just have to ask you your name," he finally said, looking up at her apologetically, as if it were his fault he didn't know it.

"Advika," she mumbled. She couldn't recall the last time a stranger had asked this of her, and she fumbled the syllables in her mouth, as if her own name were a new language to her.

"I'm sorry, my dear. I didn't catch it."

"Advika," she said, raising her voice to be heard over the brief tidal wave of applause as Ramsey winded through the center of the party.

"Aretha?"

"Sure!" she shouted back. What was the point in correcting him? The silence stretched between them as the noise swelled when the actor crossed just mere feet away from Advika's station. She had been searching the crowd gathered around Ramsey, hoping to catch sight of Dean, when J surprised Advika by circling behind the bar to stand beside her. She quickly returned her right foot back into her shoe and stifled a shriek of pain.

"Here comes young Mr. Howell," he said into her ear, pointing his Oscar in the direction of the crowd. "Or not so young anymore, is he?" They both watched as Ramsey and his entourage entered the smoker's patio, seeming to take a quarter of the party with them. "There's always a prince who feels the crown is owed to him," J mused, the violet lights giving a warm tint to his silver hair. "And this one finally got his."

Despite the sensation of her toes being fed into a meat grinder, Advika tingled with excitement. Unlike seemingly everyone else in the Dolby Ballroom, J had not been captivated by the movie star or his Oscar-winning performance. Advika had seen *The Executioner's Final Reply*, and twenty minutes in she knew that the gruesome medieval drama was Ramsey's Hail Mary, a bid to score the best actor prize that had long eluded him.

"But it's such a crock, right?" Advika met the silver-haired man's eyes and felt a frisson of connection between them. "He's the kind of guy who pretends he doesn't want accolades and awards, but he was so thirsty for them."

"Ha, yes. Exactly. So I assume you don't think he's the best actor of your generation?" J took a sip of his drink, his middle finger tapping the glass as he did so.

"He's not from *my* generation, but I think he's very good. I just wouldn't have given him an Oscar because he ate a raw bison heart and screamed at everyone like a belligerent toddler. The CGI dragon was more realistic than his performance, honestly."

The silver-haired man chuckled. "I'm Julian. You're hilarious." He held out his hand, and before shaking it, Advika wiped her damp palm on her pants. He held on to her hand a beat longer than necessary, and she looked away, embarrassed.

"Would you like another drink?" she asked. Julian was still standing next to her, crossing the invisible line separating somebodies from nobodies. This development was so discomfiting, with a splash of thrilling, that Advika needed to reestablish that boundary by reminding him she was just a service worker.

"Allow me," Julian said, sweeping a bottle of Scotch from behind the bar to refill his glass. "I hope you don't mind me joining you back here," Julian added with a wink. "It's better company." She blushed, and the tingling sensation intensified. "Would you like one too?"

Advika shook her head, feeling her face grow hot. As Julian busied himself making a new drink, Advika pinched the inside of her wrist to remind herself she wasn't dreaming, that this terrifically good-looking man was ignoring Hollywood's biggest party to chat with her. Which again brought her back to wondering who this man was, exactly, and why he would spend so much time talking with her. And what had he won the Oscar for? Unlike everyone else holding gold, he seemed pretty blasé about his award. She wouldn't have been surprised if he ambled back into the party and forgot to take it with him.

"So," Julian said, "obviously you're a fan of movies. What is it you like so much?"

Advika glanced briefly at him, then at his Oscar, glowing like a small flame on a starless night, somehow managing to still look dignified despite wearing a superhero cape made out of a cocktail napkin. To have it in such proximity made Advika feel as if she were about to speak to the movies themselves. Like a worshipper at a temple speaking directly to her deity, Advika answered Julian's question by addressing his award.

"It's the structure. The rising action, the falling action, the resolution—I can follow it like a line on my palm. Everything else can surprise you—the acting choices, the score, the direction, the plot twist even—but not the structure. When nothing else in the world is predictable, you can anticipate when each story beat will happen. If you know what kind of movie you're watching, like a rom-com, you can almost time it to the minute. I like that. Nothing else in the world feels more comfortable to me than knowing the rhythms of a movie."

Advika had never articulated that out loud before, because no one had ever asked her. Dazed by her own admission, she was about to look up to see Julian's response, when there was a sharp rap on her left shoulder: Dean had finally returned. He was breathing heavily, his forehead dotted with sweat, and his smell had gone from trash can to garbage dump.

"You can take five now if you want," he said, bending down toward her ear. Then Dean looked past her and gushed, "Julian Zelding!" He fiddled with something tucked in the back of his waistband that looked like a rolled-up screenplay.

"Don't," she hissed. Startled by Advika's admonition, Dean

seemed at a loss for what to do. Still awed by Julian, he gave him an awkward military salute.

"Stand down—I'm not your captain," Julian told Dean with a bemused smile. He picked his Oscar up off the bar and nodded at Advika, indicating he was about to leave. Advika's jaw tightened. She wanted so badly for him to stay, especially now that she knew his name and that—based upon Dean's response to him—he really was a Somebody. A Somebody whose name seemed so familiar, but she still couldn't place it.

"Excuse me!" And now Lynn was back, her half-empty champagne flute squeezed tight in her fist. "Did I not ask you for top-shelf vodka? This tastes like dog shit."

"Oh. Right." The night was beginning to take on the farcical absurdity of a Marx Brothers film. Who would stop by next— Ramsey Howell? "My mistake. Can I get you another one?"

"Like I'd trust you to tie my shoe, let alone make my drink." Lynn nodded at Dean. "You make it." She set down the champagne flute carelessly, and it toppled on its side, spilling all over. Dean stared dumbly as Advika grabbed it before it could smash to the floor. She set it down behind the bar, and as she did so, she registered that Julian, and his Oscar, was gone.

"Taking my break now," Advika announced, leaving before either Dean or Lynn had a chance to respond. Let stupid, wandering Dean deal with entitled, overserved guests. Advika limped off toward the swinging doors that would take her through the kitchen to the employee bathrooms. How she longed to chuck her loafers in the trash, and the whole night along with them. Advika never, ever drank on the job. But she was seriously considering downing a shot of tequila after she returned from her break. It might be the only way she could stand doing this job for several more hours.

Because to have had Julian's attentions, even for a brief moment, showed her how starved she was to be seen. Even now, walking past party attendees who barely acknowledged her presence reminded Advika how much her life had shrunken down to basics: work, eat, sleep, survive. And although she had been thrilled at the opportunity to work her first Governors Ball, the whole job had turned into a bright red arrow flashing in her face, a stinging reminder of all the ways she was a failure.

Advika felt fingernails dig into her skin as someone grabbed her forearm. She stumbled back and her foot connected with the square toe of a leather heel.

"You," Lynn said, pulling Advika around to face her. "You just don't walk away from me like that."

Advika was too in shock to respond. The fingernails went in deeper.

"I'm going to report you to your manager. You have no right to be so rude to me. You practically poisoned my drink!" Lynn swayed slightly, and her grip loosened. With their faces so close together, Advika could now see that this woman, with her unfocused eyes and smeared red lipstick, was full-on drunk, as if she had just downed several tequila shots in succession. "You don't treat people this way. Do you hear me?"

You're going to let her treat you this way? Anu's incredulous voice echoed in her head. *Sure,* Advika thought. *Nothing matters. I don't matter.*

"Ladies," Julian interjected. Advika's heartbeat sped up, and she was so jittery with relief she was near tears. "Mind if I join this conversation?"

Lynn finally let go of Advika's arm. "Why, Julian—I thought you had left," she slurred. "Could we chat? I think we got off on the wrong foot. I'm just such a fan, you know." She lifted her left leg as if trying to do a high kick. "I've been told I have foot-in-mouth disease. Ha ha."

"Let's go get you a drink. A real one," Julian soothed, placing his hand on the small of Lynn's back. Advika watched them go, tears streaming down her cheeks and bouncing off her chin. *Get the fuck out of here,* Anu's voice admonished. Advika fled the ballroom, through the swinging doors and the kitchen buzzing like a shaken beehive, past red-faced chefs and sous chefs chopping and sweating and shouting at each other, and through another door into a nearly empty hallway. For the first time since early that afternoon, Advika was not surrounded by a sea of other people. It should have been a relief to finally have a moment to herself, but instead the stillness only magnified her isolation. One of the overhead lights flickered in a menacing way, the dim fluorescent bulb making a *bzzz* sound as if announcing the arrival of a monster creeping toward her with unhurried steps. Advika shivered as she ran her fingers over her forearm, wincing at the three tiny half-moons left in her skin by Lynn's fingernails. From down the hall, Advika heard a door creak open. She was just about to escape to the sanctuary of the women's bathroom when she heard Julian speak.

"There you are." He strode toward her, his Oscar glinting in his hand. "Are you okay?"

Advika found herself unable to immediately respond, so stunned she was to see him. She hiccupped, then looked down at her cursed feet through tear-streaked eyelashes.

"Yes," she finally managed to say.

"I worked as a waiter about three lifetimes ago," Julian said with a sigh. "There were so many times I had to bite my tongue, when all I wanted to do instead was throw a punch. And once, I did."

"Really?" Advika said, looking up with surprise. Julian had the refined, debonair comportment of James Bond crossed with a European prince. He did not look like someone who ever had to wipe down sticky tables, plunge toilets, or refill drinks.

"This man decided to express his unhappiness with the temperature of his steak by trying to shove it down my throat.

Instead, my fist met his mouth. I lost the job, but not my dignity." He shrugged modestly, a cheeky grin lining his face. "No regrets."

"Wow," Advika said. The lighting in the hallway, which just moments ago had the hallmarks of a horror movie, now cultivated the intimacy of candlelight. Julian's presence had the effect of standing near a fireplace after being rescued from a blizzard, the surging warmth not just restorative but lifesaving.

"Did she hurt you?" Julian's eyebrows creased in concern, and his eyes traveled to Advika's arm, which she was still cradling.

"Oh, it's nothing. I just can't believe she'd grab me that way." A charred, slightly garlicky aroma emanated from the nearby kitchen, and Julian's mouth twisted into a comic grimace.

"It looks like the kitchen staff isn't having a good night either," he said. Advika felt her lips tremble into a nervous smile. "The people in this town can be obscenely awful and selfish, especially to the people who work the hardest and deserve their ire the least." Julian placed a gentle hand on Advika's shoulder. "I am so sorry you had to endure that. And I'm very sorry that I inadvertently brought that woman into your orbit. I had her escorted out of the party."

Advika gasped. "You did?"

The door opened again, accompanied by a strong burnt odor and flurry of tense voices.

"Let's go somewhere where we can have a proper conversation," Julian said, his eyes twinkling. "Without any more interruptions. What do you say?"

⁓

Advika had worked eight major after-parties in the past two years: Grammys and Golden Globes, Elton John benefits and AFI tributes. But this was her very first Governors Ball, and the very first time an A-list guest had asked her to step outside to have a chat. Not to mention whisking her away to a rooftop overlooking the entire city.

"Your bartender friend will be fine without you. The party's starting to wind down," Julian reassured Advika as they stood side by side in front of a glass-walled observation deck situated atop the ballroom. "Everyone will be heading to the *Vanity Fair* party soon. The only people left in there will be...well." He said the word "well" as if it was understood what he meant, and so Advika nodded as if she did.

Julian had mistaken her quietness for concern over leaving Dean and her post at the bar for too long. But really, she was still flummoxed that this particular Oscar winner had taken an interest in her. That, except for searching for a name tag on her blouse, he had kept his eyes firmly locked on hers, as if an Indian girl dressed in black with sweaty armpits and a half-slumped ponytail was the most invigorating sight he'd ever seen.

When Dean had first squealed Julian's name, she had experienced a vague glimmer of recognition, but his identity still remained a mystery. Only when they got outside, when she got a glimpse of his name newly engraved on his Oscar—JULIAN ZELDING, PRODUCER, BEST PICTURE, *WEST OF THE GUN*—did she realize who he was. Hollywood icon, producer of five best picture winners and ten nominees. His first Oscar win had been in 1974, more than a decade before she had been born.

Advika had always heard Julian's name as part of the industry chatter at her various day jobs. But she had no idea what he looked like until tonight. And now that she was able to really look at him without the distraction of her job and other party guests, it wasn't just his IMDb page that kept her in sort of a stunned stasis. *How could a senior citizen be hot?* There was Anu's voice in her head again. Teasing, yes, but also awed. Because he was extremely hot. Paul Newman–as–elder-statesman hot.

"Your name again, my dear?" Julian tapped the Oscar's head as if it were his pet. "I didn't catch it when we were inside."

"Advika." Her voice whimpered like a dying balloon. To try to seem less nervous, she leaned back against the wall, hoping she seemed cool and collected, rather than in serious pain from her $19.99 loafers.

"Advika," Julian said, reclining against the wall with her, then taking a cigar out of his jacket pocket. Before lighting it, he set the Oscar down on the ground, the gold statue idling between them like a third wheel. "That's beautiful. Is it Sanskrit?"

"Yes," she said, although she wasn't really sure if it was Hindi or Sanskrit. Maybe both? It's not like her parents ever told her. She had Googled it once but promptly forgot. But she always remembered her name's meaning, and after some prodding, she told Julian with a mumbling, blushing pride that her name meant "unique."

"Unique? Well, I can see that. I noticed you the moment I walked inside." The combination of the cigar smoke and his cologne enraptured her, the scent as rare and heavenly as if bottled from the dewdrops of redwoods. She found herself inching closer to him until her heel tapped his Oscar, and she drew back immediately.

"Thank you," Advika said finally, perhaps waiting a beat too long to respond to his compliment. But Julian's attentions were no longer focused on her anyhow. He was staring out into the blue-purple sky, arms folded, lost in thought.

"Handing out Academy Awards at a mall," he said with a sigh, more to himself than to her. "I miss the Shrine."

"The Shrine?"

"The Shrine Auditorium. Beautiful venue, very glamorous. That's where they used to hold these things. That and the Dorothy Chandler. Then they built this monstrosity," Julian said, waving at the neon lights and billboards surrounding

Hollywood & Highland. The entertainment and shopping complex was where both the Dolby Theatre and the Dolby Ballroom were perched like the Mount Olympus of cinema, hovering out of the reach of mortals snapping photos of the Hollywood Walk of Fame five floors below.

"I like it," Advika said softly. He gave her a questioning look. "I know it might be like a New Yorker saying they like Times Square, but it's true." Emboldened by Julian's surprised chuckle, Advika continued, getting more animated as she went along.

"LA should have a place like this. It's all a little too plasticky and generic, I know. But my parents used to talk about how when friends and relatives visited them in the eighties, they'd get disappointed there was no real quote-unquote Hollywood to visit. Just the Walk of Fame and Marilyn Monroe's handprints at Grauman's Chinese Theatre. My parents hated coming to this area, because they said it was always too hot and grimy. But look at this." Now it was Advika who waved her hand in the air, as if casting a spell. "When people think of Hollywood now, it's a real destination. Not just an ancient wooden sign up in the hills. They can come here and feel close to the magic."

She smiled even as her big right toe screamed inside its shoe. Advika shifted her weight so that her right foot balanced on her left. The pain had become agonizing, but she couldn't acknowledge it, not when this movie producer was gazing at her like she had just revealed the secrets of the Sphinx.

"So what's your dream, Advika?" he said in a warm, gravelly tone that reminded her of hot charcoal on an open grill. "Actress, writer, director. Or producer, perhaps." He waggled his eyebrows like Groucho Marx at this last suggestion, as if it were a shared joke between them.

"None of the above," she replied, tugging at her shirt collar. The unexpected question had left Advika feeling exposed, and she couldn't bear to talk about her pitiful aspirations with someone of his stature.

Julian chuckled. "The way you talked about your love of films earlier, I know that can't be true. Besides, beautiful people who work these parties didn't move to Hollywood for a career in the service industry. They want something. They're dreamers, like me." He ruminatively puffed on his cigar, then blew smoke rings into the balmy February night. "What do you want to do?"

"Write," she said, unable to mask the mortification in her voice. "I write screenplays."

"What kind?"

"Comedies, mostly." She thought of her laptop, home to three screenplays, only one of which had been read by anyone connected to the industry. Feeling like a fraud, she quickly added, "Right now, I'm trying to get staffed on a TV show, though." She had only had a handful of interviews for writer's assistant positions in the past several months, but that seemed more realistic to share than her flatlining screenwriting career.

"TV? Interesting," Julian said. "I don't believe I've seen a television series since 1992. As you can see," he said, pointing at the Oscar between them, "I have another preferred medium."

He had spoken with the polite diffidence of someone who had thought she held great promise, but was now disappointed by her. Advika's shoulders sagged. This was it. The night's plot twist had been amazing, nearly miraculous, and now it was over. Off she would go, back to her bartending alongside a surly Dean and pouring drinks for more assholes like Lynn. Her night couldn't end this way. She tried for a Hail Mary.

"I like *Columbo*," Advika said, turning to face him, subtly arching her back to better show off her chest.

"Ah, yes, I have seen that one." Julian pulled out his phone, glanced at the screen briefly, and returned it to his jacket pocket. "But that show is from my time, not yours."

"Reruns," she said with what she hoped was an alluring smile.

"Ah, ha." Julian flashed a toothy grin, his blue eyes amused. "What do you like about it?"

"Peter Falk is hilarious. He's, um…" Julian took her in with an appraising, perhaps even appreciative, stare. "I like his shtick. The rumpled coat, the pestering questions, how often he brings up his wife for no reason. And how he always has the upper hand. Just as the murderer thinks he's off the hook, Columbo will turn around and say, 'Oh, just one more thing.' And that question nails 'em. He outsmarts them every single time."

Julian laughed, and victory surged through Advika. The night still had a chance.

"My sist—" she added, and the words became dust in her mouth. She swallowed and heard Anu's voice again. *Why'd you have to go and ruin it by bringing me up?*

"Your sister what?" Julian asked quietly. He took her hand in both of his own, and the soft warmth of his palms against her own filled her with so much emotion she nearly started to cry. Advika willed herself not to give in to the grief that threatened to loosen itself from behind her heart. After counting down from ten, she finally was able to answer him.

"My sister. My twin, Anu. She hated *Columbo* as much as I liked it. Which is what made it fun to watch together." A long, choked pause. "She u-used to imitate his voice to m-make me laugh."

"I'm sorry for your loss," Julian said into her ear, the scent of the cigar on his breath eliciting goose bumps on her arms. Advika nodded and whispered a thank-you.

Below them, limousines resembling dark, languid sharks moved slowly down the valet lane before flowing into a street clogged with glinting headlights. Julian let out a little sigh, then dropped her hand. Advika retrieved it and placed it against her heart, which was beating so rapidly it filled her eardrums. She watched him bend down to pick up his Oscar, resignation washing over her. She had failed. It was over.

He took a few steps away from her, then turned around with the cigar dangling from his lips, one eye squinting just like Columbo. "Oh, just one more thing," he said in a pitch-perfect imitation of Peter Falk. "Have dinner with me?"

Over burgers and milkshakes at a diner in East Hollywood, Advika learned that Peter Falk had been one of Julian's poker buddies. He first heard the actor try out his infamous catchphrase while setting down a winning hand, winning Yul Brynner's horse in the process.

"A horse?" Advika said, dipping a French fry into a tiny pond of ketchup. She knew Yul Brynner was an old-time movie star, but couldn't remember what he starred in, and she didn't want to ask and betray her ignorance.

"We'd bet all sorts of things, just to make it interesting. One time I bet a major role in my next picture. Luckily, I won, or else Jean-Claude Van Damme would have starred in *The Feast of Souls* instead of Sean Connery."

His peculiarly hearty laughter, reminding Advika of a hic-cupping bear, echoed around the empty restaurant. On their drive over in Julian's cream-colored Bentley, he had dashed out a series of texts, his index finger moving across the screen with astounding speed. The diner's lights had flicked on just as they pulled into the deserted parking lot close to 11 p.m. A yawning waitress had opened the door to let them in, and the Formica table at which they were seated had been slightly damp, as if someone had just hurriedly wiped it down moments before.

Julian's phone, which lay on the table next to his Academy Award, buzzed. He picked it up, scrolled down the screen, and frowned. As he was reading, his phone vibrated again. With a sigh, he stood up and took the call. "One moment," he told her. Advika and the Oscar watched him walk down the diner's narrow aisle and out the door.

Admit it, she heard Anu's voice say. *He's old. Like, real old*. And it was true: inside the diner, with its bright fluorescent lighting, Julian still had a rakish handsomeness to him, but his resemblance to Paul Newman had drifted toward the final credits of the actor's IMDb page, when he was playing charming but cranky grandpa types. In the dim lighting on the rooftop and inside his car, Advika hadn't felt their age difference so acutely. But watching Julian across the table from her, she couldn't help noticing his thinning blondish-silver hair, the deep laugh lines that traced from nose to chin, and the small white whiskers blooming out of his left ear. *Google him*, Anu's voice implored.

With jittery hands, Advika took her phone out and searched "Julian Zelding age." The search results showed he was sixty-seven.

"Ha," she whispered to herself. "He's not that old." She did the math. They were forty-one years apart.

That's still pretty old, her sister huffed. Advika grimaced. She was surprised that Julian actually looked a little older than his age. Because it seemed everyone, especially with money, had discovered their own fountains of youth in Los Angeles in the form of plastic surgery and Botox and expensive skin treatments that kept them all looking preternaturally youthful. Julian seemed to have eschewed that, which Advika told herself was pretty cool. He was a rebel, an iconoclast. He believed in aging gracefully, a welcome rarity in this city. And even with his noticeable wrinkles and receding hairline, Julian was the first man who stirred feelings of attraction in Advika in three years.

His Academy Award, looking as if it were standing guard by his milkshake, gleamed under the bright white lights. Advika stared at it, marveling at how close she was to the ultimate symbol of Hollywood achievement. Her hands twitched at her sides, but she didn't dare touch it. Instead, after making sure Julian was still outside, she went on YouTube to find a clip of *West of the Gun* winning best picture. On stage were three people: a tall redhead at the center, and Julian and a bearded white man flanking her. As the woman rattled off a list of names, Advika kept her eyes trained on Julian. He seemed pleased, but not exploding with glee like his fellow Oscar winners, both of whom seemed to be about twenty years younger than him. When the orchestra played them off the stage, Julian immediately strode away while the other male producer attempted to shout his thank-yous over the insistent swell of strings.

Julian returned to the table, and Advika quickly slid her phone under her thigh.

"If I never hear the word 'congratulations' again, or at least for a year," he said, chuckling, though his eyes were unsmiling. "It just stops losing its meaning after a while."

Advika politely nodded. She hadn't heard the word since graduating from college, and she wasn't sure if she'd ever hear it again. Seeming to sense her dejection, Julian pushed aside his plate and leaned forward, his elbows on the table.

"Tell me about yourself, Ad . . . Ad-veeka. Am I saying that correctly?"

"Uh . . . sure." She waved her hand, embarrassed. Advika hated when the pronunciation of her name became a part of the conversation. "And there's not much to tell."

"I find that hard to believe." He smiled widely, then looked past her and shook his head slightly. Advika turned around to see the back of their waitress's wiry figure as she headed through the kitchen's swinging doors.

"Your life is much more interesting." She nervously tapped the floor with her socked feet, her cheap loafers abandoned inside Julian's luxury vehicle.

"I disagree," he laughed. "And I'm easy to Google," he added with a hint of slyness, and she blushed. Perhaps he had been watching her from outside earlier and had seen her frantic on her phone.

"Well, what do you want to know?"

"What's your favorite film?" Julian raised his palms. "I ask with no judgment. One of my all-time favorites is *Citizen Kane*. But another favorite is *Clash of the Titans*. The one from the eighties, with Sir Laurence Olivier and the, well, let's call them *primitive* special effects."

"Really?" Advika sputtered, delighted. She had seen a You-Tube video essay only a few weeks ago dissecting why it was one of the schlockiest movies of all time. "Not to judge," she added, raising her palms too.

"I make no apologies," Julian said with a wry grin. "It's just about what makes you feel good." He slid off his tuxedo jacket, his white shirt perfectly tailored for his lean frame, each square button shining like onyx. "So, Advika, what movie makes you feel good?"

"*Bend It Like Beckham*." Her hands sank to her lap, and she bit down on her lower lip.

"The soccer comedy." He didn't sound dismissive or judgmental, just a little confused. Then he broke out into a smile. "Oh, of course."

Julian's expression, a light bulb not just of recognition but understanding, buoyed Advika. She told him about seeing *Bend It Like Beckham* for the first time when she was fifteen, and how the sight of someone who looked like her on the big screen—specifically, the main character Jess's brown skin, dark wavy hair, and tomboyish way of dressing—had been like an electrical charge.

"We're not used to seeing ourselves onscreen, any screen. But here was this movie about an Indian girl, and she gets to be the main character. And I could relate to how she was torn between her love of family and her love of soc—Well, they call it football in the UK. I had always loved movies since, like, forever, but to see myself represented up there...I can't even describe it. It wasn't a perfect mirror for me and my life, but it didn't have to be. I just felt...seen. And nothing on TV or in the movies had made me feel that way before. The day I saw *Beckham* was the day my writing dreams were fully born."

Advika drummed her fingers against her lips, as if astonished by what came out. But what really surprised her was how Julian was able to draw all of this out of her, the deep marrow of what she considered her essentialness. Anu had known all of this, of course. When her sister was still here, sharing her thoughts with her twin was like writing in a diary. Anu had represented a safe space, and then she was gone. And Advika collapsed in on herself, not knowing how to communicate her innermost thoughts with anyone, not even in an actual diary.

But that unabashed flow of opinions and feelings had been awakened by Julian. He wanted to hear what she had to say. Advika sat up straighter and smoothed down her hair.

"Movies can be so powerful," Julian said, briefly glancing down. "Life changing, even. I know that very well." Their eyes met, and Advika's heart fluttered. "My world opened up because films awakened my imagination and let me imagine a better world. And a better version of myself." Even while in college studying film, Advika had never met someone so keyed into her specific frequency about movies and how they were her North Star.

After a few moments, he picked up a fry from his plate and playfully dabbed it in the dollop of ketchup on Advika's plate. Tickled, she reciprocated this move, eyeing him slyly. He chuckled, and the two went on like this for a few minutes while talking about their other favorite movies, until all their fries were gone. With his last fry, Julian had traced the letter A, followed by an exclamation point, in his leftover smears of ketchup. Advika, delicately licking her salt-edged finger-tips, thrilled at this small gesture, and she filed this away as something she could have one of her characters do in a future screenplay. But what Julian said next deflated her.

"Tell me more about your writing." He wiped his hands with his napkin, then balled it up and tossed it onto his plate.

"Oh." Advika slumped down in her seat. "Like I said, I wrote three screenplays. Plus, a couple of spec scripts for when I went out for some TV writing jobs."

"So you have an agent." Julian nodded approvingly.

"I did, once," she said in a forced upbeat tone, as if she didn't find this line of questioning humiliating in the slightest. "I won a major screenplay writing contest in college, and through that I got an agent. But he dropped me about a year later." Her face burned at the memory of the three-line email. Not even given the courtesy of a conversation or a phone call. There was a time she had it memorized, but now she could only recall him say-ing she was "a sparkling talent" whose work didn't have "broad appeal."

"And the TV spec scripts?"

"It was a fellowship thing to diversify writers' rooms." She paused to take a long sip of her water. "I didn't get any of them."

"Hollywood is the ficklest of the fickle," Julian said, shaking his head. "But I hope you're not giving up."

"Not at all." Advika beamed with a confidence she didn't feel. "I still write. I'll never stop writing." She thought of mentioning #OscarsSoWhite, and how she hoped the outcry over the lack of diversity in that year's nominations could initiate a change in the industry to be more inclusive of people like her. But Advika decided against it, not wanting to invoke the specter of Lynn and her asinine comments. "In the meantime," she added with a self-deprecating grin, "I do the clichéd Hollywood thing to make ends meet, as you saw tonight." To remember how they met was to remember the terrific imbalance between them: age, income, prestige. She picked up the remains of her half-eaten hamburger, which was cold and mushy, then dropped it back on the plate. "Can we change the subject?" She nodded toward his Oscar. "What it's like to hear your name called out as a winner?"

"I'll show you." Julian stretched out his arms as if taking a big yawn, then startled her by dropping them in one swift movement to loudly drum the table.

"And the winner for best original screenplay is," he said dramatically, continuing the drumroll so that the Oscar, plates, and cutlery all vibrated on the table, "Advika . . . ?"

"Srinivasan," she said shyly.

"Advika Srinivasan!" he bellowed. Cheers and applause erupted nearby, and they saw their waitress, plus a line cook and busboy, whooping enthusiastically behind the diner counter.

"I promise I didn't ask them to do that," Julian said, his eyes shining with delight. He stood up, picked up his Oscar, and handed it to her.

With confused laughter, she accepted the award, which had a welcome weightiness to it. She looked at the statuette's blank expression and saw her smile reflected back in its tiny gold face.

"So," Julian said, sliding back into the booth opposite her, "how does it feel?"

Advika looked at him, then the Oscar. "Like a million fireworks spelling out my name."

Julian flicked his right hand, and Advika heard retreating footsteps as the diner emptied to only leave the two of them. "The way you talk about films, it just gets me. Right here." He patted his heart three times. "You remind me of myself when I was younger, ambition and insecurity constantly warring inside me. My ambition won. And yours will too." Advika, surprised, gingerly set the Oscar down next to her own milkshake. The overhead fluorescent lighting dimmed, and the diner took on a warmer, familial glow.

"Do you know why I approached you tonight at the Governors Ball?" She shook her head, looking at the cross-shaped wrinkle between his eyebrows, unable to meet his gaze directly. "In that room full of preening blowhards, you had this . . . childlike wonder. Like being there meant something to you. But at the same time, your heart seemed to be breaking. You would smile so brightly, and then your face would drop. I watched you cycle through that over and over, between elation and melancholy." Advika, wide-eyed, pressed both hands against her cheeks, as if to check to see if her face was still showing those emotions. "You reminded me of someone I once knew," Julian added, his voice breaking slightly. "And I . . . I just needed to make sure you were okay."

He was silent for a moment, as if weighing something. Then he stood up and slid into the booth next to her, his leg touching hers. Julian smoothed down a tendril of Advika's hair and in one gentle motion tucked it behind her ear. The electricity of his touch rippled through her, and she shivered.

"I've known loss just like you," Julian said, his voice now hovering just above a whisper, his gaze as magnetic as a tractor beam. "And that's why I think there's this connection between us. I think you feel it too."

"Yes," she breathed. His hand alighted briefly on her shoulder, then lightly traced down the edge of her arm, to the inside of her wrist.

"I'm besotted by you, Advika." His finger danced a middle eight on her palm. "I've been blowing off people all night—my team, my colleagues, my friends—because this night didn't become important to me until I met you." Advika was shocked to feel herself tear up. It had been so long since she felt seen. Since she felt desired. Julian moved closer to her, cupped her chin between his thumb and forefinger, and kissed her.

Anu's voice was somewhere in her head, fighting to be heard. But Advika pushed it away, pushed it all away, and kissed him back.

CHAPTER TWO

Something Wild

SHE DIDN'T GET HOME UNTIL five thirty in the morning. Advika and Julian had made out in his Bentley like teenagers on the way to prom, while the vehicle coasted west through the empty streets of Los Angeles. She was shocked by how natural it felt to have her body intertwined with his, and even more so by his physicality. He might look like Paul Newman in his twilight years, but his body was muscular and firm, and he had a spry energy that even Advika's last few flings had not possessed.

Despite his protests, she insisted he return her to her car in the parking lot a few blocks away from where the Governors Ball was held. Before they parted, she gave him her phone number, not truly believing he would call her. But that was okay, she told herself as she drove down a freeway that was just starting to see its first rush of morning commuters. It was enough that the past few hours had even happened.

Advika's adrenaline from the crazy turn the night had taken kept her awake during her thirty-minute drive to her apartment in Echo Park. After pulling into her parking spot, Advika caught a glimpse of herself in the rearview mirror. She and Anu were fraternal twins, with her sister an inch taller and having a more willowy build, yet they had the same oval-shaped face, deep-set eyes, and pronounced widow's peak. Advika most often felt her sister's presence by looking at her own reflection. But this time, thankfully, she only saw herself. Her hair, pulled out of its ponytail by Julian's eager caresses, sproinged around her head like a fuzzy crown, and her lipstick had faded entirely, her lips a pink blur that stretched past the corners of her mouth. *You totally look like you were sucking face*, Anu's voice taunted. Advika ignored it. She didn't want the night's magic to wear off, even though she knew it would dissipate as soon as she walked through the front door. Which it did.

"Where've you been?" her roommate, Olive, said with a yawn when Advika crossed the threshold. Olive, wearing a low-cut top and baggy pajama bottoms, sipped a cup of coffee over the shipwreck of dishes cluttering their sink.

"Worked late. Governors Ball, remember? And I guess you're working early." Her roommate was a barista at a super-popular coffee shop in Santa Monica, favored by screenwriters much more successful than Advika.

"Ding ding ding." Olive dropped her mug onto the mountain of dirty dishes mostly made up of her coffee mugs and an entire set of porcelain rice bowls that had her surname inscribed in Mandarin with red lettering. Why Olive treated something that seemed like family heirlooms as if they were fast-food containers was beyond Advika's understanding.

"All right, then." Their dishes standoff had been going on for over a week, and Olive showed no signs of caving. But at that moment Advika was too exhausted to care. "I'm going to go collapse."

"Are you okay? You look…off." Olive dropped her pajama bottoms onto the floor, then reached for her miniskirt hanging off the oven handle between two dish towels.

"Off?" Advika brushed her fingers over her lips.

"Yeah. Like dazed." Olive peered at her, and Advika stepped

backward, bumping into the wall. "Like you're coming down off something."

"Just exhausted." *Elated.* "Long shift." *Hours of laughter and deep kisses.* "You know those Hollywood types." *Unbelievable gossip, confided solely to her.* "I'm beat. Have a good day."

"Yeah, okay." Olive was rummaging through the hall closet, already distracted by her morning routine, and Advika hobbled over to her room and shut the door.

Advika's bedroom faced west, but her sole window was a long rectangle above her bed, so she only got a tantalizingly small glimpse of the sky as the day brightened into morning and deepened into dusk. At the moment, the window rectangle was a tight gray frown, reflecting the early morning fog. The walk-in-closet-sized space had just enough room for a twin mattress, a desk, and an oak bureau foaming at the mouth with half-yanked-out pants and tee shirts. The Advika of several hours ago, ironing her blouse while wearing only a beige bra and black dress pants, rushing a dash of red lipstick over her chapped lips, forgoing eye makeup because she was running late, seemed so far away now.

Her phone's battery had dipped into the red, and so she shut it off before charging it. Then Advika slowly undressed, stripping to her underwear before crawling under the covers, not even bothering to wash her face or brush her teeth. Her body, from the top of her head to her still-stinging toes, cried out for sleep. She crushed her face into the pillow and tried to process the events of the past few hours. Advika recalled the warmth of Julian's hands on her bare back, and his lips on her neck. In those moments, entangled in each other, intoxicated with each other, the age difference didn't matter. She could imagine her sister interrogating her about this wild night, asking her point-blank if she would be attracted to him if he were just a "professor or an accountant or something else lame and boring."

And of course not, Advika would have told Anu. She couldn't deny that a huge part of Julian's allure was his connection to Hollywood. Not his power in the industry, necessarily, although that did have an impact too, but that he was a walking encyclopedia of movie history. During their meal at the diner, he must have shared at least ten anecdotes about old-time and current stars, casually tossing the information while she lapped it all up, often gasping with delight. She had been touched that he had trusted her with these amazing stories—not that she had anyone to share them with.

Advika mentally scrolled through her list of phone contacts: childhood friends from Sherman Oaks, assorted high school pals and college buddies, co-workers past and present ("Carl Wine Bar," "Delilah Catering," "Javie Boba"), a smattering of aunties and cousins from across the country. She barely talked to anyone, rarely having the energy to even respond to the "Just checking on you" or "Hey, wanna come over for dinner?" texts, and so those had now trickled to nearly nothing. The Oakies, whom she had grown up with in Sherman Oaks, stubbornly held on the longest, as she knew they would, but eventually even they drifted off, caught up in the currents of their own lives. Advika wished she knew how to do the same.

She simply didn't know how to operate in the world as just herself, without the loving, maddening presence of her three-minute-older sister, the one who sneaked them into nightclubs when they were underage, the one who had the first kiss and first boyfriend and got her driver's license first, the one who was always Advika's compass for any direction she wanted to go. Even if sometimes Anu, with her signature blunt bob hairstyle and purple lipstick, didn't agree with and sometimes mocked Advika's choices, she had been a sounding board and safe space. To lose her unmoored Advika so severely that two years after Anu's death, she pictured herself bobbing in the ocean like the movie with the scuba-diving couple abandoned in open water as great white sharks circled underneath them. Advika was barely holding on, her chin only just above the current, the sharks nipping at her feet. Her night with Julian was the first time since Anu's funeral that she felt herself not merely treading water but actively kicking her feet and starting to swim.

So Julian was old. He was a stranger. But Advika couldn't ignore the sparks spinning inside her from his lavish attention. *I get to have this*, she thought, curling her fist under the pillow, the words reverberating in her mind as she gave herself up to sleep.

Advika awoke nine hours later. By the time she pulled her face out of her pillow, reaching a stiff arm to search her bedside table for her phone, it was a little after 3 p.m. She drowsily pulled herself up, her bangs plastered to her sweaty forehead, and threw off her pale blue comforter. Despite the fact that it was February, LA was in the midst of a heatwave, and to save money, she and Olive had agreed not to use the air conditioner. But doing so turned Advika's bedroom into a sauna. She stood up on her bed and eased open the window a crack, letting in fresh air. Then she flopped back down, phone still in her hand, while she rummaged through a pile of clothes at the foot of her bed, pulling out a tank top with FINAL GIRL written on the front in red-edged black font.

"Okay, time to let reality back in," Advika said out loud, lying on her stomach on the narrow bed. She turned her phone on and closed her eyes, her thighs and legs not as sore as they would have been had she worked a full shift.

Her phone buzzed in her hands. The screen showed her messages upon messages upon messages: texts, WhatsApp messages,

social media notifications, emails. And a single voicemail. She
let out an audible *ugh*, then churned through them with sweaty
fingers.

After reading all of them, and listening to the voicemail,
her world had bent on its axis, gravity no longer keeping her
upright.

What Advika had lost:

Her job. (The high-end catering company where she had
worked for the past three years had fired her for leaving in the
middle of the shift. Advika had known this was a possibility when
she walked out on Dean, but she'd hoped that Julian's magic dust
and connections would somehow keep her employed. Her boss's
voice had been terse and tinged with incredulity, a high school
principal having no choice but to expel a star pupil.)

Her apartment... eventually. (Advika and Olive had learned
a few months prior that their landlord was upping their rent by
several hundred dollars, which neither of them could afford.
The two had asked him if they could stay on month-to-month
after their lease ended in March, until they could find a new
apartment. It was a long shot, and it had not worked, as the
email officially let them know they must vacate by the end of
next month.)

What Advika had gained:

Attention. Too much of it.

When she had her night out with Julian, first at Hollywood &
Highland and later at the diner, she had wondered if anyone
had noticed them together. If anyone would care that fresh off
his fifth Oscar win, a high-profile movie producer was seen
chatting with a "mystery woman."

The answer was yes and no.

Because they had left the party a little early, Advika and
Julian were not aware of what became the biggest story coming out of the awards show. A best supporting actor nominee

named Elyosious Payne had imbibed too much at the Governors Ball, wandered out to a nearby side street, and climbed on top of a dumpster, where he did a handstand for several minutes on end. The incident was caught on a security camera and leaked to TMZ. And in the foreground, Advika could clearly be spotted walking by, slightly limping and smiling stupidly, completely unaware of what was happening about thirty feet behind her.

About fifteen seconds after she disappeared from view, the actor fell off the dumpster, landing on his bottom, his legs and arms splayed out. Payne hadn't been seriously injured, only bruising his tailbone. So his drunken fall earned gleeful headlines like "Payne in the Butt," and the footage was being broadcast everywhere. Advika stared at the influx of messages asking if that was really her—the Oakies and old college friends, former co-workers and a few aunties too. And even though her Twitter and Instagram accounts had been dormant for years, she received several notifications asking, "Is this you, @advikasri88?"

She couldn't deal with the barrage of messages—not yet. It was around 4 a.m. in India, so it was possible her parents hadn't seen the video. Not that they'd have much to say about it, because all she did was appear on a black-and-white security camera looking giddy. But somehow they would find a way to be disappointed in her. *Will this be what brings them back?* Advika half wondered, half hoped before dismissing the thought as childish.

After Anu had died, her parents had filed and won a wrongful death suit against the high-rise where the twins had lived for only three months. The balcony's glass railing was found to have been shoddily and hastily built and "under no circumstance should have given way from Ms. Srinivasan leaning against it." Two million dollars was the sum her parents had been awarded—and in a way, the money was what caused the final fracture in their now family of three. Because in her eyes, Advika's parents had fled their grief, and their former lives, by retiring and moving back to India, without at all considering how this would affect their remaining daughter.

They used to be close, the four of them. The Srinivasans were the kind of close depicted on Disney Channel sitcoms. Mukesh was the goofy, well-meaning dad who liked to pretend he was exasperated by being outnumbered three to one but who not so secretly loved it. Rupi, lively and vivacious, thrived on the chaotic harmony of their home. She often likened managing the house and her family's schedules to conducting an orchestra. Anu's and Advika's childhoods were marked by their mother's delight in dressing them in identical candy-colored dresses and frequent visits to Disneyland, for which they had an annual pass. Their parents also had a weekly movie night in which they rewatched their favorite Indian dramas and Bollywood films from their youth. Occasionally, the daughters would be roped into watching with them. During these movie nights, the sisters would wait to see if their parents would hold hands, Anu elbowing Advika and the two exchanging private giggles whenever this rare occurrence would take place.

Even though their mom and dad favored swoony romantic melodramas, they were the rare Indian parents who didn't seem concerned about Anu's and Advika's marital prospects. Mukesh and Rupi had met while attending college in the States, and so both prized education above all else. In all other ways, they fit the archetype of traditional Indian parents: forbidding dating until Anu and Advika turned twenty-one, emphasizing SAT courses and extracurriculars that would look good on college applications. The teenage years were high on dramatics, especially between Rupi and Anu—Mukesh and Advika would witness their arguments while exchanging "here we go again" glances. Once the twins had graduated from college and started forging their paths as adults, the foursome became a tight unit again. The day after the twins turned twenty-two, Mukesh and Rupi floated the idea of introducing them to single Indian men from good families, but Anu had laughed so hard (while wearing a thin, glittery scarf to cover the hickey on her neck) that their parents all but gave up on marriage talk soon after.

But they remained adamant about their daughters finding stable careers. Anu had traveled a conventional career path, working as a social media manager for a renowned nonprofit with an eye toward one day attending law school. Advika's screenwriting prize, however, made her determined to pursue her dreams. To be chosen out of five thousand entries—as a brown person! as a woman!—had to be significant. Not just significant, but a sign she needed to see this dream through despite all the obstacles and setbacks, like being dropped by her agent. As she pursued her career, Advika couldn't envision herself working in a traditional nine-to-five role, much preferring bartending and waitressing to toiling away at an office with an endless maze of cubicles. Her refusal to get a full-time job became a growing bone of contention between her and her parents. Anu tried to play peacemaker, but the growing fissure in their family magnified to a seemingly irreparable degree after Anu's sudden death. Advika's constantly smiling, happy-go-lucky father had been broken by losing his daughter. He was a ghost, perpetually numb and haunted, barely able to utter more than a few sentences at a time. Rupi was just as devastated, but she buried herself in caretaker mode, finding it easier to tend to her husband's needs than deal with her own emotions. Which is why Rupi had agreed to move back to India with Mukesh, despite her personal misgivings.

If Advika swore off her writing ambitions and pursued a normal career, would that bring her parents back to the States?

Perhaps then her mother and father would deem her worthy again and remember they were still a family. Sometimes Advika liked to play that Sophie's choice for herself. But just as her father had chosen his grief over his only remaining daughter, Advika couldn't give up her dreams, even for the two of them. The fragility of life, of losing the person closest to her, had taught her that. Advika needed to see this goal through and succeed. If she couldn't do that, then she had absolutely nothing at all.

—

Back to the video. Advika replayed it over and over again, studiously avoiding the footage of Elyosious falling and instead staring hard at herself. She cycled through the clip over fifty times, even as she was dripping with sweat, rivulets forming under her arms and in the backs of her knees. She felt squishy, and her body odor had assumed the thick claustrophobic funk of someone who hadn't bathed in days, even though she had showered the day before. Yet she couldn't take her eyes off the thirty-two-second clip. She remembered thinking there was something strange happening in her peripheral vision, but she was too focused on the wonderful surreality of Julian's invitation to give it a lot of thought. How had Julian escaped the camera completely? In her memory, they had walked toward his waiting car side by side. She looked for a shoulder, his arm, any sign of him. But no Julian. Just Advika, her smile stretched beatifically wide, as if she herself had won an Academy Award.

She had never seen herself look so happy before. As Elyosious precariously balanced behind her, Advika watched her face flash between excitement and shock before settling on joy. The video dumbfounded her. After Anu had died, she hadn't expected to know that feeling ever again. But here it was, incontrovertible proof that it could happen. That it did happen.

Another message came in as she watched the clip for the umpteenth time: it was Julian. He had texted her a photo, and she let out a gasp of delight upon seeing the picture of his Oscar wearing a tiny Hawaiian shirt. Julian's text said, Aloha from me and ol' Oscar here. He'd like to know if you're free for dinner tomorrow night.

Of the forty-three messages Advika received, Julian's was the only one she responded to.

～

Over steak and martinis at a private social club in Santa Monica, Advika heard the inside story about the infamous night of Julian's first Academy Award win. It was often included in lists of most memorable Oscar moments, hovering somewhere between the naked streaker flashing the peace sign and James Cameron's "I'm the king of the world" speech.

"Everyone thinks I did it as a bet or a dare. But really, it was a promise to my grandfather. Pappy told me when I was seven years old that when I achieved my life's dream—and he said 'when,' rather than 'if'—I needed to take myself down a peg or two immediately. 'Take the stuffing out of your turkey,' he had said. I smuggled the champagne into the ceremony without knowing what I'd do with it. Sophia Loren sat in the row ahead of me, and so when my name was called, I swiped her shoe." He chuckled. "She was none too pleased with me. But I highly recommend sipping champagne out of Sophia's satin pump."

"Wow," Advika said, tucking her hands under her lap so she wouldn't give in to scratching her back, the itchiness caused by the price tag of her new black cashmere sweater hanging between her shoulder blades. "That's an amazing story."

Julian, who had been carving his steak with an elegant flourish, set down his knife and fork beside his plate. "Are you not bored of my stories yet?"

"Not at all," she said, beaming. And she wasn't. Listening to Julian's anecdotes about working with Brando and Bardot, Cage and Cruise was the equivalent of two semesters of film school combined with the illicit thrill of Page Six. Not only did Julian have stories, but they were all laced with juicy asides and insider information.

"You're not a secret journalist, are you?" he said, winking. "Pumping me for information?"

"You got me." Advika searched his face, wondering if he was going to bring up the fact that she appeared in the infamous "Payne in the Butt" security footage. But he hadn't referenced it all night, either out of ignorance or out of not wanting to embarrass her. Either way, she was relieved. "Just call me Hildy Johnson," she added flirtatiously as she swept her hair over her shoulder.

Julian shook his head, impressed. "I still can't believe someone your age would know *His Girl Friday*."

"I'd say about seventy percent of my knowledge of classic movies comes from my undergrad, and thirty percent from Turner Classic Movies. I even think *His Girl Friday* was the first black-and-white movie I ever watched."

A waiter stopped by to refill their water glasses, and when Julian asked him a question, Advika snuck her arm underneath the back of her blouse and scratched with all her might. But her fingers snagged on the price tag and it dropped down her back. Shit. She couldn't afford to keep a $300 sweater from Bloomingdale's. *Worry about it later*, she thought, as she busied herself with her delicious meal, which, truth be told, likely cost more than her sweater.

"So. I have to admit something to you." Julian stretched his arms grandly, then cracked his knuckles as if he were about to play a piano concerto. "I read your screenplay. *The Romance Game*."

"What?" Advika sputtered, a green fleck of creamed spinach flying from her lips. She was too mortified by the fact that he had read her work to care about the gooey green drop that landed on the cream tablecloth. "No, wait. But how?"

"As you might have heard, I have a few connections." His mischievous grin showed off the gap in his front teeth. "I found it...intriguing. I take it you're a fan of romantic comedies?"

Advika cleared her throat, trying to buy time before responding. Having Julian read her most recent screenplay was like having him read a report card in which she had failed every class. Over Christmas break, she had attempted to shake herself out of her career stasis by submitting it to every screenplay writing contest she could find, resulting in a steady, monthlong stream of rejections in her inbox. Since then, she often played a game of chicken with herself, dragging the file into the Trash icon on her laptop, daring herself to drop it in.

"I am," she said, flinching slightly, readying herself to be patronized or laughed at.

"It's nothing to be ashamed of, Advika. *Much Ado About Nothing. His Girl Friday. You've Got Mail.* They're all a part of the same wonderful tradition. And so is your screenplay."

She was so shocked by his words that she sat back in the leather banquette, eliciting a terrific squeak.

"That's very flattering, but—"

"I'm not in the business of flattery." Julian smiled, but his eyes were serious. He rested his arms on the table and clasped his hands together. "I am in the business of recognizing talent. So let me share my thoughts."

Advika's ears burned as he lauded her plot and her "zingy" dialogue. She hadn't heard anyone say something flattering about her writing in ages. And to hear it from a multi-Oscar winner (whose tongue had been inside her ear about forty-eight hours ago) was bizarre in the best possible way.

"You've taken *Cyrano de Bergerac* and turned it into a witty game of telephone. *Cyrano* times ten! It's a great deal of fun." Before she could speak and offer confused but effusive thanks, he continued, tapping his fingers on the tablecloth. "If you cut out the first ten pages of the first act and start with the group at the beach..."

He went on to speak for twenty minutes without a single pause, critiquing her screenplay structure, the "unwieldy" climax, and especially the "treacly" ending. As he did, Advika's eyes roved across the ornate room, from the waitstaff assembled like obedient penguins near the entrance, to the sparkling, gilt-edged chandelier twinkling above them, to the tiny arrow tattoo on her left ring finger.

"You're not used to feedback," Julian said, his foot brushing past her ankle.

"Oh, I am," Advika said, pulling her leg back. She wasn't some amateur, and she couldn't have him think that of her. "Four years of undergrad, dozens of writing workshops, even more rejections. But not from someone who won his fifth Oscar just two days ago. I'm going to need a moment to process—that's all."

Julian nodded, his expression hard to read. He raised his arm and snapped his fingers twice in the air. Moments later, their waiter appeared with two more martinis. From deep within, Advika felt a snap and fire that had long been dormant. Receiving faceless email rejections was hard because there was rarely any reason given. But here was someone talking about her work to her face, finding fault in the very aspects she had delighted in creating. And he had brought it up so casually in conversation too, as if he were commenting on the weather or the Dodgers game. Advika was used to feeling frustrated and upset, misunderstood and aggrieved. But righteous anger was a new glorious emotion for her. She reveled in the heat that broke through her skin, giving her an energy she had been sapped of for years. Advika opened her mouth to speak again, but Julian's next words stopped her.

"The Lily character—she was my favorite." He raised his eyebrows slightly, and the corners of his lips twitched. "She had a joie de vivre that of course drew all the men to her. And some of the ladies. A true movie heroine."

Advika's chin wobbled. Her anger messily collapsed like a melting ice-cream cone. "Oh." She jerked back in her seat again and felt the price tag slip down into her underwear. "Thanks."

"Were you going to say something?" Julian opened his mouth slightly, his pink tongue momentarily peeking through the gap in his teeth.

"No." Advika was seized by a surprising certainty: he knew that Lily was based on Anu. That Advika missed her sister so dearly that she wrote the screenplay to conjure her back into life. Writing *The Romance Game* had reawakened Anu's voice in Advika's head, and ever since writing "the end" on the final page, the voice had stayed with her. And it had become so lively and opinionated and vivid that Advika sometimes feared she had broken off a chunk of her sanity.

"Excuse me one moment," Julian said, his smooth voice breaking into her thoughts. As he walked by her, he paused and bestowed a dry kiss on her cheek. After he left, Advika began to tremble. She didn't like how much Julian seemed to know about her. And it really shouldn't bother her—of course everyone Googled each other and searched social media when meeting for the first time. But there was this cheery knowingness radiating off him that didn't sit well with her. She should at least level the playing field and know more about him than the basics of his IMDb page. Advika didn't even need Anu's voice to urge her to pull out her phone and Google "Julian Zelding." But she did imagine her sister admonishing her: *Why did you wait to learn more about him until now?*

The search results filled in the broad parameters of his life, starting with a row of black-and-white photographs lined up in a jumble of ages: a thirtysomething Julian in a black turtleneck and Don Draper hair; a current photo of Julian in aviator sunglasses, shaking someone's hand; a tuxedoed Julian with an enormous bow tie, standing next to a brunette with an impressive beehive; a twentysomething Julian, boyish and caught in midlaughter. Advika's eyes roamed past the photos to the Wikipedia-delivered stats.

Born: August 2, 1947 (age: 67 years), Bardon, Iowa

Spouse: Harley Harts (m. 2014–2014), Victoria Lizbeth Truong (m. 2008–2013), **MORE**

Awards: Academy Award for best picture, **MORE**

The first hyperlinked "more" was off-putting and intimidating, but it also dared her to click. *C'mon*, she consoled herself, *of course it makes sense that Julian had more than one wife.* That wasn't unique to Hollywood, especially for someone like him with his kind of career longevity. (*Old*, Anu said. *"Old" is the word you're looking for.*) But the word "more" also reminded her that Julian had lived a dozen lives before encountering Advika at the Governors Ball, while she had barely started living one. And that he had been married as recently as last year. *What are we even doing together?* she thought as she yanked the price tag out of the back of her underwear, then stuffed it in her purse.

Julian returned to the booth, his pale forehead creased with unshared thoughts. He saw the phone tight in her grasp, then sat back and leaned his arm across the top of the banquette. Advika, defiant, didn't put it away but held her arm in place. She matched his gaze and waited for him to speak.

"One of the reasons I've been successful for so long is that

I'm very thorough," he began. "And so I did look you up, yes. A man in my position has to be very careful whom he lets into his life. Because for all the movies I've made, the people I've met, the actors I've made stars, in my personal life, it's a very small circle. I've been burned before, more than a few times, as you might have seen," Julian said, gesturing toward her phone. "So I can be very, um, rigorous, when it comes to evaluating whom I let in. And, Advika," he said in a low, seductive voice that wrapped its tentacles around her spine, "I want to let you in."

Advika set her phone down next to her thigh. She nodded slowly, indicating she was listening.

"A person like me, I have more runway behind me than ahead of me. And I can recognize talent and ambition and drive in someone very easily—it's like the smell of garlic, immediately identifiable and undeniable. So to put it indelicately, I'm not just looking to have a fling with a young hot thing."

Garlic? Anu's voice sniffed. *Young hot thing?* Advika felt torn between her sister's brand of cynicism and the glowing affection of his words.

"What do you want, exactly?" she asked, unable to look at him.

An older couple walked past them, arm in arm. The woman was leaning on the man's shoulder as she animatedly recounted an anecdote that made him bark with laughter, and their merriment could be heard long after they exited the dining room.

"That," Julian said, turning his head briefly as they passed. "Exactly that."

Advika let out a yearning sigh. How had he managed to give her the only answer she was hoping for?

"But I'm so much younger than you," Advika said, the words spilling out before she could stop them. "And you're... well, you're you. I'm not sure how that would work."

"I'd like to show you." Julian stood up and, just as he did in the diner two nights ago, he slid into the banquette next to her. "Give me a month, and I'll show you what it can be like. I just have one request." He encircled her waist with his slender arm and leaned close so his face was half-buried in her hair. Advika was taken by Julian's scent, reminding her of a library in an English manor, all leather and old books and Scotch. She didn't pull away but shifted her weight toward him.

"Don't Google me. I'm an open book." Julian linked his fingers through hers. "There's a half million search results for my name. But get to know me for me."

"Um..." The dining room blurred into shadows and dim light, leaving Advika with the sensation that her world was only Julian, his hypnotizing presence, the warmth of his touch.

"If I do this," she said woozily, his scent overpowering her thoughts, "if I agree, I just want to know one thing."

"Anything," he murmured into her ear.

"You looked up what happened to my sister. It's why you said what you did about my screenplay—about the Lily character."

"I did, yes," Julian said. "But only after I read the screenplay. The way you wrote Lily...it moved me. I just knew." His fingers gently tapped the back of her hand. "And then I confirmed it by searching for you and your sister online. I'm so sorry."

He was still so close to her, and she could feel his empathy radiate off him like a heavy spritz of perfume. Advika nodded, tears rising up in her chest. For so long, she closed herself off to new friendships or relationships because she wanted to avoid the moment when she had to say the words, "I have a twin, but she died." To keep relating this information to every person she let into her life would have been a hammer to her heart.

And so to have Julian know this about her without her having to volunteer any of the terrible story gave her so much peace. He was an Oscar winner—from just two days ago! His movies had made millions, possibly billions, worldwide. And this man with the kind eyes and crinkle-nosed smile had taken the time to read her writing, know her story. Because he wanted to invite her into his life. The magnanimousness of his gesture was almost too much to bear.

"Thank you," she whispered. "And...okay. Yes. I can get to know you for you."

"We're going to have a lot of fun. I'm going to take care of you, Addi." No one had ever given her that particular nickname before. And although she didn't love it, she smiled and squeezed his hand.

Next to Advika, her phone screen lit up. A text message from Sunita, one of the Oakies. Where are you? We all texted you, but no one's heard back from you yet. Just send an emoji, anything, so we know you're okay. Advika sent a thumbs-up emoji. She then flipped over the phone with a decided *thwack* before dropping it inside her purse next to the crumpled price tag.

CHAPTER THREE

Heartburn

SHE COULDN'T AVOID TALKING TO the Oakies forever. The Payne video had reawakened their interest in poor, lonely Advika, and she would be barraged with more texts, and likely drop-ins, if she didn't respond within the next twenty-four hours. She texted the group after she got home, first taking care to fold the black sweater and place it in the top drawer of her bureau, then kicking off her jeans into the growing puddle of clothes near her bed.

Advika: Hey

Sunita: Hey hey!!

Vik: The superstar finally makes time to speak to us 😉

Balan: So good to hear from you, Advi

Advika: So, I'm fine. I was working the party that night, had no idea what that actor guy was doing behind me. Haha, I guess that's my 15 mins of fame

Vik: You're famous, dude!

Balan: What about the other guy?

Advika squinted, thinking she had misread the text. Other guy stared back at her, filling her with anxiety.

Sunita: What guy?

Balan: Didn't you see the new video? It has a wider angle. It showed Advi walking with some guy. You guys looked

Three dots appeared, then stopped, then appeared again. What? *What?* Advika sat at the edge of her bed and bit down hard on her thumbnail as she waited for Balan to complete his thought.

Balan: Kind of like a couple?

Sunita: Wait, who is this guy?

Balan: That's what I'm asking! Advi, who's the guy you were with? It looked like he was holding something shiny. I swear it looked like an Oscar.

Vik: Dude, what?!? 😱

Advika: I haven't seen whatever video you're talking about. Good to hear from you guys. So tired, going to bed. G'nite.

After a beat she added, Love you 🖤

She closed the chat without checking to see how they responded. No doubt the three of them would confer in their own non-Advika text group, endlessly examining the new foot-age of Advika and Julian, the same way they (and once, she and Anu with them) took joy in turning over a piece of gossip from every which side, laughing until their sides hurt.

The five of them had known each other since childhood, their families all growing up in the same neighborhood in Sher-man Oaks. They had attended elementary school, junior high, and high school together and had been in each other's lives so frequently that Anu had once joked, "We need to get restrain-ing orders against each other." And they eventually did set off on their own paths: college took Balan to Berkeley, Sunita to Stanford, and Vik to UC Santa Barbara, while Anu and Advika attended UCLA. The first two stayed in the Bay Area after grad-uation, while Vik traveled to Europe and Southeast Asia before relocating to Austin.

Even when no longer living within the same ten-mile radius, their roles within the group barely changed. Sunita was the oldest and, at four foot eleven ("and three quarters!"), also the shortest. She was the mother hen of the group, lovingly bossy and full of advice, whether anyone asked for it or not. Balan and Vik were two years younger than the twins, with Anu and Vik often teaming up for late-night escapades, though this didn't interfere with Anu's straight As. ("She's Jekyll and Hyde, man," Vik often said admiringly about Anu's ease at transition-ing between her focused, academic side and her inner wild child.) Balan and Advika liked to geek out together over pop culture, trading opinions on movies and TV shows and You-Tube stars.

And so the friendship stayed alive through group texts and holiday visits, as each of them tentatively moved toward adulthood. Until Anu died. And then Advika had withdrawn, unable to bear their constant check-ins and "Let's grab dinner when I'm back" texts and dumb GIFs of her favorite movies accompanied by "How are you?" *I'll never be fine*, she wanted to write back, *no matter how much you ask.*

While working at the Governors Ball the other night, Advika had suppressed a memory that now came into full, aching flower after seeing her friends' texts, an anvil dropping on her chest. While growing up, every Oakie had a tradition of hosting an annual event at their house: Vik claimed the Super Bowl; Sunita insisted on a post-Thanksgiving game night; Balan, with his family's enormous swimming pool, took on Fourth of July barbecues; and the Srinivasan girls held an Oscar-viewing party. Anu didn't care about the Oscars like her sister did, but she threw herself into party planning with an equal amount of enthusiasm as Advika. Each year they printed out Oscar ballots that Anu personalized by inscribing each person's name with gold lettering, and they prepared snacks inspired by the nominated films. The person with the winning ballot would get the bogus Oscar (aka "Bhaskar") procured from one of the tourist stores in Hollywood.

Their last Oscar-viewing party was six years ago, when they were all still in college (the twins were juniors, Sunita a senior, and the boys were freshmen). Advika, elated over *Slumdog Millionaire*'s ten nominations, had asked them to return to Sherman Oaks so she could host a party in her parents' living room, re-creating the bash from their high school days. Advika had seen the movie four times in theaters, once with her family, and three times by herself, mooning over Dev Patel. Beyond her crush, she was amazed that a film with an Indian cast would be recognized by the Oscars, and she wanted to mark that achievement with her closest friends. At the time, Advika was working on what would eventually be her award-winning screenplay, and so her joy from the act of writing was colliding with wonderment that the Academy would choose to honor a film starring people who looked like her. *Like all of us*, Advika thought as she happily took in the sight of the Oakies once again assembled in her parents' living room, the girls on the sofa and the guys cross-legged on the floor, just as they had watched the awards show there so many times before.

"You're glowing," Vik remarked when Advika erupted into furious applause as *Slumdog* nabbed best director, its seventh award of the night; then she made a check mark next to the correct pick on her ballot.

"Shut up; I'm not. I'm just happy—that's all." In fact, Advika had been close to crying the entire night. Nearly all acceptance speeches made her emotional. It was secretly her favorite part of any awards show: the heartfelt gratitude and heartwarming anecdotes shared by superstars and artisans alike, conveyed in a brief window of time and beamed to the entire planet.

"Well, I'm happy that you're happy. It would have sucked if your movie was scoring goose eggs all night. Especially since you forced us to come back for this when I pledged not to step foot inside my parents' house until June," Vik said.

Advika gently kicked him in the shoulder. He grinned, then reached for the bowl of The Curious Case of Benjamin Butter Cookies, named after the Brad Pitt film in which he aged backward.

"I have to admit it's pretty trippy to see a movie about Indian people getting all these Oscars," Vik said with a wry smile. "Don't they usually love movies with white people in corsets or fighting in World War Two?"

"That's what makes this so exciting!" Advika's eyes shined. "A movie like this gives us a big platform. Dev Patel is a star now. Indian people can be movie stars."

"We already are movie stars," Sunita said, looking up from her iPad, which she was using to study for one of her classes. "Bollywood, remember?"

"Exactly," Anu said, nodding. "We don't need white people to give us legitimacy, you know?"

Advika, sitting between Anu and Sunita, stiffened. "I'm not saying that. Of course Bollywood exists. I'm just saying that it's important for Indian-Americans—"

"Dev Patel is British."

"Okay fine, Anu, how about first-generation Indians? Anyway, it's nice to see that we can be stars of mainstream films. Not on the sidelines, driving cabs or whatever." Advika took a Benjamin Butter Cookie from the bowl in Vik's lap and bit into it with a satisfying crunch. "We can be up there one day, winning an Oscar," Advika added dreamily.

"But all I've seen are white men winning awards for *Slumdog*," Anu pointed out. "The sound guys, the editor. And the director's white too."

"Hey! Don't forget about A. R. Rahman," Advika countered, referring to the legendary film composer.

"But if this is a film about Indian people, then how come Dev Patel wasn't nominated? Or Freida Pinto?"

The Srinivasans' living room descended into an uneasy silence. Sunita, Vik, and Balan were all too familiar with the twins' occasional debates on a topic, usually one that Advika was passionate about and Anu was passionate about poking holes in. *Why are you ruining this for me?* Advika wanted to say to her sister. And she was about to when Mukesh and Rupi came into the living room to peek in on them.

"Wow, kids, it's so good to see you sitting here together again," said Mukesh with a wide, toothy grin. "It feels like you all never went to college."

"You don't have to go back," Rupi added. There was a sad edge to her voice. The twins exchanged worried glances. Three years after the girls had moved out, their mother still hadn't found a way to cope with the fact that her once-bustling household was now just her and Mukesh. "Just stay here forever and don't grow up, okay?"

"Okay, Aunty," Balan said cheerily.

"Well, actually, we have a surprise for you guys," Mukesh said. Rupi's face contorted with embarrassment. "We have a new member of the family." He briefly left the room, then returned with a square-shaped item in his hands, covered with a cloth. "Your amma was feeling lonely. So quiet here all the time, she says. So we got her something nearly as chatty as her." With a flourish, he removed the cloth to reveal a parrot.

"Meet Shuba," their father said.

The living room broke out into gasps and laughter, as Mukesh explained that neither of them had the energy to take care of a dog, and he was allergic to cats.

"But a bird? Really?" Anu said, peeking into the cage as the parrot eyed her warily.

"I had one when I was a little girl, also named Shuba," Rupi said, her cheeks pink. "It means 'auspicious.'" Seeing her daughters share another pointed glance, she addressed them directly. "Girls, parrots are nice. I have such sweet memories—"

"See? Look." Mukesh opened the cage's door, and a green streak shot out into the dimly lit room. For a moment, Advika felt like they were in a horror movie, their chatter devolving into full-on screams as Shuba fluttered above their heads, zipping from the ceiling fan to the television to the top of the bookshelves. The parrot squawked in alarm as she sailed and fluttered over them. Advika didn't want to be irritated by this intrusion from her mom's new weird pet, but best picture would be announced at any moment, and she didn't want to miss it.

In her memory, in the midst of the chaos, Advika's mother whistled several notes, and the parrot paused its agitated flying about and glided onto Rupi's shoulder. The Oakies applauded, and her mother smiled and nodded knowingly, as if she had planned the last few minutes all along. Then suddenly *Slumdog Millionaire* was announced as the winner of best picture, and they all stopped their conversations to whoop and applaud as the film's cast and crew took the stage. Advika tried to imagine what it was like to stand up there in front of Hollywood's elite, as she fixated on the children in the cast, their young faces radiating unadulterated wonder. Her next memory was the most distinct, the most painful upon reflection: Anu throwing an arm around her waist, understanding how moved her sister was in that moment. Anu's wordless glance—slightly raised eyebrows, crooked half grin—communicated her apology. And then Balan, Sunita, and Vik presented Advika with the Bhaskar for her Oscar ballot's near-perfect prediction of the night's winners, and she laughed along with them as she accepted it while calling herself "the biggest nerd ever." Shuba had agreed, squawking, "Nerd, nerd!" And then more hysterics, the kind in which they were all crying while doubled over with body-rattling guffaws, as if they had huffed laughing gas. It might not have played out exactly like a slapstick comedy interspersed with heartwarming, feel-good moments, but that was how Advika remembered it.

She no longer had the bogus Oscar. Advika had thrown it away after Anu's funeral, not able to bear all the memories it represented. Her last moment of pure happiness, surrounded by the people she loved the most, all of them witnessing something together that validated her ambitions. But after Anu's death, she couldn't separate the memory from the expression on her mother's face from when her father had explained Rupi got the bird to cope with her loneliness. The shame, the sadness. And even a hint of fear. Now Advika understood her mother from that time all too well.

For Advika, loneliness and silence were a yoke that tightened around her neck with every passing day, a braided rope of thorns that never ceased digging into her skin. Coming into the world with a twin meant that Advika always felt Anu's presence in her life, even if they were not in the same room. To have a twin was like a perpetual ray of sun dancing across her shoulders, a comforting warmth of just knowing and being known. Anu's passing was a cleaving of two souls that left the remaining one perpetually in the dark, searching blindly for someone she would never find.

Advika wished she could find comfort being around her friends, but their presence only made it that much clearer that Anu was missing. Sunita's maternal bossiness no longer had the counter of Anu's teasing but loving pushback, Vik no longer had his fun-loving partner in crime, and Balan no longer had someone to match his high-level ambitions and work ethic. The chorus of their voices, either in person or in a group text, stung because Anu wasn't among them. And no matter how much they cared for Advika, they couldn't make up for what she had lost. They were like family, but they *weren't* family.

When her parents were packing for their move to India, Advika had tearfully requested to keep her sister's ashes. Yet Rupi and Mukesh were adamant about wanting to hold on to this last vestige of their daughter. Advika tried to have empathy for this decision, but at her lowest and lowliest moments, the depth of her sense of abandonment and anger overwhelmed her. Their leaving the country, selling their house at a loss, and donating most of the furnishings to Goodwill, while also taking Anu's ashes with them, meant that Advika had lost her entire center of gravity. She didn't have a final resting place to visit Anu, let alone a family home to provide respite and solace. It was all gone. They were gone. And so Advika kept hitting the Delete button on the people she had once loved the most.

⌒

And then she had spotted Julian's Academy Award. Prior to seeing the gold statue with her own eyes, Advika had found that her nervousness at working the after-party was enough to keep those old memories at bay. But seeing the Oscar left alone at her bar, only inches from her face, had reminded Advika of holding her Bhaskar. With every ounce of mental strength she had, Advika had taken a fist to the memory and quashed it. It might have seeped back in like toxic fumes if not for the events with Dean, and later Julian, driving it from her mind completely. And now the memory had returned to her again, and this time Advika did not immediately dismiss it.

How was it, she wondered in amazement as she climbed into bed, the scent of Julian's cologne still singing on her fingertips, that an Oscar was now tied to two of the happiest moments of her life? Because yes, even though she had only been in his company for several hours, Advika considered meeting Julian to be one of the best things that had ever happened to her.

What she liked about him was not merely his fame or his movie connections. She liked that he was someone who made her feel happy and hopeful and had no connection to her past. The concept of her future no longer seemed exhausting or frightening, but something Advika could actually look forward to again.

CHAPTER FOUR

Crazy, Stupid Love

DURING THEIR THIRD DATE, AT a wine bar in Malibu, Julian reluctantly answered Advika's question about which of his films were his favorite.

"Well, *West of the Gun* is the most recent, and so most fresh in my mind. But I do have a fondness for *The Riders*, because it was my first, and there were a lot of headaches because we really didn't know what we were doing. But there was a beauty in that too. We were so young, like Judy and Mickey, just a couple of kids putting on a show."

"What was *The Riders* about?" Advika asked. The two were sitting side by side at a bar on a private patio just after sunset, and the surrounding palm trees sparkling with fairy lights gave the space a vibrant intimacy with a hint of enchantment. Originally, they had been seated inside, but Julian was constantly approached by people offering congratulations on last week's Oscar win—all men, all his age, and all of whom gave Advika a cursory look without speaking to her or introducing themselves. Seeming to sense her discomfort, he whispered into their waitress's ear, and they had been magically transplanted into a secluded outdoor area. She had wondered if any of those men had seen the video of her and Julian together. But the footage had been pulled off YouTube a few hours after her friends had pointed it out to her, and the two still hadn't discussed either Payne clip. When Advika had first arrived, she had apologized for her lateness, describing the drive to Malibu as a "pain in the butt." She had given him a knowing glance, and Julian had snorted in response before giving her a kiss on the cheek. He definitely knew it existed but didn't seem inclined to want to discuss it, and so she had decided to not bring it up again. Later, Advika would learn how much he despised gossip and tabloids and know she had made the right call in not asking him about the video.

"You don't know *The Riders*?" Julian said with an exaggerated gasp. "Didn't you major in film?"

"I can't help what did and didn't make the syllabus," she said teasingly.

Julian pulled his bar stool closer to hers, so their knees were touching. "It was a true indie, one of the first. We came out the same year as *Easy Rider*. You know about that one, of course?" Julian said with a small edge in his voice, as if he was testing her.

"Well, yeah." Advika didn't know why she should feel bad about knowing one of the most important films of mid-twentieth-century cinema, but Julian's tone made her unsure of herself.

"Well, yeah," he mimicked with a wink. "Anyway, we made ours on less than a shoestring budget, and it put me on the map, got me noticed, started this whole ride." Julian smiled, but the smile reminded Advika of a wolf baring his teeth. "And so I have a fondness for *The Riders* too."

Advika's cardigan, draped over the back of her chair, fell to the floor. When she stood to pick it up, Julian took her by the wrist and pulled her toward him, so she was standing between his legs. He threw his arms around her and drew her in for a kiss.

"What's that for?" Their faces were so close together she could feel his minty breath on her cheek.

"I don't ever need a reason to kiss a beautiful, intelligent woman," he said, before pressing his lips to hers. "Do I?"

"I guess not," Advika whispered, her face flushed. As they kissed, his hands tucked inside her back jeans pockets, for the first time ever she had the sensation of starring in a rom-com, with the camera panning back in a crane shot that ended on the starlit night.

On the drive home, Advika realized he never did tell her what *The Riders* was about.

⌒

At his Pacific Palisades home one week later, they were in Julian's sumptuous bed, watching the ocean slowly swallow the sun.

"This is heavenly," Advika said, wondrous at the sight of the several layers of light, the purples, pinks, and golds fanning out across the horizon.

"Surely you're talking about yourself," Julian said, nuzzling her neck.

"Oh, please," she laughed, even as she thrilled at his touch and the memory of the past few hours.

When Julian had invited her over to visit his home, Advika knew they would sleep together. With any other guy, she would have felt it necessary to indulge in facials and waxes and a new outfit. But Julian communicated his attraction to her so completely it almost felt tangible. He never once made her feel like she was lesser than but instead made her feel absolutely beautiful as she was. If anything, she had been worried about seeing him naked. The *Sex and the City* episode with Samantha debating whether to sleep with a rich octogenarian, and bailing after seeing his bony limbs and flat butt, kept running through Advika's thoughts on the drive over.

Advika forgot to be nervous upon arriving at his house, which was what the word "mansion" was invented to describe. Situated on a cliff in the exclusive, celebrity-favored Riviera neighborhood, her first view of Julian's manse made her gasp as she drove her Camry through the metal gates and parked in the circular driveway. Given the name Wildwood by its previous owner, the five-bedroom Tudor home would be the perfect setting for an elegant murder mystery.

Julian had showed her around like the world's most enthusiastic tour guide. They had held hands as he guided her through the bottom level, outfitted with a private theater, gym, and wine cellar, then the first floor with a trio of grand spaces with high ceilings and arched entryways—great room, library, and office—and a French country-style kitchen. The second floor was made up entirely of guest bedrooms, each one themed around Julian's favorite films. The anecdotes he shared as they toured his home had a practiced feel, akin to a stand-up routine performed verbatim at a year's worth of comedy clubs. Advika didn't mind; she liked how much pride he had in his home.

Their last stop was the third floor, which made up the entire master suite, a palatial bedroom with tasteful yet surprisingly muted white and gray furnishings. The only pops of color came from the bottle of Dom Pérignon chilling in an ice bucket on a silver tray, along with a single rose. *Cheesy.* Anu's voice came in unbidden, and Advika agreed, but she pretended to find it charming anyway. After two glasses of champagne and one shared joint, they began to get intimate. And as their clothes peeled off one by one, Advika's thoughts were a mad dash of prayers: *Please don't be skeletal and pasty. Please don't have a flat butt.* And he did not. He had a thankfully trim, firm physique: in fact, his body was that of someone ten to fifteen years younger.

"I can't believe you get to see this view every day. I would never get tired of it." Advika sighed happily as she stared out at the gold-lit waves and smiled even wider when Julian slipped his leg over hers.

"Good to know," he said huskily. He dripped a finger down her shoulder all the way to the inside of her wrist, then drew her toward him. Their bodies were completely entwined together, a knot neither of them was in a hurry to untangle.

Several hours later, just after midnight, Advika was roused by the murmur of conversation, a lively rat-a-tat of familiar voices playing at a low volume. She rose up slightly and swept her hair from her eyes. *The Philadelphia Story* was on the flat-screen above the fireplace, the black-and-white film saturating the darkness with a ghostly light. Advika drowsily enjoyed Katharine Hepburn and Jimmy Stewart's flirtation, their dialogue sparking against each other like flint, as the events of the past few hours dawned on her in slow-motion. It had been a long time since Advika had spent the night in another man's bed. And she liked that even though she was curled up on the edge of the mattress, facing the wall, she could sense Julian beside her. Advika turned around and gave him a sleepy wave.

"Didn't mean to awaken you, sweetheart," Julian said softly. They inched toward each other, and he draped his arm over her bare shoulders. "Sometimes when I can't sleep, I have some of the greats keep me company."

"I do that too," Advika said, nestling against his chest and marveling at how natural it felt to do so. "But my greats tend to be Ryan Gosling and Reese Witherspoon."

He chuckled. They watched the movie together in companionable silence for a while. Advika had loved rom-coms for as long as she could remember, not just as a student of the form but also envisioning them as a window into something she yearned for herself. Experiencing *The Philadelphia Story* next to Julian, in the intimacy of his embrace, bestowed the film with a nearly transcendent kind of pleasure.

"This is why I love romantic comedies," Advika said dreamily, more to herself than Julian. "The most expensive special effects in the world can't create their kind of chemistry."

"Agreed," Julian said, kissing the top of her head.

"Sparks, connection, fizzy banter—there is nothing more magical," Advika mused, even as she felt her eyes begin to close. "It can't be faked, unlike a CGI dragon," she added, referring to Ramsey Howell's Oscar-winning film.

"You're adorable. I want to put you in my pocket," Julian said, echoing what Katharine Hepburn's character told Jimmy Stewart a few scenes earlier.

"That's my favorite line too." Advika smiled. "I love the way she says it. It's so sweet."

"Katharine Hepburn was my first crush," Julian said with a sigh. "What a shame she never had children. Women like you and Katharine—smart, stylish, gorgeous—we need more of you in the world."

"Hmm?" Advika said. Katharine Hepburn being a mother was like Godzilla throwing a tea party. It just didn't work. It was antithetical to everything the iconoclastic actress had always stood for. "I don't know about that," Advika said sleepily as she eased off of Julian's shoulder and back onto the softness of her pillow.

"Never mind, darling," Julian whispered in her ear. "Get some rest." And so Advika contentedly drifted off into the welcome arms of sleep.

At a Puerto Vallarta bungalow to celebrate their one-month anniversary, they talked about their families.

"Let me put it this way: My father was General Patton. My mother, Donna Reed. No siblings—it was just the three of us. I left when I was nineteen and didn't return until I could buy them a new house."

"Wow," Advika said. They were facing each other in a hot tub, the darkness softly punctuated by a smattering of stars. Advika was wearing a white bikini he had surprised her with when they had arrived at the bungalow a few hours earlier. But she didn't feel comfortable in it, not used to exposing her midriff, so she was slumped down in the water, the bubbles bouncing against her collarbone. "They must have been so proud."

Julian snorted. He rose up and sat on the edge, swirling one foot in the water while swigging from a Corona. Advika had never seen him drink beer before. To glimpse Julian craning his neck back to take in long sips from a bottle made him seem more human somehow, like he was a guy she could have met at a barbecue.

"Have you seen *Patton*? Or learned about him in history class?"

"I know he wasn't considered a nice guy," she said carefully. Again, that feeling of being tested. "So I guess that means your father wasn't happy with a new house?"

"He thought I had emasculated him in front of my mother. Showing off and showing him up. With some people, you just can't win." Julian wrinkled his nose. "I guess I was showing off when I paid for his funeral too."

Somewhere in the darkness, a single frog repeatedly croaked, a plaintive sound that reminded Advika of deep scratches against glass. She knew it might make Julian unhappy to be asked about his family. But she had brought them up because he was always regaling her with stories of his father's father, but he never mentioned his parents.

"It seems like Pappy was more of a father to you," Advika said, her voice sounding high-pitched to her ears.

"Someone had to be," Julian muttered, wiping his perspiring brow with his still-folded towel, then tossing it into the grass. "My father didn't even have any potential to squander; cockroaches have led more meaningful lives than that man. He couldn't live up to my grandfather's expectations, and he took it out on us." Julian shuddered. Another long, deep swig of Corona, one that finished a third of the bottle.

"My mother eventually remarried. I stopped talking to her after that." Julian looked at Advika briefly, then off into the distance. "She married two weak men. One of them was a brute. But the other was a fool."

"Oh." Advika's eyes widened. Julian sniffed the air as if he smelled something peculiar, his thin lips jutting out in a pout. "So even after your films were a success and you won all these Oscars, you didn't talk to her? Because I'm sure she would have been proud of you."

"I didn't need my mother to be proud of me." He told Advika their sole communication was when she sent him Christmas cards and he mailed her five-figure checks, a wordless exchange that ended when she died on his fortieth birthday. "Pappy used to say to me that because I had idiots for parents, I had to go harder and be harder. Never give an inch. And I haven't. It's why I've been successful. In *spite* of them." Julian's face darkened. "I owe them nothing but the fact of my existence."

Change the subject, change the subject, Advika fretted as she watched him take another long mouthful of beer, then set the bottle down beside him with such force that it toppled to its side and rolled away into the grass.

"Well, I'm glad that you had your grandfather, then. I imagine he would have been so happy to see how accomplished you've become." Pappy had died several weeks after Julian earned his first Oscar nomination, never getting to witness his grandson's meteoric success.

Julian grimaced. "I don't know about that. Pappy had very high morals. He didn't exactly approve of what he called my playboy lifestyle. And he thought movies were godless." A bitter chuckle escaped his lips. "Pappy would have liked you, though."

Advika blushed. "Really? Why?"

"You have good qualities important in a...partner. An easiness about you, but also a strength. And you value family." Julian regarded her carefully. "Yes, he would have liked you," he repeated. He seemed as if he was about to say more, but instead he shook his head, his closely cropped silver hair looking white under the glare of the nearby floodlights. "No more questions, okay? When you get to be my age, you resist taking these trips down memory lane. There's no point to them."

Advika burned with guilt. She had never been whisked away on a romantic weekend before, let alone stayed in a luxurious bungalow with five-hundred-thread-count Egyptian-cotton sheets, a private pool, and a personal butler. She needed to lighten the mood and rekindle the playful spark between them. So she surprised Julian, and herself, by standing up just high enough that he could see her chest and pulling down her bikini top.

"Why, Ms. Srinivasan," Julian said with a smirk. "Are you flashing me?"

"I was just feeling hot—that's all." She pulled her top back up. "Okay, all better."

"Oh no you don't." Julian slid back into the hot tub with a tremendous splash, and Advika let out a scream mixed with a giggle. "I think they need some more air. Let me check and make sure."

They fooled around for a while, Advika sitting on his lap with her legs wrapped around his waist, the spray of the water jets tickling her feet. All the stiffness and tension inside her had dissipated in the water's relaxing heat. Advika imagined what this scene would look like in a movie, how she would describe it, what music would be playing. Something by Drake, maybe. Or Taylor Swift's "Wildest Dreams." She settled on Rihanna's "We Found Love."

"And you?" Julian asked, their faces still close together. "How would you describe yours?"

"My parents?" She pulled back from him a little. "Way to kill the mood," she added with a forced laugh.

"Well, since I shared, it's only fair for you to do so too," Julian replied, his fingers pressing methodically down her spine as if it were a flute. The heat, his touch—all of it was now stifling. She jerked away from him and floated to the opposite end of the hot tub.

"Fine." Advika didn't want to talk about her parents. She just wanted to keep existing in this bubble she found herself in with Julian. It wasn't going to last forever, and she wanted to keep out reality for as long as possible. "I don't know; they're parents. Stern but loving. He was an orthopedist; she was an accountant. Both retired. It's all kind of dull stuff."

"How long ago did they return to India?"

"About a year ago." She sighed. "I'm supposed to go visit at some point, but I keep thinking . . ."

"Keep thinking what?"

"They'll come visit me first." She swallowed a tiny ache before it became a sob in her throat. "But I'll go there. Eventually."

Julian offered gentle words of consolation, saying he imagined

Advika found the distance between her and her parents difficult. She could only nod in return, not wanting to dwell on
the subject. Which made Julian's next question sting even
more.

"I'd love to know more about your sister." His long leg
stretched and found hers, and he ran his big toe down her knee.
"How much was she like the character in your screenplay?"

If she weren't wearing the cursed bikini, Advika would have
hopped out of the hot tub and walked away, leaving wet, angry
footprints in her wake.

"I don't want to talk about her," she said, shaking off Julian's
touch as she crossed her legs underwater. Julian regarded her
warily, as if he wanted to say something, but ultimately he just
nodded. She hadn't meant to hurt him, but the mere mention of
Anu was like letting Freddy Krueger loose in an Anne Hathaway rom-com. "It's too hard, Julian. The pain is too much. I'm
sorry."

"I get it," he said, sliding over to her. "The amount of people
I've lost in my life . . . you never get used to it. You just learn to
live with it." He paused, then added, "But you have to start to
let it scar over. You're keeping the wound fresh, Addi."

"I'd really prefer if you'd not tell me how to grieve." Even
though the heat from the water began to feel overwhelming,
she sunk in farther, her chin just grazing the water. It was
all she could do to not just sink underneath and escape this
conversation.

Julian nodded, but she could sense his irritation. He reached
out to click a button on a silver, palm-sized device. "I was going
to ask the butler to bring me another beer. Would you like
something?"

"No," Advika said in a small voice. The weekend had completely curdled for her. Too many memories were battering
her on all sides, but most of all, it was the pain of her parents'

abandonment that dug into her and left marks, in the same way the bikini bottom was too tight against her skin. "I'm going to get out, actually."

"Advika." In one surprisingly fluid motion, he pulled her into his lap and rested his chin on her shoulder. "Whatever else has gone on in your life, I'll tell you this: I'm here to stay." She began to cry, not with sadness, but relief. She didn't know how much she needed to hear those words from someone, anyone. But especially him.

"Promise?" she asked, taking his arms and wrapping them both around her waist.

"Promise," he said softly into her ear.

⌒

End of April. A phone call.

"So if you aren't doing the Hollywood parties anymore, what are you doing?" Advika's mother asked, her voice sounding tight and distant.

Sex. Watching movies. Absorbing Hollywood lore. Writing, a little. "I got a freelance assignment to do some writing for . . ." She mumbled the last few words because she couldn't think of a competent lie.

"How much does it pay? Is it enough for you and Olive to keep your apartment?"

I've already moved out, Advika thought. "It pays enough." *Change the subject, change the subject.* "How is Dad doing?"

"Busy with the clinic; working too hard." Those few words told Advika all she needed to know about the state of her parents' relationship. Her father had lately become fixated on assisting at a medical clinic in a village outside Bangalore, while her mother had remained with her relatives in the city. Advika wondered when they had last seen each other. "Your avva is calling me to help in the kitchen," her mother said, then added with a hint of sadness, "Stay in touch, okay? I feel like you never text unless I write first."

"Okay. Of course." A call from Julian beeped on the other line. "Gotta go. Love you."

In the past, a conversation with her mother would plunge Advika into a bereft state. Because any phone call with one or both parents usually echoed with several voices—Advika speaking into the phone, Anu chiming in constantly in the background, or vice versa. So when it was only Advika and her mother, it was hard to ignore that what once felt like a symphony had become just one sad guitar, plucking the same stilted notes over and over.

Now she could end a phone call with her mother, resplendent with guilt and judgment, and not feel her loneliness rise up like bile in her throat. Julian's presence in her life was a dam against unpleasant emotions. Her world, for so long a muted sepia, finally flowed back into full Technicolor upon moving into Wildwood.

Julian had asked Advika to move in with him a few days after they returned from Puerto Vallarta. They had been sitting on his patio sipping mimosas and reading the *Los Angeles Times* on a crystal-blue Sunday morning in late March, and she had been detailing her fruitless search for a new apartment. Not able to afford a rental on her own, she had been disappointed that Olive had secured a room for herself in a three-bedroom apartment via a Craigslist ad.

"It's not that I necessarily expected Olive and I to look for a new place together. But the fact she hadn't even asked about finding a new place with me..." Advika pushed her white Gucci sunglasses—Julian's latest gift to her—to the top of her head. Without her sunglasses, she could see that Julian's head was starting to grow pink from the sun. "I thought we had gotten along okay. But at the same time, I don't know what her budget is. Maybe it was easier for her to just find roommates who already had their own place. Looking for apartments in this city is the worst."

"What's your budget?" Julian asked, folding up his newspaper and dropping it on the ground. "I think I know of a place that could work for you."

"Really?" Advika said, biting her lip, causing a bit of pink lipstick to flake away between her teeth. Did she really want Julian to know how little money she had in her bank account? "It's not a lot. At least not right now. I'm still on the job hunt."

"Live with me." Julian smiled, then leaned back in his chair, lacing his fingers behind his head. "I always miss you when you're gone, and I'll feel better knowing you're living somewhere safe."

Advika's mouth dropped open. She knew she should at least give the pretense of needing some time to think about it. But the idea of having to schlep to dingy apartments in crumbling buildings in the Valley, then getting rejected for having middling credit and job history, had weighed on her more than she realized. Advika stood up and threw herself into Julian's arms, her sunglasses flying off her head as she fell on him in an awkward way, half standing and half kneeling between his legs.

"I guess that means yes?" he laughed.

"Thank you," she murmured into his neck.

Being in Julian's constant company was a revelation. There was so much to discover when spending all their days and nights together. Advika hadn't been in a real relationship since college (a fact she had always been embarrassed about), so living with Julian as his girlfriend was a novel and enjoyable experience. She loved observing him, making mental lists of each new thing discovered: the silvery sweetness of cigar smoke that clung like whispers to his skin; the small scar between his pectoral muscles that resembled a comma; the blondish-gray arm hair that she loved to run her fingers over. Advika wasn't used to getting to know someone's body as well as her own. Even with Manish, her college boyfriend with whom she spent nearly every night during their sophomore year, they had mostly fumbled together in the dark on his bottom bunk. She might have seen him fully naked a handful of times, and even then only in flashes. But Manish had been a boy, with a whippet-thin torso and skinny arms, a hairless chest, and the soft belly of a Chinese Buddha.

Julian was older, sure, but he had such a worldliness about him that only magnified Advika's previous existence as a stunted millennial, marked by Ikea furniture and Trader Joe's burritos and overdue bills. She had never met someone who carried themselves with so much confidence; Julian didn't seem to second-guess himself ever. To be around him made Advika feel like an adult for the first time in her life.

But to be around Julian all the time was to also be more con-scious of how she looked beside him. From her rapidly deplet-ing savings, Advika invested in more heels and toddled around their bedroom when he wasn't around to get used to wearing them. She shopped at Marshalls looking for discounted high-end clothing by Ralph Lauren and Tommy Hilfiger. And for the first time in her life, Advika bought a straightening wand that she only used for about two weeks before abandoning it when Julian told her he preferred her curls.

Their cozy existence narrowed the world to just the two of them under Wildwood's gabled roof. Moving into Julian's home hadn't been awkward at all, because his expansive master suite included two sets of walk-in closets and bathrooms. So Advika didn't have to feel self-conscious in front of her boyfriend about the tufts of hair on the bathroom rug, the uneven sky-scrapers of hair and skin products lined up across her marble sink, several of which still had their dollar store price tags, or the electric toothbrush with traces of lipstick from the nights she was too tired to wash her makeup off before brushing her teeth. She and Julian were able to live together while not let-ting the reality of their messy human selves intrude on their romance.

If she had a friend to confide in, Advika would have told them that the moment she felt fully accepted into Julian's life wasn't even when he asked her to move in, but two weeks later, when he gave her a credit card.

"I want you to look and feel your best," he had told her, when she had unfolded her napkin at dinner and found the gold Amex inside. And so Advika had tried her best, graduating to high-end stores like Bloomingdale's and willing herself to ignore price tags and just buy what she liked. Before approach-ing the cashier to ring up her purchases, she took a photo of every item to send to Julian, just as he had asked. Julian responded to her texts with "None of them, dear." This had been repeated at every store Advika visited, until she just gave up and went home, ashamed that her tastes weren't sophisti-cated enough for her new boyfriend. When Julian had returned home that night, he had greeted her by calling Advika "my very own Eliza Doolittle."

"Eliza…?" Advika faltered. "From *My Fair Lady*?" Was she really that pathetic, to be compared to the street urchin with dirty clothes and a Cockney accent?

"I just think you need a little guidance—that's all," Julian purred, his hand lifting her shirt, his cold fingers sliding against the small of her back. "We'll go shopping together. Only the best for my sweetheart."

Advika could imagine her sister's skepticism (*You're not*

a prize poodle!), but she convinced herself that of course she needed Julian's help. Anu had been the clothes horse between the two of them, but even her twin had favored vintage shops and consignment stores. *Don't be offended*, Advika told herself. *You probably do need all the help you can get.*

One month after moving in with Julian, her walk-in closet was a museum of sleek fashions bearing the labels of designers like Céline and The Row. Nearly all of the clothes Advika had brought to Wildwood had been thrown out, along with her discount skin-care and hair-care products, at Julian's insistence. Advika's reflection in the mirror was someone she barely recognized. And she was glad for it. Her skin was soft and dewy, her mass of curls given definition and volume, and her new wardrobe was basically everything Anne Hathaway wore in *The Devil Wears Prada*. Not only that, but Advika found herself standing straighter, her shoulders high and head unbowed. The makeover had been a confidence injection into her spine. She had never expected to live out her second-favorite part of romantic comedies, but evolving from ugly duckling to graceful swan had lived up to her every fantasy.

For perhaps the first time in her life, Advika found herself truly taken care of and cherished. And she needed to do her part to make sure that she completed her transformation. When required, Advika could yield the superhuman ability to focus, which she had used when writing *The Romance Game*, and now with beauty-influencer videos. Whenever Julian was out, Advika would spend hours on YouTube, studying makeup techniques and educating herself on the most luxe brands. She made a list of products that were recommended, ordered them online, and tried them on, finally finding a use for her credit card, filling her online cart with blush and highlighter and brow gel and lip liner and fake lashes. Whereas she used to spend around fifteen minutes on her morning routine, Advika eventually found that she could spend up to an hour carefully applying her makeup.

And the best part was that when she looked in the mirror after completing her work, she didn't see Advika. And even better, she didn't see Anu either. One month after her funeral, the reality of her sister's loss caving in her insides, Advika rummaged through Anu's belongings and pulled out her signature purple lipstick. Royal Velvet, a matte lipstick, had felt rough and sticky on Advika's lips. But when her eyes met her reflection, the effect had been startling. If she looked at herself from her peripheral vision, or between her fingers, Anu appeared in the reflection like an apparition. But staring straight on at herself was a farce. Advika had looked like a clown. They had been twins, but only Anu could pull off such a daring and distinctive trademark.

Advika had not realized how much she despised the sight of herself until she found a way to change her look through makeup, giving her features a lift and color and shape. To see a new person in the mirror meant that Advika had successfully sloughed off her old life, discarding her grief-stricken and pathetic former self like a ruined garment. This was who she wanted to be now. This was who Advika *could* be. And there was no looking back. The warm but painful memories of her parents, Anu, and her friends were even easier to dismiss because they seemed to belong to a different person. Now that she had things in her life to look forward to, all Advika wanted was to live forward too.

There was one intrusion, however, although Advika tried not to see her that way.

Only Julian and Advika lived at Wildwood, but there was another constant presence who seemed to be around at all hours: Aggie, Julian's house manager. Either in her late forties or early fifties based on the thickets of grays shading her hairline and temples, Aggie always wore capri pants and silver Birkenstocks, an ensemble that Anu would have described as "audience member at a daytime talk show." As house manager, Aggie ran every facet of Wildwood, including overseeing Julian's staff, which encompassed a private chef, housekeeper, driver, and gardener. Anytime Advika asked something—where the fresh towels were kept, how to reboot the Wi-Fi, where to get a dress dry-cleaned—Julian invariably answered, "Ask Aggie." Advika thought of Aggie, with her pleasant, distant demeanor and monotone voice, as Wildwood's CEO crossed with a sentient internet search engine.

Advika wasn't used to being waited on by anyone. Her mother had raised her and Anu at an early age to be responsible for themselves, to do everything from making their own beds to vacuuming their rooms to doing their own laundry. To pass these tasks on to strangers was, in a word, strange. As part of Aggie's role in running Julian's home, she always seemed to be around: inspecting every room after Flora the housekeeper cleaned to make sure there was no dust, dirt, or smudges that went overlooked, consulting with the private chef on the grocery list, accepting all mail deliveries and packages. Advika tried not to hold it against Aggie personally, since she was just doing her job. But it was hard for her to feel like Wildwood was her home when Aggie was always underfoot, blinking at her from behind blue-framed glasses whenever they passed each other in the kitchen or hallways.

Advika would only find peace by leaving Aggie's domain and escaping to the backyard, which, honestly, seemed like too common a word to describe the sumptuous outdoor grounds. The surprisingly large lot featured a patio, a kidney-shaped pool, and then farther afield, a sizable green lawn. This was Advika's favorite spot in all of Wildwood, because at the most southern edge a pair of canopied oak trees stood together like an old married couple, with a wooden bench sheltered underneath. When the house was overflowing with staff members taking on various tasks overseen by Aggie, Advika would retreat to this magical corner of the estate, look out at the ocean below, and wait for her phone to light up with a text: On my way, love.

And then Julian would come home in the evening, Aggie and everyone else would leave, and finally Advika could breathe and relax into her new life, and her new self.

CHAPTER FIVE

Blast from the Past

EVEN WITH ADVIKA SETTLING INTO Julian's world as easily as slipping into a velvet robe, she could not avoid Julian's glittered past. Living in Julian's home was a vital escape from the tatters of her old life. But the mansion was also a shrine to his career, reflecting that Julian's DNA was practically made out of celluloid, which meant that he was in constant contact with the momentarily and eternally famous alike. While there were framed photos of him with a nearly endless parade of legendary figures—the Dalai Lama and Mandela, Springsteen and Gaga, Spielberg and Streisand—there was nothing of his family, even his beloved grandfather. Or his former wives.

And for the first several weeks of her time in Julian's home, Advika was fine with that. She didn't really want to recall the fact that he had been married several times over.

"It's healthier for me this way," she said to herself, imagining a conversation with Anu as she tried on a red paisley dress one morning in early May. Julian had surprised her with it before leaving for work and had requested she wear it out to dinner that night. "This relationship is so new, and I'm still in a really vulnerable state. I just want to focus on us."

What are you so afraid of knowing? Her sister's voice was the equivalent of an eye roll. Advika couldn't even imagine a sympathetic Anu in her head. *And where is this going?*

Advika tucked her hands underneath her chest to adjust her cleavage in the dress's constricting V-neck, trying to ignore that her stomach and thighs were already rebelling against the two sets of Spanx she had forced herself into. This was never a dress she would pick for herself. It was a little too hippie earth mother for her taste and wouldn't be flattering on anyone larger than an A cup. But she couldn't explain that to Julian.

"Do I always have to think about the future, Anu?" Advika stood on tiptoe as she appraised herself in the three-way mirror, turning from right to left. "You know better than anyone that no day is promised. I'm just enjoying my time with him, and the way he makes me feel." Could she even be falling in love with him? Advika wasn't sure. "He's so kind and thoughtful and attractive and . . . well, I actually understand the word 'lust' now."

Advika imagined her sister shutting her hands over her ears in protest. She pressed on anyway. "And I can't help feeling insecure when I think about the fact that Julian was once married to other women. I mean, they had to be gorgeous, right? I'd rather not know. I don't want to know anything about them, really. Just knowing their names is more than enough."

Advika banished Anu from her mind, tired of her sister's skepticism, which loomed just outside her waking thoughts. Besides, she didn't need anyone's opinion to tell Advika what she already knew. She could feel it in the glimmer of sweat dancing on her forehead, the tight clinch of her dress, the twist of her lips as she glanced at herself in the mirror. *Not good enough* is what her image reflected back to her.

⌒

But Advika could have lived with the mystery of the former Mrs. Zeldings, at least for a little while longer, except for what happened later that night after dinner. Julian had been oddly reserved throughout their meal at an old-fashioned steak house that had its history littered on its walls in the form of faded black-and-white photos of classic Hollywood. Advika had tried her best to initiate conversations with him, but she wasn't used to seeing Julian so withdrawn, his gaze floating past her shoulder or onto his plate, his polite mutterings to the obsequious waitstaff. Advika honestly didn't know him well enough to read his moods yet, and so by the time their porterhouse steaks had arrived, she had given up trying to engage him in chatter, and they had eaten their meal in near silence.

Once they returned to Wildwood, Julian had taken her by the hand and led her up to their bedroom. As soon as their door had closed, he gently pushed her against the wall and kissed her hard. Advika was wearing a new perfume Julian had recently given her, smelling of pears and lilies and a little too sickly sweet for her taste, but she had worn it that night at his request. And he must have been a fan of it, because he buried his face in her neck. She could feel his nose breathing her in with the urgency of an asthmatic in need of an inhaler. The Julian at dinner, taciturn verging on grim, was gone. As a screenwriter, it felt clichéd to even think this way, but she couldn't help feeling like dessert, so voluminous was his appetite for her. For the first time since they had started dating, their lovemaking was one-sided: he didn't seem to care about her pleasure. Julian was a man possessed, and while Advika didn't mind rough sex, she at least wanted to feel like she was an active participant rather than a rag doll. And then right as he came, he breathed a name that sounded like an exhalation of wonder. But it had definitely been a name.

As Advika lay next to him, Julian snoring into his pillow, his back slick with sweat and his left hand plastered onto her right breast, she panicked. Obviously, whatever had just happened between them hadn't been about her. But what was it about? Or rather, who?

⸺

After a troubled night's rest, Advika woke to the smell of bacon. She sat up with a start, taken aback by the sight of a table draped in a white tablecloth at the foot of the bed, where a silver tray of scrambled eggs, waffles, and bacon awaited her, along with a note: *Early a.m. meeting. Didn't want to wake you, but after last night I thought you might be famished. Enjoy, darling. —J.* And Advika was famished. But not for breakfast. Advika ignored the tray, even though her stomach objected to this decision, and went for her phone, not even hesitating to type "Julian Zelding wives." Despite Julian asking her not to Google him, how could she not after the weirdness of last night? (*How could you not have done it from the very beginning?* Anu's voice asked with bemusement.) With her heart somersaulting in her chest, she clicked on Julian's Wikipedia page, then skipped to the section titled "Personal Life." But her anxiety shook her focus, and Advika found she could only skim the paragraphs without being able to fully read or digest them.

From her agitated state, she was still able to pick out some pertinent facts: Julian's first wife was an actress named Evie Lockhart, and she had starred in some of Julian's earliest films; his second wife was a singer named Nova Something (she couldn't remember her last name except that it started with an M); and his third wife was Victoria Truong, who had starred on a reality TV series that had "Wives" in the title. The first and third marriages had ended in divorce, while his second had ended after Nova had passed away. Strangely, there was no mention of Harley Harts at all, even though Advika could have sworn she had seen her labeled as his most recent wife.

An actress, a singer, and a reality star. The loves of Julian's life. And possibly—probably—one of the names he had said last night. While with *her.* So what did Julian see in Advika, then? She wasn't a hundredth as accomplished as his previous wives. *Someone he's just having fun with,* came Anu's voice, her tone wavering between contempt and concern.

As Advika attempted to read the Wikipedia section again, her nerves calming down, there was a knock on the door. It was Aggie, asking if she was done with breakfast.

"No!" Advika yanked the comforter up to her chin. "I mean, not yet. I can bring it down when I'm done."

A beat of silence preceded Aggie's response. "No need. Let me know when you're ready." Each word came out like a robot practicing a monologue for an audition.

"Sure. Thanks." Advika returned to her phone, but it wouldn't turn on. Surprised and panicked by Aggie's arrival, she had accidentally turned it off from squeezing it so hard. Advika sighed. *You have a choice,* she told herself. *You can continue reading or talk to Julian yourself. But you need to know more. It's time.*

Advika believed her sister would have been proud of that choice, that she was finally drawing a line in the sand rather than continuing to bury her head like an ostrich.

⌒

Except that was what she did. Days later, while they went hiking at Runyon Canyon and took a private tour of the Getty Museum, the questions remained on Advika's tongue. And each time she was ready to finally give them air, Julian would give her a thoughtful compliment or ask her opinion on a screenplay he was reading, and she would clam up. Why disrupt what they had together? What could she possibly learn about the movie star, the music star, and the reality star that would help her feel better?

But then while they were curled up in the media room, watching *Casablanca* with his pale, knobby fingers interlaced with hers, Julian mentioned that they would be attending his pal Lenny's film premiere next week, and so she would need to go to the Versace atelier to be fitted for a new dress.

"Wait, what?" It was too much information at once. Lenny was the shorthand nickname of directing icon Leonard Bullock. A dress from Versace. And Julian didn't ask Advika if she wanted to go, just assumed she did.

"I'm going to have the most beautiful date to the ball. They'll mistake me for Prince Charming." Julian laughed, his hand squeezing hers.

"But I've never been to one. I don't know the first thing—"

Julian waved away her concerns with a doting kiss on her shoulder. "Aggie will handle it. You just get to be pampered and treated like a princess. You'll have fun."

It should have been good news—exciting, even. Hadn't Advika wanted to attend a red-carpet premiere since forever? It wasn't walking the red carpet that enthralled her, but the premiere itself. To be among the first to see a movie, and breathing the same air as the stars and director who had made it. To witness something new and potentially wonderful together was the ultimate communal experience. But movie premieres meant cameras and flashbulbs. And gossip.

"It's so public, though," Advika muttered.

"What's that, sweetheart?"

This is your chance. Anu's voice came charging in. *Ask him.* Advika looked into the crisp blue of Julian's eyes, melting from the earnestness of his gaze. If the premiere had been months away, instead of a week, she might have shut up and enjoyed the movie. But it was happening much too soon. She couldn't throw herself to the wolves of public interest to be potentially written up as Oscar winner Julian Zelding's "latest fling" or "arm candy" without at least knowing whom she could potentially be compared to.

"Are we ready for our relationship to be out in the open?"

"I didn't know we were in hiding," he teased, walking two of his fingers up and down her arm. "How cute—you have goose bumps. Should I have Aggie fetch a blanket?"

"I don't want to be compared to your wives," Advika blurted out. "You're a public figure. I'm not. And I . . . I just need to know why me, Julian? After all the amazing women you've been married to, why me?"

"Have you seen yourself? I mean, really?" He slid both hands up her forearms to her shoulders. "Darling, you're so tense." Despite her protests, Julian stood up and moved behind her leather recliner so he could give her a massage.

"Listen. You have three ex-wives. That's so . . . adult. I have an ex-boyfriend, and other guys, but no one I was serious about." As Julian kneaded his thumbs into the top of her shoulder blades, Advika started to waver. The warmth and surety of his touch had always been her Achilles' heel. *You're going to pass up answers for a dumb massage?* Anu's voice broke in. Advika forced herself to continue. "It's normal for me to want to know about them."

"I never said it wasn't." His thumbs pressed harder, and Advika winced. "I always said I'm an open book. If you prefer my boring life history to watching one of the classic films of cinema, then by all means, ask away." He returned to the chair beside hers and dramatically pushed back his seat, then closed his eyes and folded his hands across his stomach as if he were about to undergo hypnosis. Advika tentatively pushed back her seat too, so she could better see his face.

"Just tell me about them. How you met them, why you loved them, and . . . why it didn't work out." Advika bit her thumbnail, denting the magenta polish she had applied just hours before.

"I don't want to excavate your heart. But I want to know you better and where I fit in."

Julian's sigh came off as the first rumble of thunder before a storm. His eyes stayed closed and his jaw tensed as he recited words that seemed to have been memorized from his own Wikipedia page. "My first wife was an actress. Evie Lockhart. We worked on films together until it fell apart. It's not easy to be in a marriage with your leading lady. And so it ended." Deep breath. "Nova was my second wife. She was a total sweetheart, a real angel. A gifted songwriter too. Do you know *All My Desire*? Anyway, she died, and that was that." A sharper intake of breath. "Wife number three was Victoria. I think if you looked up 'gold digger' in the dictionary, her picture would be there. Beautiful, fickle, married me for my connections." Julian finally opened his eyes and slowly turned his head toward Advika. "Anything else?"

"What about Harley Harts?" Advika asked before she could stop herself.

"Harley...How would you know about her?" Julian jerked his seat back up with the sharp jab of a button. "Ah, so you did Google me after all. When I asked you not to."

"I didn't!" Advika lied, her palms leaving sweaty prints on the gray leather. "I just remember her name from the night we went out to the social club. It was our second date, and after that you asked me not to search for you." At least that part was true. Advika made a mental note to delete her search history from her phone.

"Ah. Okay. Forgiven." Julian pecked her nose with a kiss. "Harley was never my wife. She was...an aberration." He reached for her hand, and she let him take it. "And that's enough about that." Advika nodded, even though her sister's voice inside her cried out, *That's it?* "All my wives were beautiful women and talented in their own way. But Nova was special to me. And," he added, his eyes teary, "you remind me of her. Intelligent and sensitive, you feel so deeply as she did. It makes me feel protective of you."

Advika recalled with a piercing clarity that "Nova" had been the name Julian had cried out during sex. The name of the woman he loved the most. It was haunting and tragic and beautiful... and a tiny bit weird. If she were watching this conversation in a movie, she would have raised an eyebrow. But Advika was living this moment and couldn't help but be moved that she reminded Julian of Nova. To be compared to the love of one's life, especially by a legendary figure like Julian Zelding, made her special.

Didn't it?

"Wow, that's so sweet. But—"

Julian swept her hand to his face and pressed it against his cheek. "With you, I see a second chance for love, the kind of love that I shared with Nova." He pressed his lips against the inside of her palm, then let it go. "But please, let's not talk about the past anymore. Let's focus on the future. Our future."

Dumbstruck, Advika nodded. Until Julian had said the words, she hadn't let herself think about a future with him. But now that he had put it out there, that was all she cared about. And so when the two attended the film premiere at the El Capitan Theatre, Advika in a strapless lace navy blue dress perfectly molded to her body while somehow transforming her curves into a perfect hourglass figure, her sculpted hair and flawless makeup crafted by professionals for the first time in her life, she decided that she could really live this kind of life. On Julian's arm, in his world, was where she belonged.

Advika enjoyed walking the red carpet with him, taking photos by his side as the photographers dutifully snapped a few pics before the film's stars arrived, and then she headed inside with Julian as he socialized and gossiped with his powerful and famous friends. The men greeted her with everything from confused politeness to amused condescension to genuine warmth, while his women friends barely acknowledged her. Advika would have a chance to win them over in time and show them that she deserved to be there.

And that feeling was strangely vindicated when she searched for photos of the event on Getty Images and found only one photo of her, which had the caption, "Julian Zelding and guest." It was the best of both worlds. She could be a fixture in Julian's life while blessedly holding on to her anonymity, giving her time to work her way up to meriting the inclusion of her name in the caption too: "Julian Zelding and his partner, screenwriter Advika Srinivasan."

CHAPTER SIX

Ten Things I Hate About You

SEVERAL DAYS AFTER THE FILM premiere, Julian introduced
Advika to the close friends whom he thought of as family.

The dining room at Wildwood befitted a man who hosted
dinner parties as often as he produced films. An ornate spheri-
cal lantern made of crystal swept down from the ceiling, illuminating a mahogany table that could seat twenty but tonight
only seated four. Julian sat at the head of the table, with Advika
to his right and Roger Greevy, his longtime business manager,
and Eloisa Pithe, co-producer on *West of the Gun* and the daughter of Julian's late producing partner, seated to his left. For the
past two hours, first over cocktails and now at dinner, they'd
name-dropped so many people that it actually got a bit boring.

"And what about the Jamison Deeds project?" Roger asked
Julian as the group was served its main course—grilled branzino with broccoli rabe and polenta. With his leathery tan and
shock of white hair and beard, Roger was what Santa Claus
would look like after years of hard living before retiring to the
Bahamas.

"I think I heard it's still in development. You know how it is—
these adaptations are always a pain," said Eloisa. She was what
Advika thought of as "Hollywood ageless": eggshell-smooth

forehead, buoyant Angelina Jolie lips, telltale "bunny lines" at the sides of her nose that indicated a long history with Botox. Whenever her fringy bangs fell across her eyes, she tossed her head back like she was in a shampoo commercial. "Which is why you always avoid them, right, Julian?"

Talk of Jamison Deeds was their first conversation topic that actually piqued Advika's interest, since the director had long been a part of Hollywood lore. After directing three films in the early 1960s, Deeds was in the middle of postproduction for his final film, *Lessons in Objectivity*, when he disappeared. A week after police were called in to investigate, his Aston Martin was discovered in a San Diego motel parking lot, his wallet and suitcase in the trunk. Due to the talent conveyed in his film work and his unsolved disappearance, Deeds was often scrutinized and mythologized, most recently via a megapopular podcast series.

Julian grunted. "I'm not sure what's happening in this industry anymore." He scratched his elbow, his narrow face flushing pink. "First it was video games. Now it's adapting podcasts. Next it's going to be making a movie based on some idiot teen's YouTube video."

The three of them laughed. Julian caught his girlfriend's eye and looked away. Then, after several seconds passed, he purposely turned toward Advika, and his face lit up with a big grin. Advika smiled back, alternating between wishing he would include her in the conversation and feeling relieved that he had not. What could she add to their insider industry chatter anyway?

"But aren't you a fan of Jamison?" Roger continued, his white eyebrows resembling cotton balls stretched thin. "I thought you'd make an exception for him."

"Sure," Julian said with a dark burble of laughter. "But I'm also a fan of this," he added, holding up his glass of Scotch. "Doesn't mean I want to make a movie about it."

Roger roared as if that was the funniest joke he had heard in years, while Eloisa nodded smugly as she dabbed the corners of her mouth with her napkin. This gesture made Advika realize her own napkin had slipped off her lap. As she contemplated whether it was worth trying to reach down to find it, she was surprised to hear Roger say her name.

"So, Advika," Roger said, addressing her for the first time since they were introduced, "what do you think of our Julian?"

"He's great," she said, quickly swallowing a large bit of branzino. "We're having a great time. And, um, we have great conversations." She reached for her glass of water and took a healthy sip.

"Well, isn't that great," Eloisa said, curling her fingers around the stem of her wineglass.

"I still can't believe you met at the Governors Ball," Roger said, his eyes dancing from Advika to Julian and back again. "All I ever get at those things is a lousy drink and a cocktail napkin stuck to my shoe."

Advika put on a smile but gripped her fork as if it were a knife. Across from her, Eloisa examined her coolly. She was the tall redhead who won an Oscar for *West of the Gun* alongside Julian, her first-ever Academy Award win. When she had first met Advika, Eloisa had looked her up and down, then given Julian an undisguised glower that said, *Really?* She regarded her in a similar way now, but Advika refused to meet her gaze. She slipped her feet out of the six-inch black Jimmy Choos Julian had gifted her two hours earlier, and her toes gratefully grazed the cold floor.

"Julian scored more than one trophy that night," Eloisa said in a sugared purr. "Typical Julian." The three of them laughed heartily, as if this was a shared joke between them. As if Advika was the shared joke. *Don't let them get away with that shit.* Anu's voice popped up in her head for the first time since the film premiere. Advika sat up straighter. She fumbled her feet back into her Jimmy Choos.

"It was a memorable night," Advika said, looking from Julian to Roger, ignoring Eloisa. "Completely unexpected. I had no idea who he was when he approached my bar." This statement piqued the interest of both of Julian's friends. Julian took a sip of wine, and his eyes met hers. Advika couldn't read his expression.

"Is that so?" Roger said as he reached for the pepper shaker and shook it over his branzino. "See, all this time, we thought you had ensnared Julian with your charms."

"I was just doing my job, but Julian seemed a little . . ." Advika paused. Should she really tell his producing partner that he seemed bored at the Oscars? Eloisa would no doubt still be on that stage giving an acceptance speech if she could.

"Enchanted," Julian said drily. "She was the only interesting person in the entire room." With these last few words, he glanced at Eloisa, who was busying herself by digging into her salad.

"That's why we had to meet you, Addi," Roger said, between spoonfuls of polenta. "In a room with Martin Scorsese, Meryl Streep, and Al Pacino—"

"And Ramsey Howell," Julian said pointedly. Advika laughed, and now it was the two of them exchanging mischievous glances over a shared joke, excluding the other two.

"You were the most interesting thing," Eloisa said, the word "thing" caked in sarcasm. "You and Ramsey Howell."

"Not Ramsey," Advika said. "Just me."

Roger looked at Eloisa, and she gave him the faintest hint of a smirk. He then changed the conversation topic to Julian's latest movie project, a period war drama filming in Morocco. Advika used this shift of focus away from her to slip out of the dining room. Both men stood up when she did, a jarring, old-fashioned move she had only seen in the movies. Advika left the dining room, slipped off her heels, and trotted on tiptoe to the bathroom near the foyer. Once there, she reapplied her lipstick with the liquid gloss hidden in her bra, then stared at herself in the reflection. She had seen plenty of women dressed in bandage dresses, slinky and short and tight fitting, but she never thought she'd be able to pull one off. It wasn't what she would have chosen to wear, thinking the style too clubby for an intimate dinner party. But now Advika was glad Julian had requested it. To see herself in the metallic bandage dress, only a few shades darker than Julian's hair, made her feel formidable, someone not to be messed with.

On her way back to the dining room, Advika encountered Eloisa, who was staring at a wall of photos lining the hallway, a glass of chardonnay tilted in her hand.

"Addi," she said, upon spying Advika walking toward her. "They've gone into the library—you know men and their cigars. Let's you and I chat and get to know each other."

Advika had no choice but to let Eloisa link her arm through hers and lead her into the great room. Each time she stepped inside, Advika felt as if she had wandered into a forgotten wing of Downton Abbey. The room was just so aware of its own grandeur, with a stone fireplace the size of Advika's old kitchen, a massive emerald-and-silver Persian rug, and the crown jewel of a sofa, enormous and plush and resembling several camels seated in a horseshoe formation. Advika, still awed by this room, beelined toward the sofa's farthest right corner, her usual spot during the occasional instances she and Julian spent time there. She slipped off her heels and tucked her bare feet under her, because if she was going to get interrogated and insulted, she might as well be comfortable. She really didn't care about impressing this woman, figuring there was nothing she could do to seem worthy of Julian in her eyes.

"So, Addi."

"It's Advika."

"Hmm." Eloisa sat back against the cushions and crossed her legs so slowly and dramatically that, for a moment, Advika thought she was trying to emulate Sharon Stone in *Basic Instinct*. "Well, I can't really say that, so I'll stick with Addi, since Julian calls you that too."

Advika shrugged and dug her fingernails into her palms.

"So, Addi. I don't know how much Julian has told you, but the three of us are like one big family. I've known him since I was a teenager, and after my father died, he's been like a surrogate parent to me. So Roger and I, we're protective of him, especially as he gets older. I'm sure you understand that."

"Of course. I'm glad he has such good friends." Were these two only invited over so they could vet her? Or perhaps they came over to find reasons to convince Julian to dump her?

"I'm glad you understand." Eloisa drained the rest of her chardonnay and balanced the empty glass on the cushion beside her. "I'm dying to know: What makes you think you're different?" Her eyes narrowed, and her lips pricked into a knowing smile.

"Different from whom?"

"His other wives."

Those three words were the equivalent of a roundhouse kick to the heart. After their getaway during which they discussed their families, and her conversation with Julian about his exes, Advika had never felt closer to him. And she knew in her bones that this wasn't just a temporary thrill for Julian, not if he was taking her to film premieres and introducing her to Roger and Eloisa. Every new introduction to his inner circle made it clear that his future included her. But did it mean she was in love with Julian? For all the romantic comedies Advika had seen, they had never taught her how she would know when she was in love. The tin-pan crash of jealousy elicited by just the mere mention of Julian's wives told Advika that her feelings were stronger than she'd thought.

But seeing Eloisa simpering at her, resembling a cat waiting for a mouse to peek its head out from its hidey-hole, made Advika keep her face even, not wanting to give Eloisa the satisfaction of seeing she had landed a direct hit on her insecurities.

"I'm different because I'm here," Advika said, throwing her arm across the nearby sofa cushion with all the casualness she could muster. "I'm not trying to replace anyone or be like anyone else. And I'm pretty sure that's what he likes about me."

"My, my—don't we think highly of ourselves?" Eloisa recrossed her absurdly shiny legs, and the sleek movement resembled scissors slicing the air. "You think you belong in the pantheon of Julian Zelding's great loves, do you?"

The echoes of the men's raucous laughter, traveling from two doors down, burst into the room. Eloisa turned briefly around at the sound of their jocularity, and in the space of those seconds, Advika decided to play this like a scene from a movie. If Eloisa was determined to play the spoiler, the gorgeous woman with the icy heart and villainous smile set on breaking up the lovebirds, Advika would respond with the winsome confidence of a Mindy Kaling or an Emma Stone.

"Julian's much older than me, and he had a life before me. That doesn't bother me, but it seems to bother you."

"It doesn't bother me, Addi, because I know all about his life before you. And if you knew it as well as I did, you'd think twice about sitting here dressed up in starlet drag." Eloisa stood up and went to the bar cart, opened up a brand-new bottle of Scotch, and poured a large dollop into a glass, followed by a single ice cube. "You think you're the first cutesy little girl of Julian's I've met?"

"Listen, I don't—"

"No, you listen to me." Eloisa swirled her drink in Advika's direction, her voice taking on a splintered edge. "I see how you look at him. You gaze at him like he's the sun. And Julian loves attention—of course he'll drown you in flowers and romance and all that. But like you said, he's lived a life. A *legendary* life. And you're not going to be his Larry Fortensky, okay?"

"Who?" Advika shook her head uncomprehendingly.

Eloisa steamrolled past Advika's confusion, walking toward her with each stilettoed step sounding like a small dagger on the hardwood. "Harley Harts was an aberration. I put an end to that. And I'll put an end to this too."

Harley Harts. Whom Julian also dismissed as an "aberration," and who had mysteriously disappeared from Julian's Wikipedia page right after Advika had asked about his ex-wives.

"You interfered with their relationship?"

"What relationship? There was a drunken elopement in Mexico, and it was annulled five minutes later. Thanks to me." Eloisa narrowed her eyes. "You didn't know that?"

"Ladies," Julian's voice boomed, sucking all the air out of the room. He and Roger stood in the doorway, Roger's ruddy face radiating a sour delight. "How's it going in here?"

"Julian, hi," Eloisa said, raising her glass with an unsteady hand. "I was just toasting you and Addi and your new romance." Advika prickled with embarrassment, wanting to dissolve right into the cushions. It was obvious that she was doing the opposite, yet she was so brazen about her dislike of Advika right to her face, and right to Julian's too.

"How kind." Julian said this as if Eloisa had just told him he had contracted a venereal disease.

"You're back on the horse, aren't you?" Eloisa gazed at him, sounding aghast and a little wounded. "This time to win it all."

"I think you've had too much to drink, darling. It's time to go. Roger will take you home."

The two held each other's eyes, something unknowable but portentous passing between them. Even hours after Eloisa and Roger left, with Julian snoring beside her, that moment remained fixed in Advika's mind. Eloisa's strange references— Larry Fortensky, Julian being "back on the horse"—were unsettling. Her phone waited on the nightstand, a portal to all the answers about this man that still eluded her. Anu's voice crept out like a faint heartbeat. *Something's not right here.* But then Julian muttered in his sleep, turning on his side and drawing her near, his hands soft and warm against her waist, and she let herself fall into the sway of this intimacy.

In the months to come, Advika would look back at the moment and fervently wish that her intense distrust of Eloisa hadn't prevented her from looking up Larry Fortensky and learning that he had been Elizabeth Taylor's eighth and final husband. Maybe she would have understood that in her own backhanded way, Eloisa had tried to give her a warning.

CHAPTER SEVEN

Love, Actually

LATER THAT NIGHT, JULIAN AWAKENED Advika, crying and breathless, from a deep sleep.

She was sobbing into his chest, with Anu's face still floating in her vision, her sister whispering something she couldn't hear. Only once Julian said Advika's name, a short, anxious bark that broke through her haze, did the dream dissipate and Advika feel the cold splash of wakefulness.

And Anu's absence.

For several minutes, Advika couldn't speak. She was all liquid: her eyes flowing, her nose running, sweat pouring through her satin nightgown. Advika hadn't experienced a dream about Anu that intensely since the immediate weeks following her death. Only after a few false starts, her words choked by hiccupping sobs, was she able to share her dream.

"We were at our old apartment. On the balcony. We were talking about something—I don't know what." This wasn't true. She could vividly recall her dream, in which Anu kept flashing into different versions of herself: she was five years old, her lips comically smeared with their mother's lipstick; she was sixteen and wearing a glittering silver minidress for junior prom; she was twelve and wearing a Greenpeace tee. And then she finally settled into the person she was right before she died: twenty-four, mint-green bikini and matching sunglasses, buzzed from drinking too many Long Island iced teas while sunning herself on their lone piece of patio furniture, about to lean over the balcony to see what all the commotion was eighteen flights below.

No matter which version of her sister Advika was talking to in her dream, the conversation between them remained the same: how to break it to their parents that they never wanted to get married. This was a real conversation they had actually had many times. But during this dream scenario, Advika found herself not as strident about this opinion as she used to be but didn't know how to tell her sister, who scornfully dismissed marriage as "an act of self-annihilation, all in the name of a fancy diamond ring and a joint checking account."

Advika wiped her nose onto her sleeve, then immediately regretted it. The fancy nightwear had been a gift from Julian on their one-month anniversary, and her grief mucus would leave an irreparable stain on the light pink satin. She started shivering as she recalled the final moments of her dream.

"I went to get something to drink. And Anu told me not to go. I did anyway. And then, her scream. I turned around and she was gone." With her face pressed against his chest, his arms locked around her shoulders, the dream began to release its hold on her. "The thing is, when it actually happened, I didn't hear her make any noise. It happened so fast. I just heard..." *The impact.* She couldn't say it. Couldn't think it. She wept, and her tears slipped down her face and glistened on his silver chest hair.

"I'm so sorry, sweetheart," Julian murmured into her ear, his warm breath tinged with mint mouthwash. "Grief can just sneak up on you like a bastard."

"This dream felt different," Advika said, her voice cracking. "It reminded me that the pain of losing Anu is not just about missing her. I wanted to know what her life would have been. Anu would have made an incredible lawyer. I could have seen her running for office one day." Advika placed her palm on Julian's bare chest, searching for his heartbeat, and when she located its strong, persistent thrum, her own shuddering subsided. "She was the most interesting person I ever met in my entire life, and that her life was cut so short, for such a stupid reason... It's like reading a book and the last hundred pages are torn out. It's going to torment me that I'll never see her again. But also, I'll never know who she was going to become."

"Oh, Addi," he soothed, rocking her back and forth, then landing a kiss on the top of her head. "I'm so sorry for all your pain. But I'm here for you. I'm here."

This was the moment. Even in her vulnerable, half-wakened state, Advika let herself give in to the concerns stirred up by Eloisa's words and catty, dismissive glare, the question that had been etched on her tongue like a bitter flavor she couldn't shake.

"Eloisa said I couldn't compare," Advika said between shaking breaths. "She said something like I had no chance against Julian's pantheon of legendary loves." Advika gritted her teeth, already regretting giving air to the biggest worry, thereby making it real.

"She doesn't know my heart," Julian said slowly, still holding Advika close to his chest. "No one can speak for me, except for me. And what I do know is that I love you, Addi." He lifted her face toward his and kissed her, then tilted her down onto the bed and began to kiss her deeper. Advika was glad for it, because she was still in shock. Had she wanted him to say that? Maybe. But was she prepared for the reality of saying it back? Not in the slightest.

It's not that she didn't have intense feelings for him. But nothing within her rocketed with certainty. Instead, hearing

Julian say he loved her felt like a splinter embedded in her skin, an irritation communicating that maybe she wasn't ready for all of this. Advika's relationship resume was sketchy and inconsequential, with only one real relationship along with numerous short-term hookups and friends-with-benefits situations. To declare love truly meant something. Didn't she owe it to Julian, and herself, to wait to say those words until she fully meant it?

"Well, Addi?" Julian drew back and placed his cool hand underneath her chin. He was gazing into her eyes with the absurd intensity of a man locked in a staring contest.

"Wow. I didn't expect that." She feigned a smile, wishing Julian hadn't knocked the covers off the bed in a scramble to comfort her. All she wanted to do was hide for a little while and sit with her feelings.

"Is that it?"

"Yes. No. I mean, thank you." Advika gently removed his hand suctioned to her face. "I'm so sorry, Julian. I just...I didn't expect...and the dream about Anu is still in my head... and no one's ever..."

He nodded. Then without another word, Julian turned over on his side, leaving Advika staring at his back. She called out his name once, then twice, and he only lay there, his body as rigid as a statue. Advika flipped over to face the opposite direction, shivering. She curled up in a ball, listening to Julian's hard, staccato breathing, and pondered her own heart.

When she woke up the next day, Julian was gone. The bedding that had fallen off the night before was now haphazardly covering Advika, as if tossed onto the bed. On her nightstand was a stack of mail, with a yellow Post-it in blocky handwriting: *Forwarded here.* Advika took off the Post-it and sifted through the envelopes, a mix of credit card bills and bank statements, as well as the latest issue of an alumni college magazine. The Ghost of Christmas Past in the most mundane form, and not anything Advika wanted to think about. She had stopped paying the minimums on her bills because she had stopped working. Advika had a measly $325 in her savings account and only double digits in her checking. Since moving into Wildwood, she had been relying on the credit card Julian had given her.

It was the slap of reality she had been avoiding for months, but she could avoid it no longer. Advika had to figure out the direction of her life, and fast. She leaped out of bed, flinging the mail back onto the nightstand. She had to look for a job. Several of them. After showering and changing into black jeans and a white tee shirt, two of the pieces that she saved from her old wardrobe because they had been Anu's, Advika sat crosslegged on the bed. She spent all morning and early afternoon texting and calling old contacts, looking for retail and restaurant work (there was no way she could go back to working at A-list events again).

Julian walked in as the sun's amber rays were cascading across the bedroom, casting the bedroom in a rich glow. Advika had been on the phone discussing the particulars of a catering gig in the Valley when Julian sat down beside her, dropping his briefcase with a thick thud. She hung up the phone while the other person was still speaking, then reached for his hand.

"So we're leaving then, are we?" he said, his voice nearly as monotone as Aggie's.

"What do you mean?" Advika's hands fidgeted at her sides, not liking how cold he was acting.

"You're on the phone looking for jobs; you said you don't love me. I guess this is goodbye."

"Not at all! I'm just...well, I have bills, and I need to pay them." She briefly touched his elbow. "You've been so generous, but I should—"

"Make sure to leave your keys with Aggie. You don't need to worry about packing your belongings. I'll have them shipped to your next forwarding address." Advika pictured what the place might be: a shoebox with dirty carpets, iron bars in the windows, a kitchen with bare shelves and old packets of ketchup in the drawers.

And the quiet.

The intensity of the quiet of living by herself, without her family, her friends, her sister—anyone who cared about her.

"Julian, stop it!" Advika took his face in both of her hands, his blue eyes shooting fire. "I'm not leaving. I...I love you, okay? How could I ever leave the person I love?"

It wasn't as romantic as Harry telling Sally he wanted to spend the rest of his life with her as the clock struck midnight on New Year's Eve, or Noah and Allie's rain-soaked clinch after he declared he wanted her forever. But still, Advika and Julian had their moment, and it was all theirs. When Julian snaked his arm around her waist and pulled her to his lap, and they began to kiss so hard they knocked teeth, Advika clung as tightly to him as he to her.

CHAPTER EIGHT

Something's Gotta Give

DURING MEMORIAL DAY WEEKEND, ADVIKA'S childhood friends came to visit.

After the fourteenth call in the span of thirty minutes, she had to pick up. Of course the Oakies would call to wish her a happy birthday. But Advika couldn't understand the urgency of needing to say those two words to her over the phone.

"Hi!" she said blearily, still in bed even though it was noon. She and Julian had celebrated her birthday with a titanic force of early morning lovemaking, and she barely had the energy to pull on a tee shirt, let alone absorb her friends' birthday wishes. Even with Julian's loving attentions, she couldn't shake her voluminous sadness, as heavy and isolating as wearing soggy clothing at the bottom of an empty pool. This was Advika's third birthday without Anu, and she had spent the first two alone and in bed, a pillow over her face, clouds of Kleenex sprinkled on the floor. If Advika hadn't met Julian, she would have spent her and Anu's birthday this year the exact same way.

"Advi! Happy birthday! Where are you?" Sunita said over the chatter of what sounded like radio deejays.

"Thanks! I'm . . . um . . ." How to answer that question? Then again, why was Sunita asking?

"Where are you, doofus?" Vik said as the radio voices cut out, replaced by the celebratory whoops of Sunita and Balan in the background.

"Are you guys all together?" Advika sat up with a start. "Where are you?"

"We're here to surprise you on your birthday!" Vik whooped as Balan explained they had dropped by her old apartment in Echo Park only to be told she no longer lived there.

"I'll come and meet you guys," Advika said quickly. "I can't believe you're all here! That's...crazy." She didn't want to see them. Spending time with the trio was the biggest, most blatant reminder that there was someone missing from their tight-knit fivesome. But they had come all this way for her. So Advika told them to meet her at a sushi restaurant at a high-end strip mall about twenty minutes away from Wildwood.

After hanging up, Advika hovered over indecision. Should she tell Julian? Before leaving, he had promised he was taking her somewhere special to celebrate and that she should be "ready and sexy" by 6 p.m. Surely she could get rid of the Oakies before then, and her two worlds would never have to cross. Advika threw on her robe and hurried into the bathroom, her earlier lethargy replaced by a thrumming anxiety.

For the first half hour of her birthday lunch, Advika actually felt relaxed, even verging on happy. Anu's absence was still a wound, but the presence and company of her three oldest friends gave her more comfort than she would have expected. When the Oakies were together, they slipped into their familiar roles. Sunita, who would turn twenty-nine in a few weeks, was the mother hen, her signature topknot bouncing on her head as she eagerly dispensed gossip and advice in equal measure; Balan was quiet and good-natured, only turning into a chatterbox when talking about his pet dachshunds or video games; and Vik, the human equivalent of a raucous beer commercial, was quick to crack jokes to deflect from his sense of inferiority resulting from his much older and accomplished congressman brother.

Advika appreciated that they avoided asking her about her personal life beyond her plans for the day. Instead, they filled her in on the latest developments in their lives: Sunita, two years in as a junior associate at a fancy litigation firm, was mulling a change to immigration law; Balan confidently shared his plans to leave his cushy tech job to strike out on his own by year's end; and Vik, tutoring private school students while studying to be a sommelier, proselytized about why the Indian-American obsession with the National Spelling Bee was pointless.

"We need to start thinking bigger than the spelling bee—that's all I'm saying." Vik balled up his soy sauce–stained napkin and threw it on his plate next to a wad of wasabi. "These kids start memorizing the dictionary at age eight, and if they're lucky, they get what? A trophy? Some college scholarship money?"

"And an appearance on a morning talk show," Balan said, deftly reaching for the last roll on the platter with his chopsticks. "Plus, they give their parents bragging rights for, like, ten solid years." Vik huffed in frustration and rolled his eyes. "Well, it's true," Balan said.

"But that's so limiting. Do you think anyone will care when he's twenty-five or forty? The scholarship money would be long gone. All it leads to is their names on a Wikipedia page. Who cares? If Indians were really smart, we'd focus on getting kids into baseball. The big-time players get hundred-million-dollar contracts." He then playacted a conversation between an Indian parent whose child won the spelling bee and an Indian parent whose kid signed a nine-figure contract with the Yankees, an elaborate bragging contest with ludicrous one-upmanship and exaggerated accents.

Advika laughed so hard she nearly snorted her sake. It had

been a very long time since she had sat at a table with people who looked like her and who shared an understanding in
which she never had to explain herself. She was used to being
in a constant state of attention, around Julian, his friends and
employees, pasting on a smile while she patiently explained
her "Indianness" to people who didn't really seem to care about
her answers. Advika took another sip of sake, surveying her
friends as she drank from the tiny blue porcelain cup. She took
in each one—Sunita's generous, heart-shaped face, Balan's
intelligent eyes and unfairly long lashes framed behind thick
black glasses, Vik's gelled hair spiking on top of his head like a
massive wave—and told herself it was time to tell them about
Julian.

"Guys," she said after Vik wound up his story, "let me tell
you what I've been up to." As she filled them in on her fateful
meeting with Julian at the Governors Ball, and how that had
led to her moving in with him, Advika kept her nerves in check
by tending to the postmeal duties usually taken up by Sunita.
First, she methodically refilled each of their sake glasses, then
gathered their plates and soy sauce bowls and neatly stacked
them on top of the empty sushi platters, making it easier for the
waiter to clear the table. By the time she had finished—both
her story and her cleanup—Advika finally felt ready to return
their gazes. Their stunned, fascinated, anxious gazes.

"Wow," Sunita said, the first one to speak. "What do your
parents think?" Of course Sunita would ask that question,
Advika thought crossly, cracking her knuckles underneath the
table.

"They...don't really know. I just...well, you know." Sunita
nodded and flashed an understanding smile. When the waiter
approached to clear the table, the foursome sat together in a
silence Advika found disquieting. She could visualize the ticker
tape of thoughts running through each one's head—*He's so old!*

They live together! Aunty and Uncle are going to freak out!—so when she felt her phone vibrate in her pocket, a storm of sweat dampened her armpits. Shit. Julian. Advika knew it was him, because the only people who called or texted were either him, her mother, or the three people sitting at the table with her.

She bolted out of her chair and mumbled about having to use the restroom. In the tiny water closet perfumed with the cloying scent of lilacs and the previous user's flatulence, Advika pinched her nose and had an equally pinched phone conversation with Julian. When he informed her that Aggie had said she stepped out, Advika quickly filled him in on her whereabouts and her friends' arrival. She watched herself in the mirror's reflection, lips pursed and eyes panicked, when Julian insisted on dropping by. Anu's voice floated in. *How does an Oscar-winning big-shot Hollywood producer have time to crash your birthday lunch?* Advika snapped her head back as if to shake her sister's words away, then returned her phone to her pocket and stalked back to her table.

By the time she arrived, a bowl of fried green tea ice cream with a birthday candle precariously stuck on top awaited her. The Oakies stared up at her with practiced smiles she was painfully familiar with, and when Vik started singing "Happy Birthday," Sunita hushed him with a pointed look.

"Thank you," Advika said, her voice coming out like a creaky door, sharp and dry. "This is so sweet."

"Advika." Sunita said her name with a solemn seriousness, as if she were a teacher about to report her to the principal's office. "We think...I...I wanted to invite you to come stay with me in Palo Alto for a little while." She reached across the table and briefly held Advika's damp hand. "I think it'd be good for you to get away a bit, be around friends."

"Oh." Advika touched her forehead, drawing dabs of sweat from her hairline. Julian had told her he was close by and would be there in about ten minutes. "That's so nice, Sun, but I'm doing okay—really. I understand your concern; I do. But this is the happiest I've been in a long time." Advika smiled as she said those words, realizing how true they were and how good it was to share it with those closest to her. The nerves fell away like bangles slipping off a wrist.

"Julian is so kind and thoughtful. He's even helping me with my career. He helped me get a writing-assistant job on that show you like, Balan: *Agent UFO*. The one with the undercover space aliens." She looked to Balan hopefully, as he was always the nicest out of all of them, never casting judgment on the others' work decisions or disastrously bad dates. Balan raised his eyebrows and nodded, but he didn't seem all that happy for her. Advika puffed up her cheeks, then exhaled out of the left side of her mouth.

"Anu used to do that," Vik said, his face contorted by a fleeting moment of grief. "When she was frustrated, I mean," he hastened to add upon seeing the other three's confused faces. No one had mentioned Anu's name until that moment.

"You guys, listen," Advika said after a few moments of pained silence. The birthday candle had burned down to a nub on top of the melted mix of ice cream and fried dough, but the flame continued its best to flicker to the bitter end. "If I were in your shoes, I'd feel the same way as you do. I know what it must look like. On the outside," she said, stressing the last word. "But you know I've been adrift since Anu . . . since then. And if he makes me happy, and I'm actually getting to further my career, then I'd really appreciate your support." She blinked back tears, and she reached for the napkins next to the untouched dessert plates. By the time she had picked one up, Balan had clobbered her with a hug.

"I'm happy if you're happy, Advi," he said softly into her ear before letting her go.

Vik, then a reluctant Sunita, came over and also embraced her. She thanked each of them and blushed as they broke into "Happy Birthday" while Advika pretended to blow out the candle, which had long since extinguished. As they good-naturedly argued about whether to ask for a new dessert, Julian walked through the door. Advika rushed over to him, and after an awkward pause, he leaned in and gave her a kiss on the cheek.

"Come outside and see your gift, Addi." He wrapped his arm around her waist and whirled her toward the entrance. "Hello there, Addi's friends," he added, greeting them with a jaunty wave. "Come join us."

In the parking lot was a white Mercedes G Wagon with a gigantic red velvet bow on the hood. A group of white teens holding skateboards posed in front of it while taking selfies.

"No! Really? For me?" Advika said, her gaze flicking from the gleaming G Wagon to her Camry, with its smudged windshield and slightly dented fender. "I don't deserve this."

"Of course you do," Julian said, landing another kiss on her temple. "When you told me you've been driving that car since high school, I knew we had to do better. Happy birthday, love."

She wrapped him in a hug and over his shoulders glimpsed her three friends—Vik's mouth hanging open, his eyes boring into the back of Julian's head, Balan offering a subdued grin, and Sunita's lips as tight as an em dash, her hands fidgeting at her sides. Those initial reactions to Julian never really subsided or were well hidden after he came inside to the restaurant to chat with them for a few minutes, taking care of the check not just for their party, but for everyone in the dining room, before the couple had departed.

The Oakies' faces were still on her mind later that night, at a sunset dinner on the deck of a palatial beach house in which a

James Beard award–winning chef made all her favorite dishes: stuffed mushrooms, pomme frites, kung pao chicken, fettuccini alfredo, Chicken 65. She hoped to avoid the topic of her friends the entire night, but Julian brought them up during their dessert of caramel-drizzled cannoli with scoops of coffee ice cream.

"Your friends don't like me." He stated this as a casual fact, as if commenting on the crispness of the ocean breeze.

"They don't know you," Advika said. "They didn't expect to meet you, Mr. Famous Hollywood Guy." She swirled her spoon in the puddled remnants of her ice cream, averting his gaze. "It can be a little intimidating, you know."

"I guess I can forget that sometimes." The warmth in his tone prompted Advika to look up and see he had put a big dollop of ice cream on his nose. She burst out laughing and stood up from across the table and leaned toward him, licking it off. Julian pulled her in for a long kiss.

"Well, all that matters is you like me." He beamed at her, but his eyes were distant, thinking.

"You'll have time to win them over too," Advika reassured him, lighting up at the idea that just like the very disparate dishes making up her birthday dinner, her favorite people could coexist: not quite harmoniously, but at least share the same space for her sake.

⌒

She texted Sunita later that night as she and Julian drove home.

A: Thx for coming to visit—so great to see you all today. It meant a lot to me 😊

S: You mean a lot to *us,* Advi. And please come visit, anytime

A: I'd love to. Will keep you posted

S: Keep in touch 🖤

Ten minutes later, Advika's phone beeped with a new message.

S: I think we need to tell them. She's really serious about him, I can tell. What I can't figure out is his angle.

Advika stared at the screen slack-jawed, rereading the three sentences from her friend, which she had obviously meant to send to Balan and Vik. How could Sunita be so two-faced? A sob wanted to come out of her throat, but Advika pushed it down as rage surged forward instead. She maintained a pleasant facade with Julian during the rest of the ride home, the whole time gripping her phone as if it were a stress ball. As soon as they returned to Wildwood, Advika excused herself to the bathroom to regain her composure, also not wanting Julian to know what her friend had just said.

Advika opened up the text exchange with Sunita and saw that Sun had deleted her last message. She typed furiously, then clicked Send.

Too late, Sun, I already saw the message you meant to send B and V. Stop talking about me behind my back. And if your text meant you wanted to tell my parents about me and J, BUTT OUT. It's my life, and no one else gets a say. Not even you. I love you, but I'm really hurt. I don't think we should talk for a while.

With tears blurring her vision, Advika blocked Sunita, then Vik and, after some hesitation, Balan.

CHAPTER NINE

City Lights

DURING THE FIRST WEEKEND OF June, Julian had a surprise for Advika.

When Julian had suggested a spontaneous trip to New York as a belated birthday getaway, Advika initially demurred. Her new position at *Agent UFO* was scheduled to start at the end of the month, and she wanted to focus on preparing for her first-ever writing job. Her mediocre writing resume had amplified her imposter syndrome to all-new heights. So she had planned to throw herself into a self-created TV-writing boot camp by studying every single series script as well as watching classic sci-fi and spy shows, such as *Star Trek: The Next Generation* and *Alias*. And since Julian had secured the position for her, she wanted to prove she actually deserved it. But he had seemed so excited to show her "his" New York—moody, elegant bars; exquisite penthouse views; and five-star service—that she finally acquiesced to his persistent enthusiasm.

They had arrived at the Four Seasons presidential suite during magic hour, and so the city skyline had an unearthly glow, as skyscraper lights blinked on in the slowly arriving darkness. As Julian tipped the bellboy, Advika found herself drawn to the floor-to-ceiling wall of windows, catching the last shards of sun before it dipped behind Central Park. She had never seen a view like this in her life, an entire city laid out before her, as if she were a conquering hero surveying her new lands. Advika hadn't been higher than four stories since Anu had died. But the view of Manhattan from the fifty-first floor was a siren song she couldn't resist. She rested one finger on the panel, then her entire palm. She pressed down, lightly at first, then with all her strength. It didn't give. The strain in her neck that had begun upon boarding the private jet, in which she had stayed seatbelted and eyemasked the whole time, finally eased.

"I'm so glad you convinced me to—" Advika turned around to see that Julian was on one knee, holding a tiny velvet box. He opened it, revealing an obscenely large, coffin-shaped diamond inside.

"Addi," Julian said, his face lighting up as their eyes met. "Marry me."

She never thought that a proposal would feel like a sucker punch. Advika flashed to the moments before and after her sister's death. Anu was there, and then she was gone, the balcony railing hanging crooked in the open air. Julian's proposal evinced a similar sensation, dizzying and unreal and leaving her unable to breathe.

"What . . . what are you doing? You can't be. A ring?" By the time she arrived at his side, he had already stood up, one hand clutching the ring, the other gingerly pressed against his lower back. "Oh no—are you okay?"

"I'm fine." Julian snapped the ring box shut and collapsed on a nearby cream leather sofa. "That's actually kind of hard to do, balancing on one knee like that. Not a fan." His words and affect were flat, as if the act of kneeling had sapped him of all his energy and good humor. He plopped the ring box onto the cushion next to him, then unbuttoned the three top buttons of his crisp white shirt. "Would you mind pouring me a drink?"

He nodded toward the wet bar on the opposite end of the sitting room. "There should be a bottle of Scotch there. Add an ice cube too."

The whiplash from marriage proposal to drink order was too hard to process. Advika remained where she was, placing a wobbly hand on a nearby wall, her mouth opening and closing, as too many words wanted to force their way out. Where to even start?

"Julian." Advika pointed an accusing finger at the ring box idling next to him. "What is going on? Do you really want to marry me?"

"Of course I do. I'm not some addled old man, Addi. I want this. I want you."

"But why?" It was weird to be holding this conversation with several feet separating them, and for a moment she considered joining him on the sofa. But afraid that if she stepped away, her legs would give out due to sheer discombobulation, Advika chose the wall. She leaned against it and for the first time took in the room. An elaborate bouquet of white roses fanned out like a peacock's tail at the center table, with two flutes of champagne waiting next to it. Reality began to soak in. This was all really happening. The trip had been designed with this question in mind.

"It's very simple: I know my life is better with you in it." With a sigh, Julian kicked off his loafers, revealing a small hole in the heel of his left sock. "I've rarely felt as certain about someone as I am about you."

"But . . ." Advika pressed the back of her hand against her forehead. "My parents don't even know about you. I can't get engaged to someone they've never met while they're out of the country."

"So let's fly to India. I'd like to meet them."

"No! They're not going to approve. They just wouldn't."

Julian looked at her askance. "Aren't you an adult? Why should you care what your parents say?"

"You don't understand. Indian families...we don't operate like that." As she said the words, Advika realized that she hadn't spoken to her mother in a week, her father in far longer. Even her mother's texts were less frequent. "Marriage is a big deal," she added limply.

"I love you, Advika. I probably have since the moment we met. I'm offering you a life, opportunities, adventure...freedom. Anything and everything you could want."

"Why does it have to be now? Why can't we have more time? At least—"

"I'm decisive. That's who I am. I'm not very patient. I know what I want, and it's you. But if you can't see what I see, then perhaps this isn't meant to be."

Advika's head jerked up. Julian sighed, then rose from the sofa, leaving behind the ring box, which fell on its side. He went to the wet bar and poured himself a glass of Scotch, but with no ice.

"I have to decide this moment, this second?" she asked, trying to keep her voice even.

"And here I was, thinking I'm quite the catch," Julian said with a bitter laugh. The sarcasm of his words stung her. "I really had no idea there would be that much to think about."

Julian drained the glass, then set it down with a jolt that made Advika flinch. "I'm going to go out for a while. By the time I get back, I hope you'll have an answer. No sentences, no explanations. All I want is a yes or a no."

"But, Julian—"

"Feel free to go out too. There's a whole beautiful city out there, full of beautiful people." Julian arched his eyebrows at her on that last part, and Advika looked away. "Or just stay here and order in room service. Think things over." He slipped his shoes back on, then left the suite.

~

Advika lay on her stomach on the king-sized bed, wearing only her FINAL GIRL tank top and underwear as she played *Candy Crush* on her phone, trying not to worry about when, or if, the front door would open. Julian had been gone for three hours. It was just a few minutes past 8 p.m., and when she had texted him an hour earlier, he hadn't responded. Advika wondered how often, if ever, a man like Julian was rejected. Although, she hadn't actually said no. But just as she had seen in several movies, the words "I need to think about it" all but ensured there wouldn't be wedding bells in the next scene.

Julian himself—his age, his stature—wasn't her main hesitation, although it was significant. As much as she adored romantic comedies as a genre, the parts of those movies she liked best were the "meet-cutes" and the montages that depicted the couples bonding as they went on dates, met each other's friends, went on flirty strolls at farmers' markets, and kissed each other at sunset. The wedding was merely the default ending, a way to indicate to the audience that these two people they've invested their time in will remain happy and together after the credits roll.

Marriage was paperwork: mortgages, bills, bank accounts, the marriage license itself. Two lives bound together by various words printed out on various pieces of paper. Romance leaked out of the relationship over time, with the wedding just an expensive memory preserved in overpriced photos of an overpriced ceremony.

This was what Anu would be reminding her of if she were still here. Advika could have received a proposal from Drake or Dev Patel and she would have still recited a litany of all the reasons it wasn't worthwhile to tie your life, and your identity, to a man. But that was also the point: Anu was no longer here. What did

Advika have to call her own, to anchor her to the world, with her twin sister gone?

Advika repeatedly opened and closed the ring box, finding an odd comfort in the decisive snap it made each time it shut. As she did so, giving herself a second-long glimpse of the ring, Advika remembered how much she and Anu had pitied Sunita and so many women they knew who struggled with being single. Because the gift of having a twin was not needing to find a soul mate. By having each other, neither sister shared their friends' anxieties about getting married.

"If marriage is about finding a soul mate, I already have one," Anu liked to say to whoever asked—college pals, nosy aunties, their own parents—as she slung an arm around her sister's neck. "We can use our brain cells to worry about other things rather than finding 'the one.'"

If Advika were honest, she and Anu had shared a secret smugness to feel free of the scramble and anxiety that came with the search for a spouse. Anu in particular relished dating and didn't like the idea of monogamy.

"I need five different kinds of ramen and six different kinds of pickle in the kitchen at all times. So how is one person supposed to satisfy me for the rest of my life?" Anu had once said as she and Advika took refuge in the backyard of their parents' house during their college graduation party. They had fled while still wearing their caps and gowns to crouch behind a gardening shed on the left side of the house, which mostly hid them from view of a small army of aunties who viewed them as new recruits, assuming that their college degrees automatically meant they were ready to enlist in their tribe and find husbands.

"But what if it's mango pickle?" Advika had joked, wanting to temper her sister's anger. The topic of marriage always pissed off her sister more, whereas Advika was merely resigned to it.

"Okay, tempting. I could probably live with just mango pickle for a month. Two, tops. But the idea of marrying someone and living with them for the rest of your life? That's archaic. And absurd. Especially when I have you, Advi. You're the only person in the world that I could be with forever. And even then, you're a pain in the ass," Anu said with a giggle.

Advika playfully whopped her with her graduation cap. "How dare you," she said, laughing. "You love living with me."

"Sure, I love finding you on the sofa watching *You've Got Mail* for the seven hundredth time."

"And it's a joy to wake up at five a.m. to the sound of you blasting Nicki Minaj while doing the elliptical."

"That was just one time because I couldn't find my headphones!" Anu protested. A strong wind rattled through what had been an otherwise balmy evening, and the girls shivered. Even wearing their commencement gowns over their summer dresses—Anu's lilac and Advika's yellow—was not enough to keep them warm much longer.

"Ugh, we have to go back in there." Advika buried her face in her arms. "If Nandini Aunty tells me about her best friend's sister's dentist one more time . . ."

"We're going to need a distress signal to save each other from these conversations." Anu stood up and extended a hand to her sister. "It's never going to stop until one of us gets married or the entire population of aunties ages out of existence."

"How about this?" Advika said, crossing her eyes and sticking out her tongue.

"Subtle," Anu said, laughing. "C'mon, life partner. Let's get this night over with."

"Till death do us part," Advika said to her sister as they laughed and threw their arms around each other before heading back inside.

Advika stared out at the view again, now shrouded in darkness yet still alit with twinkling lights that communicated a city vibrating with people and ideas and fun. And Julian out among all of it, doing god knew what. This was her first time in New York, and to wander the streets by herself, not knowing anyone and nobody knowing her, was the equivalent of dropping herself smack-dab into a panic attack. To be out there among the humming, busy crowd would only magnify how distant she felt from people. From life itself.

At the same time, the old loneliness was creeping in. The quietude, heavy and unrelenting, that could not be buried no matter how much she cranked the volume of the TV. She avoided the clock now, not wanting to know how long Julian had been gone. But with the agitated strumming of her heart, and the gravity-drop flip of her stomach, her body was panicking as if days seemed to have passed. Advika couldn't bear her isolation one second longer. She needed to talk to someone—anyone. Advika couldn't go back to the Oakies with this piece of news—they would freak out and have an intervention waiting for her at LAX. She scrolled through her phone's list of contacts, up and down, down and up, trying to latch onto one name that she could spill her thoughts to. When her finger landed on Olive, Advika instinctively dialed her number. Olive epitomized neutrality—they weren't friends, but they had parted on decent enough terms.

"'Sup." Olive picked up on the fourth ring. "On a break right now, or else you might've not caught me."

"Oh, good. Hi, Olive. How are you?" Advika put the phone on speaker, letting Olive's deadpan voice echo through the suite.

"Fine. Um, I don't have a lot of time." The sound of traffic buzzed in the background, followed by a spray of loud barks. "Is there something you need? Is it about our old spot?"

"Oh, uh, no. This is about, well, needing advice. I figured you'd give it to me straight."

"Okaaay," Olive said. Advika imagined her rolling her eyes, taking a final drag of her cigarette in the alley behind her coffee shop, then stubbing it out with her steel-toed boot. "You got three minutes. Shoot."

"Would you be surprised by a marriage proposal after only three months of dating?" Advika grabbed one of the fluffy pillows from behind her and buried her face in it, waiting for Olive's response. Which she gave immediately.

"Wow. Is this, like, a green-card situation? Because I wouldn't—"

"It's not. He proposed, and . . . I'm thinking about it."

"Is he hot? Is he nice to you? Does he have his own money?" Olive rattled off her list of questions without seeming too invested in her former roommate's answer.

"Yes to all three." Advika blushed to realize it was all true. Olive seemed to be about to ask her something else, when a voice yelled, "Your break was over ten minutes ago." Advika listened to Olive and the high-pitched voice argue and recalled her own battles with supervisors over the years, scolded over the slightest infractions, her pay docked over dropped plates and burned aprons. The thought of returning to a life of long hours and meager tips, feet squished in cheap shoes, face muscles exhausted from smiling for hours on end, made Advika feel nauseous.

"And you're in love with him?"

Advika hesitated. Everything within her body quickened, as if she housed an ant farm inside her skin. She still didn't know the answer to this question. But what if it was simply an eventuality that would occur after some more time had passed? After all, arranged marriages had worked out for scores of Indian people over centuries, in which love arrived after the wedding day. Even a trashy reality show like *The Bachelorette*, which depicted couples getting engaged only a few weeks after meeting, had led to actual marriages that had lasted long after the cameras had moved on. Plus, she and Julian had a deep attraction to each other Advika had never experienced in her life. The slightest touch of his fingertips on her shoulder, the small of her back, the inside of her thigh sent paroxysms of delight and desire coursing through her. And most importantly, didn't she ache for Julian's presence right now? Every second without him, and not knowing where he was, felt like a withdrawal of oxygen. Wasn't this thirsty, gasping need for Julian a sign that she loved him, couldn't live without him?

"Yes," Advika said, palming the ring box in her hand, then squeezing it tight. "Of course I love him."

"Then what's the problem?" Olive's harried voice broke into her thoughts. "You seem to have got it made." Advika heard the suite's front door let out a subtle beep as a key card swiped through the lock.

"You're right. Thanks, Olive."

"Sure, yeah. Bye."

Advika hung up the phone and waited for Julian to cross the threshold to the bedroom so she could give him her answer.

CHAPTER TEN

The Marrying Man

ON THE SECOND SATURDAY OF June, they got married.

Advika never imagined herself wearing a wedding dress. If she had somehow married someone, she had at least expected to wear a red sari or lehenga trimmed with gold. But for a casual ceremony on Wildwood's outside grounds, she had impulsively chosen a lacy, long-sleeved white cocktail dress that stopped just above the knee. Because despite how often she and her college dormmates had gotten stoned and marathoned *Say Yes to the Dress*, Advika blanched at the idea of ever wearing one. She had hoped to feel less bridal by choosing a cocktail dress with a deep V in the back. But as she examined herself in the mirror, Advika mouthed, *Ugh*, at her reflection. Who was this woman who had her wild curls styled into a tight chignon, wearing an itchy, formfitting dress that kept riding up midthigh? Although, that was also the point: by choosing to wear a (non-bridal) white wedding dress rather than a sari or lehenga, she was officially leaving the old Advika behind and fully throwing herself into her new life with Julian. It was the equivalent of Angela Bassett's character tossing a lit match into her husband's car in *Waiting to Exhale*, walking away without looking back as it burst into flames. A defiant way of moving on.

And yet. In Advika's palm was a simple piece of jewelry: Anu's twenty-four-karat gold necklace with a square OM pendant. She and her sister had been given matching ones on their fourteenth birthdays. Advika had lost hers two weeks after receiving it, so her mother had taken Anu's back and stored it in the family safe. Only after Anu had died did Rupi give Advika the necklace, tearfully saying her sister would want her to have it, while also in the same breath admonishing her not to lose this one too. And so Advika had worn it every day since. Julian had noticed it the first time they had slept together, twisting his finger around the chain as it lay across her clavicle, telling her, "It's beautiful. But I prefer diamonds and pearls. Like that Prince song."

She didn't know that Prince song. All Advika knew was that in an alternate reality, she wouldn't be debating wearing a single gold chain; she would be weighed down with the most decadent and bejeweled gold chains and bangles and anklets that Rupi Srinivasan had haggled for from the finest jewelry store in Bangalore. Not that Advika minded forgoing getting drenched head to toe with gold. But when she had accepted Julian's proposal, she had envisioned wearing Anu's gold chain during the ceremony as a private tribute to her sister and retaining a small part of herself within this new woman she was constructing to join Julian's world. But it would have looked too discordant to wear the gold chain with the elaborate multistrand pearl choker Julian had surprised her with the night before, purring in her ear that he couldn't wait to see it on her when she became his wife.

A knock at the door. Eloisa calling her name. With a sigh, Advika returned the gold chain to her jewelry box, put on her silver open-toed Salvatore Ferragamos, and opened the bedroom door. Eloisa, wearing a white pantsuit with a silk red top, handed her a bouquet of lilies, then headed downstairs with

Advika trailing after her. She had purposely left her phone behind in the room, having texted her parents her news and deciding that however they responded, she would ignore it until the next day.

Julian waited at the edge of the lawn along with Roger and a justice of the peace. The trio of smiles—joyful, simpering, officious—was difficult to absorb, and so as Advika walked toward them, she watched the sun setting behind them instead. But staring too hard at the sun's fiery descent made everything in her eyesight radiate a blurry surge of light. Advika preferred this, found it fitting that her vision matched the unreality of the situation. She wished she were drunk to further blot out the happiness, fear, and pain that ricocheted inside her, making her so weak-kneed that she stumbled twice in the grass, and Roger came over and walked her the rest of the way to Julian's side. When they faced each other, Advika was shocked to see that her soon-to-be husband was teary-eyed, his hands shaking as he gently reached toward her and kissed her cheek.

"You're too beautiful for words," he whispered into her ear. His scent was entrancing, and he cut a handsome figure in his navy blue suit and gold tie. *I get to marry this man*, she thought. The unreality of the moment dissipated as she lost herself in Julian's gaze, the two grinning at each other like they just pulled off the biggest prank of all time. She handed the bouquet back to Eloisa without looking at her and held Julian's outstretched hand.

But the exchanging of vows and wedding rings punctured the bubble. How many times had she watched weddings—in movies, in television shows, a handful in person, some Indian and some not—never once believing she too would take part? Advika kept waiting for someone to call, "Cut," because she simply did not belong here, saying these words that belonged in the Cliché Hall of Fame. As if in revolt, Advika's stomach gurgled loudly after Julian said, "To have and to hold." He cocked an eyebrow at her but continued speaking, the giddy smile never once leaving his face.

When it came time for Advika to recite her vows, she became the kind of queasy that reminded her of riding a roller coaster just before the drop from a great height. The queasiness came from the anticipation of knowing the drop was coming but not knowing how it would feel, except that it would be thrilling and scary at the same time. Even taking in Julian's face, the one now most familiar to her on the planet, with his small, delicate ears and deep lines marking his forehead, his clear blue eyes and the silver tint of a beard he had just started to grow, didn't anchor her or make her feel better, as it so often did before. Saying the words "I do" out loud was a true out-of-body experience, the first word coming out as a near whisper, the second one charging out of her mouth so harshly that Julian took a step back in surprise. Only sometime afterward, as they were posing for photographs, Julian's arm around her waist as he occasionally whispered dirty talk about his plans for their wedding night, did Advika realize why she was so unsettled: this was her first time, so of course she was nervous. But Julian had done this before. Several times. And so while she was a novice who had barely memorized her lines, he had breezed through his part with the ease of a professional.

CHAPTER ELEVEN

Broadcast News

THE SCREEN WAS WHITE AND merciless, the cursor blinking at her with impatience. Despite having her own office at Wildwood (a guest bedroom outfitted with a desk, sofa, bookshelf, and framed movie posters of *His Girl Friday* and *Bend It Like Beckham*) and a new laptop (a MacBook Pro replacing her crappy Dell with a zigzag crack in the screen), Advika couldn't focus. Words were useless to her, because the only ones she wanted to write—alien spies' flirty banter while infiltrating suburban life—would never happen. Somewhere across the city, a group of people, mostly white, all word nerds like her, were gathered writing the first scripts of the new season of *Agent UFO*. And even though she had never watched the series before learning about the opportunity from Julian, Advika's entire being longed to be in that room, rather than sitting alone in an empty house, staring at an empty page.

She leaned back in her white leather chair and propped her bare feet on the desk, an enormous, stately pile of wood that would be better suited to a 1950s-era tobacco CEO constantly snapping orders at his secretaries. The view from her office showed her the simpatico sun and sky of a picture-perfect late-June afternoon, which sunk her even further into a funk.

Advika couldn't complain to Julian about how upset she still was about losing her job. He had insisted on going on a two-week honeymoon after their wedding, even though they had just returned from a trip to New York. Advika had begun tiring of all the romantic jaunts and getaways, because the endless travel disrupted her focus on writing. But how could she say no to a honeymoon? Even though she had concerns about their trip to the Turks and Caicos overlapping with the opening of the *Agent UFO* writers' room, Julian had persuaded her she'd still be able to return to her new job after "splashing in the sun in a bikini with your new husband." So the curt email she received from her new agent upon touching down at the airport—*they decided to go in a different direction*—filled Advika with a despair she was still drowning in days later. When she told Julian what had happened, he had merely kissed her forehead and said not to worry, that another opportunity would turn itself up. Well, it hadn't.

Advika's phone, which was screen down next to her laptop, buzzed. She eyed it warily and pushed it back with her big toe. Her parents' reaction to her wedding left her with a permanent stomachache, to the point that she actively feared her phone for the messages it would next communicate from them. Advika had only had one conversation with her parents since giving them the news over text right before the ceremony. Well, a conversation with her mother, since her father refused to speak to her. As if her father's silent treatment was so different from their lack of communication since they had moved to Bangalore. But her mother went through a whole rainbow of emotions—anger and sadness and bewilderment—during that lacerating call, in which all Advika could do was listen. Because she couldn't say what she wanted to say: *He's been here for me. You haven't.* Instead, she just absorbed all of her mother's pain during the two-hour call, which she took while curled up with a pillow in her master bath's soaking tub as Julian snored in the next room. Advika didn't tell him about the call, because she didn't see the point of trying to explain why her parents were so crushed by her decision to marry a man—a white man, a near stranger—that was closer in age to them than her. (For his part, Julian had cheerily asked when he could meet his new in-laws while passing her a glass of champagne during their flight to their honeymoon. Advika squirmed and took a long sip before replying, "Eventually." Julian hadn't brought them up since.)

The wreckage of that phone call still appeared in occasional WhatsApp messages her mother sent her, random diatribes that appeared at odd hours. All were long, run-on sentences lacking punctuation; some were pleading, others were merely sad. The last one Advika's mother had sent came two days ago: Come see us. We miss you. And even though she knew it was childish of her, Advika responded with, If you really missed me, you'd come here. After all this time, how could they not see how fully they had abandoned her and that, before Julian, her life had been just a series of ellipses, trailing off into nothing with no resolution in sight?

"Ugh," she said out loud as her phone buzzed again. Advika looked from that device to her laptop, which had now gone into screen saver mode from her inattention. Which was the lesser of two evils? At least her phone held the potential of sharing a message from Julian, or perhaps even her agent. Advika brought her legs down from the desk, then picked up the phone as if it were a smelly piece of laundry, holding it at arm's length between the tips of her thumb and forefinger before finally flipping it over to reveal the screen. A message awaited her, but it wasn't a text. It was a Google Alert sent to her email.

Julian Zelding's dead first wife to his "child bride": Divorce the schmuck and I'll pay you $1M

After they married, Advika had set up the alerts for her name because after the "Payne in the Butt" story, she never again wanted to be blindsided by news coverage that featured her. Yet nothing could have prepared her to see the gossip headline accompanied by an image that spliced together three photos: Julian from the recent Oscars, her own blurry face in the middle, sourced from her long-abandoned Instagram account, and a movie still of a doe-eyed brunette woman who resembled Norma Jean before her transformation into Marilyn Monroe.

Advika stared at the image, unblinking, until her eyes watered. The sense of unreality that first draped over her during her wedding came back tenfold. She walked on tiptoe to the office's adjoining bathroom and shut the door. Advika slid down to her knees, then forced herself to read the article.

JULIAN ZELDING'S DEAD FIRST WIFE TO HIS "CHILD BRIDE": DIVORCE THE SCHMUCK AND I'LL PAY YOU $1M

Julian Zelding didn't just score a trophy at the Academy Awards this year—he also scored a trophy wife. The megaproducer, 67, quietly tied the knot with Advika Srinivasan at his Pacific Palisades home earlier this month. The former bartender / aspiring screenwriter, 27, is much younger than her new husband, a fact that didn't go unnoticed by his first wife, Evie Lockhart.

The Oscar-nominated actress passed away from a long illness in her Avignon, France, home last week. We got our hands on her will, which was ho-hum (she bequeathed her fortune to nonprofits supporting girls' education and animal welfare) except for one bombshell request. Lockhart said she would bequeath a single film reel and $1,000,000 to Zelding's "latest child bride" if she divorced him.

Lockhart and Zelding married in 1970 and filmed three movies together before divorcing nine years later. Their final collaboration, *Dark, Hot Sun*, earned him his first Oscar win. She quit Hollywood and moved to France soon after, while Zelding accumulated four more Oscars and three more wives in his storied film career.

Reps for the producer did not respond to our request for comment, nor has Lockhart's lawyer.

Advika's first instinct was to call Julian, but her eyes caught on a line from the article, reminding her that in the will, she had been referred to as Julian's "latest child bride." The venom in those words, so knowing and scathing, left her breathless. Shame overwhelmed her, and she set down her phone so she could bury her face in her hands. It was humiliating to be viewed as one of Julian's young, naive wives. She had joined an ignoble club and, even worse, had done so willingly, with blinders on.

Advika picked up her phone and immediately Googled her husband. (She hadn't actually said the word "husband" aloud yet, as she had no one to introduce him to or even discuss him with. Even thinking about the word in relation to herself was odd and foreign.) Just like when she had searched for him the past two times, his Wikipedia page came up as the first search result. She let out a gasp when she saw the following:

Born: Aug 2, 1947 (age: 67 years), Bardon, Iowa

Spouse: Advika Srinivasan (m. 2015), Victoria Lizbeth Truong (m. 2008–2013), **MORE**

Awards: Academy Award for best picture, **MORE**

Her finger hovered over the "more" link next to "spouse" for a few moments, and then she clicked.

Spouse: Advika Srinivasan (m. 2015), Victoria Lizbeth Truong (m. 2008–2013), Nova Martin (m. 1982–1991), Evie Lockhart (m. 1970–1979)

Perhaps it was the shock of the tabloid report, or perhaps it was just finally seeing her name next to those of the three other women who cast such long shadows, and to whom she could never possibly measure up. But to have the one-two punch of Evie's will and seeing herself officially enshrined as one of Julian's spouses left Advika thoroughly stupefied: her fingers frozen, her vision blurred, and her mind a blank. She blinked several times, trying to jump-start the synapses in her brain. Eventually the numbness dissipated, and Advika was able to process the information onscreen, for the first time noticing the sizable gap between Julian's marriages to Nova and Victoria. The former he had called an angel, and the latter he had called a gold digger. There was so much he had left unknown and unsaid. And now here she was, a newlywed pathetically gleaning basic facts about her husband's past through Google searches.

A burst of betrayal swept through her, and she smashed the link to Julian's Wikipedia page with all the fury of someone busting through a locked door. His life story flooded onto the screen, but it was soon interrupted by a phone call from an unknown number. Advika declined it, only for another one to follow, and another after that. Then came a text from Julian: Don't pick up the phone, don't talk to anyone. Stay there, I'm coming to you.

With shaking hands, Advika powered off the phone. She found herself relieved to switch off the device and quiet the barrage of voices and opinions descending on her. After setting it down, for the second time that day she pushed her phone away with her big toe. Then she curled up into a ball on the floor and stared at a spiderweb in the corner near the bathtub, until her eyes fluttered shut.

⌒

Hours later, or maybe just minutes, there was a knock at the bathroom door.

"Advika. I need to talk to you." Julian sounded flustered, his voice coming out as a strained croak. Three more knocks in rapid succession. "Please, come out."

Advika slowly rose up, the left side of her body sore from lying on the hard tile. She opened her mouth to speak but couldn't think of what to say. She slumped toward the door and threw it open to show Julian pacing back and forth from her desk to the bookshelf, scratching his silvery beard, his sunglasses balanced carelessly on his head. When he saw her, he commandeered a hug, which she returned with limp arms. Dressed in an ocean-blue button-down dress shirt and white pants, he looked like he had just disembarked from captaining a yacht. But his expression was pure Captain Ahab, red-faced and ready to blow at any moment.

"Have you talked to anyone?" He took her by the hand and led her to the tan suede couch next to the bookshelves. She shook her head. "Good, good. This will all blow over, sweetheart. Don't worry."

"Your ex-wife's will..." Advika trailed off. Julian retracted his hand from hers and fidgeted with his sleeve cuff. "Why would she do that?"

"Why else?" he said with a dismissive growl. "She was a harpy who always had it out for me. And a flair for the dramatic. Of course she would try to ruin this. Us." He rolled up his sleeves, then pulled out his phone from his shirt pocket. "Give me yours. Let's bury these for a while. Nothing good will be on the other end."

Advika tossed her phone onto the coffee table, and Julian stacked his on top of hers after turning his device off too. "Haven't you been divorced from your first wife for more than twenty years?" she asked.

"Longer," he huffed, sliding down on the sofa and spreading his legs wide. His expression was surly, his lower lip sticking out as if he were a child forbidden to play with his favorite toy.

"Listen. Julian." Advika tentatively touched his knee. "I did what you asked when we met. I got to know you for you. But you have three lifetimes' worth of history with other people, and it's humiliating to have your past come back this way. I . . . I feel so exposed."

"You feel exposed?" Julian's voice took on a thunder Advika had never heard from him before. "That's my personal life flayed open all over the tabloids. Mine."

"I'm in that story too. I'm called a 'child bride' for fuck's sake." Advika didn't curse often, but she savored the way the word flowed off her tongue. All her anger and frustration and fear were tied up in that single word, and she realized she would have picked up something heavy and expensive and thrown it against the wall if she hadn't said it. She stood up and crossed her arms and stared down at Julian. The vantage point showed her a dime-sized bald spot sprouting at the back of his head. He looked up and faced her, his eyes narrowed.

"Advika. I love you, but nobody knows you. This is about me. She's just using you to get at me. She was always so jealous, even when we were married. She was pathetic then, and she's pathetic now."

"She's dead," Advika said quietly. "She's not anything anymore, except no longer living."

"And yet she's found a way to come between us and brought the whole bloody world along to nose into our business." Julian stood up and cupped Advika's face with both hands. The tender warmth of his touch softened her toward him, though she kept her gaze away from his. "I'll bury this, okay? In twenty-four hours, no one will care."

"How?" She briefly met his eyes before looking away again.

"I have ways. Don't worry about it." Julian's gaze flickered over to her workstation, where her laptop screen saver showed a photo taken on their wedding day, the two leaning in for a kiss with the sunset glowing behind them. "What are you working on?"

"Nothing yet," she said, placing her hands on his hips to try to steer him out of eyesight of her laptop. "I'm still... brainstorming."

But Julian was a tree firmly rooted in the ground. "If you say you're a writer, be a writer. Get words on the page."

"It's not that easy." Advika let him go and slouched back down onto the sofa. "You know how badly I wanted to work on *Agent UFO*."

He chuckled. "You didn't even know the show existed until your agent told you about it." Advika spun away from him and faced the wall, her eyes burning with tears. "Addi, come on. There'll be other opportunities—I promise." Julian took her by the hand and, with one strong pull, brought her back toward him. He walked her to her desk and sat her down in her chair.

"Can you stop?" Advika said, shuddering with held-in sobs. The wedding photo on her laptop stared back, and she hated the stupid gummy grin overtaking her face.

"You're a screenwriter. Right? That's your dream. Then focus on your dream." Standing behind her, he placed both hands on her shoulders and kneaded so hard she winced. "It's probably better for you to stay inside and keep a low profile for a little while."

"How long?" Advika's voice came out high-pitched and

trembling. She worried the engagement ring back and forth, even as the jagged edges of the diamond nipped her skin.

"We'll see. Hopefully the story goes away soon. But forget about all that." Julian bent over and touched the laptop track-pad, bringing back the white screen. "You know how many writers would love to have the free time to work on their passion project? Stop thinking about what you don't have and remember what you do. You have me. And you have your writing."

Advika wiped away her tears with the back of her hand and felt her body relax slightly when Julian walked to the other side of the room. In the reflection of her computer screen, she watched Julian pick up his phone and turn it on.

"Shit," he muttered to himself as the device began pinging with a cacophony of noises. "Addi, I have to go. I'll see you for dinner." He returned to her briefly and kissed the top of her head, then left her office and firmly shut the door. Advika glowered at the blank page still waiting for her. She smashed her fist on the keyboard over and over again, setting off small explosions of letters that filled the screen.

~

A day later, all the tabloids were chasing a story about a leaked text message exchange between a former Sexiest Man Alive and a French ingénue who had a supporting role in two of Julian's most recent films. Besides exchanging nude photos, the strange, vague wording of some of their texts seemed to hint the two had covered up some sort of crime. He posted a Notes app message about "haters conspiring against me" on Instagram, while she deleted her account altogether. (Advika had almost deactivated hers too. But deletion was tantamount to guilt, and she had nothing to feel guilty about, so she chose to make hers private instead.)

She didn't even have to ask if Julian had anything to do

with the news story: his demeanor grew sunnier as the news hopscotched from gossip sites to highbrow culture outlets to breaking-news networks. A quick online search showed that coverage of Evie Lockhart's will turned up fewer than forty stories, while the sexy and potentially incriminating text chain already had several hundred in the span of two hours. As Advika lay next to him in bed that night, she finally admitted to herself she had married a stranger. Someone whose ex-wife hated him so much she would want to dissuade Advika from staying married to him with a seven-figure check...and a reel of film.

How had she forgotten that intriguing piece of info? Advika had only seen an actual film reel when she had worked in a movie theater the summer before she went to college. She liked to hang out in the projectionist's room and watch the people watching the movies, all while the film circled nearby, the reel snapping along in a satisfying rhythm. More than the money, the film reel was what made her curious about not just her new husband, but the first woman he had married.

Julian's foot hit her ankle as he turned over and threw an arm diagonally over her chest. His long pinky toenail scratched at her skin, a minor annoyance that grew into an unrelenting irritation as the night wore on.

CHAPTER TWELVE

Working Girl

ADVIKA WAS STILL NOT QUITE used to driving the Mercedes G Wagon. Even more than a month in, she didn't like the sensation of floating above the traffic rather than being among the other cars—cars like her old Camry, which Advika had insisted on keeping despite Julian's birthday gift, because it hadn't just been her vehicle but also Anu's. But the Camry was almost out of gas, and she was desperate to get out of the house for a little while. Besides, she was on a mission.

Even with the celebrity news cycle still enraptured by the text message scandal and seemingly little else, one week after Advika spied the first report about Evie Lockhart's will, she still worried about men jumping out of the bushes to snap photos of her. So even though driving the G Wagon was akin to putting on a Bigfoot costume and stomping alongside regular people, it also helped her to feel incognito, since Los Angeles was full of similar hulking luxury vehicles.

Advika pulled into the Echo Park Public Library parking lot. She could have chosen any library in the city, but the Echo Park one had a soothing familiarity. Her life had been a whiplash of changes—new husband, new home, new car, and an exceptional number of zeros in her newly joint bank account—and to return to a place her former self had frequented gave her solace. Even though the weather was hot and dry, Advika wore a black hoodie and large, dark sunglasses as she slipped out of her car, parked as close to the front entrance as possible, and scurried up the steps into the welcoming arms of the air-conditioning.

She couldn't have anything sent to the house and didn't want to research Evie Lockhart online, petrified of running into her own name when Googling the actress. (The words "child bride" echoed in her head at all hours.) Advika's one safe resource for more information about Evie was the library, and she could only hope that none of the Echo Park librarians were gossip obsessives who would get wild-eyed at seeing Julian Zelding's current wife checking out materials related to his first dead one.

After taking a moment to revel in being in such a familiar space, eyeing the long gray tables that she once parked herself at as she worked on *The Romance Game* or read biographies of Doris Day and Ida Lupino, she jumped into research mode. This branch had only two of Evie Lockhart's films, one on DVD and one on VHS. Both featured her apple-cheeked face on the cover, one version of her serious yet smoldering, the other flirtatious. Advika was also elated to discover that there was an Evie Lockhart biography too, but since the entire Los Angeles Public Library system had only one copy, it had to be transferred from a faraway branch. Still, Advika was pleased with what she'd turned up so far.

The one remaining issue was how was she to do a deep-dive into Evie? Doing so at Wildwood would be impossible. Julian's house manager, Aggie, seemed to be underfoot more often, sitting in the kitchen and going through her to-do list while chatting on the phone. And then the housekeeper came over to clean twice a week. It was too risky. Also, who had a VCR anymore? Of the two movies, the one that Advika wanted to see more was *Lost and Gone Forever*, a 1972 drama that was one of the three movies Evie and Julian had collaborated on, and the second movie both of them ever made, three years after *The Riders*. She had lucked out and discovered that someone had uploaded *The Riders* to YouTube, and she had downloaded it in case it got pulled off the site. Now she just needed a safe place to host her Evie Lockhart mini–movie marathon in peace.

After she got back into her car, she pulled off the hoodie and threw it in the back seat and blasted the AC. Her first thought was to see if she could rent an Airbnb for the afternoon, but she couldn't risk Julian looking at her credit card statement. (He had paid off her credit card debts after they returned from their honeymoon and had told her this when he had upgraded her to an Amex black card, which Advika knew from her service job days was an invitation-only credit card for the elite.)

"This is why you need a job," she said out loud to herself. One of her and Anu's favorite songs as kids was "Independent Women Part 1." They'd drive their mother crazy by singing along with Destiny's Child, declaring in their girlish, off-key voices that they had bought the shoes on their feet and the clothes they were wearing. "I depend on me!" the two of them would shout over and over again, until their mother would declare she had a headache and switch off the radio.

She had let twelve-year-old Advika down. Because every-thing in her vicinity at that moment—the car, her clothes, the laptop stored underneath the passenger seat, even her phone, which had been upgraded to the latest, fanciest iPhone—was from Julian. Advika could no longer throw her hands up with all the women Destiny's Child saluted in their song. She really was just a trophy wife.

The self-pity came fast, but Advika didn't have time for it and slammed the heel of her hand against the steering wheel to shake herself out of her gloom. And then, the answer flashed in her head with such clarity there should have been a light bulb gleaming above her head. Advika sent a text message. Five minutes later a response came in, followed by a second message for an address in Silver Lake. Advika grinned, gunned the engine, and sped out of the parking lot.

⁓

Olive waited for her in the doorway of a Spanish-style bungalow, her quizzical expression at odds with her sparkly blue Elsa costume. Advika couldn't stifle a smile as she approached her. As much as she wanted to ask the backstory, Advika couldn't alienate her former roommate after she agreed to let her come over.

Even though they had lived together for almost two years, Advika still found Olive to be a mystery. They had met when she had answered Olive's Craigslist ad seeking a roommate. Desperate to leave her parents' house, where she temporarily moved back following her sister's death, Advika had answered every ad in the greater Los Angeles area that advertised a woman seeking a same-sex roommate. Only Olive's posting had stated she was seeking "a woman, trans, nonbinary, and/or gender-nonconforming person." This had endeared her to Advika, since Anu would have written something similar if she had ever sought a roommate who wasn't her sister. Perhaps due to that connection, Advika had imagined they would become friends after she moved in. But beyond making small talk whenever their paths crossed, Olive kept to herself, blasting her stereo in her bedroom while working on a documentary about her family. And that's as much as Advika ever really learned about her roommate, along with her love of loud music and her disdain for washing dishes.

"Thanks so much for letting me come over, Olive. And here."

She pulled out a bottle of rosé from her tote bag, but Olive ignored it and instead looked over Advika's shoulder. She let out a low whistle.

"Nice ride," Olive said, her lips pursed as she nodded toward the G Wagon parked in front of the mailbox. "You really are living the good life."

"Ha ha, I guess." Advika held up the bottle, and Olive finally took it from her with a curt thank-you. "Do you still have your VCR, by the way?" At their old apartment, Olive had a VCR hooked up to a TV in her bedroom so she could watch her family's home movies for her documentary.

"Not here." She pointed a thumb behind her, which briefly hooked into her long blond braid. "I'm house-sitting for two weeks. You really think I could afford to live here? I didn't marry Prince Charming."

"No, that was your sister," Advika joked.

"Huh?"

"I was making a *Frozen* joke. Never mind."

"Anna didn't marry a prince; she married Kristoff."

Advika burst out laughing. "Sorry! I just never figured you as a Disney expert."

"Well, you brought up the movie, not me. That's why they're paying me the big bucks, so little girls can ask me about my magic powers and Sven the reindeer." Olive finally cracked a smile. "Normally I'm Mulan, but the usual Elsa fell through. So hopefully all the kids at the hospital won't mind a Taiwanese Elsa. And if they do, too bad."

"That's wonderful!" Advika's guilt about her nonworking status resurged, which reminded her of being supported by Julian, which in turn reminded her of her paranoia at being spotted by paparazzi. Advika abruptly ran inside and slammed the door as soon as Olive followed, nearly catching her braid in the door.

"What's going on? You're acting weird."

"How much time do you have?"

Olive glanced at her watch, which, to Advika's delight, was *Frozen*-themed and also sparkly blue. "About ten minutes. Shoot."

For the first time, Advika spilled the entire story of her and Julian, not just how they met, but the ultimatum that accompanied his proposal and the new, bizarre wrinkle involving his dead ex-wife. She watched Olive's face absorb her tale, and the only time her facial muscles twitched was when Advika mentioned the specifics of Evie's will.

"She really hated him, huh?" Olive took off her synthetic wig, and her dark, asymmetrical bangs fell over her eyes. "And pitied you."

"Not just pitied." Advika took the tote bag off her shoulder and let it fall softly to the floor. "It's like she wants to *save* me."

By this time, Olive was on her phone, and Advika could see that she was reading an article about Julian and Evie and her will. "Well, shit. Yeah, I guess she did."

"And so I'm looking for answers. If I can figure out what their marriage was really like, I can try to understand why Evie is sounding the alarm from the grave."

"Wow. Your life has turned into a soap opera, Srinivasan." But her eyes were knitted together with concern, and that made Advika's pulse quicken. If Olive was worried for her, then she might be in serious trouble.

Olive gave Advika a quick tour of the one-bedroom bungalow, including the owner's cat, Deuteronomy, and his cannabis greenhouse ("I'm supposed to babysit both the cat and the weed like they were my own") before taking off, her Elsa wig in hand. Olive also noted that she was going straight to the coffeehouse after her visit to the hospital, so Advika could stay all day if she wanted.

And for the next several days, the Silver Lake bungalow

became Advika's hideaway. She told Julian she found Wild-wood too empty and quiet to get any work done and needed to be around people. With their gossip story having all but faded from the headlines, Advika received her husband's enthusiastic blessing to go to Olive's coffee shop to work on a revision of *The Romance Game* based on his feedback. But instead of making a ten-minute drive to Santa Monica, Advika wound her way thirty minutes each day to Silver Lake.

Each time she stepped over the bungalow's threshold, it was akin to stepping into an alternate life: one that included not just a full-time job and adult responsibilities—PTA meetings, property taxes, co-hosting neighborhood block parties—but a staid, respectable career that included annual bonuses and hol-iday ski vacations in Vail. Sometimes, as she nuzzled Deuter-onomy or poured herself iced tea in the galley kitchen jammed with stainless steel appliances, Advika liked to pretend that the bungalow was her home. Only under its stucco roof and within its mint-green walls did Advika feel completely relaxed and mostly free, like a teenager home alone for the weekend, ecstatic to have the place to herself but mindful of every minute ticking by until her parents' return.

During the first two days, she watched both of the mov-ies she checked out from the library, starting with the DVD. *Lost and Gone Forever* was a melodrama that featured Evie as a frazzled mother who spent a lot of time staring forlornly at her children and husband as orchestral swings swelled to echo her emotional state. The entire plot seemed to be a series of escalating arguments between Evie and her husband, as each tore into the other for being the worse parent and person. But Advika lost the thread after the first twenty minutes and focused on staring at Evie herself. She was completely miscast, in the same way Jennifer Lawrence was way too young to play a suburban housewife married to Christian Bale in *American*

Hustle. But just like J. Law, Evie sometimes transcended the miscasting and shone in her scenes doting on her two young children, though even her charm couldn't make her marriage to the droopy, weak-chinned actor playing her husband seem believable. With her creamy skin, wide green eyes, and rosy lips, her oval face framed by thick brown waves, Evie seemed to have been snatched from a 1950s California beach flick and trapped inside a dour marital drama.

Despite Evie's talent, she couldn't carry the sluggish movie on her own. Advika dozed off during the end of the second act and woke up just in time to see the credits roll. And there she spied, jumping off the screen like a boogeyman,

PRODUCED BY
Julian Zelding
Gerald Pithe

To see Julian's name on the screen, followed by his former producing partner (and Eloisa's father), hammered home that Julian had actually wanted to make this self-important movie, and so had Evie.

Before meeting Julian, Advika had only seen two of his movies: *Run*, one of his best picture winners from the '80s, which she had watched in film school, and *U-371*, a film released about five years ago, which she saw on a terrible first date with a guy obsessed with Luke Gullet, the rock star who had a lead role in the submarine drama. Thinking back to those two movies along with the one she had just watched, Advika couldn't believe the man who made the taut, mesmerizing thriller *Run* would have made the snoozy submarine movie and the equally listless melodrama. Then again, not every producer was a Jerry Bruckheimer type, specializing in high-octane blockbusters. Julian's longevity in the industry no doubt came from producing a variety of films. And *Lost and Gone Forever* was only his second movie, after all. How she wished her library had a copy of his third, *Dark, Hot Sun*, which won him his first Oscar and Evie her first and only Oscar nomination. Advika had been unable to find it on any streaming service, except as an option to buy on Amazon, which she most definitely could not do. Perhaps Olive could buy it for her, she mused to herself as she packed up her belongings and left the bungalow, sliding Olive's key under the mat before she left.

The following day, Advika was delighted to see that Olive had left her VCR waiting for her in the bungalow's living room, along with a Post-it note affixed that said, *Take care of the dishes*. Advika grinned and for the first time ever didn't mind taking care of Olive's overflowing sink filled with crusty bowls and lipstick-kissed coffee mugs. As she washed each item and placed it on the drying rack, she marveled at how she and Olive seemed to be developing a burgeoning friendship that had eluded them as roommates. Who would have thought the past few months would see her feel closer to Olive than her childhood friends?

Advika pushed away thoughts of the Oakies. Sunita had sent a letter to Wildwood a week after Advika had blocked their phone numbers, but she had never read it and instead fed it into the shredding machine in her new home office. Balan and Vik had sent DMs to her social media accounts, and she had blocked them there too. No doubt their group chat buzzed with the Evie Lockhart news story—and since the article had referred to Advika as Julian's wife, it was also likely that was how they learned she had gotten married too. Advika finished the dishes while mindlessly singing the first few songs that came into her head—Beyoncé, Robyn, Taylor Swift—to rid herself of the sensation that she was in a slow-motion car accident and her friends were watching from afar, judging her.

Once she was done, she heated up a bag of Orville

Redenbacher and then practically skipped into the living room. After inserting *The Lady and the Tiger* into the VCR, Advika pored over the VHS box, which featured half of Evie Lockhart's face and half of a tiger's face, with each eyeing the other. It only quoted a single movie critic, a man named Chester Blagg from WCTV ABC-7, who declared that the movie was "hilarious… so many laughs…a modern-day *Bringing Up Baby*!" Advika had seen the classic Katharine Hepburn–Cary Grant comedy in college as part of her comedy screenwriting class and had loved it. Although she found Hepburn's character a little too ditzy for her liking, she loved seeing her and Grant's sparkling chemistry while cavorting with a leopard.

After watching Evie in the humdrum drama Julian had produced, Advika was curious to see if she would fare any better with a four-legged co-star. And oh did she, and then some. From the opening credits, Advika was so entranced that she sat on the edge of the sofa, her popcorn forgotten in the microwave. It was like seeing Evie for the first time: even though the screenplay was dreadful and the soundtrack a slapdash of toots and synthesizers, the actress herself seemed like an entirely different person. And it wasn't just that her long tangle of brown curls was shaped into a fetching, sleek bob, but that Evie seemed looser. She even had an elegant swagger not dissimilar to Hepburn's, as she toyed with the nerdy man-child following her around Palm Springs while they searched for a tiger who had escaped from Prince Raja of Milajastan (Advika let out an "ugh" at the man in brownface and his thick accent). Evie's presence in the movie elevated it into something watchable, despite the racist and sexist humor pervading nearly every scene.

"What a waste," Advika said to herself as the credits rolled. She longed to lift Evie out of this dreck and deposit her in a film more befitting of her comedic talents. She glanced at her watch: it was only 4:30 p.m. and, even better, no check-in texts from Julian. She took out her laptop and looked up Evie's IMDb page. Advika was dismayed to see that *The Lady and the Tiger* was Evie's penultimate film; she acted in one more comedy called *Mad Chase* before moving to France. Not only that, but Evie's movie career was intriguingly brief: she had only acted in a paltry five films. Three were with Julian, all of them dramas. And then she peaced out from Hollywood after filming two comedies that, based on what Advika had just seen, were wildly different in tone from her earlier career.

Advika searched for "Evie Lockhart + France" on YouTube, curious if she could find hints of Evie's post-Hollywood career. And while there were some clips of Evie in what looked like a French TV series from the mid-1980s, in which she seemed to be an American abroad looking for love while speaking a mix of English and French, each one was only less than a minute long. So Advika instead just searched the actress's name and, after scrolling through pages of search results, came across a rich trove of interviews from the '70s. The one that had the most views was her appearance on *Dinah!*, a talk show hosted by Dinah Shore that had aired in 1974, after the release of Evie's third film and her last one with Julian. Advika bit down hard on her thumbnail, then clicked Play.

The two women were sitting in wicker chairs that were the size of thrones. Dinah wore a pantsuit as beige and unremarkable as the set of her talk show, while Evie wore her hair in a chignon and a strapless woven dress that interlaced yellows and oranges in a triangular pattern.

DINAH: You play such a serious young woman in *Dark, Hot Sun*. But you're so bright and full of joy and laughter. I guess that's why they call it acting!

[*studio audience laughs*]

EVIE: Yes, ha! That's what made it such an interesting challenge to portray Angelica. She sort of lets life happen to her, but when she finally fights back, she lets them have it. [*laughs*] It felt good to finally be able to punch back, because for most of the running time, she gets knocked around a lot.

DINAH: When playing someone who has to endure so much hardship, how do you keep your spirits up and not let it get to you?

EVIE: It's pretty simple: I take off her clothes, wipe away the makeup, and transform back into me. I look into the mirror and say, "Oh, there you are again. Hello, you." [*laughs*] Sometimes I'll sing really loud to myself on the drive home. That also helps.

DINAH: Oh really? Like what?

EVIE: [*laughs nervously*] I'll take popular songs and then twist the lyrics a bit, just have a little fun, and break myself out of a cloudy mood.

DINAH: Now, you must sing for us.

[*the audience cheers its approval*]

EVIE: Do I? Really? All right, then. Let me think. [*takes a beat*] "I wanna hold your ham; I wanna hold your ham." [*studio audience laughs*] Here's another one: "We had joy, we had fun, we had hot dogs in a bun."

[*studio audience roars*]

DINAH: Just one more!

EVIE: Um, all right. [*pauses*] "You can't worry, doves;
you just have to mate." [*sees Dinah looking at her blankly*]
Maybe that one's not so good.

DINAH: What song was that?

EVIE: You all know it, right?

[*the audience sings "You Can't Hurry Love" by The Supremes,
and Evie and Dinah both laugh heartily*]

DINAH: Of course! I should have known. Speaking of
love [*faces the camera*], Evie is married to Hollywood
producer Julian Zelding. He's one handsome devil, ladies.
You'll have to trust me on that. [*studio audience titters*] He's
produced all your films so far, correct? What's that like?

The camera switched from a wide angle on both women to
just focus on Evie. Advika leaned in closer to the laptop to study
Evie's face. Before answering, Evie smoothed out the folds of
her dress, though to Advika's eyes, her smile had become rigid,
as if roughly taped onto her face.

EVIE: We're always together, which can be wonderful . . .
most of the time. You all know what I mean, right? [*the
camera pans to appreciative laughter and applause from the
female audience*] Julian lives and breathes his work, as do I.
It helps so much that we're on the same page.

Advika paused the video, then rewound it to hear Evie's
words again. She studied her face intensely as Evie gave what

seemed to be a practiced response about Julian. *Julian lives and breathes his work, as do I.* "Independent Women" played in Advika's head again, the cherry on top of her self-loathing related to her disintegrating work ethic and stalled career. But along with that self-loathing, Advika also made room for a growing affection for the woman she had spent all day with. The woman on this talk show was miles different and a hundred times more charming than what either *Lost and Gone Forever* or *The Lady and the Tiger* had demonstrated. How could Evie only make five movies before disappearing into near obscurity? Advika paused the clip again, then zeroed in on Evie's tight jawline in the frozen image as she spoke about her then husband, and Advika's now husband.

"What a weird sisterhood we're in, Evie," Advika said softly to the screen. How she wished she could have met this woman and at least have had a conversation with her before she died. And why had Evie waited to do this "child bride" ultimatum until after she passed away? If she wanted Advika to know something about Julian, why wait until after she had married him?

She had to know more, even if it meant that Advika might see her own name pop up as part of her online research into Evie. Searching for Evie on YouTube had felt safer than a Google search, because there was little risk of encountering her own name in the search results. And even though the prospect of Googling Evie still made her anxious, Advika's curiosity now won out over her fears. Advika grabbed her phone and skimmed Evie's brief Wikipedia bio, which told her that Evie had been twenty-nine when she divorced Julian, and she passed away at only age sixty-five. The past thirty-six years of her life were summed up by just three sentences: "After moving to Avignon, France, Lockhart briefly appeared in the TV drama *Terre* before retiring for good. In 1989, her biography, *Dawn,*

Dare, Release, was published by the UK-based Granten Press. She led a quiet life in Avignon until her death in 2015."

Wikipedia also filled in some surprising details about Julian, one so shocking that Advika cross-checked it against his IMDb page. Not only was *The Riders* Evie's first-ever acting role, it was also Julian's. They had starred in the film together. In fact, they were the only two in it. Besides producing and acting in the film, he had also directed it—and written the screenplay. A perusal of his filmography showed that this was the only time Julian had done so. On all of his subsequent films, he only served as a producer or executive producer.

"A passion project," Advika said out loud, her awed voice interrupting the lazy, midafternoon hum of air-conditioning and, farther away, the grumble of a lawn mower. How had she not known this before? She searched her memory to recall if Julian had ever mentioned appearing on camera in his first movie, but she couldn't remember. So likely not. If Advika had known this, she would have found a way to watch *The Riders* immediately.

Just as Advika was about to click the link for *The Riders* on Julian's IMDb page, she was startled by an incoming text. How's my beautiful writer? I miss her. Come home and have dinner with me.

Advika glanced at her laptop, where beautiful young Evie was talking about her marriage—or talking around it, really. Had Julian been there in the studio audience, watching her too?

It was almost seven, and she had intended to be home by six thirty. Julian thought she was only ten minutes away, not thirty minutes or likely even more, based on traffic. She texted back: I'm actually on a roll! I finally figured out this scene. I'll try to be home in an hour, maybe even earlier. 🙏

Right after clicking Send, Advika booked it out of the bungalow so fast that she forgot to take her laptop with her.

$\sim$

"So, how's the writing going? You've been going hard all week." Julian asked this with his back to her, as he sautéed a pan of vegetables that Advika had just watched him chop with a chef's practiced flair. She had never seen him spend more than a couple of minutes in the kitchen before, beyond grabbing a green juice from the fridge. Any meal they didn't eat out or order in came from a personal chef that Advika had never met but whose presence was always felt by virtue of the meals left warming in the oven and the scent of Obsession left behind like a dissipating storm cloud.

"I'm sorry," Advika said. "I just didn't know you could cook. I'm still processing." Watching Julian move around the kitchen with such ease, a black apron tied around a navy blue polo shirt that showed off his strong but slender frame, reactivated Advika's attraction. All things Evie Lockhart—the stipulations in her will, her movies, the talk show interview, The Riders—still held a firm hold on her brain, but so did the way Julian's tanned biceps flexed as he lightly tossed the veggies in the skillet. Advika had been yearning for this version of Julian, the one who had a glass of wine waiting for her as she walked in, leading her by the hand into the kitchen, where chips and guacamole awaited her to snack on while he made carnitas fajitas. She hadn't seen this side of him since they returned from their honeymoon, and although her radar pinged at the sudden intensity of his attentions, Advika also reveled in them too.

"I know how to make only two things, and the other is a PB and J, if you'd rather have that," Julian said, briefly turning around to give her a sunny smile. He poured the skillet of sizzling vegetables onto a platter. "So, how's it going with your screenplay?"

"It's going great." She took a long sip of wine, avoiding his eyes. Advika longed to bring up *The Riders* and ask dozens of questions, especially about his brief stab as a screenwriter. But she couldn't risk it with the aftermath of Evie's will still hovering over them. Neither of them had discussed the story since it was published, and they were operating as if it had never happened; his ex-wife had hovered over them in the same way an extinguished fire leaves behind a smoky, charred odor. But now, the atmosphere between them was suddenly fresh and clear, and both of them could breathe again. "It, um, helps to be surrounded by other writers as I work. I feel like I can concentrate better."

"Good, good." He wiped his forehead with the back of his arm, then reached for his own wineglass. "Man, it's hot. It's been a while since I've slaved over a hot stove."

"It looks good on you," Advika offered. "I think you should do it more often."

"Is that so, Mrs. Zelding?" No one had called her by that name since their stay in Turks and Caicos, and her face went warm to hear how Julian said it, as if his hand were brushing against her thigh. Electricity rippled through Advika as he strode over to her, wineglass in hand, and toasted hers.

"Cheers, Mrs. Zelding."

"Cheers, Mr. Zelding."

Julian took her glass from her hand and set it by his. Advika tipped her face toward him, and Julian gave her a honeymoon kiss, the kind of lip-lock that dismissed the rest of the world until only the two of them remained, all scent and skin.

So much for your weird sisterhood, Anu interjected. The sharp snap of her sister's voice sounded so clear in her head, but Advika resisted letting it puncture the love bubble she was in. *Can I not just enjoy this, for however long it lasts?* she thought.

Julian's hands slid down the small of her back inside her jeans, and a curl of lust blossomed into full flower.

"What about dinner?" she murmured into his ear, as his lips smothered her neck.

"What about it?" He lifted her off the stool and set her upon the island, then slipped her lemon-yellow tank top off of her as smoothly as a banana peel. By the time both of their clothes hit the tile floor, her purple bra nestled inside the curve of his slacks, the iron grasp Evie Lockhart had on Advika's every waking thought finally began to yield.

⌒

Later, when she looked back on the night, Advika could see she was staking her claim on Julian, wresting him back from the charismatic, effervescent actress who had first won her husband's heart and then had come between them in death. It was as if she were Brandy and Evie were Monica in a bizarro, embarrassingly one-sided version of "The Boy Is Mine."

But as the two ate pizza in the great room (the fajitas had burned up while they were getting down), Julian only wearing red-checkered boxers and Advika in just her tank top and underwear, Evie was the furthest thing from her mind. Instead, she was recommitting herself to their relationship, dismissing all doubts and fears as newlywed jitters. *Maybe I really can go back to the screenplay and revise it in a way that makes us both happy*, she told herself as she tore off a pepperoni from her slice and tossed it into her mouth. *And Julian will be so impressed he'll want to produce it.*

As if reading her mind, Julian broke into her thoughts: "Tell me about *The Romance Game*. What kind of changes have you made so far?" He leaned toward Advika, eyeing her intently. She felt sweat claw under her armpits.

"Wha—What?"

"The screenplay, Addi. Tell me." He cast his thumb over her chin to remove a dab of red sauce.

"Oh. Like I said, good. Making progress."

"How so?"

"You know, rethinking the beginning, giving it a whole new structure." Julian nodded satisfactorily. Thank goodness she had absorbed his critiques so acutely that they could easily spring to her mind. "And I took out one of the supporting characters because, like you said, there were too many friends in the group," she added, even though these were the critiques she had disagreed with most.

"Mmm, wonderful. That's what I like to hear." Julian's smile was stretched so wide that Advika could spy a silver crown glinting at the back of his mouth. "I want to read it." He crossed his legs, and Advika could see a hint of his little Julian peeking out of his boxers. "Since you've been working so hard on it, I'd love to see what edits you've made."

Advika lurched upward, her arm awkwardly slapping the plate on Julian's lap. Even if there had been actual revisions to show Julian, it was too early in the editing process to show him her work, and she told him as much. "I'm a perfectionist. I can't show unfinished work." Her left foot jittered against the hardwood.

"My little Michelangelo, not ready to show her Sistine Chapel yet." Julian picked up her hand and laced his fingers through hers. "Well, this was going to be a surprise, but the reason I want to read it is because I want to show it to an important friend of mine." He raised his eyebrows to emphasize his friend's bigwig status. "She's expressed...interest."

"What? You're kidding me. Are you kidding me?" Advika exclaimed, almost tossing her pizza slice in the air with shocked delight. Then her heart fell as she recalled that she had not made a single edit to her screenplay. But here was a real opportunity dangling in front of her. Not working on someone else's dream project, but on her own.

"But I'd really like to see it before I give it to her." Julian said this genially enough, but he wasn't making a request. There was no way he would risk sharing her work with anyone without vetting it himself.

"Of course," Advika said quickly. She'd worry about that part later. "Who is she?" She grabbed a throw blanket and covered her bare thighs. If they were going to have the first real conversation about her career since the *Agent UFO* debacle, she wished she weren't in her underwear.

"You let me worry about that," Julian said, his lips shining from the pizza grease. "But let's just say she had a hand in some of your favorite rom-coms from the past few years."

Advika's eyes widened. She imagined seeing "Written by Advika Srinivasan" in the opening credits of a film on the big screen, and a smile burst from her. Julian nodded in approval at her reaction, then patted his pale, flat stomach and gave a noisy belch. Seeing her husband briefly act like a regular Joe rather than the suave gentleman she knew him as gave her pause. Enough to let Anu's voice creep in and ask, *But he wants you to make all these big changes, remember? It's not going to be the screenplay you love. The one you wrote about me.*

"Excuse me." Julian's face reddened in embarrassment, and Advika tittered and told him it was nothing. His face went soft, taking her in like he was eyeing an adorable puppy. "Are you happy with me, Addi? I couldn't wait to give you the good news."

Advika kept up the pretense of joy and showered her husband with the appreciation fireworks he expected. But in her mind's eye, the film credit with her name was already fading off the screen.

Since returning from their honeymoon, Advika had found herself waking up in the middle of the night. Each time she did,
she would reach for her phone and sigh to see that the time
hovering over her and Julian's suntanned faces in a beach selfie
was exactly 3:02 a.m. But unlike the other nights, this time she
slipped out of bed and walked on tiptoe to her office. Advika
lifted her tote bag from her desk chair and plopped down on
the seat, her fingers riffling past a cardigan, travel umbrella,
and her notebooks. But no laptop. The panic flooding Advika's
body caused her head to slam back against the chair's thankfully overcushioned headrest. Then the hurried moments
before departing for home came back to her: she had left it at
the bungalow. Advika had inadvertently sabotaged her efforts
to revise *The Romance Game* and make the edits she had pretended to have already made. And so the panic drained out
of her like butter evaporating on a heated skillet, replaced by
relief.

As much as she wanted to get her screenplay in the hands of
Julian's "bigwig" friend, Advika recognized with searing clarity that she couldn't go through with it. The nonexistent revision of *The Romance Game* wasn't something she would ever
stand behind. Not that she was naive about how screenplays
were nearly always chopped up and rewritten by script doctors
or members of the creative team, the latter sometimes nabbing
themselves co-writer credits. Yet the idea of showing Julian's
version of her screenplay to anyone now seemed wrong.

Those ninety pages had been Advika's only way out of unrelenting pain, and the hours and days she had devoted herself to
it had turned down the volume of her misery. To try to sell any
version of *The Romance Game* other than the one that existed

on her hard drive would be like renewing the agony and eras-
ing Anu all over again.

Instead, she'd write something new. Something so wonderful and in Julian's wheelhouse that he'd prefer the new script
anyway. Advika grabbed her phone and opened the Notes app
and typed

FADE IN.
INTERIOR. DAY.

The cursor bounced impatiently, waiting for her to continue.
Advika knit her eyebrows together, the phone giving off an
alien glow in the darkened room. She erased the last two words
and then wrote "EXTERIOR. NIGHT." Then deleted those too.

"Don't think; just write," she murmured to herself. Advika
leaned back in the chair, crossed her legs, and closed her eyes.
Her thumbs batted against the screen's keyboard, and she
imagined that whatever came out would be pure nonsense.
Her meditative typing was the last thing she recalled doing,
because she awoke curled up in the chair a few hours later. In
this instance, her phone had more to announce than the time
(6:52 a.m.). Advika also had two notifications: an alert from the
Echo Park library that Evie Lockhart's biography was ready to
be picked up, and an Instagram DM from someone claiming to
have known Evie and requesting to meet.

CHAPTER THIRTEEN

LA Story

DAWN, DARE, RELEASE:
A BIOGRAPHY OF EVIE LOCKHART

By Nina St. John

TABLE OF CONTENTS

Chapter 1: A Beginning

Chapter 2: Hooray for Hollywood

Chapter 3: Here Comes Handsome

Chapter 4: Break It, Then Make It . . .

Advika was tempted to turn right to chapter 3. Reunited with her laptop, comfortably ensconced at Olive's temporary bungalow, lounging on the sofa with an ice-cold green tea and Deuteronomy nestled at her feet, she couldn't wait to dig into Julian's marriage to his first wife. And even though she had been initially more excited about the Instagram DM, it now held less intrigue compared to an entire book about Evie. Because how likely was it really someone from Evie's past who wanted to connect with her? After all, over a hundred accounts had followed @advikasri88 in the minutes after the news story broke and before she made it private, which meant that any new follower could direct message her. Either this was a prank or some kind of bait from a tabloid, trying to trick Advika into talking to them. The direct message was so random and chancy. Whereas the biography would provide real information.

The front windows were wide open, letting in a delicate, delicious breeze, a rarity during what had been a scorching summer so far. Advika wanted to stay frozen inside this moment for as long as possible. To feel so safe while simultaneously twitchy with anticipation about the new information potentially awaiting her about Julian was an odd sensation, as if she were lazing in a hammock at the top of a giant cliff, glancing at the sparkling blue water as she prepared to dive off the edge. But would it be fair to ignore the early parts of Evie's life, especially since events from that time could have impacted her relationship with Julian? So she skimmed the first two chapters, gracelessly thumbing through the pages and allowing Biography.com to fill in the rest.

Evie was born and raised in a small town outside of Los Angeles. After her father, Daniel, died when she was ten years old from kidney failure, as a result of his alcoholism, Evie's mother, Lucille, raised her on her own by working as a seamstress and housekeeper. While Lucille worked hard to support herself and her daughter, they received financial help from Daniel's brother Tobias, a highly respected cinematographer hired by directors like Stanley Donen and Robert Aldrich. So when Evie graduated from high school, she moved to Los Angeles with the hopes of working in the film industry. Uncle Tobias found a job for her in the wardrobe department at Warner Bros.

Studios. Because of her five-foot-eight height, fair complexion, and slender frame, she'd occasionally be summoned to set as a stand-in.

> "In *Flight out of Buenavista*, when Telly Savalas accuses Ali MacGraw of hiding evidence of a murder plot, that's actually me," Lockhart said. "Ali had to go to a funeral and they couldn't hold up filming, so they just filmed all of Telly's scenes with me. Afterward, he told me I was a great scene partner. That might have been the moment I learned I could do the actress thing if I wanted to."

If I wanted to. Advika liked Evie's insouciance about the moment that launched her film career and changed the trajectory of her life. For the next several years, she worked in bit parts in movies and television series. But several pages in, Evie was described as spending most of her off-hours socializing with Hollywood players, befriending the right people who would introduce her up the chain to even more well-connected people, until she became a fixture at all the hottest events.

> "Evie was a gas at parties," the actress Lucia Tello said in a 1981 magazine profile. "She wouldn't seek attention, but she had such an easiness about her, a playfulness too. She always had the funniest stories and told a good dirty joke. You wanted to be around her so you wouldn't miss one tasty morsel."

So which is it? Advika wondered. *Did she fall into acting, or was she a social climber?* The woman who was so cavalier about her acting career also seemed intent on being the center of attention in her industry's social circles.

You find her likable but you don't want to like her—duh, Anu's voice teased. Advika laughed at herself, because of course that was it. She was looking to poke holes in Evie as much as she already idolized her. She was momentarily startled when Deuteronomy licked her ankle before moseying toward the kitchen. Advika's bare feet missed the warmth of the cat's white-and-ginger fur. She curled up on the sofa, tucking her feet under a throw pillow, and took a deep breath. She couldn't wait anymore. She flipped to chapter 3.

Chapter 3

Here Comes Handsome

Evie wasn't supposed to attend Loretta Mance's birthday party that cool March night in 1969. Instead, she was meant to be packing for a weekend trip to visit her mother, whom she hadn't visited in Ojai in over three months. But when Lucille phoned her to tell her that she was feeling unwell and to come the following weekend, Evie immediately dialed Lucia. Twenty minutes later, Lucia pulled up in her red Ford Mustang outside Evie's apartment, and they drove from Santa Monica to high up into the Hollywood Hills.

Loretta Mance was the then twenty-one-year-old daughter of director Ferdinand Mance, best known for his issue-oriented courtroom dramas, one of which he was awarded a Golden Globe for a few weeks earlier. His house was located on a particularly remote but picturesque spot on Mulholland Drive, and so when the women reached the party around 9:30 p.m., they were surprised to find themselves among the few in attendance. Despite assurances from the chatty birthday girl that people got lost en route to "Daddy's house all the damn tootin' time" (and the entire B-list of Hollywood descended on the party about ninety minutes later), Lucia and Evie were planning their quiet departure when Julian Zelding walked in.

Evie said in a 1975 interview with *Playboy* that her friend had let out a low whistle when Julian crossed the threshold. "Here comes Handsome," she recalled Lucia saying. And not whispering it either, but a full-throated remark that caught the attention of the fewer than twenty partygoers in attendance.

"Julian looked up at us and grinned. He strutted over to us with the swagger of a cowboy, then made a gesture of tipping his hat as if he was wearing a Stetson. 'Ladies, how are you doing tonight?'"

Advika flashed back to her own first meeting with Julian, decades later at a much fancier and very crowded party, in which he also pretended to tip an imaginary hat during their initial flirtation. *It's not that unique*, she muttered to herself. But it was still strange to see echoes of Julian's moves with other women, long before she had been born.

When she saw Julian's eyes drawn to her friend like a magnet, Lucia excused herself to get a drink. "I wasn't getting in the middle of that," she joked in various interviews about how her friend had met her husband. "From the very beginning, Julian Zelding acted like meeting Evie was destiny. If that was the case, Evie needed some more convincing."

Not that the two didn't enjoy each other's company that night. They spent most of the party sitting poolside talking. Julian had moved to Los Angeles one year earlier hoping to break into the movie business. At that moment, he had gotten as far as working at a restaurant favored by the industry. He worked as a waiter and guitar player at Jack O'Shea's, a steak-and-lobster restaurant—

A waiter . . . and a guitar player? Advika laughed out loud, trying to picture her husband earnestly strumming songs, and just couldn't see it.

—and so apologized to Evie for his "weird restaurant smell," a salty and smoky aroma that Evie found quite pleasant. Julian confided his hopes of one day directing films like his idol, Orson Welles, someone that Evie's uncle Tobias had worked with. She didn't mention this nugget. But during their poolside flirtation, in which they had to sit closely together, their bare feet swishing in the water, as the party took on a more raucous quality (several pieces of the Mances' patio furniture ended up in the pool by the end of the night), she did let slip that her uncle was a cinematographer, as part of explaining how she had come to LA.

"His face lit up. It's like I told him he had won the lottery. No, more like I was his salvation," Evie said. "He was a part of my life after that; there just wasn't a choice in the matter. He pursued me with a ruthless dedication I mistook for youthful ardor."

She stared at Evie's quote until the words blurred together. Advika could have said nearly the same thing about Julian's courtship of her. Maybe that was just his style: fall big, fall hard, like a belly flop into a swimming pool. He did have three wives before her, after all. But Evie's description of Julian reverberated within Advika, provoking a jitteriness that she couldn't shake even after she hopped off the sofa. Deuteronomy returned to take her place and nestled into the cushions, and Advika paced back and forth from the doorway to the kitchen, and back again.

Her instincts were tingling, as if she were a metal detector searching an enormous beach for treasure and beeped for the first time. Advika unearthed her phone from her tote bag. Impulsively, she opened Instagram and clicked on the DM. Before she could second-guess herself, Advika wrote back, What's your name? And how do I know you're for real? She clicked Send and then tossed the phone onto the sofa, almost hitting Deuteronomy, who scampered away.

"Sorry!" Advika said just as her phone pinged. The mystery person had written back.

Advika grabbed the phone, opened the message, and gasped at the response: Lucia Tello. I was a good friend of Evie's when she lived here. A second message then came in, a picture of Lucia and Evie wearing flapper dresses and feathered headbands, blowing kisses at the camera. The photograph was held by a tanned, freckled hand sporting a French manicure. The caption: 1972, Chasen's. This was followed by a third message: a phone number with a 323 area code. If this was truly Lucia, it seemed probable she lived in the Los Angeles area. Then one last message: I know Evie would want me to talk to you.

Could this be for real? Advika examined the Instagram account that had contacted her, but there were no posts or followers. The account @sanvicente143239521 seemed to have been created just to contact Advika. She collapsed on the sofa and closed her eyes. None of what she had learned from the biography had ameliorated the concerns first seeded by Evie's will, and now this interaction with Lucia, or someone pretending to be her, only deepened Advika's apprehension. When she heard another notification, this time a WhatsApp message,

Advika shook her head. Now was not the time to receive yet
another disapproving message from her mother. But when she
finally forced herself to take a look and get it over with, she was
surprised by what it said.

Advi, how are you? How's Julius? This marked the first time
her mother had acknowledged her husband—and that she had
a husband, even if she got his name wrong. *Come meet him and
find out* is the snarky response she would have once made. But
now, Advika just wanted to give her mother a hug.

She knew how hard it must have been for her mom to ask
about this man she'd never met, this old—older—white stranger
married to her only remaining daughter. Advika thought of her
mother, perhaps lonely, likely depressed, wrapped in a shawl
and sipping tea, her face ashen. Her permanent visage after
Anu had died. How Advika missed her. And for her mother
to swallow her pride and misgivings and ask about Julian,
Advika finally had a sense of how much her mother missed
her too. The old, terribly familiar loneliness returned, taking a
seat alongside a newly blooming disquiet. Advika wrapped her
arms around herself as tight as she could, but the tears fell anyway, spilling down her face onto her blouse's collar. Deuteronomy came out again, his ginger tail at attention as he surveilled
the brown woman in a pink skirt and white blouse make hic-
cupping sounds, the kind where a person was trying her best
not to cry and failing miserably.

The front door opened, and she heard the tread of a pair
of Doc Martens resounding on the tile entryway. Advika was
relieved that Olive had come home early, and the sudden presence of another person was strangely what caused the dam to
break. As she buried her wet face in her hands, her body shaking uncontrollably, Advika felt Olive's tentative fingers on her
shoulder.

~

"Okay!" Olive said, between loud crunches of celery-apple chips. "This is how your Julian became Movie Guy Julian."

A half hour after Olive came home, she and Advika were seated side by side in Adirondack chairs on the bungalow's outdoor patio, sipping frozen margaritas under the protection of a giant green umbrella. Olive, who came home early after a small fire at the coffeehouse ("Some meth head threw a lit cigarette into a giant wastebasket"), was paging through *Dawn, Dare, Release* and giving Advika the highlights as she worked on the bones of a new screenplay so she could have something to show Julian. So far, all she had written was

FADE IN.
EXTERIOR. DAY.

TWO WOMEN SIT OUTSIDE AND DRINK MARGARITAS.
ONE OF THEM WONDERS IF SHE HAS EFFED UP HER
LIFE.

Olive's exclamation had interrupted Advika staring at the cursor, as she tried to count how many times it blinked in the span of a minute. The effort to do so, plus the late-afternoon heat that had settled around them like a scratchy blanket, had made her drowsy. Wiping away a thin line of drool from her mouth, Advika asked Olive to share what she found.

"Julian asked Evie to meet her uncle, and she gave in after six months of dating. Once Julian met Uncle Tobias, he got him an assistant role on his new film. Julian seemed to make connections from there, like networking and all that shit, and he worked as a camera operator on a few films and then finally made his own."

"Yeah, *The Riders*." Advika tapped the side of her laptop screen. "I downloaded it here, but I haven't watched it yet."

"Why not? Chip?" Olive held out the bag to Advika, which carried the whiff of springtime and Julian's green juices.

Advika shook her head, then said after a deep sigh, "Because he's in it. With *her*."

"You're shitting me. For real?" Olive slammed the book shut and swung her legs off the side of the chair. "Movie Guy Julian is also Actor Julian?"

Advika grabbed her margarita and downed a third of it, the pleasant sting of the tequila making it easier to admit what she said next, what she hadn't had a chance to express to anyone. "I'm worried that seeing Julian as a young man will make him seem old."

"He *is* old." Olive made a funny throaty sound, like a belch crossed with a chuckle.

"But when we're together, he doesn't seem old. Well, not that old. Not like senior-citizen old. But to see him be all cute and flirty with Evie might be weird. They were in their twenties when they filmed the movie. I can't compare to a glamorous movie star."

"Wait. I thought you were trying to, like, I dunno…suss him out. See what his deal is."

"I am," Advika said. "But I'm still very attracted to him. And I'm jealous of his dead wife. But I also think she's really cool." Advika shook her head, then groaned. "I'm all mixed up. What can I say?"

"I would have never believed my life would seem boring compared to yours." Olive snorted, then ran her fingers through her long bangs.

"I'd love to be normal again." Advika closed the document she was working on, glad to see her pathetic attempt at writing disappear from view.

"Normal is overrated, though." Olive reached into the chip bag, but her fingers came up with nothing but crumbs. She licked them off, then combed through her bangs again.

Advika gaped at her, then laughed. "Olive, you're getting green chip dust all over your hair!" It felt good to laugh at the antics of her former roommate, when her sloppy habits no longer impacted Advika's quality of living. Olive cracked a self-deprecating grin, then shook her bangs out with her non-chipped hand, causing a few pieces of green crumbs to fall out.

"This is a very Ally Sheedy moment you're having."

"Who?"

"*The Breakfast Club*? When Ally shakes her dandruff out of her hair like it's snow?"

"I'm not *that* gross." The two looked at each other and smiled. Somewhere along the way, Olive had transformed from a pain in her ass to an actual friend. Gratitude overwhelmed her, especially as she remembered when Olive had stood by and given Advika space as she cried, only asking her if she was okay. When Advika tearfully nodded, Olive didn't ask her to explain herself. Just told her to go outside and she'd bring out margaritas for the two of them.

"Olive," she said, "will you watch *The Riders* with me?"

⌒

The film began with a man and woman seated at an empty restaurant next to a large picture window, the two looking out at a pickup truck parked in front and a cloud-dazed sky hovering over a vista dotted with cacti and boulders. Filmed in black and white, the scenery had a dramatic quality, majestic and a tad foreboding. The couple sipped coffee and smoked cigarettes, both stifling yawns. She looked out the window; he looked at her.

Evie's hair was swept up in a beehive of sorts, her round dark sunglasses perched atop her head like another pair of wary eyes.

Her bubblegum youthfulness didn't match her outfit, a dark blazer worn over a shift dress and a long strand of pearls that dangled just below her collarbone. Julian was dressed in a rumpled suit, the top two buttons of his shirt undone to expose a thin chain with a cross. His hair was dark and his sideburns were a little long, not quite Elvis style but still noticeable. The whole thing would be uncanny even if the man weren't Advika's husband. While she had seen plenty of photos of Julian in his younger years in framed photos at Wildwood, to see twentysomething Julian in motion, with his squinting eyes and slowly blooming smile after taking a drag from a cigarette, he was James Dean crossed with Paul Newman. Despite Evie's beauty, he was the one that commanded the viewer's gaze.

"Your guy is hot." Olive was on to her second margarita, which Advika declined, even though she didn't have to drive back home for another few hours. "Like, really hot."

"This is weird," Advika said, saucer-eyed, unable to look away from the screen. "It feels like him, but it doesn't."

Olive asked if Julian had acted in any other movies, and Advika shook her head. As the first two minutes flew by, with the soundtrack of strummed guitar and tambourine carrying the opening moments of the couple acting twitchy and exhausted, Advika wondered why Julian hadn't pursued acting when the camera clearly loved him.

Then he began to speak.

"What are you thinking about?"

"Why do you need to know?" Evie's character was listless and seemed determined not to meet his eyes.

"I don't need to. I'd just like to—that's all." Julian's character rapped his knuckles against the table. "C'mon, Phyllis. We have to talk about it."

"Do we, Ron?" Evie stubbed out her cigarette in the ashtray with three sharp jabs. "I mean, really?"

Advika gaped at the movie, the spell of Julian's handsomeness broken. Every word out of his mouth was stilted. He sounded as if he had recently learned to speak English and was trying out his language skills. For one moment, Julian even looked directly into the camera before abruptly looking away.

"This is fantastic." Olive rubbed her hands together, her eyes gleaming. "He's awful."

Advika slapped her hands over her eyes. "I don't think I can watch this." She once again recalled their conversation about *The Riders* on their third date, and how Julian had equated it to *Easy Rider*. She let out an "ugh" at the memory.

"Shhh!" Olive leaned past her and upped the volume on Advika's laptop. "I don't want to miss a moment."

For the next ninety minutes, "Phyllis" and "Ron" talked, and occasionally yelled, about whether they needed to talk about something, and why or why not. The topic remained unnamed throughout the running time, but from the way Ron tried to dissuade Phyllis from smoking and at one point snatched away her pack of cigarettes in frustration, it was very obvious. She was fidgety and diffident; he was perspiring and loud. Toward the end of the movie, Phyllis paused to look out the window to say that the rock formations reminded her of elephants, a small smile budding on her lips.

"I don't see it," Ron said, his perplexed face reflected in the window.

"I know." The two held each other's gaze for a moment, as if both wanted to say more, but neither did. Phyllis stood up from the table and slowly leaned down toward Ron, as if she was going to kiss him. Instead, she reached into his jacket and pulled out the cigarettes he had taken away from her. Without another word, she walked away. The camera followed as she walked out the door, then dimmed to black. Fade out. End credits.

"Well, that was . . . a movie," Olive said, yawning and stretching her arms. Deuteronomy leapt up onto the couch and jumped into her lap. She gave him a scratch behind the ears. "What did you think?"

"I . . . I don't know." Advika shut her laptop and rubbed her eyes. "Um, I have to get going soon. Do you have any coffee?"

"I'm off the clock, but you can make some. Just be careful— that coffeemaker was, like, invented by NASA. I never really figured out how to use it."

"Never mind." Advika didn't have the energy or attention span to figure out how to use a high-tech appliance. Her brain was on overdrive just processing everything she had seen. Julian's acting remained bad throughout the film, but despite this, he and Evie still had an incredible chemistry. In fact, Julian's acting actually improved when they started fighting in earnest. Having seen her husband erupt in paroxysms of anger, Advika knew that the fiery dynamic between Julian and Evie must have had real-life echoes. She chewed on her lip, even as she felt the minutes ticking away. Then she grabbed Evie's biography off the sofa cushion, where Olive had left it idling, and paged through so fast she nearly gave herself a paper cut.

"Looking to see what Evie had to say about it, huh?" Olive lifted the cat off her lap so she could sit closer to Advika. The two squeezed together and began reading. But Advika found she couldn't focus on the words, and asked Olive to read chapter 5, titled "Lights, Camera, Action," out loud instead.

The whole time he worked on film sets under Tobias's tutelage, Julian had been working on a movie of his own. And in late December of 1968, he finally set out to make it. *The Riders* filmed in a small town outside of Palm Springs on Christmas Day. He had rented out the dilapidated restaurant and charmed the owner's wife into playing a waitress, the only other person to appear in the film besides Evie and Julian.

Advika winced upon hearing "Evie and Julian." She glanced at her wedding band and engagement ring, both a half size too small and particularly constricting on hot days like this one. She moved them to the top part of her thumb.

They shot for three days, practically from dawn to dusk, with Evie doing her own hair and makeup and the pair wearing their own clothes. The ninety-two-minute film was largely improvised—

"That explains a lot!" Olive said, interrupting herself.
"It does, actually." Advika transferred both rings from her left thumb to her right. Julian had the nerve to shred her screenplay when he didn't even write his own? "Keep going."

The ninety-two-minute film was largely improvised after Evie refused to perform the script Julian had written. "It was barely a script," Evie wrote in a letter to her mother the following year. "He was just exorcising our personal dramas on film and wanted to call it a movie. And I went along with it, because it was the only way he could understand he wasn't an auteur," she wrote, referring to the fact that Julian had made the film with the intention of showing it to her uncle, so he would help him get representation and further his filmmaking aspirations.

"Evie's a badass." Olive slapped Advika hard on the back. "I really like her."
"Yeah." Advika's phone buzzed in her pocket, but she ignored it.

In *The Riders*, a couple named Ron and Phyllis argue about whether or not she should keep her baby, closely mirroring a conversation Julian and Evie had following a pregnancy scare. Evie, seeing the parallels between her husband's screenplay and the Ernest Hemingway classic short story "Hills Like White Elephants," references it in her final line in the film. Julian kept her ad-lib in the final cut, which he showed to Tobias in February 1969. "[Julian] insisted that he knew what I was referring to when Uncle Tobias said he liked the Hemingway homage—and it was the only thing he liked about it, he told me later. If the movie had been a hit, no doubt Julian would have claimed he wrote it," Evie continued in her letter. "Tobias let him down easy, told him to 'hone his craft' more."

The film was released in a handful of theaters and had a limited VHS release in 1982 following Julian's best picture Oscar for *Run*. But one person did see the film in 1969 besides Evie's uncle. And this man, Gerald Pithe, would permanently alter both her and Julian's careers.

"Well, that sounds ominous," Olive said, shutting the book. "I hate to say it, but your boy—I mean Julian—doesn't seem like a great guy."

"He was in his twenties and thought he was the next Orson Welles or Hitchcock. That doesn't make him...bad," Advika said lamely.

"True. Um, I might keep reading this after you leave, if you don't mind. I'm hooked."

"Sure," Advika said, staring at the biography's cover, showing Evie in profile, her face angled toward a spotlight. She remembered Lucia and her messages, the urgency with which she had wanted to meet with her. So many times throughout the afternoon, Advika had been tempted to share it with Olive but had always bitten back the words, not ready to share that her life had gotten even weirder than her friend had realized.

Olive tapped her on the shoulder. "Didn't you say you had to get going?"

"Oh shit." Advika pulled out her phone and saw a missed call and a text from Julian (Text me when you're on your way home), plus a WhatsApp message from her mother (How come you didn't respond? Are you okay???). She hurriedly tapped out texts to her mom and husband, then gathered up her things and piled them into her tote bag. She paused when picking up her laptop.

"I'm going to keep this here too along with the Evie stuff. Is that okay?"

"Yeah, sure. But the homeowner is coming back in two days."

"Oh." Another text from Julian: Please go directly upstairs when you come home. I have a surprise for you. Advika left her laptop on the coffee table and, as she did so, saw her wedding and engagement rings glinting on her right thumb. With sweaty fingers, she returned them to their rightful place on her other hand. She then stood up, and Olive followed her to the front door.

"Yeah, it blows. After paradise, I gotta return to the realm of hot-pink nail polish and the blond hairs in the bathroom sink." She paused, then added, "I would have never thought I'd miss having you as a roommate."

Advika adjusted the tote bag on her shoulder and glanced down at her feet, which she had slipped into white slides. "Me neither," she said, looking up at Olive with a sad smile.

In the space of the seconds between Olive's words and Advika's response, a single thought had taken root in her mind: *Maybe I don't want to be married. To him.*

CHAPTER FOURTEEN

Overboard

WHEN ADVIKA ARRIVED HOME, SHE went upstairs as Julian's text had instructed, anxious about what awaited her in their bedroom. She hadn't expected a dress: a slinky tomato-red silk one giving off a "sexy bridesmaid" vibe. After washing up and freshening her makeup, she changed into the dress, then took her mass of curls and tamed them in a loose bun, because she knew Julian liked it when she wore her hair up. Not sure what shoes to wear with the dress, she decided to remain barefoot until learning where she and Julian were going.

Which turned out to be not far at all. Once she finished getting ready, Advika received a second text asking her to go outside to Wildwood's back patio. She gathered up the skirt of her dress so as not to trample its hem, then marched out of their bedroom and down the stairs, not in the mood to feign excitement about what Julian had planned. For the first time since they met, Julian's romantic overtures didn't work on her. While her attraction to her husband remained, the revelations of the past day had cracked something within her, and she no longer fully felt like his wife, but merely like she was playacting.

Advika was still deep in her thoughts when she emerged outside, the sunset stapled to the sky as if commissioned by Julian, all streaky gold and amber hues flecked with wispy clouds. What was once her favorite time of day now had become rote, inextricably linked to Wildwood's ocean views. She scanned the patio for Julian, and the sight that greeted her brought her to a standstill. Fairy lights dancing in the trees. A table dressed in white linens and adorned with flower petals on the patio deck. And a string quartet next to the pool, playing a classical version of John Legend's "All of Me," the song they had danced to following their wedding.

"You look beautiful, sweetheart." Julian was at her side, his arm around her waist, the velvet scent of his cologne over-whelming her as he kissed her cheek. Advika turned toward him and took in the sight of Julian in a classic tuxedo. She had not seen him wear one since the night they had met.

"So do you." She gave him a peck on the cheek, then after a beat, one on the lips. He drew her in for a long kiss, and she acquiesced without returning his passion.

"What's wrong, Addi?"

"Nothing's wrong." She took a step back, and her bare heel hit a sharp pebble. "I just didn't expect all this. What's going on?"

"Ah." He winked, then took her hand and led her to the table. As they sat down, a man dressed as a butler brought over two glasses of champagne. Julian and Advika toasted, although for what she still had no idea. The "How is this my life?" sensation that hummed in the background most days swelled once again, even more so when the string musicians segued from their wedding song to a classical version of Katy Perry's "Firework."

"Happy anniversary, Addi." Julian flashed a satisfied smile as he sipped his champagne flute.

"Really?"

"It's our four-and-a-half-month anniversary of the day we met." He ducked his hand into his tuxedo jacket's inner pocket and pulled out the Academy Awards ticket. "A day I'll never forget."

"Oh. Happy anniversary, then."

"Thank you, my darling Addi."

Advika drummed her fingers against the table's edge, puzzled by Julian's over-the-top overtures. "Is it customary to celebrate four-and-a-half-month anniversaries?"

"It is now. Especially since I might not be here to celebrate our fifth-month one."

As the sky dimmed into evening, Julian explained that he would be departing for a work trip at the end of next week. His latest film, *War Is Death*, was in danger of stalling out due to delays in filming while on location in Morocco.

"Weather troubles, bickering stars, natives," Julian listed off with a sigh. "If there's a problem to be had, this film's experienced it." He added that while he had done his best to try to triage production troubles from LA while Eloisa ran point on location, he now had no choice but to join her and intervene directly. "I'm not sure how long I'll be there. If all goes well, no more than ten days. But it could potentially stretch longer."

"Okay." Even after a month of marriage, Advika had little idea of what Julian did all day at Zelding Productions, housed in a chic brick building in Santa Monica. She had only visited him there once following their honeymoon, and Julian had made a big show of introducing her to all twelve of his employees, nearly all of them attractive white women with names like Madison and Evangeline. The Madisons and Evangelines had greeted her with big toothy smiles and narrowed eyes, and Advika had pledged to herself right then that she would never return to Zelding Productions again. Only Julian's personal assistant, a waifish brunette woman named Mona, had shown her any real warmth upon their introduction. Advika had liked her at the time and now wondered why Mona never came to

Wildwood. Advika had spent enough time on the periphery of the Hollywood elite to know that celebrities could barely function without their assistants. Perhaps Julian was more self-sufficient than most.

"I don't know how long I can bear to be apart from you, though." Julian gave her a wolfish grin, a mirror image of how he had looked at Evie/Phyllis in *The Riders* when he suggested a quickie while they waited for their meal. "Come with me. After Morocco we can do some traveling, perhaps Italy or Spain. Have you ever been?"

"No. I haven't been anywhere, really, besides India." Advika's hand reached for her champagne flute, but then she decided to have water instead, drinking so quickly that driblets splashed onto her dress. Mentioning India reminded Advika of her mother and her forlorn text. "My mom asked about you today. For the first time."

"Oh?" Julian cocked his head as if she had started speaking Dutch. "How is she?"

"She seems pretty down. I think she might be depressed." Advika hardly ever discussed her parents with Julian after they had traded stories about their families on the Puerto Vallarta getaway. And even though Julian had asked about when he would get to meet his in-laws during the flight to their honeymoon, he had never brought them up again. "I guess I'm worried."

"Oh." Julian leaned back in his seat and slung an arm over the back of his chair. "Well, maybe you should go visit her."

Advika's grasp tightened on her water glass, a crystal goblet that felt delicate enough to shatter in her grip. "That's what I was thinking. As much as I'd love to go to Morocco, maybe I should go see her first."

"I see. Or, you could come with me to Morocco, and then afterward we can take a quick jaunt to India. Where are your parents living? Mumbai? Delhi?"

"No, they're in Bangalore—the southern part of India." Julian probably had no idea there was an India beyond what he'd seen in movies like *Gandhi* or *Slumdog Millionaire*. And he definitely didn't remember that she was South Indian, despite her explaining this more than once during their early court-ship. "Can I think about it?"

"Sure, but don't take too long."

A butler brought out two salmon watercress salads with the precision and flair of someone serving the queen of England. And as he fussed over the table, a measured silence opened up between them. There was no way she was going to Morocco. She didn't need another romantic getaway where Julian could muster the full power of his persuasive charms on her. As Advika picked at her salad, he spoke up.

"Well, it's almost Friday. I'd really love to read the screen-play you've been working so hard on." Now that she knew how lousy an actor he was, Advika could pick up the fake cheer in his voice, the way his smile stretched on his face as if pulled like a rubber band.

"Oh, yes." Advika tilted her face down, then looked up at him with Bambi eyes, fluttering her eyelashes and adding a tremulousness to her voice. "I'm having a hard time separating myself from it. I mean, it feels too close to me. I wrote it as a way to deal with losing Anu."

"But you said the revisions were going so well."

Advika shared a variation of the truth, about how each time she changed a word, even punctuation, it felt like a betrayal of the reason she had wrote it, and how it had saved her during a particularly terrible time. "And I so appreciate that you wanted your friend to read it, but I think it's become too personal to me." The words "I'm sorry" waited on her tongue, but Advika couldn't bring herself to say them.

"I see." Julian carefully placed his fork next to his plate. He reached for her hand, and she let him take it. His hand was soft yet cold, as if only recently unthawed from a block of ice. "And I do understand. I hope I didn't push you too much. I just know it's been your dream, and I wanted to help."

"Screenwriting is still my dream," Advika said, squeezing her free hand into a fist that she tucked between her thighs. "But maybe I should start something new. Start fresh." In that moment she decided she would ask her agent to submit her for every available position. She would write for game shows, talk shows, soap operas—anything that could be broadcast over an antenna, a satellite, or an internet connection. Advika just wanted to be in the industry already, no matter what shape that took or how low on the totem pole she would be. And after she secured a new job, then she would tell Julian.

Julian nodded sagely, and they returned to their salads. They made small talk about the weather, the new movies coming out that weekend, the idea of getting new curtains for their bedroom. It was all very husband-and-wife chitchat, the kind of conversation that would play as part of a montage depicting domestic tranquility. This was the part of marriage she enjoyed, the "How was your day, dear?" type of back-and-forth that helped Advika feel like she was a part of something cozy yet also solid. Almost like a family.

The string quartet began playing a song she couldn't place but found very familiar. Julian took his napkin off his lap with a magician's flourish, then stood up and extended his hand. "Dance with me? I can never resist this song."

Advika wanted to say no, but the sight of Julian in a tuxedo, coupled with his adoring smile, reawakened the stirrings of attraction. She let her husband lead her to the side of the pool, steps away from the string quartet. It was their first time dancing together since their wedding, and she hated to admit how much she loved the feel of Julian's assured hand on the curve of her back. She let herself sink into him, their bodies fitting together like puzzle pieces. The name of the song came into focus—Sade's "By Your Side"—which she knew from a *Sex and the City* episode of Samantha and her rich boyfriend... also dancing poolside. Once again, spending time with Julian reminded her of the familiar delights of a rom-com, and she allowed herself to be lulled into the fantasy again. *Don't forget Evie.* Anu's voice came in sharp and crisp. *Don't forget all she said.*

So when Julian cupped her face and brushed his thumb over her cheek, Advika tensed up. Then she told Anu's voice to zip it. After a count of three, she pulled Julian toward her and gave him the most sweeping, "Yes, I'm still in love with you" kiss she could muster. Julian responded by dipping her like they were in some sort of 1930s musical, just as the string quartet played the song's final chorus. Julian drew her back up, and they both laughed heartily, as if responding to whistles and applause.

"So, darling, I was thinking," Julian said, smoothing a few loose hairs from Advika's forehead. "If you want to take a little break from work—all work—I understand. Maybe it's time you enjoy just being Mrs. Zelding for a while and all that comes with it."

"I don't want to take a break from work, just that one screen—"

"You know what I've been thinking about a lot lately? Our trip to Mexico. And on our second day, that adorable little boy ran up to us and asked if you'd play catch with him. You remember that?"

"Uh, yeah. I do." She looked over at the string quartet, which had begun playing Ed Sheeran's "Thinking Out Loud." All four were wearing glasses and were laser focused on their sheet music except for the baby-faced violinist, who kept glancing over at the two of them, seeming wistful.

"You were so great with that kid. I chatted with his parents, and they said he didn't like strangers. At all. I think they said he was on the spectrum. Asperger's maybe." Julian flicked his hand dismissively while still holding Advika's, as the two resumed dancing. "But you made him feel comfortable. I loved seeing you like that. Because you *were* comfortable. Like you were meant to have one of your own."

Advika coughed. She took a stuttering step back and nearly tripped over the hem of her dress. Julian caught her with a devilish look in his eyes. "Got ya, Addi."

"You want to have kids?" Advika squeaked. "Now?" Her thoughts immediately returned to *The Riders* and how vehement "Ron" had been about wanting children with "Phyllis" despite her hesitations.

"Well, not this minute. That's not how biology works." His fingers dug into the side of her waist.

"But we've never once talked about it."

"Surely it was understood," he said with a hint of exasperation. Advika tore through her memories, attempting to recall when Julian had raised the idea of having a family. She remembered when he shared his weird opinion that Katharine Hepburn should have had babies, but that was truly it. How could Julian act like this was something that had always been on the table?

"I think you would love being a mother. I've always wanted to be a father. And our kids would be so beautiful. I've..." Julian looked past Advika, his eyes catching on something in the distance. He cleared his throat, as if trying to urge his voice to come out.

"Last fall, I had a health scare. I was diagnosed with dilated cardiomyopathy. It's a heart condition that left me gasping, breathless. I thought I was going to die."

"Oh my god," Advika said, partly because she was truly

surprised and partly because she thought that was the reaction Julian wanted. "That must have been so scary."

Julian's chin trembled when he shared that he had inherited the condition from his mother, and it had been the cause of her death. But his doctor had also warned him that it was due to untreated, long-term high blood pressure. "It was the wake-up call I needed to slow down and focus on what is truly important. And all the Oscars in the world are wonderful. But there's nothing I want more than a child. I was meant to be a dad. I should have been one by now, really." Julian retracted his faraway gaze and redirected it full strength onto Advika. "*We* are meant for this. I know it."

A squeamish sensation oscillated through her entire being. All she could do was nod and let him guide her body around, her toes scraping against the concrete, as she tried to grapple with what he had just said. The gauzy bubble of this romantic night had just been burst with a dramatic splat. Advika locked eyes with the violinist, as if to say, *Can you believe this?* But the musician was too busy gazing dreamily at Julian.

"Listen, Advika." He stopped dancing again and tilted her face upward with the gentle nudge of his index finger. "I know the news about Evie must have thrown you off. But don't let it get in your head, okay?"

Advika responded to Julian uttering his ex-wife's name as if she had been struck by a bolt of lightning. She stood up on her tiptoes, wanting to make sure she didn't miss whatever he had to say next.

"There's only two of us in this marriage. Gossip and other people's machinations fade. What we have is real." Julian paused, as if contemplating what to say next. "I want you. I desire you. I see a real future with you." He dipped her again, just in time to coincide with the song's ending. "You and me. And someday, a family."

The world momentarily went sideways, and this time she went so far down that her hair grazed the floor. When Julian drew her upright, it took her a moment before the dizziness passed. But Advika put on a smile for the rest of the evening, celebrating an anniversary of a marriage that was a demarcation point between her ordinary life and a future slipping out of her control.

⌒

When she awakened once again at 3:02 a.m. that night, Advika opened Instagram and found the phone number that Lucia had texted her. She copied the number, then stared at the photo of Lucia and Evie for several moments before closing the app and sending Lucia a text message: Where and when can we meet?

CHAPTER FIFTEEN

The Goodbye Girl

ADVIKA CROSSED HER LEGS, PLACING her ankle at her knee, giving up on trying to get her feet to touch the floor. The over-stuffed zebra-print sofa in Lucia Tello's living room was so high off the floor that Advika had the sensation she was floating on a cloud. While Lucia was in the kitchen, Advika examined her home, whose modest square footage housed some striking pieces, from the sofa Advika was seated on to the white baby grand piano in the corner to the adult-sized stone vase that seemed to come straight off the lot of an action-adventure movie. The apartment definitely looked like the home of someone who had been steadily employed in Hollywood on the outskirts of stardom without ever landing a breakout role.

After she had messaged Lucia and agreed to visit her home in Glendale the following morning, she had immediately Googled her. Lucia had a supporting role as a nosy neighbor in a very popular comedy franchise in the mid-1980s, and she guest starred on numerous legal and medical dramas in the '90s and early 2000s before becoming an acting coach.

"Do you still act?" Advika asked as Lucia came in with a tray of coffee mugs and a platter of multicolored macarons.

"On occasion," Lucia said, settling in beside her. "I dip my toe in acting now and then to keep my SAG card. And because I miss it sometimes."

"I see," Advika said, still finding it hard to believe she was having coffee with Evie's close friend and someone who had met Julian before he had become a Hollywood superproducer.

"So," Lucia said. "How much time do you have?"

Advika shrugged, feeling her face redden. If she had wanted to seem busy and important, she would have given a window of time. But now that Olive's house-sitting gig was ending, Advika had all the time in the world and nowhere to be. So she responded, "As much time as you have."

Lucia nodded. As they both sipped their coffees, Advika snuck glimpses of her. With her dark, short-cropped hair, oversized black silk top, and silver leather pants, she was a very tall, and very tanned, carbon copy of Liza Minnelli. Advika felt like a slouchy teenager in comparison, having decided to look and dress like the old version of herself when meeting Lucia, wearing minimal makeup, a green peasant top, and cutoff jean shorts, relics from a life when she had shopped at Forever 21. When she had first arrived, Advika had felt embarrassed by how underdressed she was for such an important meeting. But Lucia had treated her warmly, enveloping her in a long, perfumed hug. Advika should have been more shocked by such an overly friendly gesture from a stranger, but instead it helped remove her edginess and the weird sense that she was betraying Julian by being there.

"Well, thank you for reaching out," she told Lucia, starting to feel nervous about what Evie's friend would reveal to her. "I didn't know whether to believe it was you or someone trying to pull a fast one on me."

"Totally understandable." Lucia reached for a green macaron.

"It was impulsive of me, although it did take three hours and my neighbor's assistance to understand Instagram and how I might be able to contact you."

"That's impressive!" Advika said, settling back into the cushions of the sofa. "My parents would never be able to figure it out, even if they were paid, like, a million dollars."

Lucia raised an eyebrow, her green eyes expressing her surprise and a touch of amusement. Advika was momentarily confused, but once she realized she had unintentionally alluded to Evie's will, she reddened even more.

"Well, I guess that's our transition," Lucia said brightly. "I was wondering what would get us there."

"Why doesn't—didn't—Evie want me to be married to Julian?" Advika heard the plaintiveness in her voice, ashamed that she sounded like a scared little girl.

"I thought that would be your first question. So I thought the best way to start was by showing you this."

Lucia finished her macaron, then picked up the remote control and pressed a button. The flat-screen, which had been in screen saver mode, changed from a bouquet of purple petunias to the opening credits for a French TV series titled *Le Cinemax Parle*.

"It's like *Inside the Actors Studio* but wearing a red beret and holding baguettes," Lucia said, followed by a merry snort as she pulled out a cigarette from a box on the side table. "Do you mind if I smoke?" Advika shook her head, leaning forward expectantly. The air-conditioning unit switched on, and a gust of cold air quickly blanketed the room.

The half-hour episode featured an interviewer asking Evie questions about her brief but significant acting oeuvre. Filmed in 1991, fortysomething Evie radiated a chicness that was impossible to achieve, even with a black card and a stylist on speed dial. She was dressed in a cream cashmere sweater, black cigarette pants, and black flats affixed with a gold medallion at their center. Advika's eyes kept catching on Evie's shoes, as the actress seemed to have a hard time keeping still. She crossed her legs, then uncrossed them, then tucked one foot behind the other, and then crossed her legs again. So there were quick flashes of gold throughout the chat, which Advika imagined as a fairy flitting around Evie's ankles. Gradually, Evie relaxed, and so her movements stilled too.

Evie and the interviewer spoke mile-a-minute French, as each title they discussed flashed on the screen. Advika leaned forward, enjoying the musicality of the pair's language. She liked hearing the enthusiasm flow into Evie's voice the longer the interview went on, especially with *Dark, Hot Sun*.

"She loved talking about acting," Lucia said, a cigarette poised elegantly in her left hand. "Talk to her about what she was wearing or who she was dating, or later, Julian, and she clammed up. But bring up acting—especially how she prepared for roles—and Evie was the chandelier in a dark room." Lucia nodded at the screen, then took a drag of her cigarette. "See? Right now she's talking about how she decided that Angelica would always wear a silver bracelet, and that she went to several jewelry stores before finding the right one."

Advika watched Evie speak animatedly as she pointed at her bare wrist, then encircled it with thumb and forefinger. "What did the bracelet look like?"

Lucia listened for a few seconds, then paused the video. "She says she found it in an antique store in Santa Barbara. The bracelet reminded her of a handcuff, and she purposely wore it a little too tight. At the end of the movie, when she ends up naked and bleeding but alive, the bracelet's gone too." Lucia pressed Play, and Evie spoke a few more minutes, gave a brief smirk, and then looked down at her lap as the interviewer responded. "She says that no one who watched the film ever noticed. But that small detail made her feel like Angelica was her character, and that she wasn't just a director's puppet."

Advika encircled her own wrist with her thumb and forefinger. Unlike Evie, she had short fingers and wasn't able to make them connect. "Did she say what happened to the bracelet?"

Lucia shook her head. "I've only ever heard her discuss it during this interview. Even her biography doesn't mention it. Which is why I might have kept this video all these years." She sighed, and her cigarette dangled from her lips, giving Lucia the look of a Marlene Dietrich poster.

"It's nice to see her so happy like this," Advika said, running her hands over the goose bumps prickling on her thighs. "I haven't seen *Dark, Hot Sun* yet, but I want to."

Lucia shook her head. "Don't bother. It's porn."

Advika gaped. "Porn?"

Lucia threw back her head and laughed, her cigarette briefly tipping upward toward the ceiling. "Sorry, my dear. I meant to say torture porn. I read that in a review of a horror movie once, and it fits *Dark, Hot Sun*. That movie is all about putting Evie through an endless number of miseries and indignities, just to watch her suffer beautifully."

"Evie or Angelica?"

"Exactly." They sat in silence while the video continued to play. Advika resisted the urge to pull her shirt over her knees to warm them up from the intense air-conditioning. She was torn between wanting to sit in Lucia's apartment for hours, peppering her with questions, and fleeing outside into the intense LA heat.

"Have you seen *The Lady and the Tiger*?" Lucia asked abruptly. Advika nodded eagerly. "Evie loved that movie. I mean, she knew it was junk, but she liked that she had the freedom to do whatever she liked. That was a happy movie for her," she added wistfully. "She told me she based that character on me."

"That's amazing!" This information so buoyed Advika she momentarily forgot she was freezing.

"She copied my haircut, mimicked the way I spoke, even how I sipped a martini and smoked a cigarette." Lucia demonstrated by taking a long, exaggerated drag, then swept her hand toward the ceiling in an arc.

"Wow," Advika said. "That must have been so strange but also wonderful."

Lucia stubbed out her cigarette in a teal ashtray. "It was fun to see myself through her eyes. Made me like myself a little more." Without a cigarette to hold, Lucia became fidgety. She methodically slid her gold rings up and down her fingers, starting with her pinky. "But it wasn't actually me, you know? That character was an Evie creation. It's like she plucked some things from me, plucked some things from herself, and then there's the screenplay too. If she played me onscreen, that would be a lot less charming. But Evie told me she liked my 'swerve.'"

"Swerve?"

"I think she meant 'swagger,' but 'swerve' is a better word for it, don't you think?" Advika nodded. "And so she took my 'swerve' as her first building block and constructed from there." Lucia's eyes took on a faraway quality. "That was her favorite part, she told me. Not being in front of the cameras but building that person into someone before she started telling the story."

To hear about Evie's inspiration for her character reminded Advika of how she had summoned all she knew of Anu into the main character in her screenplay. It was barely creating fiction, more like resuscitating a dead person and then dropping them into a fictional world. *The Romance Game* had helped her in her grief—given her a reason to wake up each day, the sole thing to look forward to. But after it had been completed, she occasionally felt waves of self-doubt about her craft, ashamed by the lack of imagination in what she had created. To learn that Evie had done something similar with *The Lady and the Tiger* to find her way into her character was helpful. Perhaps Advika could revisit her screenplay and pry the Anu-ness out of it so Lily could be more of her own character. Maybe there could be two versions of the screenplay. The original one, which was her love letter to Anu, and a different version that took something from Anu and Advika, and created a character out of whole cloth. Just like Evie had done.

"My darling Evie," Lucia murmured. "See how much she radiated when talking about her films?" She switched off the television and fished out a second cigarette. "The end of this always saddens me, because the interviewer laments that it was a shame Evie didn't have a bigger film career. And Evie's face just becomes a broken heart." Lucia sighed, and the air-conditioning mercifully shut off with one last grumpy exhalation. "I wanted to show you this, Advika, because I think it captures Evie's essence—what she loved so much about acting. And this is what Julian took from her. He robbed her, and he robbed audiences of her too."

Lucia then began to share how Julian's ascendancy in Hollywood impacted the first Zelding marriage and eventually Evie's career. Even though Evie had hoped *The Riders* would end Julian's Hollywood aspirations, Gerald Pithe took notice after viewing the film at a private screening hosted by Julian. And he was the only one to reach out to Zelding to ask him if he wanted to help produce his next feature, *Lost and Gone Forever*, kicking off a fruitful collaborative run that would last for three decades. The duo's first films together would feature Evie as the heroine, culminating in the blockbuster commercial and critical success of 1973's *Dark, Hot Sun*.

Evie landed her first and only Oscar nomination for the film and was soon inundated with offers for new projects. All were serious dramas in the vein she had already worked, but this time, they were headed up by respected directors: Coppola, Kubrick, Altman. Yet Evie was resistant. She longed to stretch herself to make the kind of films that she had loved as a little girl, the reason she had moved to Hollywood after high school graduation. Even though she fell into acting, Evie had grown to love it and wanted to take her craft seriously. But the baggage of acting in so many dark films had started to wear at her soul. All Evie wanted was a break—a long break—from dramatic roles.

"Anyone who knew Evie was aware of her gifts for her comedy and improvisation. She was made to sparkle on the silver screen, not wail and weep," Lucia told Advika. "Everyone loved Evie—she was the sun, you know? You wouldn't know it from most of her movies. And she didn't like that."

But with his first best picture win under his belt, Julian had been elevated into one of the industry's top power players. Lucia bitterly noted that he began enjoying a newfound level of power and respect among his peers, and in his mind, he had been able to elevate himself because Evie was his muse. And he did not like the idea of Evie conducting her career without his direction. The couple spent two years trying to figure out what project to work on next following the astronomical success of their third and—what would turn out to be—final collaboration. And so began the push-pull between them that would result in the end of their marriage.

"Julian was really pushing for them to find something together," Lucia said, rearranging the folds of her silk top with delicate precision. "I think the love had fully seeped out of their marriage by that point. No, he just liked having a muse, his own Kim Novak. Do you know who that is?"

Advika nodded, her stomach sinking a half centimeter the more Lucia shared Evie and Julian's story. "She was Hitchcock's muse. She was in *Vertigo*."

"I'm surprised a young person like you would know that.

You're a smart cookie," Lucia said with an appreciative grin. "Anyway, Julian wanted a muse like that, except he wanted one on his arm, and in his home, day or night." She hesitated. "Uh, I hope this isn't making you uncomfortable. I just had to remind myself that I was talking about *your* husband."

"Honestly, same." Advika gave an uneasy laugh. The goose bumps on her arms returned. To hear Lucia discuss Julian, it felt more like she was being let in on some Hollywood gossip, rather than her spouse's backstory. "But please continue. I want to know all of it."

Lucia took a pensive puff on her cigarette, her eyes communicating regret and concern, but she continued. She said Julian wanted to one-up his idols, and as part of his self-created image, he wanted to continue his career of making serious, award-worthy dramas with his glamorous wife. Evie wanted to star in smart, sophisticated comedies and auditioned for films like *Shampoo*, *The Sunshine Boys*, and *Annie Hall*. But she didn't get any of those roles, partly because she was too closely identified with her dramatic personas, and partly because her husband was rumored to be murmuring in his peers' ears, dissuading them from hiring Evie.

As Evie went out for new acting roles with no success, Julian worked on his passion project, an adaptation of an Italian crime drama tentatively titled *Bloodwork*. He thought Evie would be perfect for the role of the mob boss's wife, but she steadfastly refused to even look at a script. Evie complained about her lack of other movie roles, and he mostly reacted with indifference. Arguments turned into screaming fights turned into separate bedrooms turned into extramarital affairs for both. In early 1976, Julian finally cut ties with his passion project and his wife. He pivoted toward working on *Adelaide, Adelaide* (a film that would garner his second best picture nod) and filed for divorce.

"The fact that Julian had filed first enraged Evie. You know, she had been ready to leave him as early as the filming of *Dark, Hot Sun* but was counseled by nearly everyone—her agent and manager, her friends, her mother—to stay for the sake of her career. I'm proud to say that I was one of the few dissenters; I wish there had been more of us who had supported her. She considered her worst acting role to be having to pretend she was happily married to Julian while they were both cheating." Lucia coughed and stubbed out the cigarette. "One day I'll quit these. Anyway, Evie hated being Julian's plus-one to industry events, helping sell this power-couple image that only really helped his career. And here's the fucked-up part: she had finally gotten so sick of it all, so sick of him. And she told me she was ready to file, and we went out to Chasen's and celebrated. That was our spot, you know. Do you know it? Anyway, not important. And then Julian files first. I think it wasn't even a week after she had told me her plans."

Advika watched the sadness creep over Lucia's lively and poised demeanor as she related the end of Evie's time in Hollywood. By the time Julian had filed for divorce, the fruitlessness of Evie's meetings and auditions, coupled with the strain of staying in her marriage, had sunk her into a deep depression. She gradually stopped appearing at parties and premieres, and so her star, which had been shining so brightly following her acclaimed performance and Oscar nomination, had dimmed completely by the time the divorce went through three years later. With no new income coming in, Evie couldn't afford to fight Julian and his phalanx of divorce lawyers for an equitable settlement. And in the divorce, Evie received their Beverly Hills home and nothing else.

"And so she left her home, her friends, her career, me. As soon as the divorce went through, Evie sold the house and departed for France."

"Did you ever see her again?" Advika asked, her voice

trembling. The chill from the air-conditioning had found its way into her bones, and she felt like every atom of her body was shivering from what Lucia had told her.

Lucia shook her head. "We stayed in touch with letters and phone calls, but we lost touch sometime in the nineties. I wish we hadn't, but time passes, people get busy. We loved each other, though. I loved her." She nodded wistfully at the television. "This DVD is actually the last thing she ever sent to me. No note, no 'How are you?' Just this. But I'm glad she did."

Advika gave her a sad smile. "Me too." After a beat, she added, "So I guess this means you don't know what's on the film reel Evie mentioned in her will."

"No idea. I'm just as curious as you." Lucia raised a perfectly arched eyebrow. "Maybe even more so."

"Did you ever, um, meet Julian's other wives?" It was a strange question to ask, but Evie's story was already sparking questions about Julian's dynamics with the other two women. She abhorred how Julian had treated Evie, but perhaps he was different with the other Mrs. Zeldings. Perhaps he got better at marriage as time went on, she thought weakly, even as Anu's voice was already charging in: *Nope, not a chance.*

"No, sweetheart. I've only met you." Advika nodded grimly. "I don't know how your romance with him happened, but please take heed of what she said in her will. When Evie's mother died, I think she was truly done with the States. It was like she didn't want to exist here anymore. So the fact that she would make this gesture—it's important. I feel like her ambassador, in a way, saying the things she'd want you to know."

"And I appreciate it. Thank you for meeting me." Advika found herself choking up, and Lucia wrapped her in another fragrant hug. Advika found it hard to pull away. It had been so long since she had been in the safe, comforting arms of a maternal figure.

"He might have changed, hon," Lucia said as Advika tied her sneakers in the foyer. "But in case he hadn't, I wanted you to know. Evie would have wanted you to know." Lucia's eyes glistened with tears.

"I'm so sorry for your loss," Advika said softly. Evie had represented so much to Advika, but in an archetypal way: as a rival, as a glimpse into Julian's past, and as someone to be admired. Seeing her from Lucia's perspective humanized Evie, reminded her she was not just a distant, curious figure in Advika's own personal history to idolize and envy. She was a real person. A real person whose dreams were dashed by Advika's own husband.

⌐

Advika sat in her car parked two blocks away from Lucia's apartment building, her hands gripping the Camry's worn steering wheel so tightly she wouldn't have been surprised if it had broken off in her grasp. She hadn't driven the Camry since her birthday in May, and returning to her old car was just like putting on a pair of comfy, broken-in sneakers after weeks of stilettos. The G Wagon was an excellent car, and Advika enjoyed driving it, but visiting Julian's ex-wife's close friend necessitated a vehicle that didn't attract attention to itself.

She thought Julian would question her for choosing to leave behind the SUV, but he had been so busy, his phone ringing constantly as he prepared for his trip to Morocco, that he had just nodded when Advika told him she needed to gas up her old car for a quick drive to make sure the battery wouldn't die. She had entreated him to keep her aged car in his massive garage because of its connection to Anu. But also Advika just liked to have something in the house that was wholly hers, that was a tangible reminder of who she was without Julian.

And to sit in the Camry now helped her process what she had learned about her husband, providing a place to sit and think where she could fully tap into her sense of self, entirely free from his influence. Because simply put, Advika was shaken. To learn about how Julian had treated Evie during their marriage—absorbing her talents and connections and beauty to launch his career, then coldly cutting ties when she was no longer of use to him—brought up parallels to her own marriage. Julian had a singular vision for Advika's screenplay, and when she didn't share it, he proposed taking a break from her career . . . in order to start a family. They disagreed one time, and so he just proposed that she fully embrace her Mrs. Zelding-ness by basically becoming his plus-one he could squire to all his big Hollywood events, while at home she would have his babies?

Advika shuddered at the idea. She didn't dwell too often on their age gap, but the prospect of having a baby with a man approaching seventy was, in a word, unappealing. It just didn't seem *right*. Prior to meeting Julian, she loved reading snarky celebrity blogs in which the writers would smartly analyze the latest gossip stories. May–December romances were often a hot topic, and after she began dating Julian, Advika gave up her beloved celeb blogs because she feared seeing her own name featured one day, followed by mean-spirited comments accusing her of being a gold digger. She could only imagine the headlines generated if silver fox Julian became a first-time father with his twentysomething wife, his twentysomething *brown* wife. He would get all the props for being a "hands-on dad," and Advika would be invisible. Her identity shrunken to being his wife, the mother of his child. She would barely exist. Just like Evie.

The sun flashed strong, and Advika winced and pulled down her visor to help protect her from the intense sunlight of early afternoon. She had about an hour before she'd have to return home. Since Julian was leaving soon, he was prioritizing "couple time" because his Morocco trip would be their first time apart. With a sigh, Advika picked up Evie's biography from the passenger seat, having gone out of her way to stop at the bungalow to pick up her things prior to driving to Lucia's. She idly flipped through the pages and decided to return it to the library. Her conversation with Lucia had told her all she needed to know; also, Advika was nervous about having it in her possession any longer. As she skimmed the book, the blur of pages revealed a blue Post-it note stuck between the final chapter and the acknowledgments. Written on it were six words: *Text me when you get here.*

What could Olive have possibly discovered? Advika set the book aside and pulled out her phone.

A: Got your note in the book!!! What's up???

Five minutes later, Olive texted back.

O: You're lucky you're texting me during a lull. Gimme a sec

O: After I finished the book, I went down an Evie rabbit hole and found a thread about her on Reddit. I'm going to send you a link but first, promise you won't search for yourself in the comments

A: You finished the book? Wow

A: And oh shit

O: Whatever you think is being said about you, it's much, much worse. So don't, okay?

A: K

O: I need you to write "ok" because "k" is nebulous and could mean anything

A: OK

A: Okay

A: 👌

O: Ugh stop. Here's the link. The thread has an interview with Evie just before she moved away. It might be the last one she did before leaving the States. She talks pretty openly about Julian and why she left

A: Thanks Olive 🌺

O: Yep

O: And seriously, don't read the comments

O: Just the story

A: 👍

Even though Lucia had given Advika the lowdown about Evie's reasons for leaving, she couldn't help clicking the link, rapacious for any and all information about the first Mrs. Zelding. The link brought Advika to a Reddit thread titled "Rare Evie Lockhart interview, May 1979." Someone had scanned in an interview with a publication titled *The Ojai Reader*, Evie's hometown newspaper. The article featured a photo still from what would be her final movie, *Mad Chase*, showing Evie sitting cross-legged on the hood of a Ferrari, with cat-eyed sunglasses and a handkerchief tied over her wavy, shoulder-length hair.

Underneath the article, the poster commented that she happened to come across the article when visiting her grand-mother in Ojai, who kept a scrapbook of "anytime movies and TV shows filmed in Ojai, and every local who became a star." The poster added that *The Ojai Reader* had stopped publish-ing a year after the story had run, and as far as she knew, "this interview was unavailable online."

Advika enlarged the scanned image of the article, quickly running through the discussion of Evie's movie until her gaze lasered in on her husband's name in the final few paragraphs.

Ms. Lockhart is unguarded and surprisingly up-front about the end of her marriage to her ex-husband, Oscar-winning film producer Julian Zelding.

"He'd like to say things like, 'No one knows you better than I do' and 'Why would I not want the best for you?' whenever we discussed my career. But I had seen him when he was a nobody, a striver, and maybe that person at one time had wanted the best for me. Or maybe it's always been that Julian only wants what's best for him."

Ms. Lockhart then leaned in and shared a surprising decla-ration: *Mad Chase* would be her last film. She was leaving the industry, and America, behind.

"I can be candid here, because you're one of my last inter-views. And I'm tired of holding my tongue—it's not benefiting me to do so anymore. But here it is: I'm no longer going to live my life as a silent scream.

"I'm ready for a fresh start. I'm ready to have my life back, on my own terms. Nothing is worth what I've been through. A pretty dress, an Oscar nod, a kind review, famous friends. Not one of them. Not anything."

Advika sat back in her seat and said, "Wow." And then, before she could stop herself, her thumb scrolled down to the comments section.

EVELYNSALT 4 DAYS AGO
Interview as therapy session. Poor Evie

TORIFIONAKATE 4 DAYS AGO
She DGAF. WOW. What a mic drop. I wish more people could see this interview

THEBONUSROOM 4 DAYS AGO
I wish more people cared about what she said in her will. This was a perfect TMZ story, why did barely anyone report on it?

FUTUREPHOENIXRISING 4 DAYS AGO
Julian is such a megalomaniac, he killed her career. What an ass

THEUNIVERSE28 4 DAYS AGO
Did that girl he just married want to write movies?

> **PersephonesGhost 3 days ago**
> That's why she married him I bet
>
> **ParisianCharm 3 days ago**
> "Write movies"—nah she a gold digger
>
> **HotDadLP 3 days ago**
> If I were her I'd take the $$$ and run
>
> **IKnowWhereUR 2 days ago**
> Child Bride doesn't deserve any of Evie's $$$

Julian had thought he squashed the story of Evie's will, and in the mainstream press, he largely had. Probably because there was nothing to be gained from earning the wrath of a powerful producer by turning his love life into soap opera fodder. Advika was glad the story hadn't died completely but had burrowed far beyond Julian's control and burned defiant in pockets of the internet. It made Advika feel like she wasn't crazy in her unease about whom she had married. Even if it made her a joke, a "gold digger," a laughingstock.

A text from Olive: You read the comments, didn't you

She wrote back: I did. But I'm okay. I agree with all of them, pretty much

Advika set down her phone, put on her sunglasses, and started driving. On the way back to Wildwood, she dropped off Evie's biography and movies at a nearby library branch. Advika then turned on the radio and flipped through the stations until she landed on an oldies station playing The Supremes' "You Can't Hurry Love." Advika cranked the volume, feeling her spirits lift. It must be a sign that Evie was watching over her.

"You can't worry, doves; you just have to mate," Advika sang along just as Evie would have, as she returned home to the man they had in common.

CHAPTER SIXTEEN

Flirting with Disaster

FOR ONE OF JULIAN'S FINAL evenings before leaving for Morocco, he wanted to go to the movies. He had insisted on dressing up for the outing and having a driver take them in his silver Maybach, which rarely left the garage. When they arrived at the Nuart Theatre, the beloved single-screen theater in West Los Angeles, Advika was surprised that Julian had rented it out for the two of them to screen one of his favorite films, Orson Welles's *Touch of Evil*.

"But you—I mean, we—have a home theater. We couldn't watch it there?" Advika asked as they walked down the aisle, each holding oversized baskets of popcorn. With her visit with Lucia from five days earlier still consuming her thoughts, Advika tried her best to pretend she was in the mood for a date with her husband. To play the part, she had worn a white summer dress with a pink flower pattern and sandals, and now regretted that choice, as the theater's air-conditioning whirred with the power of cooling a crowd of a hundred people, not two.

"That's not the same as going to the movies, Addi. I like buying popcorn, walking down the aisles, the sticky floors. Besides, I wanted to give us a date night."

"I usually go see romantic comedies on dates, not cult classics." Advika followed him into a middle row, and they both sat down in the center.

"Well, then the wrong person's been taking you on dates." Julian winked at her, then put up his arm and snapped his fingers.

As the movie unspooled before them, Advika's thoughts returned to Evie and the film reel she had promised her if Advika divorced Julian. Even as he reached for her thigh ten minutes into the film, then began kissing her neck thirty minutes later, as if the buttery scent of popcorn reawakened his inner horny teenager, Advika puzzled over what Evie could possibly want her to see. In the two brief conversations Julian and Advika had had about his ex-wife's will, he never mentioned the film reel. Surely he had to be just as curious.

Julian's warm breath was in her ear. "Addi, have you ever . . . you know."

Advika shushed him playfully, hoping he wouldn't feel rejected. "I'm trying to watch the movie. I hear it's a classic. One of Orson's best."

"We can watch it later. C'mon." He took her hand and moved it toward his pants. Advika pulled away.

"We're not teenagers, Julian." She faked a coquettish laugh.

"Send me off to Morocco with a memory I'll never forget."

"You're not going to war, babe. It's just a movie about a war." Even as she kept her tone light and her eyes focused on the screen, she could sense her husband bristling. Advika thought that was the end of it, but a few minutes later, Julian grasped her hand again, then moved it straight onto his crotch.

"No. Seriously, no." Advika yanked her hand away, then folded her arms. She watched the rest of the movie this way, while Julian seethed next to her.

⌒

They hadn't spoken the rest of the night, not in the movie theater or on the drive home. Julian went into his office once they
had arrived back at Wildwood, while Advika took the stairs
two at a time. She quickly washed her face, brushed her teeth,
and changed into the unsexiest pajamas she owned, which
were black silk shorts and a matching tank top. Advika wanted
to be able to feign slumber for whenever he came into their
bedroom, but by the time he actually climbed into bed next
to her, she was already asleep. His movements beside her, purposefully turning away from her so that she faced the back of
his head, were what woke her up, and she slept fitfully the rest
of the night.

⌒

In the morning, Julian acted as if the events of the previous
night had never happened. By the time she had showered,
dressed, and gone downstairs on tiptoe, Julian was in the breakfast room drinking his green juice, a plate of scrambled eggs
in front of him largely untouched. Advika watched him from
the kitchen, wondering whether she should try to talk to him
about the night before and how he had made her uncomfortable. Then he spotted her and waved her over.

"About yesterday, I'm sorry," Julian said as she walked over
and sat across the table from him. "I think I had one cocktail
too many before we went out. That's why we had a driver, by
the way." She didn't know whether to believe him. The words
seemed rehearsed, designed to elicit an acceptance of an apology so they could move on. With Julian leaving the following
morning, it would be better for her if her husband left on good
terms.

And yet.

Julian was staring at her, waiting. His mouth opened briefly, and she caught a glimpse of the gap in his teeth, which, when they had met, had been one of the things she had found strangely alluring about him. And now just like everything else about Julian, Advika found it off-putting. She would let Julian think she had forgiven him, for her own sake. But with Lucia's words and Evie's newspaper interview still sharp in her mind, and Julian acting like a scolded puppy admonished for peeing on the rug, Advika would twist the knife in a different way.

"I understand. Thanks for apologizing." She forced a smile.

"Oh, Addi, I'm so glad." He beamed at her. "You know how much I treasure you. It was just...stress. From the upcoming trip and some things related to work. But I could have handled myself better."

Advika nodded again and asked if he was going to finish his eggs. Julian pushed his plate toward her with a grin, his ram-rod posture quickly softening. *What a good wife*, he must have been thinking. *Young, pliable, forgiving.*

"You look incredible, sweetheart." Julian gazed at her adoringly, too much so. Advika stifled the impulse to turn into the gritted-teeth emoji. "What's the occasion?"

She had dressed up on purpose: Rag & Bone jeans, a Stella McCartney white blazer over a dark green blouse, and Anu's gold chain. It was the outfit she had planned to wear on her first day of *Agent UFO*, even though she knew she would have been overdressed in a room full of writers slouching around in baseball caps and tee shirts.

"I have a meeting," she said between bites of eggs. They were too runny and bland for her taste, but she scarfed them down anyway. "And if I don't finish up here soon, I'm going to be late. Traffic on the 405 can be so bad right now." She flashed him a grin as bland as his eggs.

"What meeting?" The tenseness returned to Julian's frame.

His legs were no longer lazily crossed; now both feet were flat on the floor. Advika relished having caused this change in him. He would be terrible at poker.

She wove a story about how she had met an agent while at Olive's coffee shop, and they had gotten to talking about Advika's work, her past award, and her career aspirations. "I like her. Um, she really understands my art and intentions."

"Is that so?" The corners of his mouth twitched. "And what about Gregory?" Gregory was the junior agent Julian had set her up with at the mega-agency that had represented Julian for the past two decades. Two days earlier, Advika had written Gregory a passionate email asking to be put up for any writing gig that came across his desk, and he had responded with "k" and a smiley face. Which could explain why Advika was only his second client.

"Gregory and I aren't really vibing." Advika fingered her necklace's pendant, then twisted the chain around her finger, the heavy gold biting into her skin. "I'm just starting out in the industry and want to keep my options open."

"That doesn't mean you need to ask him to put you up for anything and everything," Julian said, directly quoting her email to her agent. Advika gaped at him, and he sighed as he unfolded his hands on the table, his palms facing upward. "I didn't tell you this earlier, because I didn't want you to get bent out of shape. But Gregory and I agreed *Agent UFO* wasn't the right opportunity for you, and the truth is we pulled out of it." He turned on a saccharine smile. "Sweetheart, you're too talented for television. It's movies you should be focused on, if you must be focused on something."

In hearing this, Advika's finger, still wrapped up in the gold chain, jerked on it so hard she thought it would snap in her hands. Julian had cost her that job. He had sabotaged her. Just like he had sabotaged Evie when she wanted to pursue the kind of film career he deemed wasn't right for her.

"Well," Advika said, speaking rapidly in the hopes of masking her outrage, "this new agent feels differently from you. She has a new Shondaland series that she wants to put me up for." If Advika was going to make up a story about an agent, she might as well go big.

Julian shook his head in disgust, as if he had heard her say something foul. A ray of sunlight bounced off his forehead, giving him a brief angelic glow. "What's her name? Where does she work?"

"You know, I'd rather not say." Advika pushed the plate of eggs away so hard that the fork clattered onto the table. "Because it's just a meeting. And I did this on my own, without any help."

"You mean without my help. Without my name. Right?" When Advika shrugged and said yes, Julian stood up and asked her to come with him to his office. She followed him, clasping her hands behind her back to keep from fidgeting. Julian opened the door and ushered her in, then closed the door. He sat behind his desk in an imposing leather chair that reminded Advika of a sleek, cushioned Iron Throne. She took the seat opposite and made a point to look at her watch to remind Julian that she had to leave. Advika was ready to continue the illusion of her fake meeting and her puffed-up pride about scoring it on her own merits, until Julian withdrew a manila envelope from his top drawer and slid it over to her.

"You've got to be more careful, Addi."

Advika opened the envelope and pulled out photographs. She gasped. There were three photos: one of her walking to the Camry parked on the sidewalk in Lucia's neighborhood, one of her in the driver's seat talking on the phone. The last one was of her reading a book. All her anger about Julian's machinations over her career collapsed into a boulder of dread inside her chest. Advika shuffled through the photos as Julian continued to speak. But his voice was a gnat in her ear. Because she had to make sure, be absolutely positive, that the photos didn't show what she was reading in her car. After going through them several times, resisting the urge to peer closely at them so as not to tip off Julian, she was finally satisfied that the photographs did not show either the book's pages or its cover. She stifled a sigh of relief that she chose to read Evie's biography by laying the book flat against the steering wheel. But then a new paranoia emerged: Were her library records easy to access?

"I said, what are you looking for?" Julian's voice, sounding stern and a bit irate, interrupted her thoughts.

"Nothing. Well, when I was there, I thought I saw a flash, but I didn't think anything at the time..." She let her voice falter lamely. A sliver of sweat erupted above her upper lip, and Advika willed herself not to brush it away.

"The interest in us has subsided quite a bit but not completely. A part of the reason I wanted to go to the movies yesterday was to test a public outing for us and see if it generated any heat. And so when I received these photos this morning, I assumed it was the two of us." Julian cleared his throat and, for a moment, seemed uncomfortable, as if he had swallowed something large and spicy. "But it was just you."

"It's been weeks since...the news, and no one has ever approached me," Advika said. The idea that someone had been watching her unnerved her. Already on edge, she wasn't prepared for the pointedness of Julian's next question.

"Where were you?" Julian tapped the desk twice with his index finger, and Advika reluctantly handed back the photos.

Oh shit. "In Glendale. I went to visit one of my aunties. A good friend of my mom's."

"Which aunt?" Julian pursed his lips. "I thought you didn't have any family members in Southern California."

"Not aunt. Aunty. Like, a family friend." With Julian staring at her suspiciously, waiting for a name, Advika swallowed. If she showed too much hesitation, she worried that Julian would somehow squeeze the truth out of her like she were a new tube of toothpaste. She had to be forthright to the point of blasé, without offering too many details. An image of her mother's parrot zipping around her parents' living room came to mind. "I went to see Shuba Aunty. She was one of my mom's closest friends, and I wanted to go check on her—that's all."

"I see." Julian appraised her from hairline to waist, his eyes searching every part of her that he could see from his vantage point across the desk. Then just as he did earlier in the breakfast room, he softened once more, transforming from imperious ruler to lovey-dovey new husband. "I understand, sweetheart. But you should have let me know where you were going. You have to let me in and confide in me. That's what a marriage is supposed to be."

His hypocrisy was stunning. Because how much had he already kept from *her*? But Advika couldn't let herself show even a hair's breadth of her true feelings. "I'm still learning," she said, inserting a hint of tremulousness in her voice. "I'm still getting used to this wife thing."

"Not just wife. Mrs. Julian Zelding." His teeth-baring grin returned, and although he might have been trying to convey delight, all Advika could think was that he resembled what the Big Bad Wolf must have looked like as he tried to convince Little Red he wouldn't eat her. "In fact, after this paparazzi mess, I really think you should come with me to Morocco. Let's not give them one more inch to extend the story. If we take away the oxygen completely, there will be no more fire left to burn."

"That's so kind, Julian, really. But . . . my friend Olive is going through a really bad breakup. I told her I'd spend some time with her this week and help her go through the breakup woes." She sighed dramatically. "Olive was there for me during a dark time. I can't leave her when she needs me."

Julian nodded sagely, as if he were a judge hearing oral arguments in a trial. Advika scooted backward in her seat. He wouldn't force her to go to Morocco, would he? That would be crazy. Even he wouldn't do that.

"Okay, darling. Help your friend. But stay closer to home the next few days while I'm out of town. No more visits to anyone without telling Aggie. And text me too, no matter the time difference. It'll help me feel better, especially being so far away from you." Julian added with a chuckle, "Perhaps even skip the coffee shop for now. Invite your friend to stay here if you like."

Advika agreed, even as she felt that she had just consented to a glamorous sort of house arrest. She just needed Julian out of the house, out of the country. Then she'd be able to breathe a bit and figure out her next move.

"One more thing." He returned the photos to the envelope and held it up like a white flag waving surrender. "This is why you need to not keep things from me. This could have been a disaster. I was easily able to squelch this, because there's not much of a story to be told with these images. But these tabloids, Addi. They have ways of taking the most innocuous photos and spinning all sorts of stories. We can't have that—we can't give them any fodder." Julian placed the envelope inside his desk drawer, and Advika heard the tiny ping of the drawer locking shut. "Also, if you have any more meetings with agents or someone else in the business, please don't keep that from me. We shouldn't keep secrets from each other. We need to be a united front, especially right now, when there are those who want to see us hurt."

No more secrets! Anu's voice cried out from deep within. *The nerve! The gall!*

"You're right," Advika told Julian firmly, already imagining typing the name Nova Martin into a search engine. "No more secrets."

CHAPTER SEVENTEEN

Say Anything...

ADVIKA ARRIVED AT OLIVE'S APARTMENT via a private car service, something Julian had insisted upon after she had asked to check on her friend in person and invite her to visit Wildwood. When they reached the beige, two-story apartment building with a mattress on the curb and empty boxes spilled across the sidewalk, the driver asked her if she was sure she had the correct address. Advika said, "Yep, this is it," then told him she didn't know how long it would take, but she would text him to keep in touch.

Olive, dressed in her all-black barista garb, waited for her at the building's entrance. When she opened the gate, it let out a squeak sounding like a hundred mice in a choir. Upon reaching Olive, Advika whispered, "Start crying. Be mopey and sad."

Her usual deadpan expression spun into an exaggeration of grief. "Advika, I'm miserable!" she yelled, before thrusting her face straight into Advika's chest, her shoulders heaving.

"There, there." Advika clapped her friend on the back with one hand, then gave an awkward wave to the driver, who nodded back. "Let's go in, honey."

"Honey?" Olive said once they were through the gate and passing through the courtyard. "What are you, a granny?"

"Shut up." Advika had actually been priding herself on her improv earlier that day with Julian, weaving all sorts of stories on a dime and her husband none the wiser. Of course Olive had to puncture her small bubble of self-satisfaction. "I was trying to comfort you. I'll explain when we get inside."

Olive's room was like being in Olive's brain. The two windows facing the courtyard had the shades drawn, with a single bare light bulb illuminating the room, which was even smaller than the one at the apartment she and Advika shared in Echo Park. But Olive maximized the tiny space, having devised a sort of entertainment center along the back wall made entirely of multicolored packing crates, containing her television, VCR, DVD player, mini-fridge, and a breathtaking array of records, videotapes, and DVDs. A digital video camera affixed to a plastic red handle lay on Olive's desk on top of five notebooks, which were stacked neatly in front of an eight-by-ten gold picture frame featuring adolescent Olive standing stone-faced in front of her parents and grandmother. Over the twin-size bed (black comforter, purple pillows) was a single movie poster for a film called *Saving Face*. It was weird to think how Advika had never entered Olive's bedroom during the time they were roommates. While Olive had been an unapologetic slob when they lived together, her room was defined by orderliness, reflecting a sort of quiet focus and ambition that Advika found surprising.

They both sat cross-legged on the bed, and Advika shared what had transpired the past few days and the excuse she made to come see Olive.

"You want me to come to your mansion?" Olive waved her arms around as if showing off a new sports car on a game show. "And give up all this?"

"You'd be doing me a huge favor. I'm starting to hate that place."

"And what if you just left and crashed with me instead? Or with someone else?"

"I thought of that. But he wants me to stay at Wildwood 'for my own protection,'" Advika said, making quotation marks with her fingers. "And he needs to think everything's fine between us until I figure out my next move."

"Hmm." Olive tapped her left eyebrow, as if calculating Advika's request. While she nervously waited for her friend's answer, trying not to cry out, *Pleeeeeease*, Advika glanced up at the movie poster. It featured two beautiful Chinese women, the older one in a wedding dress, the younger one looking over at her. The tagline called it a romantic comedy. Since when did Olive like rom-coms? In Advika's mind, Olive was Jane Lane from *Daria* in human form: acerbic, angular, and anti anything that had the slightest whiff of sentiment.

"Is there a pool?" Olive asked after several moments. Advika nodded, and Olive's taut mouth softened into a grin. "You know what? I have to go to work in about an hour, but after that I'll take a few days off. I bet Annabella would switch shifts with me—she says she needs time off for a shoot in August, but I think she's getting her boobs done."

"Thank you so much. It'll be a relief to have you there because…it's just getting weird." Advika leaned her head against the wall. "Those paparazzi photos really creep me out. I don't think I'll ever shake the idea that someone's always watching me."

"How do you know the tabloids took 'em? Maybe he had you followed. Like with a private detective." Olive pulled out a bag of gummy bears from the fridge and started snacking on them after offering it to Advika, who declined.

"Oh god, Olive, as if I'm not paranoid enough already."

"I'm just saying. Don't take his words at face value." Olive said this while chomping on an amalgam of red, green, and gold bears, their heads and bodies bobbing on her tongue as she spoke.

"No, you're right. I can't be sure of anything he tells me. Which reminds me. When you come over tomorrow, I need you to bring me something." She took out her wallet and handed Olive a hundred-dollar bill, which Olive accepted with wide eyes.

"What do you need, Mrs. Moneybags?"

Advika reached for the pack of green Post-its on Olive's desk and scribbled several items. When she handed it to Olive, she laughed.

"It feels like James Bond crossed with *High Fidelity*."

"That's my life these days: a mash-up of movie genres that barely make sense together." Advika stood up and grabbed her bag. "Looking forward to rooming with you again."

"Same," Olive said. "But just so you know, I still don't do dishes."

They exchanged goodbyes, and as Advika left her apartment and walked through the courtyard, with its rusted patio furniture, dead leaves in dusty corners, and piles of newspaper coupons and take-out menus scattered all over the ground like confetti, she longed to stay. This was where she belonged and where she wanted to be again. Somewhere real. Where she was a nobody with other nobodies, living their lives in blessed anonymity.

~

For Advika's final night with Julian before he departed for Morocco, he wanted to watch another movie, but this time in their home theater. When Advika initially demurred, the memory of their night at the Nuart still uncomfortably fresh in her mind, Julian vowed to be on his best behavior. Despite her misgivings, she agreed. After all, Advika wanted him to leave

Los Angeles feeling that their marriage was on firm ground and that he had a wife who was still deeply invested in their relationship.

The movie they screened was one Julian had produced, which didn't surprise her. Early on in their courtship, Advika had admitted she had only seen two of his films, which Julian had pretended didn't bother him, even as his blank smile and constant blinking indicated otherwise. So here they were, sitting in a darkened room, Advika with a cashmere blanket draped over her up to her neck and Julian sitting with his legs stretched out and crossed at the ankles as the words MADRE VALLEY flashed on the screen.

It was one of Julian's best picture winners, released in 1987—one year before Advika was even born, a fact that made her uneasy. Did Julian care that this prize-winning film existed before she did? Probably not. Although *Madre Valley* had received seven nominations and three wins, including the biggest prize, Advika hadn't really heard of it before. Some films are of their time and leave no impression beyond that; Julian's third Oscar-winning film was a prime example.

Madre Valley was a study in clichés that must have seemed groundbreaking in the mid-1980s. It was a Western overstocked with guns, shoot-outs, saloon girls, and rampaging Native Americans on horseback, yet it also tackled contemporary "issues": mental illness, domestic abuse, and an interracial relationship between a Mexican maid gradually going blind and the white priest determined to help her. Advika could barely keep her eyes open throughout. She always hated Westerns, but this one was particularly dull and imbecilic. She couldn't believe Julian had produced such a mess and then had been awarded for it.

Her thoughts drifted as she steeled herself to get through these final few hours with her husband. Advika feared what

Julian could do if he realized how much she knew about him, especially from her conversation with Lucia. Perhaps he already knew, but at this point, she could tell when Julian was guarded or suspicious of her actions by the degree to which his jaw would tense and how much he would crack his knuckles. At the moment, he seemed content, playing the attentive husband, which was a huge relief. Advika briefly closed her eyes, only to be startled by a dramatic crescendo in the film's score booming through the speakers.

"I see I have your undivided attention," Julian said, grabbing her wrist.

"I'm sorry?" She must have drifted off, but hopefully not for too long.

"You fell asleep, Addi," he muttered. He shook his head, adding, "The worst critics are those who merely aspire."

Smarting from his words, Advika wrenched away from his grip. "I'm just tired—that's all. It's no slight to you or your movie. Also, Westerns really aren't my thing." She gingerly massaged her wrist, surprised by the intensity of his hold on her.

"Ah." He muted the movie, which showed the priest and the maid having noisy, clothes-ripping sex in a barn. "Listen, Addi. You can't stay in your little rom-com bubble. You're limiting yourself and your talent. It's important to be exposed to all kinds of films. It will make you a better screenwriter and a more well-rounded person."

Advika's head whipped back as if she had been struck. Urging herself to breathe, Advika purposely looked past Julian, instead fixing her eyes on the Hollywood sign mural painted along the far wall. All Julian ever did was live, talk, and breathe movies. And just because she didn't like his shitty, xenophobic Western, Advika wasn't a talented writer or a well-rounded person? Everything within her wanted to push back on what he said. But to her surprise, Anu's voice calmed her down. *We need him to be happy when he leaves. Don't push his buttons.*

"I . . . I see your point." She took his hand in hers and kissed the tops of his knuckles. "I didn't mean to offend you. I'm sorry."

But for the first time perhaps ever in their marriage, Julian was not placated by one of her apologies. "I've given you everything, and you can't even keep an open mind."

"But I just said—"

"You probably think I'm old-fashioned, but you're the narrow-minded one. I've given you everything: a home, help with your career, a comfortable life. And yet you refuse to think seriously about starting a family, even though you know how important it is to me. You'll go see some aunty or a friend and take care of their needs. But what about me, Addi? What about your husband?" His voice caught in his throat. "I'm not getting any younger. And this is important to me."

To her shock, Julian bent forward and covered his face with his hands. Was he for real? It didn't matter. She had to ensure that he didn't get more emotional or start spinning out and finding reasons for him to stay or for her to go with him. And so she spilled out a monologue interspersed with all the words he wanted to hear: children, family, babies, home, love.

"You changed my life," she said, her voice crackling with genuine conviction, because that part was undoubtedly true. "I want to do this with you. We can talk about it when you get back—I promise. And we'll make a plan." Advika kneeled down at his side and carefully peeled back his hands. His mouth quivered, tears glinting in his eyes, and her affection for him briefly returned. Advika couldn't bear to see anyone in pain, even Julian. "Come on, baby; let's go upstairs." They stood up and embraced, and she let herself stay in his arms, listening to his heart beat through his cotton pullover.

"You'll be a wonderful mother," Julian whispered in her ear before they left the home theater. Advika hoped her face didn't betray her true feelings. She glanced at her watch before they climbed the stairs, his arm firm around her waist, wishing that time would fly faster to the hour that he would leave, putting an ocean between them.

CHAPTER EIGHTEEN

They Came Together

OLIVE'S ARRIVAL AT WILDWOOD WAS like throwing a New Year's Eve party in a mausoleum. Luckily, Aggie was out running errands and so missed Olive flouncing through the front door with a skip in her step, dropping a duffel bag and rolling suitcase with a clatter to the floor, then spinning in a circle as she marveled at Advika's home.

"You're supposed to be getting over a breakup, remember?" Advika murmured into her ear as she caught her in a hug midtwirl. "Try to be more sad. There's no one here, but I never know when one of the staff will pop in."

Olive eyed her strangely but nodded. After Advika led her to a guest room on the second floor, a bedroom that rivaled only the master in its ocean views ("Holy shit—I can feel my heartbreak healing already"), Olive took a gray plastic bag with the label MIKE'S MUSIC HOUSE from her duffel, which held the items Advika had requested. She brought it with her as Advika led her back downstairs and to a wooden bench at the far edge of the backyard.

"Here you go," Olive said, looking over her shoulder before giving Advika the bag. She peered inside and was relieved to see a prepaid smartphone, a Discman, and three CDs. "The first album was really hard to find. I nearly ordered it off of eBay until I saw Mike's had it."

"Thank you so much." Advika looked behind her as well and, satisfied that no one was home yet, took the burner phone from its box.

"Is this really necessary, this James Bond stuff?"

"I feel better having a phone he doesn't know about. Especially when it's just me and Mrs. Danvers." Olive looked at her blankly. "You never read *Rebecca*? Never mind."

Julian had left for the airport at 6:30 a.m., and before he left, he gave her a gift-wrapped box that he asked her to open if he didn't come home in time for their five-month anniversary. A few weeks ago, Advika would have melted at the gesture. But now, it was just the latest part of their relationship that called upon Advika to use the acting skills she didn't know she had. In this performance, which would turn out to be her final one in the limited series *The Zeldings*, she threw her arms around Julian, thanked him for being a thoughtful husband, and in a spontaneous gesture she quickly regretted, patted his butt. He offered to catch a later flight and squeezed her butt in return, noting that they hadn't had sex since their kitchen rendezvous about a week earlier. "Why not start trying now?" he said with a lascivious grin. Advika hurried him out by promising a "mind-blowing, sexy surprise" on their anniversary, whether they were reunited in Los Angeles or she came out for a visit. This promise was enough to finally get Julian on his way out the door.

But earlier that morning, before he thought she was awake, Advika had overheard him on the phone. It was a conversation that had not just confirmed her suspicions but raised new ones too.

"So I think Julian might be spying on me." Between furtive looks over her shoulder, she told Olive that upon returning from their honeymoon, Julian had given her a new laptop and brand-new phone, both the latest, priciest upgrades. Advika hadn't thought much about it, but once she learned about Evie and her will, and how little she knew of her husband's past, Advika had a nagging unease that grew over the past two weeks. She had thought the prospect of being followed by paparazzi was what had made her feel skittish and paranoid. But Julian's phone call before leaving Wildwood had enlightened her that the source of her paranoia was coming from inside her house.

"I overheard him talking to Mona, his assistant, before he left early this morning. The weird thing is that Mona is like a nonpresence in our lives. I met her once at his office. I kind of forgot that she exists. But Julian thought I was still asleep and took a call from her in my office."

"Ooh." Olive lightly slapped her thigh. "You listened outside the door?"

Advika nodded. "I heard him say something like, 'It's here. Yes, Mona, I'm sure.' And I heard him open my laptop and then close it. Then he added, 'I don't know. Come over and check yourself.'"

"Whoa." Olive sat at attention, and her feet crunched on a pile of dead leaves.

"Yeah. Whoa."

"But how could you tell he was opening your laptop?"

"I dropped it like two days after I got it. Yeah, I'm not proud. But ever since I did, it makes this creaking noise when I put the screen up or down."

"So you think that he's spying on you with these devices? But he's old. He wouldn't have the ability to do something that high-tech."

Advika pulled at a loose thread on the hem of her blouse. "Which is why I think Mona is doing it for him. Why else would she have to come here and check on something herself?"

She paused, then gritted her teeth. "Okay, I'm about to say something else that I know makes me sound like a basket case. You don't have to agree or disagree, but I just need to say it out loud."

"Okay. Shoot."

"After Julian left, I got a text from Mona asking me if I needed anything while Julian's away. And I told her not to worry about it, that Aggie—the house manager—picks up everything I need. And she texted back, 'Actually, I do that.' Mona said she either gives my stuff to Julian or drops it off with Aggie, and one of them passes it along to me. And now I'm wondering, how much of my business does Mona know? She picks up my dry cleaning, my prescriptions…my birth control." Advika said these last three words in a hushed tone. "Like, if she messed with it, how would I know?" In reaction to Olive's incredulous stare, Advika responded, "I know, I know. It all sounds crazy. But I can't trust anything here."

"Okay, yeah. Calm down. There's something not quite right with your husband—I one hundred percent agree. But all this other conspiracy and spy stuff—you're spinning out a bit. And I don't blame you!" Olive put her arm around Advika's shoulder. "But you are."

"But that's what it feels like to live here. I doubt everything, including myself. I need to get out."

"You mean…leave him?"

"That's why I wanted the burner phone. There's someone I need to speak to. Immediately."

⌒

A: Hi Sun, it's Advika. When you have a chance, can we talk?

(One minute later.)

S: Advi! I can be free in about 20 minutes. Does that work?

A: Yes! 🖤

S: 🖤🖤🖤

Advika broke out into weepy, relieved tears. She sensed that Sunita would be receptive if she reached out to her despite blocking the Oakies over a month earlier. But the reality of Sunita's enthusiasm caused all the fluttering emotions she had been keeping inside since Julian's departure to leak out like a punctured balloon.

Olive, who had gone inside to use the restroom, returned with two bottles of beer and a bag of pretzels. "I know it's only noon, but I figured you could use one. Also," she said, lowering her voice, "I met the house manager. She wasn't surprised to see me at all—knew my name, where I worked. It was kinda strange."

Advika wiped her tears away with a crumpled tissue she found in her jeans pocket. "Huh. I guess I should be surprised, but I'm not." Advika told Olive that she had gotten in contact with Sunita, and she would call her in a little while. "After we talk, I can give you a tour of this place if you like. And then maybe we can get some lunch?"

"Sure. Are you okay?"

"Yeah. I just got emotional after texting with Sun. It's been so long, and I didn't know for sure if she'd want to talk to me." Advika paused, then admitted, "I blocked her and my other childhood friends after they tried to dissuade me from being with Julian. They wanted to hold an intervention."

"Can I ask you something?" Olive said, a tiny piece of pretzel flying from her mouth. Advika nodded. "Why *did* you marry him?"

"You said I should!" She swallowed hard. Advika hadn't expected the question, and it felt like a kick in the face. For so long, she had been blaming herself for her predicament. As illogical as it was, she was now ready to blame someone else. "I called you and asked if I should get married, and you said yes." As soon as it was out of her mouth, she regretted it.

Olive snorted. "I only knew the broad strokes: he was rich, handsome, and worked in the movies. And he seemed good to you. I didn't know you had barely Googled the guy." She chugged her beer, then set it down hard next to her. "Don't put this on me."

"No." Advika sighed. "It's on me. I saw a happy ending and I leapt for it. If you had said no, I think I would have found a way to say yes." She turned to Olive and placed her hand on her forearm. "I'm sorry. Like you said, I'm spiraling. It's outta control."

"Well, if I were in your shoes, I don't know if I'd be any better."

"You wouldn't be in my shoes, Olive." Advika smiled sadly, then took a sip of her beer, which had gotten warm from sitting out in the sun.

The burner phone rang, and both of them jumped. Advika's heart sang to see that it was Sunita.

"Sun, hi," she said softly as she answered the call, holding in a sob with all her might. "Thanks for calling me. I know I don't—"

"Advika, I love you. Tell me what you need." Sunita's voice was laced with concern and urgency, unleashing Advika's tears for a second time.

"I don't deserve it, but I need your help. I'm going to mail you a copy of my prenup. Will you review it for me?"

Sunita didn't respond right away, but Advika heard her exhale, followed by her typing furiously on a keyboard. "Of course. Send it right now, and I'll take a look. Am I looking for anything in particular?"

"I don't know. I didn't even look—" Advika's voice faltered, and she pressed the back of her hand to her forehead, the extent of her naivety making her dizzy.

"That's okay," Sunita replied quickly. "I'll take a look. I'm just so happy to hear your voice."

"Ditto."

After they hung up, Advika picked up her warm beer and stared into the horizon for several moments, reflecting on the past few weeks. Then she stood up and poured it slowly out on the grass.

"What are you doing?" Olive jumped up and moved out of the path of the spilled beer.

"Pouring one out for Evie. If it weren't for her and her will, I'd still be . . . well, god knows what."

Olive grinned. "To Evie," she said, and then poured the remaining drops of her own beer on the ground too.

⌒

Advika made a show of taking Olive around Wildwood, using the tone of a braggy trophy wife as they toured the mansion. Both Aggie and Flora the housekeeper were downstairs when they came inside, and so Advika plastered on a smile as she showed Olive around, who didn't have to fake her awe at the sprawling, tastefully expensive manse. But she did have to fake being heartbroken when Advika formally introduced Olive to the two women, who clucked sympathetically as Olive sniffled and emitted several dramatic sighs.

"You're quite the actor," Advika whispered as they went up the staircase to Olive's guest room.

"Maybe I can win an Oscar." They opened the door and

plopped onto the bed. "By the way, where are Julian's Oscars? I don't remember seeing them around the house."

"He keeps them in his office. He has, like, fifty awards on his shelf, and he basically treats them all like bookends." Advika recalled holding one of Julian's Academy Awards at the diner on the night they met, and then the photo of the trophy wearing a Hawaiian shirt. How long ago that seemed, as if she had seen it in a movie years ago. "He's not really into awards."

"How come I didn't get to see his office?"

"Uh, he keeps it locked."

"Interesting," Olive said, stroking her chin as if she were a detective on a cop show. "No doubt all his skeletons are in that room."

"No doubt," Advika mused. Olive's question about his Oscars triggered a second, more recent memory, when Julian had shown her the paparazzi photos in his office. She was almost positive she had only seen four Oscars there, not five. Including one still wearing a Hawaiian shirt.

"Earth to Advika," Olive said, tapping her shoulder. "Are we, like, stuck here? Can we go and get a drink or something?"

"If we do, I'm supposed to tell Aggie and text Julian. For my protection, in case we get swarmed by paparazzi." Advika rolled her eyes. "I think let's just keep the peace for today, and I'll nurse you through your broken heart—"

"Ugh." Olive pulled off one sock and threw it on the floor.

"—and once they're lulled into complacency, we'll scale the palace walls."

"Got it." Olive yanked off the second sock and slingshotted it in Advika's direction. It landed on her knee.

"Gross." Even as she flicked it off, Advika couldn't stop smiling. How awesome to have someone in Wildwood actually on her side. She opened the Mike's Music House bag and took out a CD with Nova Martin's face on the cover. "I'm dying to give this a listen."

"Contestant number two, come on down." Olive took out the Discman and waved it in the air. "Let's see what you're all about."

CHAPTER NINETEEN

Music and Lyrics

THE MOOD OF THE HOUR (released September 2, 1981, by Mezzanine Records)

1. Lemon Trees
2. At Your Side
3. Paper Moon
4. Valentina
5. Wanderlust
6. Downbeat
7. Shadow Dance
8. Dream It Away
9. Martinis All the Time
10. No Chance
11. The Mood of the Hour

Vocals, guitar: Nova Martin
Bass, vocals: Dan Forworth
Keyboards: Phillip Stern
Drums: G. Henry

All songs by Nova Martin
(Adlana Publishing)

Produced by Hector T. Cano

Recorded at Hilgard Sound, Los Angeles

El amor es como el agua que no se seca.

They listened to the entire album three times in a row, occasionally talking but mostly just listening, lost in their own thoughts. The music was very lo-fi, mostly acoustic instruments that sounded like four people jamming together in a room. But to be honest, all the songs seemed a little samey-sounding. What Advika liked most was the pleasant silkiness of Nova's voice and her lyrics, which had a gentle simplicity, seemingly about the highs and lows of a relationship.

As the last song played, Advika's stomach grumbled. She and Olive had only had that bag of pretzels, having inadvertently skipped lunch to come upstairs for privacy. She craved Indian food, but not restaurant Indian food. Her mother's sambar, keema, and homemade mango pickle—that's what she suddenly wanted more than anything. But she'd settle for anything edible as long as it was available in supersized quantity. With Julian out of the country, was his private chef still going to prepare dinner for them? How lame that she barely knew how her house was run, or what she was supposed to do when her husband was not there.

"What time is it?" Olive said sleepily, curled up into a shell at the foot of the bed. She glanced at the time on her phone, then set it down. "How is it almost six already? Right about this time I'd be making some asshole writer his fourth latte with almond milk. Or emptying the trash." She rose up reluctantly, stretching her arms above her, first left, then right, then center. "This bed is incredible. If you told me it was made from angel wings, I'd believe you."

"What did you think of the music?" Advika didn't want to focus on the fact that at this time, if she would be doing anything, it would be staring at a computer screen, waging a silent war against her nemesis, the blinking cursor.

"Wait, so is this what you get to do all day? Hang out in these beautiful rooms, lead a life of leisure?" Olive stood up and walked to the window, which had an ocean view partially obscured by the oak trees.

"I don't get to do *anything.*" Advika tried not to sound exasperated. "I'm just expected to be his...I dunno. His wife."

"But you can still write, though, right?" Olive asked, still facing the window. With her drapey black blouse with bell sleeves, she had the silhouette of a bat. "He can't control that."

"It's complicated. He does control it, in his own way." Advika grabbed the CD case and stared at Nova's face on the cover. *I bet you would understand,* she thought. To Olive, she said, hoping to change the subject, "But what else about the music?"

"She sorta sounds like Eva Cassidy, maybe a little bit of Christine McVie." Olive finally turned around and sat down on the bed, landing on the edge with such force that Advika bounced up from the mattress.

"Who?"

"Do you listen to anything made before 2005?"

"Ha ha. I'm not a superbig music fan," Advika said, picking intently at her cuticles. "I know what I like, and I like Nova's voice." It was her first time saying Julian's second wife's name aloud. *Nova. Evie. Advika.* What was his last wife's name? Oh yeah—*Victoria.* How funny and strange that all four women had the letter *v* in their names. What else did the four of them have in common besides Julian?

"Oh good." Olive was looking at her phone, and Advika moved an inch closer to see that she was scrolling through Twitter. "There's a major protest happening at HappyFunTimes this weekend."

"What happened?" Advika said idly, her eyes trained on her nails, where she had snagged a loose piece of skin and revealed a pinprick of blood.

"What do you mean 'What happened?'" Olive threw a surprised glance at Advika. "It's been all over the news for days." She explained that the family-entertainment megaconglomerate was under fire after a whistleblower revealed the extensive and appalling human rights violations at the factories used to manufacture their apparel. "HappyFunTimes breaks the law, but the whistleblower is the one who gets thrown in jail on trumped-up charges. Like, what the fuck?"

"Oh." Advika couldn't think about that right now. Not when her own life was so screwed up.

"You don't care?"

"Of course I do." Advika didn't sound convincing, even to herself. "But what can I do about it?" She gestured at her friend's phone clenched in her hand. "See? That's why I quit Twitter a long time ago," she added. "It's a bad-news parade. I can't take it."

"You can't put your head in the sand." Olive's know-it-all tone reminded Advika of Anu. "This affects—"

"I get it. But I'm stressed as it is." This was the one part of her sister she didn't need back in her life. Anu's earnest, verging-on-sanctimonious, "save the world" speechifying resulted in a lot of arguments between them. But she didn't want to fight with Olive. "I just have a lot going on right now, you know?"

Olive opened her mouth, as if wanting to say more. Advika steeled herself for a self-righteous response, so she was surprised when her friend changed the subject.

"I'm getting hungry." Olive jammed her phone into her back pocket. "What do you have to eat around here? Because you know, I'm so heartbroken over my ex, Sven—"

"Sven?"

"Sure—Sven. Why not?" Olive shrugged. "He's a masseur. I really miss the free massages. Anyway, what's for dinner?"

"We can Postmate something. Pick a place—whatever you want," Advika said eagerly, glad to be talking about something else. She checked her phone, then Googled the time difference between LA and Morocco. "I wonder if he's landed yet. He hasn't texted."

"It's a pretty long flight, at least ten hours. Enjoy the silence." Olive picked up her socks from the floor and put them back on. "That was a Depeche Mode reference, by the way."

"Who?" Advika asked distractedly, weighing whether she should ask Aggie if she had heard from Julian yet.

"Who, who? What are you, an owl?" Olive laughed.

"I don't know why you're testing me. I never claimed to be a music expert." Advika was tempted to throw a pillow at her head. "C'mon—let's go figure out dinner."

Advika listened to Nova's second album, *Nova Martin*, by herself after dinner. The private chef had been retained after all, and a white Margherita pizza with calamari and garlic bread awaited them in the kitchen. Advika's last memory of dining on pizza at Wildwood wasn't a happy one, and so she had eaten mechanically while having the title track of *The Mood of the Hour* stuck in her head. Olive had gobbled her slices while playing a game on her phone, and they hadn't talked much as they ate. Aggie, who was staying on full-time in Julian's absence, had peeked in on them before retiring to the pool house. After she had gone, Olive got up from the table and announced she was going to bed. When Advika pointed out it was only seven thirty, Olive straight-facedly replied, "A long bath in my very large bathtub should help soothe my broken heart." Advika had winced as Olive dropped her plate, glass, and cutlery in the farmhouse sink with a clatter and murmured, "Good night," before leaving the dining room.

Something had changed between them while they were listening to Nova's first album. The source of Olive's sudden irritability was a total mystery. Who cared if Advika didn't follow every news headline or know some stupid songs from before she was born? She was fighting for her freedom from a very powerful man. A man who had called her at 8 p.m. as she lay prostrate in bed, facedown on the mattress. Julian's phone call was thankfully brief, just long enough for him to tell her the trip was exhausting, the food on the flight was no better than McDonald's, and he couldn't wait to pass out in his hotel room before having to be on set in a few hours. He neglected to ask how she was doing, which was fine by her, because she didn't want to prolong the conversation.

After they hung up, Advika reached for the Discman on the bedside table. She had picked up the CD player and Nova's albums from Olive's room on the way to her own. When Advika had opened the door after knocking several times, Olive had been in the en suite bath with the door closed and some hard rock music playing at medium volume, just like she used to do when they shared an apartment. By becoming roommates again, even temporarily, the passive aggression and pointed silences of their former relationship seemed to have been reawakened. She couldn't deal with Olive's out-of-nowhere about-face on top of everything related to Julian. With a deep sigh, she popped *The Mood of the Hour* out of the Discman and replaced it with *Nova Martin*.

NOVA MARTIN (released April 5, 1984, by Warner Bros.)

1. **Silence (Sunrise)**
2. **Prelude to a Dream**
3. **Rainbow High Above**

4. Love Don't Stop
5. If Only You Knew
6. Honey
7. All Your Roses
8. Right Away
9. Feathers on the Grass
10. Sunset

Vocals, guitar: Nova Martin
Electric and slide guitar: Roger Deans
Bass, vocals: Dan Forworth
Keyboards: Phillip Stern
Drums: G. Henry

All songs by Nova Martin
(Adlana Publishing)

Produced by Trevor Johns

Recorded at BeachRide Studios, Los Angeles

This album felt more expensive, for lack of a better word. There were more instruments in Advika's ears—tambourines and strings and something zippy and electric—plus more-prominent background vocals singing along with Nova. She didn't dislike it, but now Advika had a warmer feeling for Nova's first album and how spare and simple it was compared to this collection of songs, which, to her ears, sounded like a bunch of musicians all trying to be heard above the others. Nova was still wonderful despite it; strangely, her voice was what kept the whole thing from sounding like a runaway train in danger of skidding off the tracks.

In the dim lamplight of her bedside table, Advika pored over the album cover and liner notes. The cover artwork was an arresting black-and-white image showing only Nova's deep-set eyes and forehead, which was covered by a lush fringe of bangs. Her name was spelled out above her head in graffiti-like font. Unlike *The Mood of the Hour*, Nova's second album featured more photos as well as lyrics to all of the songs. As Advika studied the lyrics, identifying the ones she liked, her eyes latched onto three words in the corner.

FOR DARLING JULIAN

Advika's shock at seeing the dedication dissipated once she remembered that Julian and Nova had already been married for two years when the album came out. The word "darling" conveyed so much sweetness and warmth, and rather than the stabs of jealousy Advika experienced when reading about Julian's marriage to Evie, this glimpse of his relationship with Nova only made Advika uneasy.

The middle of the CD booklet included a series of photos of Nova in a studio setting, alternately smiling and frowning, wearing an asymmetrical sweatshirt that artfully exposed her left shoulder and clavicle. Only one photo featured two people: a man and woman shown from the back, the wind tousling their hair, as they walked hand in hand along the beach. Nova and Julian. Advika found herself trying to enlarge the photo with her thumb and index finger, just as she would have done on a phone or tablet screen, before shaking her head at herself. But that's how much she wanted to peer closely at these two, who radiated an easy intimacy Advika never really saw with photos of Julian and Evie.

It was time to learn more about Nova Martin. A Google search of her name reminded Advika of her one and only brief conversation with Julian about his ex-wives, and Nova was the only one he had spoken about with actual feeling. Not only that, but he had even compared Advika to Nova. Something about them both having "sensitive souls." Was it just a line he fed Advika, or did Julian truly mean it?

As she clicked through the lineup of photos of dead, gorgeous Nova, she listened to *Nova Martin* on repeat. A song called "If Only You Knew" played as Advika scrolled through photos of Nova with luscious brown waves and Cleopatra-esque eyeliner, tenderly holding a guitar; Nova with superteased hair resembling a frizzed-out waterfall careening off the side of her head, singing into a microphone; Nova in a white toga-like gown at a party, smiling as she stood next to Julian; Nova with stick-straight hair, looking away from the camera, her eyelashes superlong and her lips pouty and sad. As she took in these various versions of Nova, Advika listened to her sing the following:

If only you knew
The effect of your heart
If only you knew
This love would never start
But you knew
And I did too

Advika didn't really pay attention to the lyrics. But she was drawn by the way Nova elongated the word "you," holding the note for several long, impressive beats, so it sounded like "But youuuuuuuuuuuuuuu knew," followed by the quick and resigned way she sang, "And I did too." Later on, once she learned more about Nova's life and untimely death, Advika would revisit these lyrics—and how these words summing up the essence of Nova and Julian's relationship would be heartbreaking.

For hours she clicked through the first fifty results for *Nova Martin*: fan sites, lyric pages, anniversary tributes. Too many of these remarked on the irony of her sharing a name with a type of star that burned out bright and fast. But this wasn't entirely accurate, since the Merriam-Webster definition for "nova" was "a star that suddenly increases its light output tremendously and then fades away to its former obscurity in a few months or years." To Advika, that truly seemed to capture the trajectory of Nova's career, as she learned from the singer's VH1 *Behind the Music* episode, which IMDb stated had aired in 2002. Only a few clips had been uploaded, ranging from three to five minutes in length, leaving Advika to fill in the blanks via Nova's Wikipedia page and a brief biography on Billboard.com.

BEHIND THE MUSIC: NOVA MARTIN (part 3 of 15)

NARRATOR: Nova Martin met her future husband, Julian Zelding, at a party in May 1981.

LARK TENNER [*best friend*]: I was there that night. These two were magnets. It was just like this. [*she moves her hands apart, then makes a whizzing sound as she quickly claps them together*] But Nova was still not over her breakup with Emilio. I think Julian tried his best to charm her, but Nova wasn't ready for that.

According to Wikipedia and then doing the math based on their birth years, Julian was thirty-three and Nova was twenty-three when they met. Advika raised an eyebrow when she learned their age difference.

NARRATOR: But Julian seemed determined to woo the young singer. A month after the release of *The Mood of the Hour*, Julian arranged for a business lunch between them. He told her he was a fan of her album and wanted to include one of her songs in one of his movies.

ANDIE MCPILL: [*Mezzanine Records label mate and friend*]: "Andie, Andie!" Nova had said, running up to me. "He said I was better than Joni Mitchell! I told him he needed to get his ears checked." We both laughed.

But Nova had been flattered—I could tell. The business meeting had just been a pretense to see her again, and they started dating not long after that.

NARRATOR: In fact, one of their first dates was to the 1982 Academy Awards. Nova was Julian's date to the ceremony, where he won his second Oscar for best picture as a producer for *Run*. [*A video clip shows Julian and Nova reacting as* Run *is announced as the winner. Nova wears a glittery baby-blue sheath dress with white gloves. When Julian's name is announced, he leans over, grabs Nova's face, and kisses her hard, before leaping out of his seat.*] Nine months later, they were married.

"Ugh," Advika said as the clip ended. She replayed the Oscar win a few more times, trying to gauge if Nova was as enthusiastic to receive the kiss as Julian was to give it. But the clip cut off right after the word "married," so it was too hard to tell. Since she couldn't find part 4 online, she moved on to the next clip, right into the midst of Nova's ascendant career.

BEHIND THE MUSIC: NOVA MARTIN (part 5 of 15)

NARRATOR: Buoyed by the success of her second album, *Nova Martin*, including a Top 20 single with "Love Don't Stop," Martin's record label wanted her to make a push for mainstream stardom.

LARK TENNER: She didn't really want to be the next Madonna or Whitney. She liked writing songs on a guitar, playing at small venues like the Troubadour. But the record label was pushing for it, thinking she had the potential to break big. And so did Julian. Nova didn't like letting people down. I heard someone once refer to her attitude as "being a good soldier."

NARRATOR: Julian had been instrumental in bringing Martin to Warner Bros. for her second album and now took on an even more prominent role in Nova's career. With 1987's *All My Desire*, he asked some of the biggest songwriters and producers in the industry to work on her album, including highly respected veterans who had produced number-one hits for Heart, Jefferson Starship, and more.

HERB LAWRENCE [*Nova Martin's manager, 1981–1984*]: He went from her de facto manager to her official manager. It wasn't a coincidence that once his movies started tanking, he got more interested in his wife's career. She didn't fight for me, but I think she would have preferred I stayed on. I know for a fact she didn't want to give up writing her own songs in favor of those dimwitted guys with too much hair spray. But out of all the people who had a vested interest in Nova Martin Inc., Nova herself had the least input.

NARRATOR: Many from Nova's inner circle point to the "Diamond Nights" music video as a symbol of the clash between Nova's sensibilities and those of Julian and her record label. It was the lead single off of her third album and represented the pop direction they wanted her to go.

ANDIE MCPILL: She hated it. You can see it in her face!

[*A music video clip plays with Nova lip-syncing as she drives around in a convertible, arriving at a dinner party where all the guests are movie star impersonators: Elvis, Marilyn Monroe, James Dean, Judy Garland, Elizabeth Taylor. She frets as the guests get into a food fight, smashing dishes and throwing pies in each other's faces. The video is a sloppy, colorful mess, and Nova's lip sync is so half-hearted that the editing can't always hide how out of sync she is with the words. In fact, the Marilyn Monroe impersonator, with her bounteous chest and overdrawn red lips, seems to be more prominent in the video than Nova.*]

That's not Nova's style. Anyone who heard "The Mood of the Hour" and "Diamond Nights" wouldn't think these two singers existed on the same planet. This is the one time she put her foot down, though: she never filmed another music video again.

NARRATOR: Nova may have disliked the video, but it caught on at MTV, which put it into heavy rotation one week before her album came out. *All My Desire* debuted at number twelve on the Billboard album charts, and "Diamond Nights" peaked at number seven on the singles chart. Nova's first-ever national tour, which was supposed to take place in theaters, got bumped up to bigger venues, including some arenas. But despite all her success, she was misera—[*clip cuts off*]

The next clips—parts 7, 9, 13, and 14—painted an increasingly tragic picture of Nova plunging into depression over the shiny pop trajectory of her career. Her national tour skidded to a halt after only one-third of the dates. Her management claimed she had to take time off the road for exhaustion, but rumors swirled, ranging from depression to rehab. As Nova's tale of woe continued, with her friends sharing how she decided to quit the music business rather than continue on with a path that didn't feel authentic to her, Advika tingled with recognition. Just like Evie, Nova left behind something she loved after interference from Julian. No matter how well-intentioned he might have been, he only wanted her to succeed on the terms he deemed worthy. Even though Julian seemed to truly love his second wife, in the end he had driven her out of the industry.

One final *Behind the Music* clip of Nova's remained, but Advika wasn't ready to watch the conclusion. Nova's death could bring back too many echoes of Anu's. The shock, the grief, the beautiful words expressed about a young life gone too soon. Maybe Olive could watch it with her, lend her a little moral support.

Another aspect troubled Advika. She had waited for Julian to make an appearance in the episode to discuss Nova, but he never had. In fact, Julian seemed markedly disinterested in participating in upholding her legacy, a sentiment she picked up from her online research. After her death in 1991, Nova gradually returned to the obscurity in which she had begun her career. Her musical output neatly fell into two categories— cult singer-songwriter and two-hit wonder—yet neither type of music seemed to have much staying power in the public consciousness. Nova hadn't ever experienced a major revival in popularity like some of her peers, and it appeared largely due to the unavailability of her music, which could not be streamed on Spotify. Her hit singles and music videos were on YouTube, and someone named "SuperNovaFan72" had uploaded ninety-second clips of each song from *The Mood of the Hour* onto the site. But otherwise, Nova's music was hard to find, at least on the internet. In the comments for a fan-made lyric video for one of the songs on *All My Desire*, there was a spirited conversation about why Nova's music wasn't more widely available. "It's her husband," one commenter wrote. "He owns the rights to her music but has done shit with them. I read about it in an interview with her mother and brother. They hate the guy."

"Ooh," Advika said softly, stifling a yawn. That was a tantalizing detail worth pursuing tomorrow. She stretched out in bed, the first time she had the plush, king-sized mattress to herself since getting married, and tried to envision Julian curled up with Nova, wondering if he had wrapped his arms around her waist and kissed her left shoulder, then her right, as they drifted off to sleep together. Nova and Julian were still tangled in Advika's thoughts as she fell asleep, and in her dream, she was at the dinner party from the "Diamond Nights" music video. But the only guests were Evie, Nova, and the real Marilyn Monroe, the three of them staring at Advika with judgment but also concern.

CHAPTER TWENTY

That Uncertain Feeling

OLIVE WASN'T IN HER ROOM. Advika had knocked softly, then entered on tiptoe at 8:45 a.m., even though she had planned to wait until nine before checking on her. But it didn't matter, because Olive was gone. Her duffel bag slumped in the corner and a wad of socks at the center of the unmade bed were the only evidence she had even slept there that night. Advika wiped away the sleep crusts from her eyes, as if clearer vision would help communicate why her friend had left and where she had gone. At least Olive had to come back, if for nothing else than to retrieve her belongings. Advika surveyed the room, bemused by how Olive's haphazard messiness had once been such an irritant and was now strangely reassuring.

Advika returned to her room and found a text message waiting for her from Julian: How are you, love? Miss you. Advika didn't respond. Instead, she busied herself getting ready, going through the motions of teeth brushing and showering and the rest of the morning rituals, resentful and exhausted at having to even bother. If there was no house manager lurking around, Advika would have put on sweats and an oversized tee. Why bother getting dressed up when sitting around the house? But to live in a place like Wildwood was to always feel the need to be presentable, to prove you belonged among the expensive furniture and expansive ocean views.

But as she came downstairs, wearing dark jeans and a billowy scarlet top with matching lipstick, Advika was relieved she had made an effort. Someone was chatting with Aggie in the kitchen, and it wasn't Olive. She slowed her steps so that she could perhaps overhear what was being discussed, but the staircase squeaked on the lowest step, and the low, chatty hum of voices paused, then resumed. Advika entered the kitchen and nearly stubbed her toe on the entryway when she saw whom the house manager was chatting with: Mona. The two stood on opposite ends of the island, and when Aggie saw Advika gaping at them, she nodded in Advika's direction. Mona whipped around and hurried toward Advika. She was dressed like a stylish librarian, with chic, wire-frame glasses and a navy blue shirtdress and black heels, and her chestnut hair was swept up in an immaculate ponytail. Advika ran her fingers through her bangs, fluffing them nervously.

"Addi! How are you?" Mona swallowed her in a hug, the force of which caused Advika to stumble backward.

"Hi, Mona; nice to see you," Advika said right before they disentangled from each other, Mona's tennis bracelet crashing against Advika's watch.

"Are you missing Julian? It's the first time you newlyweds have been apart, right?" Mona had the Los Angeles quality of seeming ageless; depending on the angle, she either looked twenty-five or forty-five. She had struck Advika as much more serious and interesting during their first meeting. Now, Mona was acting like her gal pal. Advika faked a smile.

"Yeah. It's been a little tough, but we're making it work." She remembered Julian's good-morning text, which she still hadn't responded to. "The time difference makes it a bit challenging, though." They both walked over to the island and sat on adjacent stools. Aggie had disappeared but could be heard around the corner on her phone. "What brings you by?"

Between loud sips of coffee, Mona told Advika that because of the recent tabloid attention, Zelding Productions was upgrading security features on all the office computers. Julian had recommended that his and Advika's personal laptops be upgraded as well.

"Oh." Advika said. *Shit.* She should have been prepared for this; she had basically heard her husband tell Mona to come over and check Advika's computer. But it still caught her off guard, especially since last night after going on a tear doing Google searches about Nova. Had she used an incognito browser? Did she have time to delete her search history? "Well, I kind of need it. I'm working on something."

"Oh yeah?" Mona said brightly. "I promise it won't take more than twenty-four hours tops." Advika was sitting so closely to Mona that she could see how tautly her skin was stretched over her features, all covered in a thick layer of makeup. Despite this, she still looked effortless. "Um, is something wrong? Is there something in my teeth?"

"Sorry—didn't mean to stare! But your skin is beautiful. What kind of products do you use?" Advika patted her cheeks with her fingertips, as if tucking away stray pimples.

"Thank you!" Everything Mona said had the overdone exuberance of three exclamation points. She tucked a strand of hair behind her ear, then examined Advika's face and looked her up and down. "Actually, I'm so glad you brought it up." She lowered her voice. "You are so gorgeous. I mean, wow. But listen. Julian will never say it, but you have to start looking the part more, you know?"

Advika sat back, smarting as if Mona had doused her with ice-cold water. "What part?"

"He's a big deal. You know that. And he gets invited to a lot of big events and parties, especially come fall. Now's a good time to work on developing your look. You know, so it can be complementary to Julian." Mona returned to her former sunshine tone. "I can help! We can get you a glam squad just like the Kardashians..."

Advika nodded, equal parts mortified and relieved. She was happy to have a reason to distract Mona from her laptop, but doing so by letting Mona rattle on with a detailed critique of her face and body was torture. Advika thought of delicate, doomed Nova and how she was barefaced and radiant on the cover of her first album, and by the third one, she looked like a child had applied her makeup with crayon, coloring outside the lines with wild neons. Nova, whose face was the first thing Mona would see if she opened her laptop. She had to get rid of Mona—now.

"Oh, that'd be great," Advika said, cutting her off. She rose up off her stool. "Could we start now? I've...I've been embarrassed and didn't know who to talk to about it. I've actually been watching makeup tutorials, trying to improve my game, but obviously I could do better. But how great would it be to surprise Julian with all this? I'd love to stun him."

"Uh, sure!" Mona said, surprise splattered all over her face. "But first, let me get that laptop. Really got to make sure you're protected." She stood up too, then looked at her watch. "Actually, I gotta get to the office soon. What about tomorrow afternoon? We could go to Rodeo Drive, give you a whole *Pretty Woman* makeover thing."

"Oh, I can't. I have—" Advika didn't have to make up an excuse, because at that moment, the doorbell rang. "That must be my friend Olive. She's staying with me while Julian's out of town."

"Is that so? Well, you go tend to your friend, and if you could just point me to—"

Advika heard the front door open and Olive's hurried steps heading to the staircase.

"Olive!" she cried out, then hopped off her stool, hoping to wave her down. To Advika's relief, Olive entered the kitchen. She was wearing a blue mesh tank top, black shorts, and white running sneakers. Her chest sparkled with perspiration. "Hey, what's up?" She gave Mona a curious glance.

"This is Mona, Julian's assistant." It occurred to Advika how strange it was to have Olive staying in Julian's home, meeting several of Julian's employees, yet not having met her husband. "This is my good friend Olive. Mona's come by to pick up my laptop." When Mona turned around and said hello, Advika raised her eyebrows and gave her friend a pointed look.

"Oh. Cool. Well, I was about to go upstairs. I can go grab it for you."

"Oh, wonderful!" Mona clapped her hands in delight.

Advika sank back onto her stool. She barely listened as Mona recommended she straighten her hair and follow an intensive thirty-day skin care routine that would clean up her "trouble spots." Olive's behavior yesterday was confusing, but now it was like she was replaced by a pod person. Her heart sank when Olive returned to the kitchen, her laptop in hand. Mona grabbed it like she was afraid it would disappear, gave Advika an air kiss, and hustled toward the door. Once it slammed shut, Olive groaned and said she was going to take a shower. Advika followed her upstairs, walking behind so closely she nearly stepped on her heels. Olive entered the guest bedroom, and Advika followed her in and closed the door.

"What the hell, Olive?" she hissed. "How could you—"

"Don't worry. I saved all your stuff on a flash drive, then gave it a hard reset. It's pretty much like giving her a blank page of paper."

"Ohmigod. Thank you." Advika collapsed onto the bed like

wet spaghetti. "I thought it was like *Invasion of the Body Snatchers*. Like you had been turned by them."

"Nah," Olive said. "But if they bribed me enough, I could be tempted." There was the slightest edge in her voice on that last word. "Can I talk to you, though?"

"Sure. Of course. Sorry to have doubted you. I wasn't expecting Mona here and she just arrived out of nowhere and—"

"I think I'm gonna go." Olive peeled off her tank top, revealing a gray sports bra splotched with sweat. "Like, go back home."

"But why?" Advika sat up, shocked.

"Because this isn't working for me. I'm not the Watson to your Sherlock Holmes. I have a life. I have credit card debt. I have to get back to the real world."

"You can't leave me here—"

"What—I can't leave you in a mansion, waited on hand and foot by a staff?" Olive kicked off her sneakers, and a rubbery, sweaty odor soon filled the room. "You're not Rapunzel, you know. Stranded in a tower. You have autonomy."

"But I literally don't. That's why I asked you to stay here. To help me out."

"I feel bad for you, Advika—I do. But being here...it's not good for me."

"Where is this all coming from?" Advika sprang up and resisted the urge to shake Olive by her narrow shoulders. "You just gave Mona my laptop, knowing she's going to spy on me with it. I'm surrounded by people I can't trust. And now you're just going to leave?"

"My life doesn't revolve around you, okay?" Olive wriggled out of her shorts and kicked them toward her duffel bag. "Listen, you have Sunita and your other friends. But I can't keep losing myself in your problems. I have my own stuff to worry about. As long as Julian's not here, you'll be fine." She walked into the bathroom and shut the door. Advika stared after her for several moments, then fell back onto the bed, smacking her hand over her eyes.

⁓

After Olive had silently packed up and abandoned her, Advika went into her office and shut the door. She ordered herself not to cry. Because maybe Olive was right, and Advika had been depending on her too much, almost using her as a substitute twin. (That included asking Olive to do one last thing for her before she left: mailing her prenup paperwork to Sunita using next-day delivery.) Advika had to figure out her predicament on her own.

And that started with retrieving her original Dell laptop from the bottom drawer of her desk, the one with a zigzag crack that she had gratefully retired after Julian had given her a MacBook Pro. Somehow it still worked, but only when the screen was exactly bent back at a specific angle; otherwise, the screen would fritz over like television filled with static. As she moved it up and down and then back again, trying to find the right angle, Advika's thoughts again went to Nova. What was there to know about her beyond what was presented in the media, especially when Julian seemed to exert so much control over her music? Speaking with Lucia had been so important to understanding Evie better, Advika mused as she shuffled Nova's CDs like an oversized pack of cards. And then: a lightning flash of inspiration.

At first she went to log in to Facebook, but the sight of the blue-and-white logo reminded her that she had deactivated her account several weeks after Anu's death. So instead, she logged in to her LinkedIn account, which embarrassingly had not been updated since her college graduation. If Facebook had been a quagmire of painful memories, then LinkedIn was a sad litany of internships and part-time gigs, a graveyard of her professional failures. And even though the latter account was set to private, she winced as she saw fifty-two messages waiting for her, some from as recent as last week. If it was anything like her Instagram account, more than half were inquiries about Julian and Evie's will. Advika closed her eyes and shook her head. She was tired of how much of her life seemed to revolve around the past, and not just hers, but also her husband's.

Once her nerves were steadier, Advika took out the CD booklet for *The Mood of the Hour* and set about seeing if she could find any of the names listed in the liner notes on LinkedIn. She found three of them: the album's cover art designer, and two of the people included in Nova's list of thank-yous, Alma and Inez. With tingles revving along her spine, Advika sent them the same message, introducing herself as Julian Zelding's wife and wanting to ask a few questions about Nova and her marriage. It was a gamble, because there was a chance one of them could tip off the press. But considering how much the people in Nova's orbit seemed to dislike Julian, she doubted that would happen.

As Advika downloaded the LinkedIn app to her burner phone so she would receive alerts if anyone wrote her back, she heard a large clatter on the first floor as if something heavy had fallen to the ground. A quick run to the banister and a peek downstairs showed that the fancy vacuum cleaner had toppled on its side, resembling a beached whale. Without thinking, she went down and lifted it back up and met the gaze of a frightened older woman she had never seen before.

"So sorry!" the woman repeated over and over.

"It's okay. It's fine—not even a scratch." The woman looked vaguely familiar, having the same pointy chin and hangdog expression as Flora. "Are you . . . do you know Flora?"

The woman beamed and nodded emphatically. "My daughter. She needed to go to the doctor's at the last minute. I came in her place." She peered closely at Advika. "Mrs. Zelding?"

"Yes. That's me." Advika realized she was stepping on the cord and moved off it. She looked from the vacuum to Flora's mother and then back again. This machine was way too heavy for the older woman to maneuver by herself.

"Let me help you. Where are you going?" Mrs. Flora gestured toward Julian's office and fished a set of keys out of her pocket. How could the Flora family (she regretfully didn't know Flora's last name) have access to Julian's office and not her? Inwardly, Advika fumed. Outwardly, she smiled solicitously and helped steer the monster vacuum toward the office two doors away.

After they had both entered, Mrs. Flora set about her work, dusting and vacuuming and emptying wastebaskets while Advika stayed in the room, pretending as if it were natural to sit at her husband's desk and read the various scripts piled on it. She watched Flora's mother fastidiously clean the office, waiting for the moment that she would finish her work and expect Advika to leave Julian's office with her. But Mrs. Flora didn't. She wrapped up her final tasks, then thanked Advika for her help. Advika's heart seized and magnified in her chest as the door shut, leaving her in the only room in Wildwood she had never visited solo.

It was just past 1 p.m., which meant that Aggie was having her weekly lunch date with her goddaughter. But if she was acting as Julian's watchdog, she wouldn't be gone very long. Advika leapt out of the chair and made a beeline toward the bookcase. The wall of shelves was crowded with books and trophies and a few framed photos, all of which seemed to have been taken at least twenty years ago. She double-checked Julian's Oscars and indeed only saw four of them. Even though Julian no longer seemed to care about winning Oscars, did that really mean he wouldn't keep all of them together in one place? She spotted the *West of the Gun* Oscar on the bottom right shelf, next to three Philip Roth novels and a framed photo of a gap-toothed little boy sitting on an old man's lap, his expression stern and a pipe emanating from his lips like a stuck-out tongue. Julian and Pappy, his beloved grandfather. Little Julian had his tiny hand wrapped around something hanging from his grandfather's neck. *Pappy's cross*, Julian had told Advika on their fifth date when she had asked him about his most valuable possession. But Advika had never once seen it—he didn't wear it and had never mentioned it again. Where did Julian keep his most valuable possessions? *Hidden, of course.* Anu's voice came in bright and clear like an elbow jabbed playfully in her side.

First, Advika tried Julian's desk, but all the drawers were locked. Then she returned to the bookcase, scanning every shelf from top to bottom, not knowing what she was looking for. Julian had to have a safe. Didn't he? One of those old-fashioned kinds she'd seen on *Columbo*, with a gigantic combination lock that a safecracker could open with a stick of dynamite. The top level of books had a coat of dust on them that neither Flora nor her mother could reach. So likely not anywhere near there. Advika tried her best to jog her memory and see if anything seemed changed since she had last been in this office a few days ago. After several minutes of furtive scanning while listening for the opening of the front or side doors, Advika noticed something odd. All the books lining the shelves had titles on their spines. But at the far-left end of the middle row were two black leather books with blank spines. With a deep breath while standing on her tiptoes, she tried pulling out the first book, then the second. Neither budged. So Advika yanked on both at the same time, and a wood panel at the bottom of the center shelf nudged open a crack. Advika pried it open with the hem of her shirt, not wanting to leave fingerprints. And there it was: Julian's safe.

It was a slim wall of dark blue concrete with a giant combination lock at its center. Advika didn't think twice. Having already memorized Nova's birthday, she tried the combination and had flashbacks to being assigned her first-ever high school locker. At the time, she had struggled to get it open, not understanding the right-left-right turns that granted access. But now, Advika's fingers were flying on instinct: 11-left, 04-right, 57-left. With a dramatic snap, the lock's tumblers gave way and the safe door opened. Advika glanced at her watch. It was only 1:30. Advika prayed to the LA traffic gods that Aggie was smack-dab in the middle of afternoon traffic somewhere on the 101. Just as she was about to reach inside, Advika stopped herself and took out her phone. In a move borrowed from her twin sister when a not-yet-licensed Anu took her parents' car keys before sneaking out in the middle of the night, Advika snapped a photo of the safe's contents so she could put everything back exactly as Julian had it, and hopefully he'd never know she had entered his inner sanctum. At last, rather than being spied upon, Advika could now nose around in his business for once.

Sitting cross-legged on the Persian rug, Advika carefully took out each item and placed it in a semicircle across from her. A white jewelry box containing a gold cross, which had to have belonged to Julian's grandfather. A stack of cassette tapes, labeled with dates ranging from 1981 to 1991 in swoopy handwriting and written in faded pencil. An almost-empty bottle of perfume called Bienvenue, a fragrance Advika had never heard of before. She took off the seashell-shaped top and sniffed it, getting the faintest aroma of lilies. There was also a small manila envelope with several photographs: some black-and-white prints but mostly Polaroids. And finally, a notebook.

Save for Pappy's cross, this was fully a shrine to Nova—there were no jewelry or pricey watches or gold bars or anything else that the wealthy usually stored in their safes. Just these simple items. Did Julian visit it often? Every item seemed surprisingly free of dust, so perhaps. Advika tried to picture Julian with the contents of the safe spread out before him, examining each artifact of his past, maybe even shedding a few tears over the memory of his late wife. As she surveyed the physical remnants of Nova Martin, Advika had to decide quickly what she should investigate first. She glanced at the time on her phone, then at the sun shining through a crack in the heavy velvet curtains. Advika looked at each of the items again and made a decision. The tapes would have to remain a mystery, since she had no device to play them on.

So she would focus on the photos and the notebook. She turned to the latter first, and after seeing that the first several pages featured delicate handwriting, a far cry from Julian's blocky style, she took a photo of each page, so she could read Nova's words at her leisure later. Then Advika flipped through the photographs. Nearly all of them featured Julian and Nova in bed, the two of them making funny faces at the camera with a loose bedsheet carelessly draping over their bodies. In some photographs, that meant Nova's breasts peeked out, as if playing peekaboo, her chest small and lovely as two perfect oranges. Advika's fascination was tempered by a sickly wave of self-disgust. She was violating Nova's—and even Julian's—privacy, but she couldn't stop looking. Julian, besides being vibrantly young and strikingly handsome, had a looseness to him she had never experienced herself. He was a total goofball in the photos, and no matter how blurred or off-kilter the angle, Julian's exuberance came through. The last photo showed the two of them kissing as both kneeled on the bed, their knees touching, Julian's hand parked along the small dip of Nova's lower back. He was biting her bottom lip, a move Advika herself was familiar with, and she tried to picture herself and this younger Julian, cavorting naked in bed and taking selfies with old-fashioned cameras. But she couldn't, because the man in these photographs was a total stranger.

Oh shit. Julian. She had never texted him back—not that he seemed too concerned, since she hadn't received any follow-up texts. But just the thought of him waiting for her response led Advika to scramble to put everything back in the safe, just as she found it. Except for the notebook, which she grabbed and hid underneath her shirt, not knowing why she did so when she already had taken photos of its pages. Advika slipped out of the room and hurried upstairs, waiting until she was in her own office before she fired off a series of cheery texts to Julian, proclaiming how much she missed him too. Then she dashed off one more text message to Aggie, called a Lyft, and left Wildwood.

⁓

Advika couldn't read Nova's private thoughts in Julian's house. She needed more distance and space, even if that meant pissing everyone off by leaving Wildwood when she had been expressly told not to. But did they really think any person could stay cooped up inside the same place, even a mansion, for days on end? It was madness. Ludicrous. She needed to get out.

And so she had her Lyft take her to a place where she knew no paparazzi lurked in the corners, waiting to catch celebs coming out of Pilates class or carrying a smoothie or air-kissing their equally famous friends at lunch. A place where everyone looked like her, and no one would (should?) notice or care if she was there: Artesia. Otherwise known as Little India, a nondescript neighborhood marked by Indian grocery markets and sari and jewelry stores. She and Anu used to hate being dragged to Artesia every other weekend as their parents did their "Indian stuff" shopping, while the twins slumped bored in the stores' aisles, the thickness of competing aromas of spices and stale air making them irritable. But now, Advika hungered for it. A place where she could just blend in, belong, and *be.* And read Nova's journal entries in peace.

After an hour's drive, surprisingly smooth and free of traffic, her driver deposited her outside a local sweets shop in a strip mall, which Advika chose because she recalled it from visits with her family, and it was the only store that had outdoor seating. She ordered a mango lassi and sat with it at a rickety table dusted with cobwebs. Staring out at the sea of cars, the musical murmur of conversations from aunties and uncles that felt thrillingly familiar, Advika took a sip of the lassi, and the sweetness of the cool drink relaxed her even further. The morning had been such a blur of intense activity—Mona's arrival, Olive's departure, and the discovery of Julian's safe— and Advika found comfort in having a treat that reminded her of her childhood. Rather than rushing to read Nova's notebook, she took her time savoring the lassi. After wiping her hands on her jeans to get rid of the condensation from the cup, Advika used a napkin to flip the notebook cover open.

The first page was filled with words, doodles, little poems in the margins. So were the second, third, fourth ones—in fact, all the first ten pages. But Advika couldn't read a single word, because it was all written in Spanish.

Her burner phone buzzed. Advika gave a start and knocked her lassi over, but she had drunk so much of it that only a few yellow drops flew down from the metal table to the sidewalk. She scooped up the notebook, hugged it to her chest, and saw that she had received a text from Sunita.

Heads up. I told Vik about this phone number and he wants to talk to you. Can I give it to him? After Advika finished reading the first text, a second one came in. He said Austin didn't pan out, and he's living at home for a while.

Advika tapped the slim phone on her chin, thinking. She wrote back: Okay. And tell him if he's free, he can come see me right now. I'm in Artesia.

Two minutes and forty-seven seconds later, a text from a new phone number came in: Dude! Give me your address, I'll be right there.

⌒

Vik looked from Advika to the notebook, then back at her. "Whoa."

It was the first word he said after they had embraced each other with a tight hug and she had unloaded on him everything that had happened since her wedding—just like she had done with Olive at the bungalow. She had started speaking so fast that he hadn't even had time to order a lassi; he had just sat there and listened to her waterfall of words. Advika had kept her tone low for fear of being overheard, so Vik had to lean in closely, their knees touching, to catch everything she said.

"Yeah," Advika said, wiping away a sliver of sweat running down her temple. "It's a lot."

"Do you think you're being watched now? By paps or one of his minions?"

They both scanned the strip mall and surrounding parking lot. Two middle-aged men smoked next to a wastebasket in front of a fabric store. A harried mother loaded her trunk with groceries as her two kids squabbled over a comic book. Otherwise, it was just a sea of vehicles with dusty dashboards and elementary school stickers affixed to their bumpers. If a paparazzo or a private investigator was hidden among their midst, they should apply for the CIA.

"There's always a chance, I guess," she mused. Vik's face tensed, and his hands were two fists that seemed ready to throw out at the slightest provocation. He had always been the bodyguard of their group, his six-foot-one height giving him prime position to watch over the rest of the Oakies—all of whom were five foot eight and under—at bars and parties. Advika felt grateful for his protective big-brother energy, especially when her loneliness was particularly acute in the face of Olive's desertion. "But right now it seems pretty remote." She reached for his hand and squeezed it. "Look at me, talking your ear off. You haven't even had a chance to get anything," Advika said, nodding toward the sweets shop. "It's stinkin' hot out here. Can I buy you a lassi or an orange soda?"

"So Sunita's looking into your prenup because you want a divorce?"

"I want to know all my options. But that's on the table. Go get something to drink, will you?"

After Vik returned with a strawberry lassi, Advika asked him how much Spanish he remembered from high school. When he pointed out she had taken Spanish too, she gave him an embarrassed grin.

"All I remember are a few random phrases and translating the lyrics to Justin Bieber's 'Baby.'"

"But why is it written in Spanish anyway?" Vik asked, after taking a long, noisy sip of his drink. "Like, did she want to record her thoughts in secret? And do you think your guy has ever had it translated?"

Neither question had occurred to her. Advika recalled the line of Spanish in the liner notes for Nova's first album, which hadn't been replicated in subsequent albums. "I'm still looking into it. But maybe you could hold on to this for me? And if you have the time, see if you can translate it?"

"Well," he said, scratching his stubbled chin. "Between looking for jobs and avoiding my parents' eternal disappointment, I think I can make the time."

Shamefaced, Advika lambasted herself for not having asked Vik how he was doing. "What happened with sommelier school?"

"It was fucking hard, Advi." He set down his drink and cracked the knuckles on his right hand, then the left. "It wasn't a waste of money to study something I loved, but I just wasn't cutting it. I don't know what I'm cut out for."

Advika's iPhone buzzed, rattling the metal table. Julian was calling. "Ugh," she said, showing her friend the phone.

"Do you have to go back there? Come stay with me. You know my parents would love to have you over for as long as you want." The idea of crashing at Vik's house was simultaneously comforting and mortifying. Vik's parents would be sweet and welcoming, but she could only imagine the whispered conversations behind closed doors, gossip exchanged in the form of expressing concern. They wouldn't be able to resist sharing their firsthand accounts of taking in Mukesh and Rupi's only remaining daughter, already one foot out of her hasty marriage to the rich Hollywood white man.

"He's not home; he's in Morocco. And I'll be fine." She declined Julian's call, then messaged and asked him if they could FaceTime later that day, followed by a ridiculous number of heart emojis. "I have to pretend everything's normal until I talk to Sun and figure out my next move."

"Well, if you need anything, you got me. And I'll get started on this." Vik tapped on the notebook with his index finger.

"You're the best, Vik. Oh, and sorry for blocking you guys. I was such a shithead."

"Don't call my friend a shithead. But just don't ever do that again." He pretended he was about to grab her around the shoulders to give her a noogie, which he did often when they were kids. Advika squealed and playfully batted him back.

"Deal." They shook hands and smiled at each other.

"Now, can we get out of here?" Vik said, standing up and throwing his drink away with a one-handed hook shot into a nearby trash can. "If I have to come back to SoCal, I want to go to the beach and the clubs, not freakin' Artesia."

CHAPTER TWENTY-ONE

The Awful Truth

BY THE TIME VIK DROPPED her off at Wildwood, it was close to 6 p.m. Advika entered the house furtively, as if she were a teenager sneaking in past curfew, but the place seemed empty. The only lights on were in the kitchen, where she was shocked to see her laptop waiting for her on the island. There was a Post-it attached: *Here you go! Call me and we'll go shopping. XOXO—M.* Advika eyed it suspiciously, then opened the fridge and took out the pizza left over from yesterday. After quickly chowing down two slices, then taking a shot of tequila to calm her nerves, she went upstairs to her bedroom to FaceTime Julian, bringing the MacBook with her.

It was past 2 a.m. in Morocco, but Julian answered her call. "My wife, where have you been?" He peered at her closely, his smile all teeth and gums. "Been keeping busy without me?"

"More like trying to keep myself busy while you're gone. It's not the same without you." Advika could see a chandelier's reflection behind him, which gave Julian a hazy, beatific glow. A curdle of angst pulled at her skin, as she found a small part of her actually missed him. Not Julian himself, but just the companionship of having someone she shared her days and nights with. With Olive gone and Aggie in the pool house, Wildwood felt startlingly empty. A whisper of the old loneliness could be heard in every creak and random noise reverberating through the cavernous home.

"I miss you, honey. Can I get a peek?" Julian momentarily stepped out of the chandelier's light, and his shadowed face revealed him to briefly look like an old man.

"Now, now," Advika said, hoping she sounded flirty. "The faster you get back here, the faster you can see all this. Live and in person." But Julian insisted, and so she pulled up her top and briefly revealed her white bra. "That's all you're going to get right now. Tell me how it's going over there."

For twenty minutes, Julian droned on about inhospitable locals, challenging film locations, clashing co-stars, and multiple references to "losing the light." Advika nodded as she watched the sun's descent behind the horizon, pink and fiery as usual. The sky had turned a violent shade of peacock blue when Julian finally wound up his complaints, by which time any lingering remnants of affection Advika had felt for her husband had long dissipated. She told him about Mona's visit to Wildwood.

"She said I need to start looking the part. Of your wife, I mean. All shiny and pretty." Advika relayed this to Julian with a big smile, as if it was all just one big joke.

"Is that so?" Julian ran his hand through his hair, revealing a glimpse of his wedding band. "Well, you know I think you're adorable. But Mona could help. If you want it."

Advika had been FaceTiming him while sitting on the edge of the bed, her bare feet firmly on the floor. Now she scooted backward to lean against the headrest, then briefly picked up the MacBook so Julian could see it. His face changed, just for a moment. He nodded slightly as if pleased, and his mouth twitched at the corners.

"Did Mona do anything else for you? She mentioned to me that there was an issue at our offices—"

"You're cutting out. I can't hear you. What?" Advika brought the phone closer to her face, as if Julian were falling away from her.

"I said—"

Advika hung up the call. She counted to fifteen, then messaged Julian that her phone was fritzing and she had to restart it. Let him think his spyware was malfunctioning and preventing them from talking. She then opened the MacBook and spent several minutes online, hopping from IndieWire to Lainey Gossip to Save the Cat, her usual go-to sites. Advika also threw in a few Google searches for fancy makeup, luxe lingerie, and phrases like "being a mom in your twenties" and "balancing writing and motherhood." She weirdly enjoyed spreading around these crumbs for Julian and Mona and hoped they were lulled into thinking Advika was all about being the Mrs. Zelding they desired. After wrapping up her fake online searches, Advika took a long, hot shower and changed into her pajamas, feeling so exhausted she was ready to fall asleep on her feet. But upon returning to her bedroom, there were text messages waiting on both of her phones.

From Vik on the burner phone: I did some notebook translating. It was kinda uncomfortable TBH. 😱 Call me

From Julian: Baby, if the phone issues keep happening, let Mona know. Goodnight xoxo

From Olive: How's it going? Or do I not exist unless you need something from me?

Advika was taken aback. The amount of passive aggressiveness packed into so few words was almost impressive. How had she hurt Olive so badly and not even realized it? Had she been too preoccupied with her own issues that she had failed to see something was bothering her friend? As Advika started to reply to Vik while mulling whether or not to respond to Olive, she received a new alert on her burner phone.

From LinkedIn: Alma Betters has replied to your message.

⌒

In reflecting on it afterward, Advika's Skype conversation with Alma reminded her of calling long-distance to speak with her relatives in India before there were Wi-Fi and smartphones. When her mother would hand Advika the phone to chat with a cousin or aunty or her grandmother, the line connecting them would go through bouts of lucidity and distortion, necessitating shouts of "What?" or "What did you say?" about every five minutes. Advika recalled the warmth and affection that flowed between her and whomever she spoke to, making the disruptions even more frustrating.

Between Advika's busted laptop and Alma's intermittent Wi-Fi connection, their conversation was interspersed with sentence fragments and frozen screens. But despite the obstacles to their communication, the relief Advika and Alma felt in connecting with one another was palpable. Advika could see it in Alma's eyes, overflowing with kindness and sadness, the way her hand fluttered to her heart every time she uttered Nova's name. Alma was a childhood friend whom Nova had remained close to her entire life, and Alma's pain at losing Nova was still very raw. If grief could be a garment, Alma would be clad head to toe in a dark, scratchy fabric wrapped so snugly that no skin peeked through.

Advika thanked Alma for speaking with her, then shared a brief sketch of her time with Julian and how she was starting to have doubts about him based on what she had learned about his ex-wives, including Nova.

"Could you keep this confidential? That I reached out?" It was close to 11 p.m., but paranoid that Aggie might stop by and overhear, Advika was crouched in her en suite bathroom with her back against the door, speaking in a low voice.

"Of course. Believe me—I understand." Alma seemed to be in her early sixties, with a cloud of grayish chestnut hair and a swanlike neck. She held herself with a graceful rigidity, as if she were standing at a barre, executing perfect pliés. "Nova shared a lot with me. About *him*." During the entire conversation, Alma never said Julian's name.

But what she did offer was insight into the final, tragic year of Nova's life. Once Nova left her music career behind, she decided to focus on starting a family. But she suffered two miscarriages over the course of two years, so when her third pregnancy had safely progressed past the first trimester, Alma recalled Nova's joy and relief.

"She was the happiest I'd ever seen. Truly radiant. She often said to me, 'Am I dreaming? I must be dreaming.'" Alma's lips twisted into a grimace. "I could tell this meant everything to her. Both of them."

Alma's screen froze, and Advika whispered a string of expletives. When Advika had first responded to her message, she had proposed communicating by FaceTime or WhatsApp. But Alma had requested Skype, because that was what she felt comfortable with when making international calls, since she was based in Mexico City. While waiting for the connection to resume, Advika Googled "Nova Martin" + "Alma Betters," but the search results were scant, mostly referring to Alma as a name in the *Mood of the Hour* liner notes. Considering how long Alma had known Nova, Advika found that strange.

"Hello? Are you there? I think I've been talking to myself." Frozen again, Alma's brows furrowed as she pointed to something offscreen. "Okay. I had my son jigger with the Wi-Fi. We should be better now."

And for several minutes, the connection stayed steady. Alma

shared that Nova had become dependent on benzodiazepines and sleeping pills when first starting out as a recording artist to help cope with industry pressures and stage fright. And as much as she wanted to stay clean and clearheaded, the anxiety that had plagued Nova during her career resurfaced during the early months of her pregnancy.

"She couldn't sleep at night. Sometimes during her second trimester, she'd wake up early in the morning, around two or three a.m.—"

Advika shuddered upon hearing this: another thing she and Nova had in common.

"—and he would tell me he would find her curled up in a rocking chair in the room they designated to be the baby's nursery. The only thing slightly redeeming about him is that he loved Nova—I'll give him that." Alma sighed. "He would call me more than Nova sometimes, telling me how worried he was for her. The one thing we agreed upon is that she needed to see a doctor, but Nova could be stubborn when she wanted to be." A crumpled tissue fell out of Alma's hand, and she bent down to grab it but then seemed to think better of it. "I'm always using and dropping tissues," she said with a wan smile.

During the middle of Nova's second trimester, Julian postponed all his film projects to be at home to watch over his wife. But in Alma's view, that only increased her friend's anxiety and erratic behavior because he wouldn't let anyone else visit with her until she was, in his words, "back to his sweet, happy Nova." After several impassioned phone calls from Alma and Nova's mother, Julian finally relented and let them both come stay in the Zeldings' home for the weekend. But two days before their arrival, Alma received a midnight phone call from Julian.

"He had found her unconscious in their bed. He said he

didn't even wait for an ambulance; he carried her into their car and drove her to the ER. As if this made him a hero." Alma winced at the memory of his panicked call from the hospital. "He pleaded with me to come right away, as if he weren't the reason Nova's family and friends hadn't felt welcome in their home. I was on the line with him when he was told she was gone."

An autopsy had revealed her death was caused by an overdose from a mix of Xanax, Valium, and sleeping pills. Nova had died exactly three months before her due date, which on that year would have fallen on Mother's Day. Nova had planned to give their daughter the middle name of May, in honor of her birth month.

As Alma narrated the awful details, her voice remained calm and measured even as her face was a slowly breaking dam, fracturing with every word she uttered. After she had concluded her story, the two sat in silence for a few moments, as the faint noise of city traffic emanated from Alma's open window behind her. Even through Advika's damaged laptop screen, she could see how agonized Alma still was for her lost friend. It had been a long time since Advika had seen her own ongoing anguish reflected so clearly in another person, and deep within her the embers of her own primal grief threatened to catch flame. To counter thoughts of Anu and her heartbreak for Nova, Advika ruminated on Julian. Now she finally grasped why he had understood her loss so well: he had lost a wife *and* a child. This new information renewed her sympathy for him and explained his intense desire to start a family. Even in learning about Nova's tragic fate—

Wait a minute.

"Alma," she said abruptly. "Sorry to ask this so bluntly, but what was Nova's due date?" This was something Advika could have searched online, but her need for an answer was too urgent to even do that.

"May twelfth," she said, blowing her nose into a new tissue that had been handed to her by a beefy hand. "Gracias, mijo." Alma dabbed at her eyes with the same tissue. "You know, I'm not sure why I'm so emotional while speaking with you. I think it's the idea that he has another young wife. Even younger than Nova."

Advika's entire body went numb. That night with Julian when they had weird sex and he had called out Nova's name had been May 12. And he had asked her to wear that red earth-mother dress, style her hair in a certain way, wear a certain perfume that she now remembered had odd echoes of the fragrance in Julian's safe.

She had been Julian's dress-up doll, unknowingly playacting his dead wife.

"Are you okay?" Alma's voice came out distorted, and Advika looked up to see that the screen was stalled again, her features frozen in concern.

"Yes, I am." With new answers came many more questions. "I know it's late, and our connection is bad. How much longer can we talk? There's so much I still need to know." Advika was plagued by a nagging sense that she was missing something vitally important. Because there had to be more to the story than what Advika had learned so far. And it wasn't even just the mystery contents of Nova's notebook, which she still had to talk to Vik about. It was as if Advika were staring at a thousand-piece puzzle of an iconic landmark like the Taj Mahal that had a hundred missing pieces: you could easily grasp what the puzzle was supposed to be, but those empty spaces still made the picture feel maddeningly incomplete.

"I...bad...send...see..." Alma disappeared, and the Skype

call ended. Advika tried calling back four more times, but it went unanswered. Just as she was about to give up, go to bed, and resign herself to a sleepless night, she received a trio of messages in her Skype chat box from Alma.

Hector Cano, Indigo Studios.

Good luck, dear.

And be safe.

The old loneliness descended on her, heavy and unrelenting, along with a new, twitchy companion: fear. Alma's final words flickering in and out of view on the fritzing screen had an ominous effect, as if they were a warning uttered to the final girl in a horror movie before she decided to leap out of her hiding place and take on the monster once and for all. The loneliness Advika was used to, but this jumbled heartbeat of slow-building dread was new to her. She didn't think she had to physically fear for her life and safety, but Alma's words acknowledged what she had already known for some time: she was in a very vulnerable position by being legally bound to a very powerful man.

"You're okay," Advika whispered to herself. "You're okay." She sought out the clarity of Anu's voice but couldn't access her. So she shakily rose up off the cold bathroom floor and fled into the bedroom. After switching on both her and Julian's lamps on their nightstands to shoo out the darkness, she reached for her Discman, which she had hidden under the mattress. To listen to Nova's lovely, tremulous voice on *The Mood of the Hour* after all she had learned pierced Advika's heart, but it calmed her down too. Especially once she remembered that Hector Cano had produced this album, and Alma had specifically

pointed Advika in his direction. This realization serendipi-
tously occurred as Advika heard Nova sing the title track, and
the lyrics helped ease her jumpiness enough to allow her to
drift off to sleep.

Between us there lives
A small glow, a shy hope.
This is not the end, not yet.
Not forever,
Not yet.

CHAPTER TWENTY-TWO

Who's That Girl?

ADVIKA HAD VIK READ NOVA'S words to her over the phone four times. The first time was because she had been lost in thought ruminating over her conversation with Alma the night before, and the subsequent times were so that she could copy down what Vik said. She wanted to be able to read it over at her leisure and have a record of Nova's words after she returned Nova's notebook to Julian's safe. The only reason Advika didn't meet Vik in person was that she didn't want to raise any red flags with the Wildwood staff, especially with Olive's whirl-wind departure following Mona's drop-by visit the day before, and then Advika leaving for a few hours too. One full day at Wildwood seemed important, even mandatory, in order to keep presenting as Julian's young, naive wife.

But staying at Wildwood didn't have to mean staying inside. She took Vik's call in the early afternoon while sitting on the wooden bench. To Advika's surprise, Aggie had prepared a weirdly sumptuous breakfast for both of them that morning—eggs Benedict, blueberry-lemon waffles, and turkey bacon and avocado. The two had spoken about trivial things, and Advika let herself be chatted up, nodding along and breaking into polite laughter at appropriate times. As soon as the house manager excused herself, Advika went outside. She wandered the grounds a bit, needing to burn off the heavy meal she had consumed, before she walked all the way down to the bench, which she had started thinking of as her own. In fact, it was the only thing in all of Wildwood that felt like hers.

After she felt assured that no one had followed her, Advika phoned Vik, and he relayed the contents of the final entry in the notebook, which was undated. Sometimes the noise of revving car engines and hoots of laughter caused Advika to miss certain words ("Sorry, I'm at Starbucks on Sunset; it's like a high school *Game of Thrones* over here"), and he had to repeat them. But after a half hour, Advika had successfully copied all of Nova's words into her own notebook. She could have just had Vik snap a photo and send it to the burner phone, but somehow Nova's words felt more real to Advika if she could see them on the page in front of her, as if she were finally meeting Nova herself.

It's time. It's time, it's time, it's time. Perhaps if I say the words here, I can convince myself what I've known for so long, maybe since the day we married. There was no room for me in this marriage.

Maybe I could have stayed inside this kind of love, full and bright and like a diamond necklace tight around one's neck. As it is I've already cut out pieces of my heart to fit in with him here. To realize one dream is to have lost another, perhaps forever.

No more looking back, no more fearing the future. No more fog, no more numbness. We have to leave for your sake. My heart. My little girl, a beautiful seed waiting to blossom.

The days happened, the memories exist, nothing can be changed. But now, everything can be changed. I want

to be able to breathe. No more constriction, no more
acquiescing, no more no more no more. I never want that
for you, dear one. Whether that means here or elsewhere,
we'll be free.

"Oh," Advika said as one long exhalation, more to herself than Vik, whom she could hear chewing on the phone. He had waited on the line with her, as she reread Nova's words over and over, sometimes to herself, and sometimes in a low whisper. "She was going to leave him. She was going to take her child and go." The revelations from speaking with Alma took on an even more tragic dimension.

"This is all so, like, heartbreaking," said Vik. "I don't know who she is and I feel all shook up over this." His apologetic, consoling tone was at odds with the whoops of merriment in the background.

"I don't get . . . I don't get why she died." A light breeze curled itself around Advika, rustling the leaves above as if they also commiserated with her. "She wanted a new life for herself and her child. So why the pills? Why overdose?"

"She probably didn't mean to, you know," Vik said. "Drug dependency doesn't go away just because you want it to. Maybe she was anxious and scared to leave him, and she needed a way to cope."

"True," Advika responded, batting away a tear streaking across her cheek. The catch in Vik's voice reminded her that he had relied heavily on Ritalin in his junior and senior years of high school, desperate to achieve the test scores and grades that would get him, in his words, into a "good enough" college. Though his parents had never found out, Vik had been so alarmed by its effects on him—dizziness, nausea, loss of appetite—that he had stopped taking it as soon as he got into UC Santa Barbara, recognizing that while the school wasn't good enough for his parents, it was more than good enough for him. "How are you doing, Vik?"

"At the moment, I feel like I'm trapped inside a really bad high school movie. But really, every moment…I just feel trapped. By my choices, you know?" He paused. "Maybe that's why I related so much to what Nova had written."

"Yeah." Advika chucked herself on the chin and sighed. "Yeah." Rihanna's "We Found Love" began blasting loudly next to Vik. She shook her head, recalling how she had once thought the song would be the perfect soundtrack to the romantic comedy she imagined herself to be in with Julian. How long ago that time now seemed, though it had only been a few months. "We all make choices, but we don't have to be trapped by them."

"What?" Vik yelled, as the song increased in volume. "Okay, hold on. I'm getting out of here."

Advika picked up the notebook and stared at Nova's words translated from Spanish, itching to leave Wildwood and investigate further. While she didn't want to raise suspicions with Julian and his staff, or attract the attentions of any bored paparazzi, she couldn't just sit at home and wait for Julian to come home. Because then what?

"Actually, Vik, could you meet me somewhere? I can fill you in on the details when I see you."

⌒

Indigo Studios was located in Culver City, a one-story white cement building in a series of them, save for the red headphones logo etched in the front door's windowpane. Advika stared at the entrance, willing herself to go inside, with Vik hovering protectively behind her like a bodyguard, his broadshouldered shadow dwarfing hers.

"I don't feel comfortable with you standing outside, Advi."

Vik squinted into the sunlight as he glanced down the sidewalk, which was empty except for the two of them.

"Well, let's go in, then," Advika said, watching her shadow flit in and out of existence as she stepped forward, then back again. "I think we can just walk inside. Right?"

Vik shrugged, and from the dazed look on his face, Advika imagined he was still processing all she had shared from her Skype call with Alma. He seemed to be taking Nova's story to heart as much as Advika, which she found to be so sweet. The only thing Advika hadn't told him about was that day in May, because she could barely think about it without feeling sick, and there was no reason to inflict that on her friend.

"I think we go in," she repeated, this time with more conviction. "The worst that happens is that we get asked to leave." Before she could chicken out, Advika opened the door with a determined twist of the doorknob. Upon stepping inside, a ferocious blast of air-conditioning nearly blew her back on her heels, and she was glad she had thought to take a cardigan on this second field trip as part of her research into the former Mrs. Zeldings.

"Hi, can I help you?" A petite twentysomething woman with a short brown ponytail and jean jacket sat at the front desk, eyeing them quizzically.

"We're here to see Hector Cano?" Advika asked with the timidity of a teenager seeking permission to drive her parents' car for the first time. To seem more confident, she added, "My name is Advika Srinivasan. He's expecting me." She bit her lip, hoping she sounded believable.

"Oh yes. One second." The receptionist shot up out of her chair so fast that it was still spinning when she exited the room.

Advika and Vik only had time to clap each other on the back in astonishment before they were approached by a tall, lanky man with wire-frame glasses and a white goatee, dressed in tan khakis and a black tee shirt. "Advi . . . acka?"

"Advika," she replied, her face still configured in a rictus of shock that her gambit had worked. "Mr. Cano?"

"Come on inside. Alma told me to expect you." She and Vik followed Hector down a long, dimly lit hallway, a kaleidoscope of sounds and voices flowing softly from the various doors they passed, each one of them marked with a different colored set of headphones in its windowpane. Hector opened a green door at the end of the hall, the only one that had the outline of a guitar etched in the glass instead. It was a recording studio the size of her walk-in closet. Unlike the sleek but unremarkable reception area and hallway, this room was like a portal to the *Brady Bunch* era: wood paneling; a round yellow shag carpet; and a quartet of lava lamps holding court on top of a horizontal shelf teeming with vinyl records. Hector gestured toward a black leather sofa against the wall, and he took a seat next to the mixing board.

"I spoke to Alma," he said with a grin, his hands alighting on both armrests. "She told me to apologize to you about the internet connection, by the way. She would have loved to speak with you longer."

"Me too. Also, before I forget . . ." Advika took a deep breath, then willed herself into a smile despite the tears welling behind her eyes. "*The Mood of the Hour* is absolutely gorgeous. It's just . . . it's just . . . I love it." Embarrassed by her emotion, and surprised by it too, Advika turned away from Hector and Vik to take her cardigan out of her bag. She slipped it on, then hastily wiped a tear dangling off her eyelash. When she finally felt ready, she looked up to see Hector gazing at something above her head. Advika followed his eyes, and her breath caught in her throat as she saw that it was *The Mood of the Hour*'s album sleeve and vinyl record, mounted in a silver frame.

"Thank you, Advika," Hector said, clasping his hands together before doing a small bow. "It's the best thing I've ever done, or will do. Which is why I wanted to meet with you."

Hector told them that Nova's first album was recorded at Hilgard Sound, a semipopular recording studio in the late '70s and early '80s. *Mood* had been his first time as a producer and hers as an artist, so they had gone into the project feeling like they had something to prove.

"There aren't many creative experiences when you feel perfectly in sync with your collaborators," he said. "But it was a very special time. We went in there feeling like novices and came out of the sessions charged up with confidence and ambition—we knew we were meant for this." When Hilgard closed a few years later, Hector, who by that time had a few more albums under his belt, took several of the furnishings from the studio space in which they had recorded *Mood* with the hope of one day opening his own recording studio. And he did with Indigo Studios, but the commercial side—ADR, voice-over, radio ads—gradually became the predominant aspect of his business.

"My music career didn't last beyond the late eighties, but I cherish that part of my life. I like having this space as sort of a living memory of the time. When I thought youth and passion were enough to conquer the world, you know?" Hector chuckled. "So that's why that sofa you're sitting on sags in the middle and feels as comfortable as a pound of rocks," Hector added with an apologetic laugh. "Sorry. I'm just a sentimental guy like that. But Nova sat on that sofa, and so did Carole King and Joan Armatrading. It feels like a part of music history."

"She should have been a part of music history," Advika said emphatically.

"Yes, exactly," Hector replied, drawing back in his chair, then exhaling hard. "I'm glad you feel that way. She was an exquisite artist, and it has always gnawed at me that she didn't get to fulfill the promise she had on her first album. I don't say that as her producer, but just as a person with ears who knows good music. She had *it*."

"How come she didn't work with you on the second album?" Vik asked, scooting forward on the sofa, causing it to respond with a groan. "I imagine she wanted to, but it wasn't her decision."

Hector nodded. "After she released *The Mood of the Hour*, Nova wanted to record some songs in Spanish. She had adopted the name Nova on a lark, thinking it would help her be more easily accepted by the industry. And for her second album—"

Spanish. Advika clapped her hand over her forehead, the errant pieces finally coming together for her: the single line of Spanish in the first album's liner notes and Nova's journal written in the same language—the language she had felt at home in and used to express her deepest thoughts.

"What was Nova's real name?"

"Nalda. Nalda Martinez." Hector smiled as if doing so caused him pain. "She was Mexican-American, just like me. And Alma. The three of us grew up together in the same neighborhood in San Diego."

He explained that once she had a taste of success, Nova regretted her choice to change her name and wanted to move forward in her career with her real one. But by that time, she had started dating Julian, who encouraged her to stick with "Nova Martin" because she already had established herself in the industry with that name.

"And no doubt he's a good reason why she recorded *Nova Martin*—that was her second album—with Warner Bros. I was happy for her when I learned she had signed with a major label, because I thought she deserved to break into the mainstream. Sad to say, I mostly lost touch with Nova once she became a bigger star. But Alma told me that the whole situation for her was a nightmare."

When she signed with Warner Bros., Nova was encouraged not to discuss her heritage because of fears she wouldn't be seen as marketable in a mainstream way. "Her management told her they didn't want her to get pigeonholed as the 'Mexican Madonna.' They just wanted her to be known as the next Madonna. No matter how ill-fitting that designation was for Nova. What she wanted was to be the next Joni Mitchell." But there was no room for Joni Mitchells in '80s MTV pop culture, let alone a nonwhite one.

"So they made Nova—Nalda—keep quiet?" Vik said, sliding forward again, wincing slightly as he stretched out his long legs.

"Not quite," Hector said, shaking his head. "I don't think her management and her husband were actively trying to silence her. But they told her that embracing her heritage, especially when she was fair skinned and had the quote-unquote advantage of looking white, or perhaps Italian or Mediterranean, would be a mistake. Alma said that Nova felt she had to keep this part of herself out of the public eye for the sake of her career. And it really troubled her."

There was a knock at the door. As Hector stepped outside, Advika pulled the cardigan so tight around her body she felt the seams give at the shoulders.

"Holy shit, right?" Vik whispered. "But now the notebook makes so much more sense." Advika responded with a faint nod, her mind scrolling through every single image of Nova she had ever seen. Even after staring at so many of Nova's photos, Advika never once thought Julian's late wife wasn't white. It reminded Advika of her shock after her father offhandedly told her that Queen's Freddie Mercury was from a Parsi-Indian family. For both singers, she saw their light skin, lighter than hers, and just assumed they were Caucasian. But shouldn't she have known, despite the prescribed narrative? The revelation about Nova's true heritage made Advika sick and angry, both for Nova and at Advika's own ignorance.

Hector returned to the studio and cocked his head to the side at the sight of Advika hugging her arms around herself. "Are you cold?"

"Oh, I'm fine. Just mad at myself. I'm ashamed to say I didn't know that Nova was Mexican."

"Unless you knew Nova personally, or are a superfan, there was no reason to know. It doesn't seem to be common knowledge, even after all this time."

Vik, who had been squirming beside Advika for most of the conversation so far, shot up out of his seat. "Sorry. Just need to stretch a bit. The sofa is a little tough."

"There's sentimentality, and then there's holding on to junk," Hector said drily. "Sit here. I'll go get another chair for you... I'm so sorry—I never caught your name."

"Vik. That would be great."

In between the time Hector rolled in two more chairs and positioned them near the mixing board, and he and Vik chatted for a few moments about the best quality headphones, Advika responded to a text from Aggie, who had asked when she would be home. Before she left Wildwood, Advika had told Aggie that she was visiting a sick aunty, her go-to excuse with Julian and his crew. Shuba Aunty asked me to stay and have lunch, she wrote back. Expect to be back around 4.

Aggie texted back immediately. Isn't she sick?

Advika responded, I guess you've never met an Indian aunty before, and included a laughing emoji. Ever since their weirdly chatty breakfast earlier that day, she hoped this kind of convivial, conversational exchange would soften Aggie, and she wouldn't just view Advika as a person to keep tabs on. When Aggie replied with a thumbs-up emoji, the knot in Advika's stomach loosened from a triple to a double.

"I wanted to play you something," Hector said, once all three of them were seated together, with him in the middle. Vik's stomach grumbled as loudly as a bowling ball hitting a strike, and they all laughed. "Don't worry—this won't take too long."

His fingers flew up and down the console, and a few seconds later, Nova's voice filled the room. She was singing in Spanish. The melody was reminiscent of one of the rare upbeat songs on *The Mood of the Hour*, with what sounded like a flamenco guitar and maracas providing sunlight and texture. Advika's jaw dropped, her face cradling a huge grin.

"It's good, right? This is the music she wanted to do."

"She sounds so happy," Advika said.

They listened to the song in a warm, easy silence. Hector closed his eyes and sang softly along with the chorus. Vik nodded his approval, even as his stomach rumbled loudly a second time.

"One story that isn't known about Nova is the real reason she walked away from her music career," Hector said as the song faded out. "She idolized Linda Ronstadt. Her and Joni. But Linda had been personal for her, because Linda was a superstar, but she also had Mexican heritage on her father's side.

"Nova didn't like the direction her music was taking on her third album, *All My Desire*. That's pretty widely known. But what wasn't common knowledge was her hope to incorporate the musical traditions she had been raised on: Mexican folk ballads, mariachi, banda. But no one was on her side." Julian and her management had nixed her plans because they wanted to build on the momentum from the success of her second album and not alienate listeners. When Linda Ronstadt's Spanish-language album was released the same day as *All My Desire*, Nova was heartbroken. "She saw there was a way to be authentically herself and be accepted in the pop marketplace. But when she told Julian this, he retorted that Linda was a superstar who could record 'three monkeys banging pans together' and it'd be a hit."

If Julian had been in the room, Advika would have marched up to him and punched him in the stomach.

"Nova decided she couldn't record another album again, not the way she was being pushed to do." Hector took off his glasses to dab at the corners of his eyes with the heel of his hand. "But a month before she died, she mailed this to Alma and asked her to give it to me. At some point she had started recording, likely in secret. Since this song is addressed to a 'niña,' she was—"

"Oh my god," Advika said, jerking up in her chair. "She was working on new music while she was pregnant?"

"This is the only evidence I have of it, plus some remarks she made to Alma and her family. But there's no real way to know."

The tapes in Julian's safe. Advika exhaled, even as her heartbeat sped up. Why else would he have them locked in there, hidden away? Just as she was about to tentatively reveal what she had discovered, Hector turned toward her, his eyes pleading.

"Next year is the thirty-fifth anniversary of *The Mood of the Hour*. I want this music out there, Advika. And this new song too." Hector shared that he wanted to make a documentary about Nova and her music, but he needed her help. Specifically, with Julian.

"Your husband has full control of her song publishing, which means he has full control of her legacy. And Nova's full story has never really been told. *Behind the Music* did an episode about her, but that was just to mark the fifteenth anniversary of *All My Desire*. Her family refused to even participate in it."

Ever since Nova's death, the Martinez family had tried repeatedly to reach out to Julian, begging for him to allow her pre–Warner Bros. music to be reissued or licensed for film and TV use, but Julian never responded to them. They had some measure of hope when they heard he was cooperating with *Behind the Music*. But when Nova's family learned Julian had refused to allow the show's producers to use songs from

The Mood of the Hour—and only *The Mood of the Hour*—in the episode, they issued a statement to the producers that they "couldn't be involved with a production that ignores Nova's heritage" and also blasted Julian for being a "toxic and damaging influence on our beloved daughter's life and memory." While the Martinezes' statement was featured in the original airing of the episode, it was deleted from subsequent airings.

"Her family wanted to share with the world the Nova they knew, and the Nova they still grieve for," Hector said. "With this anniversary coming up, I want to try to make things right for them. And for her."

"But why do that?" Vik stretched his legs again, causing his chair to roll back and gently bump into the sofa adjacent to them. "Why block that album?"

"It's not about him, or written for him," Advika murmured. "It's about someone else."

"That's what we think, Alma and I. The album was about her first love. I guess your husband doesn't like that."

The words "your husband" came out like a rebuke, and Advika reacted as if she had been reprimanded. "What can I do?" she said quickly.

"Talk to him. See if you can get him to change his mind about the reissues and the documentary." Hector put his glasses back on. "At the very least, if he has no interest in Nova's early music, then give the publishing rights to her parents, for god's sake."

"What about just releasing this song you have?" Vik rolled himself back to the console while still seated, his long legs giving him the look of a spider inching along the floor. "Upload it to YouTube, or SoundCloud?"

"He's very . . . litigious. I don't want him to ever know about this, until we have an agreement of some kind, legally speaking," Hector said.

Advika's heart sank. Julian was a stone pillar, silent and unmovable, when it came to being asked to do something that didn't benefit him. But she would try anyway. And that's what she told Hector.

"Thank you. This is the closest we've ever been to getting somewhere." As he walked them out of the studios into the haze of the late-afternoon light, he hummed a tune to himself. "All these years, and her music is still in my head. I think about her every day, you know."

"I'll do my very best to make this right," Advika responded, shaking his outstretched hand and then standing on her tiptoes to give him a hug.

She was lost in thought as she and Vik walked back to his car, her mind in a frenetic whirl, not just about Nova or even Julian, but about fragments of her own life before her marriage. As she got in the car and shut the door, all the disparate thoughts coalesced into one single urgent need.

"Vik, could we make one more stop?"

"Sure. Where?" He zipped his seatbelt into place, then flipped down his overhead mirror to retrieve his Ray-Bans.

"Wait. I mean, you don't have to. I've already asked a lot of you today." Advika tried to yank her own seatbelt over her body, but the belt kept catching midway.

"Dude, I don't mind. This has been hella fascinating." He fumbled with his sunglasses before putting them on. "I feel so directionless. I'm just drifting. Meanwhile, Nova was so passionate about her music, and Hector is so passionate about getting her story told. You have your writing..." Vik trailed off, staring ahead at the pickup truck parked in front of them. "What do I have?"

Advika stopped battling her seatbelt and let it zip out of her hands. "You have a lot to offer. Passion is great, but it's not everything," she added, thinking of how little progress she had made in her work. "Sommelier school is just a setback. You'll figure it out."

"When, though? Like, seriously? Sun is making a big career transition, Balan is making a move to strike out on his own, and I'm here. Back with my parents, confirming to them, and me, that I'm a screwup."

"No. You're not." Advika thought of Anu from her nightmare, in which her sister changed from different ages but never progressed past twenty-four. "Anu would be the first one to tell you how special you are and not to be so hard on yourself. We're not even thirty. We still have a lot of time," she said to Vik, and also to herself. "Nova, and Anu—their lives were cut short for stupid, senseless reasons. We're still here, and as long as we're walking and talking and breathing oxygen, we'll take every day that we have to figure it out. In their honor. Okay?"

Still staring straight ahead, Vik held out his hand to her as a fist. "Okay," he said softly. They bumped fists, and as Vik started the car, Advika reached for her seatbelt, which, after several tugs, still didn't yield to her. Sensing Vik watching her with amusement, she pulled even harder for comic effect.

"Don't break it!" Vik laughed, and Advika was relieved that his spirits seemed to be lifting. "Just let it go, all the way. Then try again, and the seatbelt will give on its own."

She complied, and at last she was able to buckle herself in. "That could be applied to a lot of things, couldn't it?" Advika said. "Like, as a life philosophy."

"That sounds about right." He turned on the radio, and the beginning notes of "California Love" spilled out. "So, where did you want to go?"

~

The Shop, which is how everyone referred to the coffee shop where Olive was a barista, was a darkly lit, circular space that had always reminded Advika of a hipster spaceship: blinking lights, murmuring, lo-fi music, and several leather chairs that seemed fancy enough for a starship captain, although these highly prized seats were always taken by the same pale white men with MacBooks and neatly trimmed beards. Not that Advika was inside to see for herself this time.

"Okay, so I'm here," Vik told her in a loud whisper. "What does she look like?" When Advika had decided she wanted to speak with Olive, it had been an ambulance siren careening through her whole being. But by the time they actually arrived and spent several minutes looking for a parking space, her driving need evaporated into shivery anxiety. What if Olive didn't want to see her? To experience that rejection in person would devastate her. So she had sent Vik inside the coffee shop while she waited a block away in his car, lying flat on the passenger side with her seat all the way down.

"She's Taiwanese. And she has a punky kind of haircut— long in the front, buzzed in the back. She's Balan's height. And she never smiles and is probably cussing out a customer right now."

Vik laughed. "Okay, so I think I found her. What's her name again? Olivia?"

"Olive." To know Vik was now likely just mere feet away from her friend made Advika's heart race. Vik would be a good buffer for the two of them. A sort of Cyrano de Bergerac, but for friendship. At least, that's what she told herself.

"Excuse me, miss," Advika heard Vik say, and the phone became slippery in her grasp. The soaring July temperatures washed over her in stiff bricks of heat, and she was starting to sweat through her tee shirt. The car was stuffy from a lack of ventilation because the air-conditioning was off and the windows sealed tight, due to her paranoia about being spotted and photographed again. She switched hands, wiping her palm on her jeans while staring up at the car's ceiling. With a frustrated sigh, Advika turned up the phone's volume to its highest level and pressed it to her ear, wanting to hear Vik and Olive's exchange. But all she heard was the drone of coffee grinders and the generic chill beats pumped over the speakers. Advika was finally about to give in and go inside when Olive's voice bulldozed her ear.

"Yeah?" Even though Olive sounded like her usual aggrieved, disdainful self, Advika was thrilled to hear her voice. She deeply missed her friend, more than she realized.

"Olive, hey." Advika cleared her throat. "How are you? I've been...thinking a lot about you."

"Oh. Cool." Olive wasn't bending an inch. Behind her, the buzz of customers intensified. "Hold on—I'm going to step out a minute. Do you wanna come?" Olive said to Vik.

The low chatter and chill beats dissipated into a blinking stillness. Advika waited with her eyes closed and her heart racing. She couldn't shake the fear that Olive would disappear again, and this time for good.

"Okay." Now it was Olive's turn to clear her throat. "So I have about five minutes. I didn't even take my break, just walked out. So." The silence following the "so" was pregnant with expectation. Advika couldn't mess this up.

"I want to apologize. You've been such a great friend to me. I wouldn't have survived these past few weeks without you." The onrush of tears surprised her for the second time that day, and she bit them back by curling her toes in her sandals. "I'm so sorry if I made you feel...I don't know, less than."

"Less than what?" Olive's words came taut and caustic, like the snap of a whip.

"Lesser than. Maybe I was using you as an emotional sounding board, and..." Advika thought about yesterday and the tidal waves of information and feelings she had unleashed on

Vik without ever once thinking about him and what he was going through. "I never asked you about you." Saying the words aloud, Advika knew they were true. The truth of how she had treated Olive clicked into place like a combination lock snapping shut.

Olive let out a long, deep breath. "This is true. You never asked about me. Not when I was at your house, not when you were at mine, or when I was house-sitting. And not ever before—when we lived together. And I got tired of not existing as a breathing human until you had use for me."

Advika wished she could melt into a puddle, seep right through the car seat and disappear into the asphalt beneath her. What must Vik be thinking, only hearing Olive's side of the conversation? He already knew she could be a total shithead after she had blocked the Oakies, and now he was seeing evidence of it from the only non-Oakie person she could currently call a friend.

"You're right. All of it. I'm truly sorry. I need to be a better friend to you. And I will be, if you still want to be friends. And if you need some time, I get that too."

"Okay," Olive said after a long pause. "So what's new in your saga? And who is this guy, anyway?" Advika heard Vik say something, but she couldn't understand it.

"That's my friend Vik. He can fill you in."

"Cool. Gotta go." After a few moments, Vik spoke. "Can I tell her what I learned about Nova? The stuff from the notebook?"

"Sure." Advika started to get woozy. She was probably feeling the ill effects of the sun and could also be a little dehydrated. She shut her eyes and listened to them speak, the heat pressing in on her on all sides. She hadn't realized she had fallen asleep until Vik opened the car door. A glimpse at her phone's clock told her a half hour had passed.

"Sorry—we ended up chatting for a few minutes. Once I got

started on the whole Nova thing, she was hooked. I basically followed her behind the bar to fill her in." Vik paused, lifting his sunglasses to the top of his head. "You okay? Didn't mean to keep you waiting for so long. Did anyone bother you?" He had his hands clenched into fists, as if he was expecting to have to defend her from paparazzi at any moment.

"I'm fine. Just tired. Thanks so much for everything, Vik. You're a real knight in shining armor."

"So are you. Thanks for the pep talk earlier." Advika reached for Vik's hand on the steering wheel and squeezed it affectionately. He turned to look at her briefly and smiled. "We would do anything for each other, right?"

"Right," Advika said. "Once an Oakie, always an Oakie."

"And don't you forget it." Vik started the car and pulled into the bumptious flow of traffic on Santa Monica Boulevard. "It's already past four. Are you sure you want me to take you back to his house?" It seemed that once people knew Julian, the real Julian, their distaste for Advika's husband meant they couldn't even say his name.

Advika nodded, thankful that the woozy feeling had dissipated in the first blast of cool air from their drive. "Yeah. You heard what Hector said about Julian being litigious. I need to pretend to be the happy wife a little longer while figuring out a plan. It helps that he's out of town." Seeing her friend's worried expression, she added, "It's fine, Vik. And Sunita's helping me with the legal stuff."

"Oh good." They both flew a few inches out of their seats as the car hit a pothole, and Advika giggled while Vik apologized and swore about the shitty conditions of LA streets. They chatted about other things—living at home with his parents, Balan's bizarre love of PowerPoint presentations for the mildest of tasks—but both quieted as they got closer to the Palisades.

"Are you sure you'll be safe?" Vik asked as he turned onto the street that cascaded up to the gleaming manses of the Riviera's gated community.

"I am," she said, although she didn't entirely feel that way. Advika had Vik drop her off outside of the security entryway. As she waved to the guard and saw the gates close behind her, each step taken back to Wildwood held the dread of someone reentering prison.

⌒

After returning home, she sat down for a dinner of fettuccini alfredo in the kitchen, making sure Aggie saw her eat while Advika pretended to read on her iPhone. Aggie seemed more watchful than usual, but this time they barely exchanged words as Advika finished her meal. Only when Advika washed her plate and put it away did Aggie's watchfulness dial back a few degrees, and they made some small talk about the weather before Aggie exited for the pool house.

Feeling as if she had passed some sort of test, Advika retreated to her bedroom, collapsing onto the bed, kicking off her shoes, and then burrowing under the sheets. She fell asleep, only to be awakened an hour later when a text came in from Sunita, informing her she had set up a Proton Mail secure email account for her, along with info on how to access it.

I sent you some information re: prenup. Take some time reviewing it. Let me know if you have any questions.

On the surface, the prenup seemed to be standard and what Advika had agreed to during the one time she and Julian had discussed it before she had signed it. Even though California was a community property state, Julian would retain sole intellectual property rights as well as all the income and royalties derived from his films preceding and during their marriage, which the prenup stated as having a value of $62 million. Instead, Advika would receive a $1.5 million lump sum and an extra $550,000 allotted for the purchase of a new home. As someone who had never exceeded four figures in her bank account, and not wanting to demand more from her soon-to-be husband when she was bringing so little into the marriage, Advika had found these terms generous. But Julian hadn't informed her that while he had protected his intellectual property rights, he had not extended the same courtesy to her. In the event of their divorce, the prenup stated that he would receive 50 percent of royalties from any of her written work.

"And this doesn't just include work produced during the course of the marriage," Sunita wrote in a comment box within the document. "He argues that because you worked on *The Romance Game* during the marriage and incorporated his advice in reworking the screenplay, he is entitled to fifty percent of the copyright as well."

Advika's eyes blurred, the words on the screen becoming a black fuzz of text. She had cried into his arms just weeks before the prenup signing, in which she had confided how this screenplay had saved her during the darkest, most painful period of her life, and how she didn't believe she would have survived Anu's death if she hadn't found a creative outlet for her loss.

"Motherfucking bastard," Advika murmured, tucking her fists under her armpits, squeezing down with all her might. If she didn't, every single item in their bedroom—framed photos, bedside lamps, the flat-screen TV—would find themselves smashed, cracked, and broken. Her eyes alighted on Julian's anniversary gift, still waiting for her on the bureau. She snatched it up by its extravagant velvet bow and stalked into the bathroom. Advika tore open the gift and gasped when the velvet box revealed a diamond necklace and matching earrings. She snapped a photo of the flashy jewels on the bathroom counter, her toothbrush in the background. Advika then sent a text message and Proton Mail before slinking back into her bedroom and dragging the covers over her head, where she would remain for the next forty-eight hours.

To Vik, she sent a photo of the jewels, along with a request he come by to pick them up so he could appraise their value. When he texted back immediately to ask why, she wrote, I need to hire a divorce lawyer.

In Proton, she wrote the email she had thought about writing since their four-and-a-half-month anniversary celebration and was now ready to send. The email was to Evie Lockhart's lawyer, and the subject title was simply "Film Reel."

CHAPTER TWENTY-THREE

Trainwreck

FADE IN

INT. SRINIVASAN HOUSE—DINING ROOM—NIGHT

The Srinivasan family sit at the dinner table they have
gathered around since the twin daughters were infants
in high chairs. MUKESH sits at the head of the table,
with wife, RUPI, to his right. ADVIKA is at his left, and
ANU sits opposite her father. Their plates are mostly
empty, as they've just finished eating.

> MUKESH
>
> So, Advika...anything new with your writing?

> ADVIKA
> (flustered)
>
> No, Dad. You know if there was, I'd tell you.

ADVIKA glares at her plate. MUKESH and RUPI
exchange looks. ANU glances at her parents, then her
sister. She seems to be steeling herself for something
unpleasant.

MUKESH

Well, if that's the case…maybe it's time to—

RUPI

—put writing on hold. Just for a little while.

ADVIKA

(still staring at her plate)

Not this again.

MUKESH

Now, Advika, listen. Writing isn't getting you anywhere. It's time to take your future seriously.

ADVIKA

I do take it seriously. And writing is my future.

ADVIKA gives ANU a "Can you believe this?" look, but her sister won't look at her.

MUKESH

No one is saying you have to give it up forever. But you can start thinking about a full-time career or graduate school.

RUPI

Or what about teaching?

ADVIKA

I'm not cut out for teaching. Or office life. I'm a screenwriter—I don't know how many times I have to say that. I get that it's not a

traditional path, but it doesn't mean it's not a
valid one.

RUPI
We can't be your safety net forever.

ADVIKA is startled—her parents have never spoken
so plainly to her before. When she looks to her sister
for support, ANU'S hands are clasped on the table, her
expression unreadable.

ADVIKA
You're acting like I don't pay my own bills.
Sometimes I'm a little short, and I'm always
grateful when you can help me out...but fine.
I'll never ask for a dime again. I'll take on
ten, twenty, thirty bartending jobs if I have to.
Whatever it takes. Because I'm not the kind of
person who gives up easily. You raised me—
us—that way.

(beat)
But I'm not going to give up. So, can we
please just stop talking about this, now and
forever?

CUT TO:

INT. ADVIKA AND ANU'S CAR—NIGHT

ANU is driving, and ADVIKA sits beside her. ANU'S
eyes are locked on the road while ADVIKA fiddles with
the radio.

                              ADVIKA
Ugh, the radio sucks.

ADVIKA glances at ANU. Her sister continues to look
straight ahead.

    Just say it. Say something.

                               ANU
                             (sighing)

    I can say what you want to hear. Or I can say
    that I agree with them.

ADVIKA turns up the volume on the radio, an ear-
splitting car commercial. ANU shuts it off.

                               ANU
You know I love your writing. And I believe
you'll make it someday. But there's nothing
wrong with being practical too. A plan B isn't
the worst thing in the world.

                              ADVIKA
             (voice barely above a whisper)
You know it is. For me, you know that.

                               ANU
Why do you think I've taken your side every
time this conversation has come up for the
last five years? But now—god, I hate to say
it—but we're on the climb to thirty. This can't
go on forever.

ADVIKA
(muttering)
You and your perfect life and your law school
applications...What do you know about
creative struggles?

ANU
I could have done graphic design. I really
wanted to. But the law interests me too. I still
think maybe I can do both. I'm not giving up
anything.

ADVIKA
I'm not going to make writing into some sad
little hobby! I don't have to make the same
choices you do.

ANU
(sighs)
Obviously.

Both go silent, wearing matching sour looks on their
faces.

CUT TO:

INT. ADVIKA AND ANU'S APARTMENT—DAY

ADVIKA is in the kitchen washing dishes the following
afternoon. She has her back to the balcony, where ANU
is lying out on a patio chair in a mint-green bikini and
sunglasses. A Pink song wafts in softly from ANU'S
phone. The two haven't spoken since last night's car

ride home—more specifically, ADVIKA hasn't spoken to
ANU.

ANU sings along to the music. She stops and stands up
when she hears a crashing sound on the street below.

                    ANU
  Whoa, what was that?

ADVIKA, being a stubborn ass, hears her but doesn't
respond. She turns off the sink but remains facing the
wall.

                    ANU
  I think there was an accident! It sounded
  pretty brutal. I hope everyone's okay.

ADVIKA rolls her eyes and shakes her head. She's not
ready to stop being irritated, even though she's also
curious about what happened on their street.

                    ANU
  Oh wow, a car hit a fire hydrant. There's
  water everywhere! Everyone's crowding
  around near the car. I'm going to call 911.
  Unless you think someone else has called?

ADVIKA maintains her silence.

                    ANU
  I'm sure someone else called. Okay, Advi,
  this crowd is getting really big. And they're
  pointing at something.

ANU leans over the balcony. The Pink song segues into a Nicki Minaj song.

ANU

I think someone got hit—oh no. (pauses)
Whoa, this is a little wobbly.

ADVIKA storms off into the bathroom and halfway shuts the door. She stares at herself, watching the anger radiating off her in the mirror's reflection. She looks away when she hears a strange noise. In the days and months and years following this moment, she'll never quite remember what the noise sounded like, except that it was unnatural and unsettling. She leaves the bathroom to find its source. On the balcony, the Nicki Minaj song is fading out. One of the glass balcony panels hangs off into the edge of the sky, then falls right in front of her eyes. And then where there was silence, there is noise. Screams, sirens, chatter, the sound of glass breaking. ADVIKA falls to her knees. She doesn't step foot on the balcony then, or ever again.

CHAPTER TWENTY-FOUR

How to Marry a Millionaire

FOR TWO DAYS, ADVIKA DIDN'T leave her bed. She texted Aggie that she was feeling under the weather and was not to be disturbed. Yet the house manager persisted in bringing her meals three times throughout the day and then leaving them outside her closed door. Each time she dropped off food, she'd text her breakfast or lunch, depending on the meal, followed by the "yum" emoji. Advika always texted back Thx but never ate any of it. She had a water bottle at her bedside and sometimes had the energy to take a few sips. But otherwise, Advika stayed in bed, the covers enshrouding her past her head.

Advika's phone buzzed a lot, and she never responded, except to Julian. Even buried in the throes of depression and rage, she never wanted him to be too alarmed about her and cause him to return early. She texted him messages like Just under the weather, my love, I need some rest and quiet time, and he'd text back XOXO and heart emojis. Advika was surprised he didn't inquire too much more, or at least ask her what was ailing her, but no doubt Julian was mostly consumed by production woes. As long as he had in-house spies, he wouldn't be too concerned. It was probably enough that she was waiting for him in Wildwood, barely alive to the world like Sleeping Beauty.

Vik and Sunita had left a series of messages, the tenor of each getting more worried and desperate. To her message about hocking Julian's anniversary gift, Vik had replied that he would come over immediately but needed clearance to drive through security. When faced with the idea of having a piece of home cross the threshold of the fractured fairy tale she found herself trapped in, Advika couldn't respond. The idea made her panicky and nauseous, at a loss for what to say or how to explain herself. So the messages piled up for forty-eight hours, until Advika finally told them I'm fine. Will be in touch. And then proceeded to sink into a soundless sleep that she didn't awaken from until there was a knock at her door.

"Go away," she said, but her voice bounced harmlessly against the comforter drawn over her nose. The knock returned— three sharp, insistent raps. Advika threw an arm over her eyes. "Please, go," she whispered hoarsely. The doorknob turned, and footsteps arrived haltingly at her bed.

"Advika?" Olive's voice. Olive was back—back at Wildwood. Advika burst into tears, so surprised and moved that her friend had returned, even as Julian's betrayal and her own resurgent guilt over Anu still throbbed inside her like the slimy creature from *Alien*, close to bursting through her skin.

"Ahehhhmooorrrr" was the pained sound that came out of Advika's mouth.

"Hey, hey, it's okay," Olive murmured. Advika felt Olive climb under the covers and place a warm hand between her shoulder blades. "We're all worried about you. Did something happen?" Advika heard Aggie's low, rumbly voice, sounding like the teacher in *A Charlie Brown Christmas*. "I think she's fine," Olive called out, even as Advika felt herself tremble uncontrollably in her friend's embrace. "I'm going to sit with her a bit, and then we'll have dinner."

Dinner? Really? The curtained windows gave Advika no sense of time, but her appetite came alive like a race car driver gunning the engine of his vehicle. She pondered the profound depth of her hunger as Olive momentarily slipped out of bed and had a hushed conversation with Aggie. Once the door clicked shut, Advika heard Olive unzipping her boots, the sound of them clattering to the floor, and then her friend was back beside her.

"Advika, you're not alone," she whispered into her ear. "We're worried about you. We're here for you."

"I'm…a…terrible…person," Advika managed to say, the emotions burbling in her throat impeding her ability to speak. "Terrible…friend. And…sister." She couldn't bear to open her eyes and see how Olive regarded her. With pity maybe, and likely annoyance.

"Listen, you're not terrible. You made some mistakes—we all do."

"All…I do…is take," Advika said between hiccupping breaths. "Only care…myself. I'm…a…narcississs," she added, finding it too hard to add *t* to the end of the word.

"Narcissists don't feel bad about being narcissists," Olive said, her voice knocking with gentle humor. "We all get self-involved sometimes. I know I do. I shouldn't have made you feel guilty about that."

"But it's true." The iceberg of self-disgust and misery encasing Advika finally began to thaw, but even with Olive's empathetic words, she wasn't ready to let herself off the hook. "All I ever care about is myself. Never asked about you. Or Vik. Don't…don't even know what's happening with Sun and Balan or the world. And then my sis…" She couldn't even finish that thought, wanting to sidestep the quicksand that would come from speaking her guilt about Anu out loud.

"You've been through a lot. I knew that even when you moved into our old apartment. I could have been kinder too, you know. I knew that you were grieving your sister." Olive tapped Advika on the shoulder, and Advika turned around to face her. She was surprised to see tears in her friend's eyes. As she spoke, they were lying side by side in the king-sized bed, only inches apart. Olive's gaze remained watery, but she never spilled a single tear.

"But I was going through my own shit. If you're a narcissist, then that makes me King Narcissist. All I think about is my documentary. I have no time for anything else: friendships, relationships—nothing. I'm on this treadmill running nowhere. I perpetually feel like I'm running out of my time to fulfill...to fulfill the potential of what I think I'm capable of." Advika nodded, understanding that feeling all too well. "I've been working on the documentary since graduation, and I still feel miles away from finishing. My family has stopped asking me about it; that's how I know they've given up on me. And the hardest thing is that I think this doc could be really special, but it's just...I just don't see an end in sight. Meanwhile, I'm going from apartment to apartment every time my lease is up, working at the same coffeehouse for three years...I'll be pouring coffee until I'm fifty."

"That's not true," Advika said softly.

"But it feels true. And then seeing you in this magnificent house drove it home for me: my life has hit a dead end. I craved what you have, Advika. I want a gigantic flat-screen TV and a swimming pool and not having to think about my bank account balance ever. And I began hating myself for how much I wanted it. I even began thinking of starting a YouTube channel. YouTube! Like some kind of lame influencer. Anyway, I got jealous of you, which was shitty. And I'm sorry."

Advika looked at herself and her current circumstances through Olive's eyes. And she was ashamed of herself and her behavior. Olive was being too easy on her; she really had treated her friend shabbily while caught up in her own drama, and she told Olive so.

"Thanks, I appreciate that." Olive gave her a small smile, revealing that her black lipstick was starting to fade along her lower lip. "Now that we've had our Dr. Phil moment, we've got to get you out of this bed. You're not going to be stuck here until you're fifty, okay?"

The self-pity Advika found herself mired in began to slowly abate. Olive's words were not only a salve, but also a firing pistol, reminding her that she had already lost two precious days in her goal of finding a "free yourself from your marriage" card before Julian returned. The sadness gave way to a growing roar. And now Advika herself was the slimy creature from *Alien*, ready to come flying out, no longer willing to hide or be contained.

That feeling was only amplified by a DVD that Olive pulled out of her backpack and placed in front of her.

"I tracked down the entire season of *Luxury Wives* with Julian and Victoria, his third ex-wife," Olive said. "I thought you might be interested."

~

Over the course of twelve episodes, *Luxury Wives* proved itself to be an unrepentant rip-off of the *Real Housewives* franchise, starting with the opening credits. Five women in their thirties and forties, all sporting bounteous hair, overplucked eyebrows, and sparkling gold gowns resembling wedding dresses, whipped around to face the camera with a smile, as their catchphrases played in voice-over. Each catchphrase was a bad pun based on where each luxury wife derived her wealth. Two were CEOs of dubious-sounding "wellness" enterprises, with a Google search revealing that one had gone bankrupt and the other had been felled by a class-action lawsuit. The remaining three wives were the spouses of very wealthy men: a real estate magnate, an '80s pop star turned Tony-nominated Broadway star, and Julian Zelding.

"Lights, camera, action." Victoria Truong whipped around, hands on hips, her waist-long hair gathering around her like a silken waterfall. "All eyes on me."

And she wasn't wrong. Not just because she was Vietnamese-American and therefore the only person of color on the show, but because at age thirty-five, she was the youngest of the group by a decade and therefore lacked their shiny, immobile faces. At five foot eleven, Victoria towered over all the women, and even her husband. She also had a delightful potty mouth and a tendency to walk around in skimpy clothing ("I'm warm-blooded!" she often protested) that kept the editors busy bleeping her swears and blurring her chest.

To watch *Luxury Wives*, which Advika and Olive did mostly nonstop from 6 p.m. to 6 a.m. the following morning, was an experience on par with déjà vu but turned on its head and then angled sideways. It was shocking to see Julian appear on some of the episodes. But what truly stupefied Advika was that Mr. and (the third) Mrs. Zelding lived at Wildwood during the filming of the show. She shouldn't have been that surprised, but it was deeply weird to watch Julian's relationship with Victoria depicted onscreen—and take place where Advika now lived.

Perhaps because he kept zero photographic evidence of them at Wildwood, it had never occurred to Advika that Julian might have occupied their home with one of his exes. By watching *Luxury Wives*, she learned that Julian had lived for nearly two decades in Beverly Hills but had bought Wildwood for his new bride because she "needed—like, desperately needed—an ocean view." Hearing this made Advika feel foolish. Julian had always talked about his home as if he had been its sole resident, and since he barely discussed his former wives, Advika had just assumed Julian had moved into Wildwood as a single man. Binging the series was almost like watching home videos, except that Advika had been snipped out of the frame and replaced by a gorgeous supermodel type whose expertise included makeup, Pilates, and transforming Julian into her personal lapdog.

"Is he like that with you?" Olive said during the end of the first episode, in which Julian massaged Victoria's sparkly, pedicured feet while she lamented a long day at her private fitness club, where she worked as a personal trainer. The couple were lounging on a lavender leather sofa in the great room, a much more feminine piece of furniture than the enormous camel-colored one that currently took up the cavernous space.

"Sort of? Maybe in the beginning?" Advika said, wrinkling her nose. And then they both made "ewww" noises as Julian sucked on Victoria's big toe, making her squeal.

"Ohmigod, make it stop." Olive covered her eyes.

"Julian hates paparazzi more than anything else on the planet. Why would he agree to appear on this show?"

"Men get stupid when they're in love. Or lust. I mean, she's superhot." Olive leaned back against the headboard, then crossed her legs at the ankles. "She obviously turned off his brain and turned on his . . ." She raised her eyebrows at Advika, who responded with "Ugh."

A Julian-less episode—episode four—revealed why Wildwood's entire top floor had been converted into a master bedroom suite, and how Victoria had masterminded the his and her bathrooms.

"We need to retain a little mystery, you know?" she told Taylor, the wife of the real estate magnate, as they surveyed Victoria's bathroom palace, which looked much better on TV than in person.

"Ooh yes," Taylor giggled. "Gotta keep it sexy, girl."

"Not just for him, but for me too, right? I don't need to hear his farts, and he doesn't need to see me pluck my chin hair." Taylor reacted with a gasp, followed by a clutch of fake giggles.

"Thank you," Advika exhaled, clasping her hands in gratitude. "Having my own bathroom here has been a lifesaver."

The scene jumped to Taylor in a talking-head interview, a tiny white Pomeranian on her lap. "I think Victoria's a sweetheart, but I don't understand that kind of classless talk. Maybe that's okay where she comes from," the woman added, eyes narrowing, as the dog licked her elbow, "but I wasn't raised like that."

Victoria, when told what Taylor had said, shot back in her talking head: "Listen: she told me about her vaginal rejuvenation at a children's birthday party, and I can't say the word 'fart' in front of her?" She rolled her eyes, then tapped her temple, showing off a gold ruby ring on her index finger. "Taylor has a hard time understanding anyone who doesn't look like her. Did you know the first time we met she thought I had come over to pick up her laundry?" Victoria grimaced, then shook her head, as if expelling dark thoughts. "I just keep hashtag winning because I'm me. And Taylor is . . ." Victoria gave a Cheshire grin. "Taylor."

The scene cut back to Taylor in her talking-head segment, holding up the Pomeranian to her face and planting kisses on its tiny, wiggling head, only to make a retching noise, then spit out something that had been stuck to her pet's fur.

"Oh, gross," Olive said. "How did Victoria put up with these women?"

"Because she's better than them," Advika replied. Having served and waited on many Taylors throughout her career, it was so satisfying to see how often Victoria was able to put the Luxury Wives in their place with a combination of wit, wiles, and pure glee. As Advika enjoyed watching Victoria on the show, she shamefully realized that she hadn't been nearly as invested in researching her as Julian's first two wives, because she had just taken his "gold digger" assignation at his word, an opinion that was solidified by the fact that Victoria had been a reality star. She could now understand what had attracted Julian to Victoria besides her beauty; she also seemed incredibly fun to be around. As much as her co-stars threw passive-aggressive remarks her way, mostly about her Asianness, they all gravitated toward Victoria too and wanted her favor.

As did her husband. Julian's sporadic appearances on the show were primarily to fawn over and compliment his wife just before she was about to leave for an event: a dog fashion show or a launch party for a vegan lingerie line. Victoria would always look stunning and accepted his lavish words of praise ("You are a feast for the eyes, my dear") with a bemused acceptance, responding, "Oh, Jules."

But there was a standout moment in episode six that seemed to neatly encapsulate their relationship. Victoria gave a talking-head interview listing everything she had bought or asked for in the past six months, interspersed with said items and occasionally cutting to a shot of Julian.

VICTORIA
[counting on her fingers]
Let's see. A hot pink Bentley.

Victoria in a photo shoot while wearing a fur bikini as she reclines on the hood of the Bentley.

VICTORIA
[proudly raises right arm]
This diamond-and-jade bracelet. A twenty-four-karat
gold toilet bowl.

A zoom in on the toilet bowl in Victoria's bathroom,
followed by a flushing noise.

"Is your toilet gold?" Olive asked, mouth open.
"Not anymore." Advika sighed. "But damn, I would have loved
to have seen it."
"I wonder if she got it in the divorce," Olive said.
"Wouldn't be surprised."

VICTORIA
[tucks her hair behind her ears]
These earrings. Black diamonds. Only one of ten in the
entire world. Also went on a lingerie shopping spree at
Fleur du Mal.

Victoria modeling several sheer and lacy bras, panties,
and bustiers in a three-paneled mirror in her walk-in
closet. At the last ensemble, the camera panned in closer to
show Julian in the mirror's reflection, watching her with a
lascivious grin.

VICTORIA
Lots of donations for causes that are really important
to me.

Victoria posing for photos while presenting big checks:
$50,000 for UNICEF, $25,000 for Save the Children.

VICTORIA

And the swimming pool. Well, not the pool itself—that was there already, right? But the water was imported from a freshwater pool in Indonesia. We get it refreshed every month. It costs a lot, but trust me—it's worth it.

Victoria doing laps in the pool as Julian sits poolside, eyeing her while talking on his phone.

"He doesn't know how to say no to me," Victoria said at the end of the montage, shrugging coquettishly but with a twinkle of merriment in her eyes. *Teach me your ways*, Advika thought, impressed by how wholly Victoria had Julian in her sway.

Throughout their binge watch, Olive would Google facts about Victoria and the show. From online deep dives of old entertainment and gossip stories, and the tidbits that emerged whenever Victoria was onscreen, a story started to emerge that made Victoria seem much more interesting than her reality TV persona. Born in Vietnam, she and her parents and older brother had emigrated to the US following the end of the Vietnam War. Like many Vietnamese refugees who left the country during the fall of Saigon, the Truong family resettled in Westminster, a city in Orange County that had one of the largest populations of Vietnamese people in the United States. Victoria lost her older brother to a car accident when they were both teenagers, and at age twenty-one, she married her high school boyfriend, only to divorce a year later. She moved to LA soon after, where she carved out a career for herself as a personal trainer and occasional model and actress.

"This is how Julian and Victoria met, according to *Us Weekly*," Olive read out loud over a muted scene of Taylor and the pop star's wife, Cleotina, drinking wine while painting—but mostly ogling—a nude male model.

"The glamorous couple met at Kitson, where Zelding had asked Truong for advice on buying a gift for his goddaughter.

"'Victoria has exquisite taste,' a source told *Us Weekly*, 'and he was enamored with her immediately.' After a sushi date that night, the two had a whirlwind courtship before eloping at Maui's Four Seasons—"

"Ughhhhhh," Advika said, pulling the covers over her head.

Olive snorted. "I don't mean to laugh, but man, this guy loves to wine and dine Asian women until they marry him. He has a type."

"He *is* a type too," Advika groused, throwing back the comforter. "But why isn't this show more well-known? How has it not stuck to him?" Advika flopped down onto her stomach on the bed. "This is an embarrassment."

"Because (a), the show was canceled after one season, and (b), the Women First network went off the air a year after that." Olive flopped down next to Advika. "There are no reruns on cable and it never went on streaming. It's not even on YouTube. So it's almost like it never existed." She explained that from the moment Advika had told her about Julian's ex-wives, Olive had been searching for anything she could about *Luxury Wives*, finally striking pay dirt on a Japanese auction site similar to eBay.

"Shit—was that expensive?" Advika said. "I can pay you back."

Olive waved her away. "No need. To be honest, it wasn't just for you. I was curious about what it'd be like to see an Asian-American woman on a show like this."

"And?" Advika said, pausing the DVD.

"She's not what I expected."

"Me neither," Advika said with a smile.

⌒

The sun was just starting to peek over the horizon by the time the two made it to the season finale. Advika had been close to giving in to sleepy exhaustion when Victoria made an announcement at the end of the penultimate episode that elicited shrieks of joy from her castmates. Throughout the series, the Luxury Wives threw events so that the whole cast had an opportunity to gather in front of the cameras to snipe at and gossip about each other. But Victoria seemed to have trumped them all by throwing a wedding-vow renewal and cannily timing it so that it would air during the two-hour finale. The news jerked Advika out of her drowsiness, especially when Victoria noted that it would be taking place at Wildwood.

Julian had only appeared intermittently throughout *Luxury Wives*, but since he was the groom, Advika expected him to appear for a good chunk of screen time. That clawing sense of déjà vu at seeing Victoria living with Julian as his wife had diminished with every passing episode, but resurfaced full force as she saw the preparations taking place. Advika's own wedding seemed hurried and inconsequential compared to the extravagant lead-up to this main event. Victoria indulged in nearly all the bridal clichés: trying on dresses in front of the Luxury Wives at a Beverly Hills salon, cake tasting with her best friend / hairdresser, a bachelorette party in Vegas, a titanic freak-out over flowers and seating charts with her frazzled wedding planner, and a shouting match between two of her castmates, which Victoria calmly refereed while getting her makeup done.

As for Julian, he oddly didn't make an appearance at all until the ceremony itself. Clad in an aubergine velvet tuxedo jacket and matching bow tie, he stood at a white altar laced with ropes of gardenias, looking happy but also strangely nervous, his eyes often flickering to the bride's side of the audience. Whereas Julian's side had about thirty or so people, mostly white and middle-aged, Victoria's side seemed double that. And nearly all of them were Vietnamese. As the camera panned over them,

Victoria said in voice-over that the main reason she wanted to renew her vows after only two years of marriage was for her family's sake.

"Eloping was kinda selfish when you have a family like mine," Victoria said as a series of family members were shown conversing and laughing in the crowd, along with their names and relationship to the bride. Victoria's parents were in attendance, as well as scads of aunties, uncles, and cousins. When an off-camera producer asked her if they were all her blood relatives, Victoria laughed.

"We don't have to be related to be family. We're all very close—I've known most of them since I was in diapers. Many of us came over to America at the same time. It wasn't easy at all, but we had each other." Advika and Olive both groaned when stereotypical Oriental-sounding music played during a montage of photographs of baby Victoria, then toddler Victoria and her older brother dressed up as a witch and the Hulk for Halloween, and several shots of Victoria and her extended family at Disneyland, at the beach, and having meals together.

Advika watched all this with some interest, but she was jittering to get to the wedding part. She couldn't help wanting to compare her memories of her own simple wedding with this extravaganza and judge how heartfelt Julian was saying "I do" to Victoria compared to her. Advika found herself grabbing Olive's arm when the wedding march began, as Victoria, wearing a Vera Wang mermaid gown and tiara, walked down the aisle. The camera showed close-ups of Julian's face as he gazed at his wife gliding toward him with a pink, rigid smile, her eye makeup glittering in the waning light of late afternoon. Julian seemed as besotted as ever upon seeing Victoria.

"This must be weird for you, huh?" Olive said, drawing her arm away.

"You have no idea."

The wedding march was replaced with faux-romantic syn-
thesizer music as a profusely sweating man in an ill-fitting suit
recounted how Julian and Victoria had met at Kitson ("It was
love at first sight"), then asked them to recite their vows.

"Two years ago, you made me the happiest man alive. Every
day I take a moment to reflect on how lucky I am to have you in
my life." Julian's eyes, which were fixed on Victoria's, briefly
swept down her body. "I want to reaffirm the vows I made to
you on that perfect day in Maui in front of everyone here, our
nearest and dearest. Victoria, I pledge to love you and honor
you through all our tomorrows, in sickness and health, for better or for worse, until death do us part. May God continue to
bless us and bless this marriage."

"God?" Advika said incredulously. "He's not religious." She
remembered Julian's grandfather's cross that she discovered in
his safe. Did he care more about religion than he let on?

"Shhh!" Olive was sitting at the edge of the bed. Unlike
Advika, she hadn't yawned at all during the entire binge watch.

After Julian concluded his vows, Victoria dabbed at her eyes
with a handkerchief that she had tucked inside her bouquet.
Her voice trembled as she surveyed her side of the aisle. The
camera intercut Victoria's vows with shots of her family members watching her with pride.

"I'm so overcome. To have my family here on such a momen-
tous day. These are the people who cared for me, watched out
for me, gave me lectures when I didn't want to hear them." Both
sides of the aisle laughed. "I wouldn't be here without you. I
only wish Max could have been here. I keep looking out at all
of you and expecting to see him. You'd think that feeling would
go away after a few years, but during important moments like
this, boom—they're back," she said with a forced laugh that
did not mask the sadness in her voice. In a jarring contrast to

her princessy bridal look, the episode then cut to Victoria in a talking-head interview, wearing a black one-shouldered top and muted makeup, her voluptuous hair snaking down her shoulder in a braided ponytail.

"Nothing is more important to me than my family," Victoria said in the interview, briefly raising a Kleenex to her eyes. "We're loud and noisy and always in each other's business. Lately I've been thinking that we're this way all the time to compensate for the fact that Max isn't here." She sniffled, then continued. "I do everything a million percent, full throttle, full volume, so I don't have to think about him. I used to try to run away from those feelings in all the ways you can imagine—partying, booze, men—but at the end of the day, I learned I just have to live with it. On a day like our vow renewal, those feelings come back like a tidal wave." Victoria shrugged. "But what can you do? I have to go on."

The episode returned to the wedding, with Victoria saying in a joking tone, "Okay, sorry; I'm rambling now." The crowd let out a collective "awww" as Victoria dabbed at her eyes again. Then she pulled out a folded piece of paper from her décolletage. "Now, I have a few words for this man right here."

Advika didn't listen to any of Victoria's wedding vows. The image of Victoria in her interview, sad-faced yet stoic when discussing her dead brother, remained frozen in her mind. Advika barely registered the rest of the ceremony, or even the episode. She was lost in thought when Olive exclaimed, "Okay, plot twist!"

"Huh? What?"

"Are you okay?" Olive paused the DVD, and as she did so, the remote control slipped out of her grasp and clattered to the floor. Startled by the noise, Advika jumped up, then sagged to the ground next to the remote. "Seriously, is something wrong?"

"I...my sister. It's my fault." Saying the words out loud that she had berated herself with daily for the past two years gave her a shot of nervous energy.

Advika sat up halfway and grabbed the remote and squeezed it, the buttons digging into her palm. "I never told anyone what I did, what I could have done to save her."

In halting sentences, Advika unspooled the whole story to Olive, about how dinner at her parents' led Anu to agreeing with them about Advika's writing career, which in turn caused Advika to give her the silent treatment, right until the very end of her sister's life. "I was childish and stupid and insecure, and if I had just talked to her, or gone out on the balcony, none of this would have happened. She'd still be here."

Olive huddled next to her on the floor but didn't say anything. She patted Advika's back with gentle, rhythmic taps, the kind one would give to a baby when trying to calm her or get her to nap.

"I know...what you're thinking," Advika said, her words coming out breathy and stuttered. "It's not...my fault...I can't...blame myself. But I was there! I was there."

"You were there, but you didn't cause the balcony to collapse. Or the car accident that caused her to look out over the balcony in the first place." Olive sounded maddeningly logical. "It was just a terrible accident."

"I'll never not feel responsible, because she was my sister," Advika said after several deep breaths, and her voice became steady again. "I've been trying to outrun my emotions, stuff them away in a box, or turn my life upside down just to escape them. And I'm exhausted. I can't do it anymore. But at the same time, I don't know what to do with myself either."

"I think it starts with learning to forgive yourself. I think therapy can help with that."

"You're the first person I've confessed this to. It will scrape my insides to have to say those words again to anyone." But already Advika felt lighter. Maybe she'd be ready to try in time.

"Everyone's grief is on a different timetable. You'll know when you're ready." Olive leaned back against the bed, her fingers brushing the jade bracelet on her wrist. "I lost my grandmother when I was nine, and while it's not the same as your loss, the grief was like a piece of gum. The longer I chewed it, the less flavor it had. And then one day I swallowed it. So I'm not chewing it every day, but it's still inside me. And I heard that gum takes, like, seventy-two years to digest, so..." Olive covered her face with both hands, but a few moments later, she let out a terrific snort.

"Are *you* okay?" Advika asked as Olive doubled over with laughter.

"That analogy," Olive said, gasping for air, "was terrible. I can't believe I compared grief"—another loud snort—"to gum."

"I liked it," Advika said, even as she began to laugh too. She got up from the floor and grabbed a tissue from her nightstand, then took the whole box and tossed it to Olive. Advika's aim was off and it bounced off Olive's shoulder, which for some reason made both of them laugh harder.

As they collected themselves, stretching their arms and yawning, Advika wondered if Aggie was downstairs, or perhaps creeping up the steps to overhear what the two were talking and laughing about. When Olive had first produced the DVD, Advika had been grateful the master bedroom's entertainment setup included a DVD player, allowing them to watch the entire series through the night behind closed doors, since the only other option would have been the home movie theater on the lower level. The whole night and early morning had taken on a surreal quality, like standing inside the eye of a hurricane, with anxiety, angst, and drama still surrounding Advika, while also being able to momentarily step outside of it.

But two floors below them, Wildwood had begun to stir, and with it, the reminder of the real world. Advika's immense hunger pangs, which had been momentarily satiated by Olive's stash of candy bars and Taiwanese fruit jellies, also reemerged. Her stomach rumbled so loudly she patted her belly, as if to reassure it they'd be eating soon. Doing so reminded her of the night before final exams during her and Anu's senior year in college. While they were studying in their bunk beds, Anu on top and Advika on the bottom, Advika let out a fantastically loud fart that sounded like a battalion of exploding balloons. Anu had swung down from her bunk and lovingly patted Advika's butt. "There, there," she had said, loopy from nonstop studying and little sleep. The twins had howled with laughter until they were barely able to breathe.

The memory made Advika smile, without the usual accompaniment of pummeling guilt and chest-beating remorse. Maybe there really was a way to live with it, she thought, recalling both Victoria's words and Olive's strange but strangely apt gum metaphor.

"Do you want to wash up, and then we could go get some breakfast?" Advika asked.

"Wait." Olive picked up the remote, which Advika had dropped at the foot of the bed. "There's something you need to see. I think you missed it earlier." She rewound the episode to the final two minutes, which, in *Real Housewives* fashion, concluded with a pithy summary of each Luxury Wife's life, a sort of "Where are they now?"

> *After their vow renewals, Julian surprised Victoria with a second honeymoon to Vietnam and Thailand. And now that they're back from their romantic getaway, the couple is eyeing a second car for Victoria: a hot pink minivan.*

The bland pop song soundtracking the title cards abruptly transitioned to a rocking version of "Rock-a-Bye Baby" before segueing to the end credits.

"Holy...wait, what?" Advika's eyes widened.

"My thoughts exactly," Olive said with a yawn, as she snacked on the last of the fruit jellies.

CHAPTER TWENTY-FIVE

Down with Love

EXHAUSTION HAD FINALLY HIT OLIVE, and she needed some rest before her afternoon shift at the coffeehouse. So Advika let her snooze while she went downstairs to check in and gather some snacks to eat. It was close to 7 a.m., and just as she expected, Aggie was seated at the island, sipping coffee while typing intently on her phone.

"Hi there," Advika called out, mustering up the friendliest tone possible.

"Morning." Aggie spun around on her stool, her Birken-stocked feet slapping the floor. "Looks like a visit from your friend has done wonders."

Advika ignored the condescending tone and went about opening the pantry cabinets to gather some quick breakfast items like blueberry muffins and croissants. As she did so, she flashed to a scene from *Luxury Wives*, in which Victoria dressed up in a French maid's outfit and did a sexy shimmy for Julian before treating him like her personal chef as she asked him to make her dinner. The scene seemed to sum up their dynamic in a nutshell, and for a brief moment, Advika wanted to ask Aggie if she had ever met Victoria, but thought better of it.

"I'm feeling much better," Advika said, her head buried deep in a cabinet so she didn't have to make eye contact with her. "I think I might have eaten something bad, and it just needed some time to work through my system."

"Oh, you had an upset stomach? Or nausea?"

What is it to you? "Something like that," Advika said, picking up some bananas and sticking them under her armpits. "Olive's feeling down about her breakup, and she barely slept. So I'm trying to get a little food in her before she has to go to work." Was her story too detailed? Or would it have been worse to pretend she hadn't taken to her bed for the past two days?

"Well, you two take care of each other," the house manager said as Advika finally turned around and faced her. She was looking at Advika through her glasses, which had slipped down her nose, one eyebrow raised as if it were an antenna. Advika smiled at her and nodded, then hurried back up the stairs with the baked goods gathered precariously in her hands. When she reached the bedroom, she managed to open the door without dropping anything. Olive was fast asleep on the bed, her arms and limbs splayed out like she was in the middle of making a snow angel. So Advika left the breakfast items on top of her bureau, except for a blueberry muffin that she finished in four big bites. Then she grabbed her janky Dell laptop and got to Googling.

What she learned about Victoria surprised her. In the US, Victoria had minimal fame and presence and remained mostly known as Julian Zelding's third wife. There were also occasional references to *Luxury Wives* and the fact that she had carved out a niche for herself on reality television—but not in America. Just like Evie, Victoria had seemingly absconded to another country as soon as the ink dried on her divorce papers. But rather than hide away in southern France, Victoria chased the spotlight and achieved reality stardom in the UK. *Luxury Wives* was a minor blip on her resume compared to the steady stream of shows she appeared on from 2013 to the present day: *Bikinis and Abs*; *Ladies and Gentlemen, Let's Get Sexy*; *The Essex Star Challenge*. She eventually became so popular that she earned a place on *Celebrity Big Brother*. But as far as Advika could tell, Victoria never mentioned *Luxury Wives* or her marriage to Julian—not on any of her series, in the press, or on social media. Usually, a reality TV star would milk her connection to Hollywood, or at least the media would salivate over that angle. And there were some gossip stories about Victoria and her "successful Hollywood producer ex" in some initial news coverage of her. The bio for her first UK reality series also made mention of it, describing Victoria as "twice divorced" and the "former wife of Julian Zelding, Oscar-winning movie mogul."

But as *Bikinis and Abs* aired, Victoria emerged as the breakout star. Besides displaying the same charm and self-deprecating sense of humor she had shown in *Luxury Wives*, Victoria also benefited from having steamy romances with two of the "abs." Judging by the news stories and blog posts about the show, viewers were divided into two vocal factions: "Team Nasrat" and "Team Robbie D." The frenzied coverage of the love triangle augmented Victoria's star power to the point that references to Julian in the press dribbled down to nearly nothing—and not just when the show aired, but afterward too. Advika marveled at how Victoria had successfully distanced herself from a marriage that could have easily defined her for the rest of her life.

"Seriously, teach me your ways," Advika murmured.

Advika clicked through page after page of search results, hoping something would catch her eye. By page 37, Advika was ready to give up and give in to her fatigue but willed herself to try one more page. And she was rewarded for her doggedness by coming across a link titled "Victoria Trang talks second marriage to movie mogul." A careless (or purposeful?) spelling error had caused the link to be buried in the search results. Advika bounced excitedly on the bed, stirring Olive out of sleep. But Advika's elation soon turned to disappointment when, upon clicking the link, she learned that Victoria's interview was only accessible to those who lived in the UK.

"Are we having an earthquake?" Olive murmured, burrowing her head inside her tee shirt like a turtle hiding in its shell.

"Nope, it's just me," Advika said, massaging her temples as a tiny headache erupted behind her eyes. After twelve hours of watching TV and then hopping on her laptop, her head was finally rebelling against all the screen time. "Sorry to wake you. I thought I found something about Victoria, but I'm blocked from watching it because I'm not in the UK."

"Oh, that's easy. Let me wash up and I'll show you how to get around that."

Advika scarfed down a banana and a croissant as she impatiently waited for Olive to finish showering. Just as she contemplated a second croissant, Olive emerged from Advika's bathroom, shaking her head.

"It's kinda trippy using your bathroom after seeing what it used to look like. I think you should have kept the pink zebra-print wallpaper and the chandelier."

"All of Victoria's touches were gone by the time I got here." The two sat side by side on the bed as Olive showed Advika how she could use a VPN so that her laptop had a UK IP address and could therefore access any of their content. Advika marveled at Olive's skills and ingenuity and told her friend so.

"It's nothing."

"No, it's everything." Advika gave her a side hug, which Olive gamely withstood. "If you hadn't been there for me...I don't know what would have happened. And I promise that I won't be a one-way friend. Let me just figure out this whole husband thing." Advika shook her head. "God, that sounds lame."

"Ha! Well, you said it, not me. But seriously, I'm glad to

have been there for you. And you better be ready for the whole friendship thing, because I'm going to make a lot of demands. There will be tattoos, for starters." Advika and Olive exchanged grins.

Later, they gave each other a proper hug before Olive left for work. In Olive's backpack next to her headphones and car keys was Julian's anniversary present. Olive had promised to deliver the diamond jewelry to Vik so he could get its value appraised. As she watched Olive descend the staircase, Advika had no idea that it would be the last time she saw her friend for several years.

⌒

VICTORIA TRANG TALKS SECOND MARRIAGE TO MOVIE MOGUL

"Chatterbox with Laina and Nigel," RadioStarUK
Runtime: 7:56

It was a videotaped radio interview, and based on the awkward segue, the undated clip seemed to take place after the filming of *Bikinis and Abs*.

NIGEL: So we've been talking Victoria's love life on the show, but can we talk about your real-world relationships?

VICTORIA: Well, I haven't been so lucky in love. [*laughs*] I'm twice divorced. That's why I thought I'd change my mojo and see what you all have for me across the pond.

LAINA: Your second husband is the film mogul Julian Zelding.

VICTORIA: Is there a question in there?

Not only did Victoria weave in and out of a British accent, but she also slurred a bit when answering the question. This is what led Advika, initially focused on staring at the weird feathery hat perched on Victoria's head like a cockatoo, to notice that the interviewers and interviewee all had filled shot glasses in front of them.

LAINA: Tell us, love! What was it like to be married to a Hollywood movie man?

VICTORIA: Well, you know, this isn't my first reality show. Julian and I [*hiccups*] were on a reality show together. I was on the show—I was the star—and he made appearances. You can't see it, kids; it's canceled. Thank God.

NIGEL: I think I remember reading that! I would have loved to see it. I bet the camera loved you even then. I can just see you running around the pool, wearing a skimpy bikini—whoops! [*he rings a bell*]

VICTORIA: Now, c'mon. You did that on purpose.

Advika was dismayed to see all three reach for their shot glasses and down whatever was in them. Who knew how often vile Nigel had inserted "bikini" into the conversation. Although, she realized with equal parts excitement and self-loathing that an inebriated Victoria might be more forthcoming about life with Julian. She turned up the volume.

> VICTORIA: Blech. Okay, that's the last one for me. Anyway, I was a good wife, and for a while, he was a good husband. We had some fun times. I met a lot of movie stars. They were all shorter than me, though. [*giggles*]

> LAINA: I'm surprised that a man of his stature—he's won a few Oscars, yes?—would agree to do a reality show with you.

> VICTORIA: Well, you know. [*she tosses her hair dramatically behind her, and the radio interviewers laugh*] He couldn't resist. And I told him that if he would be on the show with me, then we could talk about starting a family.

Even as Advika's stomach churned from eating the pastries and banana so quickly, her headache magically receded. She leaned forward, as if by having her eyes just inches from the screen, she could be closer to the truth.

> VICTORIA: I wanted that series to be my launching pad to bigger things. I didn't want to just be a wife with furs and jewelry, you know? But my ex wanted me [*scrunches up her face*] to stay at home and be pretty and have his babies. And we had some miscommunication... Anyway. Don't you want to ask me about the—

> NIGEL: Wait, wait. This is so interesting. So is that why the two of you split up? He wanted little Victorias and Juliuses—

VICTORIA: Julians. Whatever. Listen, you want a
story? I'll tell you a story. People want to paint me as a
gold digger, but guess what? We didn't have a prenup.
[*picks up glass, sees it's empty*] Bikini!

The shot glasses are refilled, and the three immediately
down them. Nigel is delighted, but Laina looks a bit
green.

VICTORIA: [*slams glass down*] So listen. We had no
prenup, and I asked for no money from him. But in
exchange for no money, no alimony, I only requested
one thing. [*pause for dramatic effect, followed by a devious
smile*] One of his Oscars.

"Ohhhhh," Advika exhaled, a smile of wonderment curling
on her lips. So she hadn't been imagining it when she thought
one was missing from Julian's office. There really were only
four Oscars in there, not five.

VICTORIA: I didn't want a long, drawn-out fight. I just
wanted out. But I needed to take something from him,
you know? He has this whole affect that he doesn't
care about awards. That's bullshit. He cares. Deeply.
He made it impossible for me to carve out a career in
the States. He took something important to me, so I
returned the favor.

Two things then happened at once: A birdlike woman in
glasses entered into the frame and covered the microphone
with her hand. And then Laina made a terrible retching noise,
but thankfully the video cut off right then.

Advika sat back, a sense of elation washing over her. Victoria had defeated Julian! After Evie's and Nova's stories, she wanted to stand up and cheer that the third Mrs. Zelding had managed to get away from him and, even better, achieve the career she wanted. She had to contact Victoria right now. There was so much they could talk about, so much they could share. To know there was another woman out there who could relate to Advika's experiences was like fireworks spinning inside her, making her dizzy with hope.

Except that Victoria had just started filming *Escape from Reality Island*, which saw her stranded on a desert island with other reality stars. Advika discovered this when she was searching for the most recent news coverage about her. It would be impossible to communicate with her for who knew how long. Still, to know Victoria was out there thriving, specifically by defying Julian, gave Advika strength. And also clarity. Because she could now clearly see Julian's pattern of marrying women with the intention of them giving him a child. As he had gotten older, his wives became younger and, even more importantly, had less clout and power.

After an actress and a pop star, then a reality wannabe, he finally landed himself a wife who was a pure nobody, someone whom he could easily control. And just like with his previous wives, Julian had sought to undermine Advika's career aspirations and keep her homebound. *No more of this*, she fumed, pounding the bed with a tight fist. *I am done.*

And for once, Advika's timing worked out for her. Because no sooner had she decided to file for divorce immediately than her burner phone pinged with a new email. Evie Lockhart's lawyer had written her back.

CHAPTER TWENTY-SIX

You've Got Mail

Dear Ms. Srinivasan,

I was quite delighted to receive your email, as I wasn't sure if you would contact me regarding the stipulations in Ms. Lockhart's will. I will gladly share with you what Ms. Lockhart authorized me to communicate to you, but as a part of the conditions of her will, she requires you to travel to Avignon and meet with me in person, and alone.

I am leaving on Aug. 4 for a three-week holiday, so if you are able to come before month's end, that would be most ideal. Please let me know at your earliest convenience if you will be able to come here and meet with me. I truly hope you can, as we have much of interest to discuss.

Sincerely,
David Renaud, Esq.
Bedioux, Renaud, and Associates
Avignon, France

"Knock, knock!" The unfamiliar voice outside Advika's bedroom was followed by several urgent knocks. Still absorbing the email from Evie's lawyer, she froze in place, not able to identify who was at her door. "Addi, are you in there?"

Oh shit—Mona. Advika scrambled to hide the Dell laptop and burner phone underneath the mattress. With the bed already believably rumpled, she yanked her bathrobe off the chaise lounge. Before opening the door, she cast a quick glance around the room. Julian's elegant master suite looked like a group of freshmen had just had a dorm room cram session. Oh well. Advika brushed her hair out of her eyes, then opened the door.

"Hi, Mona," she said with a sleepy but solicitous grin. "I guess you heard I was under the weather."

"Yes, I did. How are you?" Mona didn't ask to be let in but instead stepped past Advika and surveyed her bedroom. "You're feeling better now?"

"I am, yeah. I think it might have been something I ate. Whatever it was, it felled me for a bit. But I started to feel better this morning." With a wry smile, she added, "You can let Julian know I'm okay."

Mona kicked away some candy wrappers with the pointed toe of her black stiletto. "What makes you say that?"

"I just get a feeling that you're his eyes and ears when he's not here." Advika sat down on the bed, grateful she had tucked her secret electronics on the other side of the mattress. "And I don't think he believed me when I told him myself."

"You know Julian—he's such a worrier." Mona sidestepped a pair of Advika's socks on the rug and sat down beside her. "You know, if you ever need to talk, I'm here for you. I'm his assistant, but I'm also his friend. And I can be yours too."

"I appreciate that." Advika rubbed her temples again, not because her headache had returned but because she wanted to delay responding to her. Finally, she had an idea, and she dropped her hands to her sides, as if finally ready to come clean.

"I haven't wanted to worry Julian with this. My friend Olive—you remember her from the other day, right? She's been a good listener, but..." Advika trailed off, then let her throat catch before continuing. "I miss my parents. And I'm worried about them. After the wedding, they kinda cut me off."

"Oh no," Mona said, patting her knee. After a moment's hesitation, she leaned in and gave Advika a quick hug, briefly overwhelming her with the scent of her cinnamonesque perfume. "That must be so hard. And now with Julian out of the country too. Are you feeling alone, maybe a little depressed?"

"Yeah," Advika said, nodding slowly. "I think the only thing that will help at this point is going to see them. Things are just so, um, unfinished between us. And I'm their only child. I can't let this estrangement go on." Even though she was talking to one of Julian's surrogates, every word Advika told her was true. She hadn't ever said it out loud before, or even to herself. "Thanks for asking about me. I appreciate it."

"Of course, Addi! We're friends now. You can tell me anything." Mona looked Advika over from head to toe, her eyes briefly, and weirdly, alighting on her chest. "Like, if you ever feel under the weather again, tell me ASAP. We can't just have you suffering in here alone."

"You got it," Advika said, hoping she radiated gratitude instead of disdain.

"Well, I gotta run." Mona stood up and brushed off lint from her pencil skirt. "And I wasn't supposed to tell you this, but I think I'll be doing you a favor." She flashed a smile that showed off her absurdly white, Tic Tac–shaped teeth. "Julian's coming home early. He's catching a red-eye tonight. He just can't wait to see you. Ohmigod, you have no idea how much he talks about you. Addi this and Addi that!" She giggled and clapped her hands, causing her bracelets to clang noisily against each other. "I have a few things I've got to take care of, but why don't

I swing by later this afternoon and take you out for a girls' day? We can go to the salon, get a mani-pedi. And finally go on that shopping spree." Mona waved her pocketbook in the air. "I have Julian's black card, so sky's the limit!"

Advika deserved one of Julian's Oscars for the performance she staged for Mona as she walked her out the door, exulting over Julian's surprise return and their plans to "knock him dead" with a four-figure makeover before he got home. After Mona left, Advika stood near the doorway and waited for her footsteps to recede and echo down the stairs. She counted to sixty, then one hundred, and after counting to five hundred, she locked the door. Advika made a beeline toward her closet, pulled out her largest carry-on bag from the top shelf, and began to pack.

CHAPTER TWENTY-SEVEN

Woman of the Year

ADVIKA'S SNEAKERED FOOT FLUTTERED AGAINST the tile floor, giving off a rat-a-tat noise that echoed loudly in the empty reception room. The office of Bedioux, Renaud, and Associates was located in one of the most stunning buildings Advika had ever seen. The grand, elegant structure, reminiscent of a nineteenth-century opera house, made her wish she had dressed up for her visit to Evie's lawyer, rather than looking like a broke, twentysomething tourist.

But she had packed her carry-on in a hurry, not thinking she would need to add a more formal outfit to her repertoire. The past forty-eight hours had been so urgent and adrenaline-fueled Advika still couldn't believe she was in France and not just having a waking dream. Once she had made her decision, Advika had surprised herself by how forthrightly she had acted. No nerves, no doubts, just forward movement. This meant cranking up the volume on *His Girl Friday* in her bedroom to give the impression she was inside, then flushing several of Julian's socks down the toilet in the downstairs bathroom that was farthest away from the front door. As soon as she heard Aggie and Flora react to the gales of flooding that seemed to have even seeped into the kitchen, she sneaked out of the home with her bag clutched to her chest, sprinting the half mile out of the gated community and having a Lyft meet her at the bottom of the hill. This also meant texting Mona, just minutes before her plane taxied from the gate, that she had decided to fly to India after speaking to her parents and learning there was a family emergency.

Before her text to Mona, Advika had also called Sunita to discuss meeting with Evie's lawyer and get her input on that and some other things related to her prenup with Julian. Vik had come through on the diamonds front, contacting a friend's uncle who owned a jewelry store. Not only had Vik gotten the diamonds appraised at $30,000, but he also had a lead about how she could sell them. And then lastly, prior to texting Mona, Advika had messaged Olive that she was off to France to meet with Evie's lawyer and would call her in a few days. Wish me luck, she had signed off in her text to Olive.

"Mademoiselle," a voice called out. "Come." Advika hurriedly stood up, and her purse dropped from her lap. After collecting the items sprawled on the floor and stuffing them into her bag, Advika followed the receptionist into the law office, a byzantine lair of gorgeous but dimly lit wood-paneled hallways, until she was at last led into an antechamber, where she was then requested to wait again. Advika sighed and plopped down into her seat, hoping her entire day wouldn't be spent waiting. Avignon was in the midst of hosting its annual Festival d'Avignon, a three-week arts festival that had seen the city reverberating with a cultural vibrancy that Advika found invigorating and so opposite of what she was used to in LA. She was itching to experience the festival, since she had no idea how long she would be in Avignon. Advika had studiously avoided checking her phone since landing in France, fearing the likely bombardment of emails and texts would throw her off her game. Just as she was about to give in and finally check, the door opposite her opened and a man in a trim navy blue suit stepped out. He resembled the actor who starred in *Fifty Shades of Grey*, and his youth and obeisant manner indicated that he was just one more assistant who would lead Advika through longer hallways to smaller rooms.

"Ms. Sri...Sri..." The man looked at her with embarrassment.

"Yes, hi," Advika said, this time remembering to pick up her purse before standing. "I'm Advika Srinivasan."

"David Renaud." This was the lawyer? He seemed more likely to walk the runways of Milan than handle the legal affairs of old ladies.

"Oh! So nice to meet you." They shook hands, and Advika found herself deeply inhaling his cologne, a scent she couldn't identify but would describe as "expensive" and "handsome." *You think he's hot*, came Anu's voice, sly and amused. Advika couldn't remember the last time her twin sister had come to her unbidden in this way, but it was not the most opportune time. As if she wasn't nervous enough, she didn't want to have to fumble through one of the most important conversations of her life while feeling the pleasant sting of attraction.

After they sat down in his office and exchanged pleasantries, during which Advika tried to resist the charm of his French accent, David pulled out a thick manila folder and a thin slate-colored sealed envelope.

"This is Ms. Lockhart's will. I wanted you to see the documents for yourself, and I also can send an e-copy to your attorney, if you have one and would like them to review these things." Advika nodded but barely glanced at the will. Her eyes were fixated on the envelope that she assumed held the film reel, as it was key to untangling so much of what had consumed her life over the past few months. David noticed where she was looking and gave a nod. He slid the envelope across his desk, and it touched the tips of Advika's fingers.

"This is the film reel; there is no other copy."

Advika picked it up with trembling fingers, then returned it to the desk. "I need to know what's on this. I've flown so far, and I have barely slept because I couldn't stop—"

"I understand." He twisted a gold band on his ring finger, which Advika noticed with a mixture of consternation and relief. "This is what Ms. Lockhart has told me. I've also looked at the images, and while I cannot corroborate her story, the intensity of her conviction made me inclined to believe her."

Advika leaned forward, her breath quickening as Evie's lawyer laid out the story of her mysterious bequeathment. According to Evie, the reel contained ninety seconds of a scene from a film called *Lessons in Objectivity*.

"Jamison Deeds!" Advika exclaimed, half standing up, then collapsing in her seat. She recalled the dinner conversation with Roger and Eloisa, and how Julian had acted oddly when Roger suggested making a film about the director.

"So you know him. And about his disappearance?" When Advika nodded, David told her that when Deeds disappeared, so did the last third of his final film. Because Deeds was known for being relentlessly self-critical and never happy with his work, many theorized he had destroyed the footage before leaving the country or causing himself harm.

"Evie said she had proof it was neither of these." He offered a nervous smile as he shared what Evie had told him: that the climactic scene in *Dark, Hot Sun*—the film that had won Julian his first Oscar and earned Evie her sole acting nomination—had been plagiarized from Deeds's film. Specifically, a scene taken from the missing footage of *Lessons in Objectivity*.

"Whoa." Advika again picked up the envelope with a delicate touch, examining it in wonder.

"Yes." David cleared his throat. "It's an audacious claim. But she told me that anyone who saw what's on there," he said, nodding toward her shaking hand, "and then watched her husband's film would automatically know he had plagiarized it."

"What's her evidence that this is even from Deeds's movie?"

"The very first image is the film slate that states the scene is take four from *Lessons in Objectivity*."

"So you've seen this?" Advika said, raising it toward him.

He nodded. "Evie wanted me to. First, I examined the film reel, and then I watched the scene from Mr. Zelding's movie. And based on what I have seen, they do seem nearly identical. And even though he wasn't the film's director—"

"No, I get it. I've done some reading about my husband's work." Advika recalled that part of *Dark, Hot Sun*'s lore was that Charlie Etherwald, the film's director, was well-documented as having said that Julian advised him on how to shoot the climax, down to camera angles and blocking. "He was burning with a vision, like a man obsessed," Etherwald had said. "It's unusual for a producer to be that directorial on set, but his ideas were so sound, so inspired. I would have been a fool to not listen."

"So, you see," David said. "Again, I don't know if Ms. Lockhart's claims are true. But she did say she had a way to verify." His phone rang, and he answered in a string of musical French while giving her an apologetic look. Advika gestured it was fine, and examined the envelope while she waited. For the first time, she noticed the handwriting gracing the front. In gentle, sloping penmanship was one simple word: *proof.* Advika smiled and teared up to be holding something that had once been in the possession of Evie Lockhart. As she ruminated over Evie's handwriting, a question sprang to mind, which she communicated to David as soon as he got off the phone.

"She had this in her possession for such a long time, and she never did anything with it. Why?"

"For protection." David gazed at Advika with concern. "She said the film reel has Mr. Zelding's fingerprints on it."

"Oh my god." Advika sunk down in the leather chair, as all the revelations weighed her down.

"That I cannot verify, as I said earlier. I'm taking her word for it."

"And how did she get this, anyway?"

"I do not know. She did not tell me when I asked. But after she gained possession, she moved here because she wanted to put as much distance between her and Julian as possible. She said that after spending much of her married life controlled by him, once she moved to Avignon, he never tried to insert himself into her life again."

Advika stared at the word "proof" and thought about the reverberations of what it meant for Evie's life and her own, the magnitude of which took her several moments to wrap her head around. Inside this paper-thin envelope was a shield whose power extended across oceans, across time. The magnanimousness of Evie's gesture moved her deeply. But why only help Advika? Two ex-wives preceded her. When she asked David, he said that during one of their final conversations, Evie had expressed regret over this very thing.

"Ms. Lockhart knew about Mr. Zelding's marriage to his second wife. But she said that she feared to speak out then, not wanting to get tangled in his web again. By the time she became aware of Mr. Zelding's third marriage, it had already ended, and she had been relieved. When Ms. Lockhart learned about you, her illness was already terminal." His voice became hushed. "She had only weeks to live. But getting her affairs in order, in relation to you, is what she focused on with the time she had left."

"She spent the last moments of her life trying to help me," Advika whispered to herself as this revelation sunk in. "Giving me my life back."

To David, Advika said with an authoritativeness she had

never heard from herself before, "I do plan to divorce. What would you need from me so I can...fulfill Evie's request?" Her eyes traveled to the envelope in her hands.

"Once the paperwork is filed, and you can send me a copy, I am authorized to execute the terms of Ms. Lockhart's will." David gazed at her sympathetically. "But to be honest, she told me to judge your character, and if you were in immediate need, to go forward with it."

"That's so kind. She was so kind." After taking a few deep breaths to gather herself and fully shake off her emotions, Advika stood up. "I need to think on a few things. This can stay here until we talk again?"

"Of course; take your time." David stood up too and took the film reel from her. "How long will you be with us here?"

"In Avignon?" Advika said. *Of course, dummy,* Anu's voice said, butting in again. "I'm not sure yet. I have a one-way ticket, but I've booked a week's stay at the Hôtel Le Bristol."

"Well, before you leave, you must do a little sightseeing. And you must enjoy the festival." David opened a drawer and took out his business card, then turned it over and wrote something on the back. "My cell phone number. If you ever want a guide around town, let me know. My wife, Cecile, is a painter, just like Evie, and during the afternoons I know she'd love to show you around—the museums, especially."

Boo, a wife, came Anu's voice, but it was crowded out by Advika's own: *Evie was a painter?* As she thanked David and he escorted her out through the maze of hallways to the law office's front entrance, she made a mental note to call David's wife the next day, hoping to learn more about Evie and her artistic side.

After she left, Advika was intent on exploring Avignon, since up until that point all she had seen of it was the airport, her hotel, and David's office. She was awed by how the city was

completely encircled by ramparts and that the stone fortifica-
tions dated back to the twelfth century. To see the majestic
medieval walls surrounding Avignon was the closest thing to
experiencing actual time travel. In contrast, Los Angeles, where
she had lived all her life and barely left except for a handful of
vacations, now seemed like the equivalent of fluorescent lighting: too harsh, too bright, too modern. Avignon reminded her
of the serene glow of magic hour—the kind of soft, shimmering
light Angelenos sought when taking selfies. It wasn't a perfect
metaphor, but Advika, so used to highways and strip malls and
beaches, reveled in how Avignon's history was impressed upon
its streets and architecture and worn proudly on its beautiful,
aged shoulders.

The main streets and markets were overcrowded with
happy, chatty people wearing backpacks and sneakers, and
the walls were covered with posters for the hundreds of theater
shows taking place as part of the festival. The poster Advika
saw most frequently—papered over walls and lampposts and
mailboxes—showed two girls in hijabs, one whispering into
the other's ear, both sporting secret smiles. The sheer number
of posters popping up all over Avignon advertised the pair's
ambitions, and Advika was happy for them, but she also felt
a stab of jealousy. To be surrounded by all this creative energy
and excitement should have been inspiring. But instead, the
festival and its attendees amplified Advika's sense of stagna-
tion. Her failure.

Even with her feet sore and her limbs and brain exhausted
from the nine-hour time difference, Advika couldn't stop moving. She was a pet dog left off its leash for the first time, dizzy
with the freedom of just getting to roam around wherever she
liked, not needing to worry about a tug on her collar, restricting
her movements. But by late afternoon, she was famished and
forced herself to stop and get a bite to eat. As Advika searched

for a cafe, she turned a corner and walked down a quiet alley that had a multitude of giant sunflowers dangling down from wires strung up overhead. When Advika stopped to look up, watching the flowers sway in a soft breeze, she was taken by the lovely contrast between all the yellow petals and the brilliant blue sky. It was such a simple thing, but the thought that went into creating this small piece of magic thoroughly buoyed her. For a moment as she gazed upward, she forgot all about her problems and just soaked in the wonder of being in this city at this particular time. The blaring ambulance siren of her failure subsided.

For so long, her life had felt burdensome and, on her worst days, pointless. So to be reminded that living didn't have to always feel like a weight hung around her neck, that there could be beauty and grace too, seconds intertwined that could make you feel lucky to be alive? She breathed in, closed her eyes, and tilted her face toward the sun, happy to feel a genuine smile lifting her lips.

So Evie had never fulfilled the promise of her talents. What had she said in the *Ojai Reader* interview? *I'm ready to have my life back, on my own terms.* Surely Avignon had given her the space and freedom to do that. Evie had started painting, which meant she had found a new form of creative expression. Evie in Avignon was a happy ending. Just the thought of her living here as someone's friend and neighbor gave Advika so much solace.

Advika spent the remainder of the day sampling sweet treats at a variety of stalls and watching music performances in the square. Exhausted but electrified by all she had seen, she made her way back to her hotel room around dusk. As she took the elevator up to the fifth floor, Advika finally took out both phones and turned them on. A dozen messages greeted her, some she wasn't expecting and some she had anticipated. She briefly read through them as she exited the elevator and walked down the hall to her room. Advika fished her hotel key out of her purse and opened the door.

Julian stood at the window, gazing out at the parking lot and city beyond. Her suitcase had been opened and its contents dumped into a haphazard mountain peak on the bed. Dressed in a gray tee shirt and matching slacks, Julian's ensemble emphasized how much his skin had tanned from his stay in Morocco.

Julian turned around and took her in, his gaze traveling from her feet up to her eyes.

"Hello, Addi." He gave her an icy smile. "We're quite a ways from India, aren't we?"

CHAPTER TWENTY-EIGHT

The Proposal

ADVIKA CROSSED THE THRESHOLD AND closed the door most of the way, leaving it open a crack. "Hi, Julian. How was your flight?"

For a split second, Advika could see the confusion in Julian's eyes. He had expected her to be surprised, furious, scared. Instead, she came off as nonchalant, even bored. Julian watched her carefully, and she matched his gaze. He opened his arms. "It was wonderful because I knew I was on my way to see you. It's been too long. I missed you."

She crossed her arms and stayed near the doorway. She eyed her belongings, so ignobly searched and abandoned by Julian, and inwardly smiled. Advika had texted Olive about her whereabouts on her iPhone, knowing that Mona would see the message and immediately tell her boss. Julian would have been just returning or would have already landed in LA by the time he had seen his assistant's message, necessitating an immediate turnaround toward Europe. Advika knew Julian's mid-Atlantic travels would last long enough to ensure he wouldn't arrive in France before her meeting with Evie's lawyer. Even so, from the moment her plane landed in Avignon, Advika had expected to

see Julian at every turn, on street corners or cafes or even waiting at David's law office. But as the two appraised each other in
the waning light of day, Advika realized that of course Julian
would confront her in this way, when she was alone and seemingly helpless.

"You missed me? Like, what did you miss about me?" As she
spoke, Advika ticked off each item on her fingers. "My naivety?
My youth? My lack of power?"

Julian shook his head slightly, as if the conversation he
wanted to have wasn't going the way he had expected. "Oh, so
is this who you're trying to be? Acting like, what is it? Hashtag
girlboss?"

Advika laughed. She had never expected her husband to
utter those last two words, and he looked ridiculous doing so.
"Sure, let's go with that."

Julian grimaced, or perhaps stifled a yawn. He rocked his
shoulders back and forth, as if gearing himself up for a physically arduous undertaking. Julian then took a few steps toward
her, and Advika put her hand in her back pocket and grasped
her burner phone.

"What—you think I'd actually harm you? You're my wife."

"How did you know I was here?" Advika's grasp on the
phone tightened.

Julian flinched but masked it with a smile. "It's not as sinister
as you make it sound. You told Mona about going to see your
family in India, and yet you booked a ticket to France. I do
check our credit card activity, after all."

"Why check, though? You don't trust me?"

Julian let out a short, dismissive bark of laughter. "Look
where we are, Addi."

Would he ever admit it, the constant monitoring and pry-
ing into her privacy? And did it matter? Advika thought of
the film reel and the word "proof" defiantly scrawled in Evie's

handwriting. Despite the exhaustion roiling through her body, she stood up straighter, elongating her neck and holding her chin high. It was time to end this.

"How about this: Do you know why I'm here?" Her eyes flickered to her overturned suitcase. "Seems like you were searching for something."

Julian's nostrils flared, and he made a *pfft* sound. "Let's cut the shit. Where is it?"

"Where's what?" she asked innocently. He took another step closer, and Advika pulled out her phone.

"You want to make me say it? So, what—you can record me?"

"I have no intention of recording you. But I have every intention of protecting myself. Just like you, it seems." She held her phone close to her chest. "Let's just say it: this marriage isn't working. I want a divorce."

Julian smirked. He walked back toward the window and leaned against it, then clapped his hands together.

"It's not for you to decide. I'm not granting one." He sniffed. "It wouldn't look good for me to divorce my wife after just a few months. Especially not after what happened with Harley. I'd look like a fool."

"I don't care. I want out." Advika uttered each word deliberately, raising her voice for the first time. "If you think your reputation will be damaged by a quickie wedding and breakup, that's laughable compared to how much I know about you now." Her hands and wrists began to ache from gripping the phone so fervently, but she remained rigid. "And I'll do what it takes to end this marriage."

"So now you're threatening me?" Julian's Adam's apple bobbed up and down.

"No threats, just knowledge. And then you can decide what to do with it." Advika shrugged. "And where we go from here." As she had practiced on the plane ride numerous times, without looking at her phone she opened up her texts, where a prewritten message awaited. She pressed Send.

"I hold your reputation in my hands," she continued. "However the world thinks of you I can change instantly. So it's in your best interests just to let this marriage go. Let me go," she added softly.

"This film reel thing is a joke." Julian did his short, bark-like laugh again. "Whatever *she* said, whatever the lawyer said—it's nonsense. Pure fiction."

"Good to know," Advika deadpanned, nodding toward her upturned suitcase. "We have a prenup, but I'm willing to void it if you'll grant me two other things instead. One, forfeiture of any rights to my screenplays."

Julian snorted. "My, we think highly of ourselves, don't we?"

"And two, the publishing rights to Nova Martin's music."

Even with his deep tan, Julian's face still exploded into a terrifying shade of red. "How dare you. You little bitch."

Advika had never seen this side of her husband before. But rather than being fearful, she was relieved. She knew there was this side lurking in him, which he masked behind luxurious cologne and incessant romantic getaways. To finally see his real self gave Advika the same sort of weird exultance she experienced when watching the end of *Iron Man*, when Tony Stark brashly revealed his superhero alter ego to the public.

"We're going to end this right now," he said, scolding her as if she were a child. "You—"

"I know what's on the film reel, Julian. And the lawyer has seen it too."

"Is that so?" He tried to keep his composure and rearrange his features into a blasé haughtiness, but as Advika learned when watching him in *The Riders*, Julian was a terrible actor.

She nodded. "He had some pretty interesting things to tell

me. Courtesy of Evie. She really did everything she could to keep you out of her life."

Julian made another, louder *pfft* sound. "That's ridiculous. Once we were divorced, I didn't give a flying fuck about her. She was washed-up, useless. I have no idea what's even on this 'film reel,'" he said, making quotation marks with his fingers.

Advika's phone buzzed in her hand. A text had come in, and although she couldn't look at it, she knew what it said. It was time to push things forward. And fast.

"*Lessons in Objectivity*," Advika said. "It's oddly similar to *Dark, Hot Sun.*"

Julian's face paled. His eyes bulged, and his mouth opened, then closed, then opened again. Julian grabbed a chair from a nearby desk and collapsed into it, his arms dropping inelegantly at his sides. When he didn't speak, Advika pressed on.

"It would be a major scandal if their similarities came out. Maybe you'd even lose a second Oscar—but this time it'll be the Academy taking it from you." Julian absorbed Advika's words, including her Victoria-related dig at his precious trophies, with all the calm of a bull right before being let loose in the streets of Pamplona. He seemed to want to leap out of his chair toward Advika, but with his short breaths and pained demeanor, he looked like he had just been socked in the gut.

"Evie was full of it. And now you're full of it. Ingesting her lies," he panted.

Advika took a small step backward toward the door. "I don't care what you believe, but you obviously believe *something*," she said. "Let's just call this, Julian. We were never meant to get married."

"There will be no divorce," Julian said with a contemptuous snort. "But there will be some changes. Obviously, I've left you alone too long. Running around with your little friend, sitting at home, being idle. You need . . ."

"I really don't want to hear the end of that sentence," Advika muttered, her stomach churning. She didn't know what time it was, but she guessed it was between 7:00 and 7:30 p.m. based on how the evening sky was just starting to darken. It was the dinner hour, and she expected to hear the traffic of hotel guests coming and going out for the evening. Her room was right across from the elevator, and she had chosen the location purposefully. Advika kept an ear out for the ding of the elevator bell, needing to know the exact moment when she wouldn't be alone with Julian.

"This isn't the movies, Addi. You're no match for me and my lawyers. Let's go get some dinner, start afresh, talk things out." The gentlemanly, smooth Julian reappeared, or at least tried to. There was the gap-toothed smile, the warm demeanor. But his eyes were hard. Advika stifled a nervous laugh at how he was trying to play her. Two months ago, maybe two weeks ago, it would have worked. But not now.

"For the first time in our marriage, can we have an honest conversation?" she asked.

"I've always been honest."

"But not forthcoming." Advika took another step backward, her shoulder brushing against the edge of the wall. "Why didn't you talk to me about your ex-wives before we got engaged? I mean, really?"

Julian pressed his palm to his forehead. "Because it wasn't your business. Because my past shouldn't have any reflection on what we were going to share together."

He would never admit to anything. Why was she still trying to get him to budge on this? Advika thought of Evie, of Nova, of Victoria. Their weird sisterhood. Each of them had radiated talent and ambition, and that was what drew them to Julian, who had basically acted as a parasite, draining them of what made them special to benefit his own needs. From Evie, he gained his entrance into the film world, and once he had clout, he used it to bully his wife into taking movie roles of his choosing. With Nova, he pressured her to give up her heritage, her very sense of self and identity, in order to fit into his cookie-cutter picture of what her music career should be. Even Victoria, who ultimately escaped him, still had to reinvent herself and pursue her ambitions in a different country, which took her away from her beloved family and community.

Advika wanted Julian to admit he had taken something vital from each of the women he had pledged to love, honor, and cherish. But why would he? He never thought of anyone but himself.

"What were we going to share together, though?" Advika recalled Nova's tragic end, and Victoria's reality star dreams, and what both women had in common. "You just married me so I'd give you a child."

"I want a family with you. What—does that make me a bad person?" Julian's exasperation was so real that for a moment, Advika doubted herself. But only for a moment.

"I had—have—dreams. That doesn't include a child, at least not right now. So it makes you a bad person if you took away all my choices and opportunities just as a means to your own selfish ends."

"I'm not going to apologize for desiring children." Julian's words were choked with a mix of sadness and anger. "It's what we were put on this earth to do."

Advika thought of Pappy's cross and the religious overtones in Julian's wedding vows to Victoria. Time was ticking, and every second precious, but her curiosity got the better of her. "But you've had, like, fifty years to have kids. Why now, and why with me?"

"I just didn't want to knock some woman up. I wasn't raised that way."

"Julian Zelding," Advika said mockingly. "Man of morals."

He grunted, and a flush of scarlet swished along his collarbone. "You're so young, you know that? Thinking that life will go on forever, the minutes extending on and on like a rolled-out red carpet. Well, it won't." Advika didn't respond, her ears straining to catch any noise of people in the hallway. But Julian took that as a dismissal of his words, and he slammed his fist on top of a nearby chest of drawers.

"What do you want to hear? That my health scare realigned my priorities? And reminded me of my relationship with God? Well, fine. If that's what helps you understand how important this is to me. That it's *the* most important thing." He used his wiry forearms to push himself out of the chair. "And you, Addi—you were never going to be some great screenwriter. The world is not waiting with bated breath for your work. At the very least, the two of us coming together to have a child—that would mean something. Give your life, and mine, meaning."

It was now Advika's turn to feel socked in the gut. All those beautiful things he had said early on in their courtship were really just a means to an end. She'd had a dim awareness of this for quite some time, ever since he had told her about sabotaging the *Agent UFO* gig, but she was not prepared to hear Julian admit it so cavalierly. Advika's knees nearly buckled from hearing the truth from him. This man would have taken so much from her and felt no remorse. Julian coolly regarded how his words had affected her. He dropped his shoulders back and grinned at her broadly.

Advika's phone buzzed again, bringing her back to the present moment. It was time to drop the hammer.

"So here's the deal," she said, trying to keep her nerves from invading her voice. "Before leaving home, I had my lawyer ready an annulment filing based on fraud." Julian's smile drooped off his lips like melting wax. "And as proof of that fraud, I'm ready to share everything. Not just the story of our marriage, but how you treated your ex-wives—these incredible women you just stomped over."

"I loved all of my wives. Some more than others, I admit. But every single one."

"You do understand that two of your wives left the country after divorcing you. They wanted to put an ocean between them and you."

He seemed befuddled by this, as if he had never thought of it before. "Their choices had nothing to do with me."

"Are you kidding me?" Advika shook her head in astonishment. "Your need to dictate our choices is what we all have in common. What you did to each of them—"

Julian sneered. "That's not fraud, little girl. That's tabloid fare, gossip."

"Exactly," Advika said brightly. "You know that sites like TMZ love nothing more than to trawl legal filings for their headlines. And they'd have a lot to talk about based on what I know. And what I have in my possession. And I don't mean just the film reel," Advika added, thinking of Nova's journal, which was safe with Vik. "Right now, you're the handsome, multi-Oscar-winning film producer. But what happens to your legacy when even a tenth of what I know comes out?"

"So what are you saying, exactly?" Julian scratched manically behind his ear. His neck veins pulsed. *You're getting to him,* came Anu's voice. *Now knock him out.*

Advika glanced at her phone. Four minutes had passed since she had sent the text to Sunita.

"If my friends don't hear from me in one minute, the

annulment paperwork will be filed, and the story is going to be leaked to all your favorite gossip blogs. How you treated Evie and Nova and Victoria. Not to mention Jamison Deeds."

Julian's mouth dropped open. "You're serious? Where... where did you even get a lawyer?"

Advika thought of letting Julian in on how his anniversary gift, which in an alternate life she would have worn to the Oscars as his date, the diamonds cutting into her skin like a dog collar, instead had secured her the ability to engage a divorce attorney for sixty billable hours. But there was no reason to inform him of that irony.

Her phone buzzed. A new text from Sunita. The earlier one had said, Standing by. And the new message: One more minute, and I'm getting the ball rolling.

"What should I tell them? It's up to you. Is this marriage really worth more to you than your reputation?"

Julian glared at her, continuing to scratch behind his ear so hard Advika wondered if he was having an allergic reaction. No doubt his mind was racing, trying to think of ways to maneuver and manipulate his way out of this.

"Ten, nine, eight..." Advika called out, inching another step back.

"Fine," he bellowed, his hand dropping to his side. "Just... let's end this."

Advika told him that she would send a text asking to hold on filing, at least for now. But Julian would need to have his lawyer draw up paperwork in the next twelve hours acquiescing to her wishes regarding the voided prenup in exchange for the rights to her and Nova's work. If not, Advika would move forward with the filing immediately. Over the next twelve hours, Advika would check in with her friends every sixty minutes with a code word. If they failed to hear from her within those intervals, they would instruct her attorney to go ahead and file.

Just as Advika finished telling him this, her body sagged with relief as the elevator dinged, and she heard the footsteps of several people enter her floor. With her right foot, she gently swung open her hotel room door.

"Now, leave," she said. Advika backed out into the hallway, as a group of fortysomething British women in pastel-colored tees and culottes walked past her, eyeing her curiously. Her whole body trembled as she watched Julian exit her hotel room, then press the button for the elevator. The ladies, sensing something was off between Advika and Julian, stayed in the hallway with her, all of them staring at Julian until the elevator arrived and he got on it.

Julian stood inside the cramped compartment with a slight bend in his knees, his neck veins still throbbing. He raked his fingers through his silver hair, and his mouth was agape, as if he couldn't breathe through his nose. Advika didn't break eye contact with him until the elevator doors closed.

After Julian left, one of the women asked Advika, "Are you okay, love?"

Advika thought about the word "okay" and all it signified. Not great, not terrible. But still standing. Still going. She smiled at the woman, teary-eyed, and nodded.

Waiting to Exhale

Four Years Later

ADVIKA YAWNED. A HALF-EMPTY TEACUP dangled from her fingers, and she managed to lift it back up just before any drops could fall to the floor. She had never in her life been a morning person, and even after the past few years, she still had trouble adjusting to awakening when the sun was still young and not quite at full strength. Advika let out a louder yawn and then set down the teacup on the kitchen table with the flourish of a chess master moving her queen into position for checkmate. Doing these kinds of over-the-top gestures helped her feel more awake. They also tended to make Anu laugh.

"Silly!" Anu giggled. Her daughter was seated across from her at the table, painstakingly writing her name on a birthday card for Olive.

"I am silly," Advika agreed, smiling. "Almost done, love?"

Anu, who, like her namesake, tended to wear an oversized pout when frustrated, pushed the card away. "I don't like you."

"You don't like me?" Advika said, pressing the back of her hand against her forehead as if feeling faint.

The dramatic gesture had its intended effect, and Anu

erupted into peals of laughter. "Not you," Anu said, pointing at her. "*Uuuu.*" She tapped the birthday card with her green marker, where she had crookedly spelled her own name.

"Your *u* looks fine. And I'm sure Aunty Olive will love it. Did you have enough to eat?" Advika examined Anu's bowl of cereal, in which several Cheerios and blueberries bobbed in a sea of milk.

"Can I have a lolly?"

"Lollies aren't breakfast. Two more bites of cereal, please."

"And then we can play Legos?"

Advika sighed. "Yes, then we can play."

After two quick bites of cereal ("Chew, please!"), Anu ran out of the kitchen into the living room. From this vantage point, Advika could watch her daughter empty a box of Legos onto the floor while still retaining a few more moments of solitude along with the last sips of her tea. She reached for her iPad and checked her email, even though she rarely expected to receive anything this early on a Saturday morning, since most of her friends were halfway around the world, still asleep. But waiting for her were eight messages, all alerting her to the same news, with Sunita's providing a link. Advika sat back in her chair, making an ugly scraping noise against the tile, then read through the "Thinking of yous" from Vik and Balan and the "What now???" from Olive.

After glancing up at Anu, who was humming a Taylor Swift song while busying herself with her Legos, Advika clicked the link Sunita had sent her.

JULIAN ZELDING, OSCAR-WINNING FILM PRODUCER, DEAD AT 72

Lucia J. Valdez
September 20, 2019, 11:14 p.m. PST
THR.com

Julian Zelding, the producer of five Oscar-winning films, including *West of the Gun* and *Run*, has died at age 72. Eloisa Pithe, Zelding's producing partner and goddaughter, announced the news Friday night on Twitter.

Advika stared at the photograph of Julian, snapped in the 2015 Oscars press room, in which his fellow winners were edited out. A few hours after it was taken, she would meet him. How strange to see this photograph, a window into her past and a reminder of the moment that led to Advika's future. She waited to feel some emotion, any emotion, about the fact that Julian was dead. But none came.

"Vroom, vroom!" Anu called out. She had built a garden car, one of her favorites to make with Legos: pink plastic tulips planted on top of a green Lego wedge with wheels affixed to it. "Mama, coming?"

"Yes, baby, one second. I'll be right there."

Advika quickly scrolled down, past the summing up of Julian's achievements and career, toward the end of the obituary, which covered his personal life.

Zelding was previously married to Oscar-nominated actress Evie Lockhart, pop singer Nova Martin, and reality star Victoria Truong, with whom he appeared on their short-lived series, *Luxury Wives*. He was most recently married to aspiring screenwriter Advika Srinivasan; their three-month marriage ended in 2015.

Advika enlarged the final paragraph on her iPad, then reread every word. She had never seen her name in print alongside Julian's previous wives in a major publication. Advika barely minded being called an "aspiring screenwriter," considering she could have been designated a "bartender" or just a nobody instead. But more importantly, the obituary said that Julian wasn't survived by anyone.

He died without knowing.

He died with no one.

Advika deposited her teacup and Anu's bowl in the sink and stopped to gaze out the picture window at the pink-gold sky. Living in Avignon always made her wish she were a painter, someone who could capture the godlike light that illuminated this miracle of a small town that had kept Anu happy and safe.

From the moment she had discovered she was pregnant, Advika had never stopped worrying that Julian would find out, sue her for custody, or spirit away her daughter in the middle of the night. If he'd had the smallest inkling of the truth, her life would have been an operatic nightmare. But a month after their divorce was finalized, Julian had to undergo surgery related to his heart condition, and complications from the procedure had left him weak and unable to travel. So staying in Avignon had turned out to be a blessing in more ways than one.

Advika joined Anu in the living room and sat cross-legged next to her little girl. Even though Anu was only three and a half years old, she was tall for her age, already outgrowing the pink cotton pants and matching flamingo tee shirt Advika's mother had sent her just a few months ago. Sometimes Advika was alarmed by how quickly Anu was growing up, a heartbreaking reminder of how easily time could slip away. That the red-faced newborn squalling in Advika's arms could now pedal a tricycle and sing Taylor Swift songs in French and English could stun her at random moments. The news of Julian's death hadn't yet fully sunk in, but it was starting to as she stared at her daughter. The angular curve of her chin, tiny ears, and dimpled smile twisted Advika's heart. Anu was an echo of two people whom she would never know.

Every once in a while, Advika would wake up during the

night and not know where she was. Or she'd wake up and be bewildered at where her life had taken her, the events that brought her to this picturesque cottage with a leaky roof and peeling paint, now and forever a mother. Her daughter's existence was the moment when Advika's life officially branched into somewhere new, taking her far away from the ambitions she had long burned for. And it was a soft pain that gnawed at her sometimes, especially late at night, when she would feel so far away from all that she loved and missed and that defined her. She would give up the world for her Anu. And in a way, she had.

As her thoughts darted between the past and the present, Advika busied herself layering different-colored Legos on top of each other—red and blue, yellow and green, orange and white. With Julian's death, her life was about to be different again, branching off in an entirely unknown direction, yet endlessly moving forward.

"What is that, Mama?" Anu dropped the garden car and pulled the block of Legos out of Advika's hands.

"I'm not sure. What do you think it is?"

Anu scratched her forehead. "Ummm . . . maybe a rainbow?"

Advika beamed. "Oh yes, I can see it now." She kissed the top of her daughter's head, luxuriating in the honeyed scent of her shampoo. "You know how much I love you, right?"

Anu nodded, still examining the colorful stack of Legos. "As big as the ocean, as bright as rainbows."

Advika leaned forward, surprised. "Did you learn that from a cartoon?"

Anu handed the Legos back to Advika. "No, Mama. That's how much you love me."

"You came up with those words?"

"Yeahhhhh." The withering, exasperated look Anu shot Advika gave her a preview of what she would be like as a teenager.

"Well, you're right. That's how I feel about you. Always and always." She peppered Anu with kisses until the little girl squirmed from all the affection and ran back into the kitchen to get a lollipop. Advika watched her go, joy and sadness rippling inside her.

In the evening, after Anu had gone to bed, Advika sat at her desk and stared at the ceiling. She hadn't responded to any of her emails, texts, or phone calls yet, except for briefly thanking them for reaching out. It was in these quiet moments when she allowed herself to put her "mother" self on pause and either ruminate or brood, depending on how she felt about herself that day. It was important to her sanity to carve out at least a half hour daily when she could sip a glass of whiskey and contemplate the stars, pinpricks of light that emerged out of the blue-black sky. Tonight felt different. The old her, the part that was briefly a wife, flickered in her mind. Only once she stopped being a wife did she fully comprehend how suffocating that role had turned out to be, just as she and her sister had imagined all those years ago when they pledged to each other, and later their parents, that they would never marry.

Here's the question that plagued Advika during her darkest moments: *What would my life look like if Anu had never died?* Losing her sister meant gaining her daughter. That equation was as heart-wrenching as it was true: Advika would have never had them both in her life simultaneously. She was over-the-moon thankful for her daughter, but on her worst days, Advika admonished herself for thinking that having a child would ever replace her kinship with her sister as she had hoped it would when she decided to have the baby.

But there were also the needier, greedier questions. Would she have been a happier person, a more accomplished person, if her sister, Anu, were still here? Sometimes Advika felt the presence of a shadow person, this other Advika who would have existed if her sister were still alive. During her first draining months of motherhood, Advika sensed this shadow person standing in corners, watching her with judgment, tsk-tsking that this was how Advika had ended up, covered in throw-up, rank from sporadic showering, and singing off-key to a tiny creature who wouldn't stop crying.

Gradually, that person had faded away, especially as Anu got older and the two of them developed their own relationship and rhythm as mother and daughter. But the news about Julian had reawakened this shadowy second self, reminding Advika of the terrifically strange journey she had gone on to end up as a mother and ex-wife living in chosen exile.

Actress. Pop singer. Reality star. Aspiring screenwriter. That is what differentiated Advika from the previous wives: she hadn't yet realized her particular ambition. If the world remembered her at all, it would be in connection with this list of names. Yet even within them, she was the outlier. Advika liked her job at the Musée Calvet well enough, enjoying the flexibility of working at the gift shop and offering guided tours to American and British tourists. She also liked being around all the art, in the casual company of genius, and she thought of the paintings by Mignard and Bonnard as her co-workers. But now that Julian was dead, Advika could see her job for the life preserver it really was, an occupation to fill her days. She had purchased the cottage with the inheritance from Evie, then put 10 percent into a retirement fund and the rest into a trust fund for her daughter, which meant that all other living expenses came from her income. Advika thought over her work history, a haphazard series of jobs largely in the service industry. There was no shame in it, as she had always been a hard and dedicated worker. But that shadow self held up a mirror to all her unrealized potential.

With a sigh, Advika looked down from the ceiling and began straightening up her desk, a housewarming gift from David and his wife, Cecile. The antique desk's surface was in the shape of a half-moon topped with three horizontal shelves, and its drawers were outfitted with brass pulls that resembled rosebuds. It had belonged to Evie, who of course had impeccable taste. The stateliness of the walnut desk was obscured by a mess of books and photographs, framed and unframed, plus so much paper: cards, receipts, Anu's drawings, and a stack of Generation Equality pamphlets and signs emblazoned with BRISEZ LE SILENCE, PAS LES FEMMES and À BAS LE PATRIARCAT. Over the years, anything that didn't need Advika's urgent attention ended up tossed on the desk with a vague promise to herself that she would get to it eventually, and she barely paid attention to the mess as it expanded its domain over every inch of space. But all at once, the clutter became too much to bear. And anyway, she needed to do something physical. She needed a distraction.

So Advika skipped her nightly whiskey and star-gazing ritual to clean up her desk, accompanied by the *Sleepless in Seattle* soundtrack at a low volume, a movie she returned to frequently when her stay in France became permanent. The warm blanket of familiar sounds kept her company as she sorted and separated the detritus, choosing what to toss or keep. After an hour, the desk's regal beauty began to reemerge, and for the first time in ages, it no longer seemed like a storage place for her daily worries.

Advika went into the kitchen, this time pouring herself a glass of Riesling. Before returning to her bedroom, she pressed her ear to Anu's door, then opened it a crack. Anu was sleeping with her stuffed flamingo clutched to her side and a stuffed parrot sharing her pillow. Advika listened to her daughter's wispy breaths for a few moments, then closed the door and returned to her own room.

As she sat back down at her desk, she paged through the mail and notecards she had intended to frame. One was a thank-you letter from the Martinez family after she had returned Nova's publishing rights to them. The letter accompanied a photo of a teenage Nova smiling gleefully at the camera, holding a guitar with her birth name, Nalda, written on its body in thin red cursive. Another was an old postcard from Victoria, which showed a stunning photo of the enormous stone statues on Easter Island. The two DMed each other occasionally on Instagram, but Advika was always more thrilled to receive these one-of-a-kind postcards, which Victoria liked to create from photographs she had taken of places she had visited while filming her various reality shows. Whenever the two texted, they discussed trying to meet in Paris, but Victoria's busy schedule so far had not allowed it. Advika fished out her phone from her back pocket and sent her a message: Did you hear? She could only imagine that Victoria was also somewhere in a dark room, processing the news.

Advika took a giant sip of her wine before tackling her last task: deciding which photos to frame and set up on the desk's top shelf. She chose one from Olive's visit a year before, the two of them squinting in the sun and wearing swimsuits, the blur of Anu's arm at the bottom edge of the frame. Olive had been in town for a screening of her film at the documentary festival happening concurrently with the main one at Cannes. The photo had been snapped two days after her film received third place, and Advika loved that it captured Olive's unabashed smile, which she never stopped wearing for her entire visit. Next to it she placed a framed photo of herself, her belly the size of a beachball, with Sunita, Vik, and Balan. All three Oakies had surprised her with a visit a month before Anu's birth, and their picture showed the foursome with their arms around each other in front of her newly purchased cottage. The trio were planning a return visit in the spring, and Vik had promised to bring a rough cut of the Nova Martin documentary he was helping Hector produce.

Bookending both images were two photos that Advika considered the most dear to her. The first was a picture of her and Anu from their college graduation party, wearing matching caps and gowns and sticking out their tongues at the camera. The other was of Advika in the hospital with newborn Anu, her parents hovering on either side. All of them looked tired, with Advika's eyes half-closed, but Rupi and Mukesh were beaming as they gazed down at their grandchild. And at the center of her desk sat a laptop. Not the old, banged-up Dell, which had gone kaput long ago. But a new MacBook Air, the only other purchase Advika had allowed herself from Evie's inheritance. It had sat unused since she bought it, hidden away under years of accumulated clutter, neglected in favor of her iPad.

"Julian is dead," Advika said, her eyes traveling from the laptop to the smiling images of herself in the picture frames. "He's gone." Stating the fact out loud brought home how long she had lived her life as one long held breath, waiting for the other shoe to drop. Even though she had the incriminating film reel (stashed away in a safety-deposit box), Advika had never let her guard down and had never let herself believe that Julian would truly leave her alone. The ability to dream had been lost to her, having spent the past several years running in place on a treadmill powered by her worst fears. But in the meantime, hadn't she carved out a life for herself? Not the one her twenty-something self had envisioned. But this cottage was filled with love. Anu was loved and never questioned it—she even came up with her own vocabulary for it.

A text came in from Victoria. It was the popular GIF of the four characters from *Anchorman* gleefully jumping up in unison. This was followed by just two words: Sure did.

Advika laughed. How nice to know there was someone else

in the world who had walked in her shoes and therefore greeted the news about Julian with joy—and felt no guilt about it. She wanted to send back a GIF in return but couldn't find the right one to express her own kaleidoscope of emotions, all bright colors bouncing against each other that made her feel like she was glowing from within. Advika tried searching for GIFs using several words: yay, applause, celebration. None of them were right. Advika looked up at the framed photos again, the photos of her loved ones from whom she had lived apart for so long, not daring to step foot back in the States after all this time.

Advika typed in one last word: freedom. And one of the first images that came up was a white woman behind the wheel of a car, raising her arms high in triumph as the wind tousled her hair. This is what she sent to Victoria, along with the following: Forget Paris. Let's meet in LA. Victoria responded immediately with a row of thumbs-up emojis.

Later on, the two would meet and discuss the immense relief that had coursed through their bodies that day, how they had no idea of the degree of tension they were carrying until it flowed out of them like lava from a seething volcano. But on that night, there was still an edginess nettling Advika that she couldn't quite name. She stood up from her desk and wandered the cottage with her wineglass in hand. As she moved from room to room, her footsteps creaking on the old floors, Advika considered how the life she had created for herself and Anu had not been accomplished on her own. She had the support of her parents and her friends, and the grace of her sister's memory. And she was in a sisterhood with three other women who knew what it meant to be married to a man whose desires and narcissism threatened to blot out their spark, the essence of what made them whole. These women were a constellation in her sky, and even if some of the stars had burned out long ago, their light still traveled through the darkness to reach her.

She wanted to tell their stories. She wanted to tell her own story. Advika thought of the bridal tradition of wearing "something old, something new, something borrowed, and something blue." She hadn't incorporated it in her one and only wedding day, but these elements from her life and theirs she would wear now. And weave them into something new.

Advika returned to her bedroom. The *Sleepless in Seattle* soundtrack was on a loop, and she listened to several songs as she reclined in her seat. Advika strummed her fingers on the edge of the desk as the sad, dreamy "In the Wee Small Hours of the Morning" played in the background, and she had a quiet chuckle when it transitioned into the jaunty "Back in the Saddle Again." She squared up her shoulders, placed her bare feet firmly on the floor, and counted backward from ten. Then she pulled the laptop toward her.

For the first time since leaving Julian, Advika began to write.

Acknowledgments

Thank you to literary agent extraordinaire Andrea Somberg, whom I've no doubt sent over a hundred emails with the words "quick question" in the subject heading, and who always answers promptly with so much patience and grace. Also my utmost thanks and appreciation to my TV/film agent Rich Green at the Gotham Group.

It was a pleasure to once again work with the incredible team at Grand Central Publishing. Thank you to my amazing editor Karen Kosztolnyik, whose astute feedback was absolutely transformative at a crucial time. Thanks so much to Rachael Kelly and Andy Dodds (both gracious recipients of their fair share of "quick question" emails), as well as Ben Sevier, Theresa DeLucci, Brian McLendon, Albert Tang, Luria Rittenberg, Kristen Lemire, Kristin Nappier, Erin Cain, Ali Cutrone, Karen Torres, and Melanie Schmidt. Thanks also to Sarah Congdon for yet another brilliant cover design.

Writing is such a solitary affair, and I'm grateful to those who made it feel less so: Daphne Palasi Andreades, Colleen Hubbard, Saumya Dave, Juhea Kim, Rachel Krantz, Erin Mayer, Shannon McLeod, Kate Racculia, Qian Julie Wang, and Liv Stratman, the ideal accountability partner in every way. Also thanks to the Is This Anything crew: Jennifer Keishin Armstrong, Saul Austerlitz, Erin Carlson, and Thea Glassman, whom I think of as the Avengers of pop culture writers.

My thanks to Joel Lyons, Lauren Maxwell, Meghan McNamara, Reena Shah, Suzanne Strempek Shea, and Laura Uyeda for our meaningful conversations and correspondences over the years, especially during the beginning months of the pandemic. A special thank you to Jessica Wells-Hasan, whose kindheartedness and generosity inspire me to no end.

The friend group in my novel was inspired by my own family friends, who are the most loving and hilarious and loyal people, and who provided me a measure of belonging that I appreciate more with every passing year. Heartfelt thanks to everyone who ever spent time in the bonus room: Sailaja, Sairam, Salitha, Sudhir, Kavita, Kshema, Rahul, Leena, Anil, Jayashree, Jayant, Rama, and Vani, and my cousins Sunil and Sailesh. And of course my brother and sister, Pavan and Anjali, who are not just members of the above group, but also the best siblings a little sister could ask for.

Flamingos and hearts to my niece Leela, and so much love to her namesake, my beloved grandmother Leela. And thanks also to dearest Rekha Aunty for all her support, and also for introducing me to the deliciousness of Chicken 65.

Thank you to my parents, Dattatreya Kumar and Shuba, for instilling in me a love of reading that has blossomed to a point that I can express my gratitude to them in the acknowledgments of a novel.

My gratitude to my husband, Corey, who has given me the universe.

Thank you, readers. I will forever be awed that anyone takes the time to read my work, and grateful to those who send me kind messages, discuss my novel in their book clubs, or recommend my writing to others. Books are magic, and so are readers.

Thank you to bookstores and libraries for providing an oasis of words within your communities. It will never stop being an honor to have my book on your shelves.

And this novel is an ode to the women whose accomplishments have been diminished, whose careers have been unjustly derailed, or whose worthy stories have never been told. Thank you for your sacrifices and perseverance. Your light reaches us still.

About the Author

Kirthana Ramisetti earned her MFA in creative writing from Emerson College, and has had her work published in the *New York Times*, the *Wall Street Journal*, and more. Her debut novel, *Dava Shastri's Last Day*, was a *Good Morning America* Book Club pick and is currently in development as a television series for HBO Max. She lives with her husband in New York City.